Jessie Running

Chris Lewando

Published in 2017 by Independent Publisher

First Edition

A CIP catalogue record for this title is available from the British Library.

The Way of the Warrior is a resolute acceptance
of death. This is the true virtue of strategy.
The Way of the Sword is to defeat the enemy
in a fight, nothing other than this.

The Book of Five Rings
Miyamoto Musashi

Chapter 1

Gary left London in the early hours of a wet Sunday morning in the Volvo automatic estate provided by his firm. The wide road was empty, the beam of his headlights cutting through a fine drizzle.

The dry squeak of the windscreen wiper blades passing across the glass set his teeth on edge. Irritably, he flipped them onto intermittent and began to relax as they flashed sporadically, allowing him the occasional glimpse of shining tarmac.

Yawning, he began to put his latest victory behind him, already planning the next. The signing of a contract and a sexual conquest provided the same kind of buzz, and nothing was better than getting high on both at the same time as he had last night. Without that, life would be pretty unbearable, after all.

He was heading for his enviable four-bed show-piece house which was no longer a home. The dream had turned sour somewhere over the last few years. The same went for his wife. Sought, reeled in and landed, but not so easily dispatched. The bitch knew which side her bread was buttered, and wasn't going to do the honourable thing and leave him, oh, no; she was hanging onto her meal ticket by her glossy red fingernails.

At night, lying awake, staring at her back, he fantasised, in gory, blood-gushing detail, about sticking a knife into it.

Driving towards the outskirts of London's grey sprawl, with the major part of his journey still ahead, Gary stretched, staring down the tunnel of dancing raindrops. With the remains of the Chablis pressing on his temples and Joanne's soft, white expanse of flesh in his mind's eye, he had slipped into the realms of self-satisfaction when a figure shot unexpectedly across the road in front of him.

Dream jolted into nightmare.

His brain shot into overdrive. His foot slammed on the brake and the car slewed in a barely-controlled emergency stop. There were a sickening series of lurches as the tyres thudded over something on the road. The car stalled. He pulled on the hand brake, knocked the gear-change out of drive, and climbed slowly from the car to stand dazed in the drizzle, waiting for someone to turn up and do something.

Who he expected, or what they'd do, he didn't know, but someone had to have seen it wasn't his fault, someone had to take charge.

It hadn't happened. It wasn't real.

Yet deep inside his mind a quiet voice whispered that he'd driven over someone.

Then he saw the girl lying in an unnatural sprawl around the curb of the central reservation where the force of the impact had thrown her.

Oh, God.

He sidled hesitantly closer, glancing around guiltily, regretting the impulse that had made him stop. She moved and groaned. A vivid image of blue lights and sirens filled his mind, and a whole heap of other stuff followed, like police, losing his driving licence, losing his job. It was surprising what the brain could come up with in the space of a few seconds.

It also came up with a very good solution: run.

The girl's eyes flicked open.

There was a moment of disorientation before her eyes focused. She whimpered slightly, seeing a figure looming above her, threw up an arm as if to ward away danger, and screamed at the unexpected pain of that sudden movement.

'Oh, God, shush!' Gary hissed, making calming,

flapping motions with his hands. The desperate fear in her eyes drained, to be replaced by something else: a flat, almost inhuman expression.

His mind notched into a lower gear.

What normal person would have been out on a night like this? Who had she been running from, and why? Torn between a slim social conscience and a huge fear of the consequences of doing the right thing, he hovered uncertainly. He sensed the presence of witnesses, faceless eyes peering out from behind shielded windows. Certain of his high alcohol level, self-preservation once again raised its head. Someone would have made an anonymous call by now, and his career depended on retaining his driving licence.

He took a step back.

As if some animal instinct let her know his intentions, her fist clenched around a handful of his trouser leg.

'Get me up.'

The harsh timbre of her voice made him jump.

He obeyed the command without realising he'd done so. As he hauled her to her feet she gasped with pain. Her face paled. She swayed against him for a moment until will-power alone overcame the weakness.

'Is he alive?'

Gary's eyes reluctantly followed her line of sight.

His stomach lurched horribly. It was the event he'd been refusing to accept. There was a crumpled lump on the road behind them, lying in a widening, viscous pool spreading out over the dark tarmac.

Oh, God.

He knew he'd gone over something, but his relief at finding the girl alive had made him avoid the memory, pretend for a second that it hadn't really happened.

The girl clutched at his sleeve, pulling him along, using him to help her. He avoided looking directly at the mess of what had once been a human being, but the girl bent over, trying unsuccessfully to pull it over onto its back.

'Jesus, don't!'

He touched the girl's shoulder, adding more softly, 'You can't do anything.'

She moved awkwardly, trying not to use her right arm, and her voice was thick with pain.

'Help me! I can see he's dead. If he wasn't I'd finish the job. Bastard!'

Realising that the dead man rather than himself was the object of her hatred, Gary took hold of the shoulder of the body, and pulled. Most of the face was gone and blood was seeping from various gaps in the man's clothing.

As the body flopped onto its back he turned away and was violently sick. Finally he mastered the nausea that had turned his insides to liquid fire, and swung back to the girl, keeping his eyes averted from the corpse.

She was surprisingly calm: no hysteria, no tears or accusations. Then he realised that while he had been emptying the contents of his stomach, she'd been searching through the dead man's pockets. He watched in disbelief as she pulled a wallet from an inner pocket, rummaged briefly, then threw it aside to join a small pile of scattered possessions, including a leather fob of keys and a pile of screwed-up papers. There was a sudden pause, a small intake of breath, and he knew she'd found whatever she was looking for. He couldn't quite make it out, but she slipped the trophy into her pocket. He was shocked out of his horror by her callousness.

'What the hell are you doing?'

She glanced up at him. In the glare of the street light her face was a sullen yellow mask, but her eyes burned with a hatred that seared him into silence. He'd supposed, at the girl's obvious flight, that the man was attacking her: a jealous boyfriend, a rapist, a mugger.

Now he wondered if she'd been the aggressor.

Maybe the dead man had been her trick, her mark. Maybe she'd already stolen from him and was being chased with some justification.

He took a step towards his car.

From somewhere she pulled a gun, and pointed it at him. She grinned slightly, but there was no humour in that baring of teeth. It was an animal reaction, one of survival.

'Get my bag and get me out of here,' she said.

He'd never seen a real gun before. The rather small dark hole which stared at him was more menacing than he would have guessed, now that he was looking straight into it. It was only minutes since the impact, and yet he felt as if he'd been trapped in a nightmare forever. He stared at the girl, sure that he should do something clever, take the gun from her or just walk away, daring her to shoot, but he was frightened and confused. He bent and lifted the sports bag, surprised at the heavy bulk of it. Part of his mind wondered what the hell was in there; another said things were so bloody awful, what the hell did it matter, anyway?

There was rapid pattering of feet on damp tarmac. A flood of relief burst upon him as he heard the cavalry arrive, but in the same second the girl lifted the gun, fired it into the air, then pointed it back towards him. The report echoed loudly against the shuttered shop-fronts. The running figures doubled back like rabbits, and disappeared. He was left, standing in the drizzle with what he now knew was a loaded gun pointed at him, and still the police didn't arrive.

The girl levered herself to her feet. He wondered hopefully if she would pass out or something, but she wasn't that considerate. She wavered a bit then took a step.

'Your car,' she said.

He walked gingerly toward the Volvo, his horror at the dead man now taking second place to his own, more immediate danger. The girl limped to the passenger side. For a moment the car was between them. He felt a sense of security buoy him up. He could get in and drive off. She leaned against the car, obviously needing something to support her, but the muzzle pointing straight at the passenger window didn't waver.

'I can shoot you through the glass.'

Having never before been threatened with anything other than words, he was unsure of a gun's true capabilities, and folded once more. He threw the bag into the back and climbed in, while she slid in the other side with a wince of pain.

'Now drive!'

He rammed the car angrily into drive and gunned away, as fast as the automatic would let him, slamming the girl back into the seat.

She grunted with pain.

Now he was back in his car, his own space, he regained some measure of self-respect. No one would argue against the threat of a weapon. No one would blame him for doing as he'd been told; it wasn't a sign of weakness.

The girl's gaze alternated between him and the road.

Would she really shoot?

'Left here,' she said.

He squealed the car too fast around the corner.

She drew breath sharply.

Next left, a few blocks, then right.

For a while they wiggled through a maze of smaller roads. She knew her way around all right. Now they were in suburbia; miles of faceless homes, parks, and small shopping malls shot by. He was completely lost.

In the distance, police sirens blossomed and faded.

Then there was just the night, the open road, and the rain. Eventually he came to a wide junction he recognised.

His glance sidled towards her. Although she was still conscious, her skin was grey and speckled with sweat, her mouth compressed to a thin slit.

She said nothing.

He hesitated for just a moment, then turned left automatically, heading for home. Every so often he

10

glanced at her, but she didn't move, just sat there, back to the door, the injured arm resting on her lap, and the gun still pointing towards him.

When she spoke he almost jumped.

'Where are we headed?'

'Southampton.'

'You live there?'

'Yes.'

'That'll do.'

'You want me to take you home?'

His voice rose fractionally. He'd never seen a female he disliked more. Hard, dirty and, judging by her actions, from the seamier side of London. He didn't want to have anything to do with her. Besides, what the hell would he say to his wife? Except it was more about what she'd say to him.

The girl laughed, as if she could read his mind.

'Just keep driving. I'll tell you where to drop me off, and then we can both keep quiet, can't we?'

Gary scowled, irritated.

'Put that thing away. You're not going to shoot me when I'm driving.'

Her eyes flashed darkly, met his.

'Trust me, I will. I haven't got a lot to lose. If they find me now, they'll kill me.'

'Who will? What did you do to that poor bastard?'

He was left to conjecture his own answer.

His eyes flicked towards her again.

She was a lot younger than he'd first supposed. Christ, possibly only late teens. He'd get done for child-molesting, too. Dressed in ill-fitting jeans, a sweatshirt, and a grimy three-quarter length coat, she was certainly not something he'd make a pass at, but who would believe him? Her dark blonde hair was lank, greasy, and unkempt. He didn't know whether the rank smell was coming from her or the coat she wore; whichever, it offended his sensibilities. Dirt belonged to the underclass, with people who didn't move in his circles, and he resented the fact that she was in his nice car.

He felt violated.

Beyond the warmth of the car, rain continued to fall, the windscreen wipers and lights carving a path through the gloom. Towards what, he didn't know.

No one need know he'd killed a man.

He could get back to his life, pretend all this never happened. It hadn't been his fault; he hadn't intended it, for God's sake. He'd simply been caught up in someone else's nightmare, and it wasn't fair.

But though weary to the point of exhaustion, he knew that even if he was presented with a bed now, sleep would evade him. He wondered what was happening back at the scene of the accident; no, crime. It might have been an accident, but now it was a hit and run.

He didn't know which carried the greater penalty; running someone down while inebriated, or running someone down and scarpering. Either would lose him his driving licence and, ergo, his job. A nasty premonition of the future shuddered through him. He wondered whether anyone had the number of his car, or his description, but with forensics being what they were, these days, and bloody cameras everywhere, they might trace him anyway.

Hit and run.

Christ, they'd be all out to find him. He should have called the police. But the girl wouldn't have let him, and that was the truth.

Filled with guilt, and expecting at any moment to be hauled out of his car by an irate seven-foot policeman with a chip on his shoulder, he was becoming dangerous.

'Pull in here,' she said.

He jumped.

His passenger had sat in virtual silence for the last hour, and although he kept hoping that she would pass out, her eyes had burned him for the whole journey.

They were on a dual carriageway heading into

Southampton, and there was a slip-road ahead, indicating a layby with picnic facilities. He knew it well. It had once been part of the old road, and disappeared behind some trees, to emerge a bit further along the duel carriageway. It was the kind of place lorry drivers would stop to put their feet on the dashboard and wait for time to catch up with their hours of driving.

But the lay-by was empty.

The safety of Southampton was an orange halo ahead, but the lay-by was dark and menacing. They were in no-man's land.

Coldness flooded his gut.

She was going to kill him.

She was going to shoot him and leave his body to be found whenever someone chose to pull in for a snack or a leak. He indicated, slowed down, and came to a halt, clutching the wheel with white hands, while mentally getting ready to attack her.

'Put the hand-brake on. Put the car into neutral. Turn off the engine. Put the key on the dashboard. Put your hand back on the wheel.'

As if guessing his desperation, she enunciated each command sharply, lifting the gun slightly. She held it steady, her hand white and tense, and he was once more intimidated into obedience.

Low and harsh, her voice was honeyed with the promise of death. He was going to die. He clutched the wheel, kept his eyes to the front, afraid to breathe, afraid to look. He heard the window slide down. Then the door opened. The car lifted fractionally as she backed out.

'Get out.'

He whimpered, hating the sound of his own fear.

'Don't. Please, don't.'

'Throw out my bag.'

He opened the back door and pulled the green kitbag on to the road. The dull thud sounded like a falling body. He pushed the door shut slowly. Was this it? He realised he was making a keening sound under his breath, and swallowed hard. Beads of sweat broke out on his forehead.

'Now get back in the car. Put your hands on the steering wheel.'

He clambered back into the driver's seat. Her elbow was on the window frame, the gun pointing unerringly at his head. A small noise escaped his tight throat.

'Take out your wallet.'

After everything he'd gone through she was going to rob him? It added insult to his already injured pride, his eyes glared murderously, but the tiny black hole of the gun faced him down.

'Open it. With one hand! That's good. Now, tell me what you've got in there.'

'Bitch!' He flipped the wallet open. 'About seventy quid.'

'Not the money. Papers, cards, driving licence. There, give me that. Gary Bryant,' she said in a harsh whisper. 'I know you. I know where you live. Go to the police, and I'll destroy you. I'll destroy everything you hold dear: your house, your finances, your wife, your children, your career. I'll make you wish I'd killed you here, today.'

To his surprise she backed off.

He didn't have to be told. He wrestled the key into the slot, hit the door locking mechanism and the button to raise the window, slammed into drive, and gunned off with an angry squeal of tyres. It wasn't until several minutes had passed without the sound of a following gunshot that a great shuddering sob wrenched out of his throat.

Breathing heavily, he slowed his erratic driving down to something approaching control, and let the miles slide between himself and the girl with the eyes of a snake.

More sober than at any time in his life, reality hit him between the eyes. Shit, fuck, he thought, slamming both hands angrily on the wheel several times. It wasn't fair. It really just wasn't fair. He thought back over the

14

last couple of hours. A night of passion, a good deal finalised, the world was his oyster, then Bam!

Out of nowhere, an accident resulting in manslaughter or even murder, and he was instantly a criminal. The implications terrified him. He could still go to the police, tell them what had happened. They would come up here straight away, sirens and lights shattering the night, and even if she holed up like the wounded animal she was, they'd find her.

But he knew he wouldn't.

Her threat and all the other the implications raced each other around in his mind, police, prison, job, wife. Shit, it was just too big to handle.

He drove on down the road towards home, alone with his recollections and his fuming anger. And besides, even if they believed him, when the shit flew, some of it would stick. He'd seen it happen to others. His reputation would be mud, his career finished. He'd never be able to walk away. Exaggerated out of all proportion by the press, they'd drag every sordid little detail out into the open; every odd liaison, every cut corner in his business transactions. He'd never get another job.

Shaking, he finally made it home.

His wife, Charlene, realising something was badly wrong, hooked the story out of him piecemeal in a long, angry session the following day. It took her a lot less time to decide what to do about it. They watched the evening news together, he in a cold sweat, she in chilled silence.

The hit and run made single day headlines.

Shots were thought to have been heard, but the man who died was known to the police; a pimp and drug dealer, with, not surprisingly, a reputation for being vicious.

No one mentioned a girl.

'She was obviously running from him when I hit her,' Gary commented tightly. 'She was probably one of his women. No one's going to spend time searching for

15

a missing whore, even if they did know. It'd be a waste of the tax-payer's money.'

Her eyes narrowed. 'You said she stole from him after he was dead. What did she take?'

'Christ, I don't know! Something tiny: a book maybe, or a phone. I couldn't see. It was dark. I was busy bringing my guts up. Then she came up with the gun. Probably got that off him, too.'

'And, well done, you helped her over there so she could get it.'

The cold derision in her voice shrank his self-worth more effectively than the blonde girl's gun.

'As far as I can see there's nothing that can tie any of that to you. Just say nothing. There's no point in courting trouble.'

'OK,' he agreed meekly.

Chapter 2

Redwall squeezed his bulk between two filing cabinets to get to his desk. Old and scratched, the bare wood bore the hallmarks of thirty years' use, but he had refused to swap it out when the place was refurbished. After a year, his was the only desk that didn't wobble when he leaned his elbows on it.

Sunlight was barred by vertical blinds in deference to computer screens. The office walls were apple green, the carpet the colour of scuffed shoes, and the large notice board couldn't be seen beneath the clutter of official notifications which choked the department on a regular basis.

He shared the tiny space with his colleague and partner, Jim, who now shoved a fact sheet and a photo over his way. Vince Bertini. He recognised the dead guy's face from several minor incidents over the last few years. The mug shot, of course, not the one which had been snapped last night, after half his face had been smeared along the A 406.

While he knew his search for the H&R driver would be as diligent as he could make it, he felt a measure of relief in the fact that the dead man wasn't someone's loving father or husband. It wouldn't have been the first time he'd knocked on a door to bring the sort of news that only a police officer could bring. That never got any easier. You just learned to hide it better.

He had two children of his own: a boy of sixteen who was desperate to get a motorbike, and a headstrong girl of fourteen. The sheer pressure of worrying about them sometimes drove him to distraction.

He shook his head to clear the morbid sense of failure that overwhelmed him in the presence of violent death.

'Did you find out if he's got any relatives?' he asked.

'None that we know of.'

Jim was overweight, more inclined towards a pint and a game than a conquest and, to Redwall's mind, thought rather less about his appearance than might have been expected in a young, unmarried man. His slow manner of speech, thickened by a west country burr, wasn't going to further his career. He wondered if Jim was destined for a non-eventful bachelor's existence, or whether he minded. Theirs wasn't the kind of relationship that engendered personal confidences.

Jim carried on in his unhurried way.

'Barnes told me Vince's father died in a brawl a couple of years back, and it was rumoured the son had something to do with it. He's got a file going back to the age of nine, and has been pretty intimate with other known thugs most of his life.'

'He ever do time?'

'A year in juvey in his teens. Apparently he thanked the warden when he was released, told him it had been a real education.'

'I don't doubt it. Give me the profile.'

Jim flipped open a daffodil yellow folder as he sat down, the seat creaking in complaint.

'From what we know, he made most of his money from the girls, but wasn't above dabbling in anything at all money-lending, drugs, guns, extortion; you know the score. All small time stuff, but he was keen to get in on the real action. He was twenty-eight, good looking, in a spiv kind of way, and seems he thought the underworld was his oyster. Only it seems he wasn't that bright. Nasty but dumb. I heard on the vine that he was acting as go-between for some larger dealers up country. Distribution, they think. Seems he was under surveillance for a bit, a year or so back, but by who, I

18

don't know. Probably narcs, but they didn't admit to it.'

Interdepartmental secrecy. The bane of the Force.

They were all supposed to be working towards he same end, weren't they? How was he supposed to do his job?

'Anyway, we've got nothing concrete. He had a stable of his own and a reputation for being violent enough to keep 'em.'

'Illegals?'

Jim was scanning the file.

'Maybe some. But I heard recently he was seen hanging around the station.'

He put on a sultry voice with the merest hint of Italian charm. 'Are you hungry, you poor leetle girl? Was daddy nasty to you? Is that why you ran away? Never mind, come with me, I'll look after you. Everything will be very deefferent from now on.'

He flushed slightly, at Redwall's amused expression. 'Well, Christ, don't they know nothing's ever free?'

'People who are desperate, hope. And you've only got to see his photo to realise why the girls believed him. He had the look of Valentino about him.'

'Not anymore,' Jim said.

'Not anymore,' Redwall agreed.

His eyes dropped to the mug shot, probably taken several years previously. It could have been that of a high school footballer, complete with a cow's lick and a cheeky smile with dimples. 'He was a pretty boy, sure enough. On the surface.'

'Whether his toms will be pleased or unhappy about the demise of their lord and master I don't know, but there'll be a scrabble on for ownership, you wait and see. But that's not all. It now appears he inherited quite a sizeable chunk of warehousing from his late, unlamented father. That should bring some relatives out of the woodwork.'

'I don't doubt it. Can we get an order to go and have a rummage? You can bet he was moving hot goods around.'

19

'It's in hand.'

Redwall flipped a few more sheets over. 'Do you think this was a hit?'

'Doesn't have the hallmarks, but something went down. Even if it was a genuine hit and run, how come he'd run into a car on a near empty road?'

'Well, we know he wasn't drunk or high. Chasing, or being chased, maybe? There was a gunshot.'

'Apparently; that's what I wondered. I guess we'd better have a chat with his toms.'

You never got anything out of toms, he knew from experience. 'I'd like to look round his house, first.'

They drove down to Victoria Street.

The row of identical terraced houses, built of red brick, were squashed into a narrow street dating from the thirties or thereabouts. Set back from the street behind brick walls, the tiny front gardens of most had been paved for bins and bikes. This was a known red-light area, holding all the seedy promise of the underground skin trade. The street lamps leaning drunkenly down the uneven pavement were mostly smashed, and most of the houses had the grubby appeal of years of neglect. Vince's house, number 18, was no exception. Paint hung in strips from rotten fascia boards, the roof had more growth on it than the garden, and the grimy windows were backed by blankets nailed to the frames.

A sad come-down for a once-upmarket family home.

It was not a salubrious area by anyone's standards, now.

There was a Fiat Panda parked outside, with a uniform standing guard by the open door when they arrived, and a search was already underway. Though they were ostensibly searching for something that could lead to a motive for Vince's murderer, they knew what he'd been and were simply looking for anything and everything.

Two women, aged respectively around fifteen and eighteen at initial appearance, had been asleep inside when the house had been entered, and were now down at the station with a WPC, awaiting the arrival of a social worker. The tattooed thug, who had turned up later, scratching a two-day stubble, was venting abuse in a holding cell for impeding them in their duties.

From the front door a corridor stretched alongside a set of stairs that marched in a single flight to a landing. On the ground floor, two doors on the left and one on the right were open, betraying the stench of the women's trade: heavy perfume mingled with the after effects of sex, stale sweat and a hint of vomit. The kitchen, once a scullery, was tacked onto the back, at the end of the corridor.

The house was larger than it appeared from outside, having three storeys, and the rooms surprisingly tall and airy once the makeshift curtains had been ripped down from the rattling, sash cord windows.

On superficial inspection there was little to find of any interest in any of the downstairs and first floor rooms, just the sad evidence that the young women who occupied and plied their trade in them had few personal possessions. Anything of value had probably long gone to buy drugs or had been claimed by Vince. After all, to him the women themselves had been no more than commodities, to be acquired and used.

Redwall headed for Vince's apartment at the top of the building; the Penthouse Suite as one detective derisively labelled it. Unlike the lower rooms, this boasted a scattering of expensive furnishings: white leather TV chairs, a chrome coffee table, some rugs and pictures. It tried to give the impression of designer-chic, but missed the mark by a motorway mile.

Aside from the living room, there was a bathroom, a tiny kitchen, and two bedrooms, one of which was functional, the other done out in black paint and purple satin. It contained a concealed video set-up; whether for porn or blackmail would be anybody's guess.

Not even here, though, was there evidence of cleanliness, and Redwall's face set with grim determination as they methodically worked their way through the piles of porn magazines, papers, and personal items.

Given Vince's rather unsavoury reputation, it was highly unlikely that he would have trusted banks, so the search rapidly progressed to the level of tapping for wall cavities and lifting floor boards, but, although a couple of fairly well-hidden hidey-holes were exposed, there was little of interest in them.

When they finished, his stretch of warehousing would be the next port of call. Redwall was just waiting for the search warrant to come through. Though, by the time they got it, it was likely that anything suspect would be long gone. He was actually looking for something that would give him a handle on the dead man; who his colleagues might have been, and what scams he'd been running that might have upset someone enough to murder him.

The search revealed surprisingly little of Vince as a character, and he was left feeling largely unsatisfied. He stared at the one more recent photograph of Vince they had discovered, as if trying to see past the gloss to the man within. Dark, heavy-lashed eyes stared back from a face thickened slightly with age. He had retained that arrogant curl to his lips Redwall recalled from the earlier image, though it was now framed by a carved, designer beard.

Redwall imagined that the first sight of such a vision must have touched the heartstrings of the sad and lonely girls who'd climbed on board the London Express to seek the better life.

But not anymore, as Jim had said.

Vince had been identified in the early hours by virtue of the contents of a wallet that lay scattered around, and Redwall wasn't expecting any surprises when the coroner finally got round to his examination.

Aside from the obvious physical attraction, however, his character was as flat and insubstantial as the photograph. He just didn't exist in the house as a person.

He wondered who actually owned the house and the warehouse on paper, and what kind of a legal mess this was all going to end up in. No wiser, he left the house to the team and drove back to the station in the miserable kind of drizzle that usually set in for days.

Back at the station, he tried talking to the man first.

Dressed in once-expensive suit, the jacket of which stretched thinly across his massive frame, he could have passed for a bouncer except that Redwall deduced most of the muscle was between his ears.

He was an assistant, he told them.

In what?

Oh, anything, you know. He helped with stuff. He hadn't been with Vince for long. Yeah, there were girls, lodgers who paid rent. Nice girls. Vince was a paragon of virtue, giving them cheap rooms until they could find jobs. Were they prostitutes? Nah. But was he going to be allowed to keep his room in the house? Never mind Vince was dead, it was awkward. He had no place else to go. After a little persuasion he managed to recall the names of four girls, but that was all.

The two girls waiting at the Station for whatever life was going to thrust at them, were obviously exhausted. Ladies of the night, they had probably not long fallen asleep when they'd been hauled out of bed. Their nervousness was visible only in the tiny, rapid movements of the eyes, but it was clear from the hardness of their faces that ignorance had become a way of life: they saw nothing, knew nothing.

Redwall recalled his vivacious daughter, thinking, there but for the grace of God...

Toms all looked the same after a while.

Not in physical appearance, but in the blank emptiness behind their eyes, as if the thing that made them individual humans had been amputated. Worn out husks of the women they might have been, their young faces reflected lack of respect for themselves and everyone else. Their inadequate clothes, skimpy skirts, lacy tops and heeled shoes simply betrayed their profession.

They'd been told Vince was dead, but not how he'd died. It was doubtful they'd liked him or would mourn him, but their situation was now unstable. No one liked that.

He turned to the taller of the two; dark haired, pale skinned, anorexic, he'd come across her before. She had her arms crossed tightly around meagre breasts. He imagined her playing the part of the schoolgirl. He thought school was probably where she should still be.

'Alice, I'm Inspector Redwall. I know you've been told Vince died last night. I'd just like to ask you a few questions about it.'

'I dunno anything about it.'

'About Vince, then.'

'Am I in trouble?'

'No. We're just trying to establish what happened. Were you at home last night?'

'Home?' She snorted with amusement. 'Yeah, I was in. Mostly.'

'Was Vince at home?

'How would I know? He doesn't ask my permission to come and go.'

'Do you know if he recently had dealings that resulted in arguments with anyone?'

'You mean anyone want to top him? Try half London. He was well into his wheeling and dealing. You don't mess with those guys.'

'What guys?'

Her eyes shuttered. She shrugged. 'Any of 'em. So he was murdered? Kinda not a surprise. I heard it was hit and run, though.'

Where the hell had she got that from?

'We don't know what happened, that's what we're trying to establish.'

She examined her nails, showing how little she cared.

'Did Vince carry?'

Her eyes flashed to his.

'Dunno. Never saw anything. Was he shot?'

He turned to the other girl. Blonde-from-a-bottle, with half an inch of black roots, she was shorter, but with the same lack of substance that suggested she survived on less than an adequate diet. She stank of cigarettes.

'Sandy, were you at home last night?'

'Some.'

'And where were you when you weren't asleep?

'Walking.'

'Where?'

'Around.'

'Did you see Vince last night?'

'Yeah, he was in some.'

'Did he have anyone with him?'

'Dunno.'

'Did he go out?'

'I guess.'

'Was he with anyone?'

'Dunno.'

'Where did he go?'

'Think he asks my permission? Tells me what he's at? Gimme a break. He went out. That's all.'

'Do you know what time?'

'Nah.'

'Alice, do you know what time Vince went out?'

'No.'

'Was someone with him?'

She yawned pointedly, pale eyes assessing him from below shuttered lids. He knew why, of course. It was more dangerous to talk than not. Pigs could put you in prison, but the others could smack you bad, break your arms, or worse.

'Who else was in the house last night?'

Eyes half closed, she gave a faint, derisory smile.

'We're not after you, this isn't about turning tricks.'

'Tricks?' she asked ingenuously, and crossed her arms with slow deliberation. Co-operation was at an end.

'Give us a break, here. We just want to find out *why* he was *where* he was at that time in the morning.'

'Give *us* a break. How in hell do we know?' she said. 'You woke us up breaking into the house.'

The 'we' wasn't royal. It was a threat, a promise binding the two girls together: you don't talk, neither do I, and maybe we get out of this thing alive; go back on the streets and have another go at earning enough to break out of the cage.

'We didn't break in. We used Vince's keys. He didn't need them anymore.'

There was a potent silence.

'Has anyone given you anything to eat?'

'Yeah. Could do with a fag, though.'

'Go and find some cigarettes, Jim.'

Jim slipped out, came back with his own brand. The girls both lit up, inhaling eagerly. The red glow was a useful, impersonal focus.

Jim asked, 'Anyone see you in the house last night?'

Alice laughed. 'What d'you think?'

They probably had lots of alibis, but not ones that were going to come forward, and they probably didn't have names.

'Can we go now?'

'Not yet. The social worker just needs to verify your ages. She's likely to offer you a way out, a place to stay, if you want out.'

'And a job as a till tart, too? Can you see me behind a till. Yes, ma'am, no ma'am, up yours ma'am.'

She was right, he couldn't.

They just wanted to get out of there, take stock of their situation, find out who owned them now. They didn't care about Vince, but his demise left them in an unenviable position, up for grabs by the next pimp with a fist.

'Do you know where the other girls are?' Redwall asked.

'What other girls?'

He studied Sandy's face, wondering if he'd even recognise her again. She sucked at her cigarette, small, hard puffs that imploded her cheeks.

'Gill and Jessie, for starters.'

There was a brief silence.

He sighed theatrically, stretched, and settled into the hard-backed chair. 'I can keep you here for as long as it takes. It's something I can find out, so you won't be giving anything away. When was the last time you saw either of them?'

There was a small pause, then Sandy stubbed out her cigarette with deliberation. 'Gill was at some hotel with a client for a few days. Don't know which one, but he's a regular of hers. He pays good.'

A travelling businessman or salesman, probably taking time out from his wife.

'Thank you. And Jessie?'

Redwall picked up on the almost infinitesimal hesitation. He could feel something emanating from the woman. He'd felt it before: hatred.

'What do you know about Jessie?' he said softly.

He watched her face set into hard plastic; doll-like in its youth.

'Was she with Vince last night?'

He looked searchingly at each woman in turn.

Alice spat into the silence, 'She can look after herself, that one. Wouldn't 'ave put it past her to have killed the bastard, and good luck to 'er. But what about us? What're we gonna do now? You tell me that.'

Later, Redwall sat, thinking, chin on his hand. It had taken a while, but the girls had finally started to talk.

They had been working that night, and Vince had taken their money as usual around three am, and would have come for more, later. Instead, they had been roused the next morning by the police, not realising at that time Vince had even left the house, let alone the fact he was dead.

What were they, his keepers?

27

But even so, his death had obviously shaken them. It had probably left them homeless, vulnerable to any pimp who wanted to add them to his stable. As it turned out, they were both over twenty-one, so social services couldn't intervene, and as the girls didn't take advantage of their help, later in the day they walked out into the streets and were gone.

With a sigh, he phoned his wife to say he might be back late and got back to the statements from the hit and run witnesses. A few people had come forward with wary social conscience. No one wanted to be involved with the police; with the media, maybe, for a moment of transient celebrity, but the police? No.

No-one had actually seen what went down. Most had run towards the scene after the sound of the impact; probably more had run the other way. They had seen a car stopped in the road and a man standing by what later turned out to be a body. Then the man had walked to his car and had driven off in a hurry. But who had fired a shot, if it had been a shot, and who it had been fired at, remained a mystery. They found no cartridge case at the scene, and didn't have the manpower to spread the search.

Not for someone like Vince, anyway.

It had been a cold, drizzly night, just like tonight, and no one had been near enough to get a good look at anything. They couldn't describe the driver who scarpered, and their descriptions of the car were vague. It had possibly been of a light-ish colour, it had been hard to tell, what with the rain and reflections from the orange street lights. It had been bigger than a saloon, possibly an estate or a bigger four by four. And that was all they had, except for the one man who thought he'd seen a woman at the scene.

Someone had been sent out to take a 360 image from the point of impact, and was scanning it now for security cameras. The statement that you couldn't do anything without being caught on camera these days, wasn't backed by his experience. Half the time the cameras were fake, hadn't been switched on, overwrote their own images on a twenty-four hour basis, or were recorded onto dodgy media. But you had to look.

The witness, David Finch, was mid-twenties, clean, and relatively tidy, but there was something indefinable about him that made Redwall uneasy.

He shook his hand and introduced himself.

'Detective Inspector Redwall. Thank you for coming in, David. Take a seat. I understand you saw the accident we're investigating?'

'I didn't see before they stopped. I didn't see anyone go under the car, which is what I heard after, on the news. I just heard the brakes, and the skid, and a bang. Didn't sound right, so I went to have a look.'

'What kind of bang?'

'You know, when a car's pranged. A thump I guess.'

'I understand you saw the driver?'

'Not really *saw* him. I was too far away.'

'Was he alone?'

'No, there were definitely two people. No doubt about it. It seemed as if they were arguing, or something.'

'Can you describe them?'

'Really, I was too far away. I think it was a bloke and a woman; just struck me, the way they were standing, or something. She was smaller than the bloke, anyway. She might have been blonde, but with the rain and all...'

'How close were you?'

'I was about as far as...' he looked around, then out of the window. 'See that lamp-post? I guess I was about as far as that. But it was night, and it was drizzling.'

'Did it look as if he was coercing her in some way?'

'It seemed as if he was holding onto her arm. I just thought she was a whore, or it was a lover's tiff or something.'

His tone was defensive.

'Other than the thump, did you hear anything unusual?'

'No. By the time I could see anything, the car was stopped, and these two were gassing in the middle of the road. Then they both went over and got in the car and drove off pretty smartish. I only called you 'cos I heard it on the news. I didn't see a body or anything.'

'Did you see what sort of car it was?'

'No. But it was an estate, big, like a Mercedes or something. Not one of those little city jobs. I didn't see the registration. And I couldn't see the colour, not in the night.'

'Did they both get in the same side?'

'Why would anyone do that?'

'If she was being coerced.'

'Oh.'

He thought about it. 'No, they both got in different sides. I think she got in the passenger side, but I couldn't swear to it.'

'And there wasn't anything else at all that struck you at the time?'

'I told you what I saw, that's all. I wasn't really paying much attention. You don't, you know.'

Redwall knew. In the city you didn't see, didn't hear, and didn't look anyone in the eye. In a city where millions lived shoulder to shoulder, no one ever really saw anyone else. Especially at night.

'What do you do for a living, David?'

'What's that got to do with anything?'

'You don't have to answer. I'm just getting a handle on who you are.'

'I push paper. In M&S head office. In accounting.'

'Can you tell me what you were doing on the street at that time in the morning?'

He flushed, bristling. 'I'd been to a night club, Maxim's. I thought you were interested in what I saw.'

'I'm simply trying to establish your credence as a witness, if it should come to that. Had you been drinking?'

'What do you think?'

'How much had you had to drink?'

'I don't know, do I? But they'd stopped serving a while before.'

'They'd been closed for over an hour by that time. Where were you?'

'Walking. Clearing my head. I can't sleep after a nightclub, too wired.'

'Of course.'

Not buying drugs, not looking for a quick blow job on the corner, simply walking to clear his head. There was a slim possibility it was the truth.

Eventually the statement was typed and signed.

'If we need to ask anything else, we'll call,' he said.

David muttered that he hoped not.

'He came forward, he didn't have to,' Redwall told Jim. 'And he's reluctant enough to not be lying. But what do we make of it? A car stopped. A man and woman were having a tiff over a dead body. And one of them rifled Vince's pockets. They must have been together. If she got in the car on the opposite side to the man, she wasn't under duress, was she? Perhaps it was a lover's tiff after all. Or a partners-in-crime tiff.'

'I'm not convinced it was anything but an accident. Sure, there are people out there who would have done Vince for a variety of reasons, but if he'd been a target, the middle of a main dual carriageway seems an unlikely place to choose. Running a guy down isn't a particularly controlled way of topping a bloke. If it was a hit, the killer would have been up close and personal. a knife or bullet, or using a long-distance rifle.'

'H'm. And if it wasn't for the fact that someone went through Vince's pockets, I'd put this down as a plain old H&R. But...' Redwall paused, drumming his fingers on the desk. 'Why the shot?'

'It could be a gangland whack that just went squiffy? If Vince was running from someone who had a gun, he could have dived under the car by accident.'

'If there was a shot at all.'

'Yes no-one is absolutely sure. It could have been a

back-fire. David Finch is the best witness we have, and he didn't mention a shot.'

'I actually have more faith in him as a witness because of that. He probably heard that a shot was possibly fired, yet he didn't add that to his story, so isn't inventing things to make his story more plausible to us.'

'We're missing something, aren't we?'

'I guess. We're missing something big.'

He scraped his chair back. 'Let's go check out that warehouse.'

Chapter 3

With a strange sense of loss Jessie watched the Volvo swerve back up onto the duel carriageway. For a brief while she'd sunk into the expensive upholstery, feeling it wrap around her like protective arms. It had been difficult not to fall asleep, and now she was standing in the cold night again, as alone as she had ever been.

She looked down at the blood smeared on her hands, Vince's blood, but all she felt was vindication. He'd hurt her plenty. He hurt all the women, that's what he did, so it was a fitting end. If she hadn't been hurt in the accident she would have danced a jig on his dead body. It was definitely worth the pain of a broken arm to know that Vince was no more than a smut of tissue spread on a London road.

It had been one hell of a night, though, and while she'd been reluctant to leave the illusion of safety the car provided, the angry, narrow-faced man driving it had been close to breakdown.

He'd been scared shitless, but his fear had reached saturation point, and he'd been on the verge of turning. If he'd attacked her she would have been done for, and she didn't want to murder him, twat though he was. Her lips narrowed. But if he'd given her no choice, it would have been his bad luck.

She loathed the weakness of being female, never mind one with a broken arm. Damn, she should have been born a man. They did ops for women trapped in men's bodies they slit their dicks and turned them outside in, she'd seen it on TV. But could they do for a

33

man trapped in a woman's body? Not that she felt like a man, really, she just wanted the strength, the power to be her own boss.

She moved, and pain shot through her arm. She didn't need a doctor to tell her it was broken, yet didn't dare go to one to get it fixed. Life was just so much pain. God knows why she kept trying to live, yet that was just the way it was.

She wondered about the driver, Gary.

She'd put the wind up him, but he might have been calling the cops the moment he drove off. She doubted it, though. Never mind her threats, once you've run away from something, it's kind of fait accompli. You don't go back and invite trouble.

At the side of a strange road in a new dawn, wondering what the hell she should do now, she heaved the heavy bag onto her good shoulder and began to walk. She had money, so finding a motel would be easy enough once she got cleaned up, but the broken arm was a problem.

The moment she entered a hospital, there would be a paper trail. They'd take one look at her and start asking all sorts of awkward questions and probably bring in social workers. If her father had anything to do with it, she'd end up in one of those homes that were more like prisons. Oh, yes, he'd loved that.

She clutched the large army bag, and felt the first thrill of excitement. Money meant freedom, independence.

Gary didn't realise it, but he'd been her lucky Joker in the pack just as the deck seemed stacked against her. When the same fates that had given her a glimpse of the money and let her run with it, in a spirit of malicious spite they had also sent Vince back for something he'd forgotten just as she was on her way.

If it hadn't been for Gary, he would have killed her, for sure. You just didn't muck about with drugs money, because the bastards were not very amused by it. But with Vince dead, they wouldn't know where it had

34

gone. They would probably think Vince had it stashed somewhere, so that was that. Life, which had seemed not worth bothering with, opened up before her.

The glow of Southampton disappeared as the streetlights faded into dawn. She'd never been there before, but what the hell. One city was as good as another. But one thing was for sure: she would no longer allow any man to rule her life. Not her, not any more. Who needed to invent bogeymen when men were rotten to the core?

Her muscles were beginning to cramp a bit, but she knew to expect that, and her gait was slow and ungainly, favouring the extensive bruising that was paralysing her left side, where she'd been belted by the car. Must have caught the wing and been bounced off. A couple of seconds either way, and she'd be dead; either the car would have flattened her, or Vince would have.

For a while she listened for sirens, looked for flashing lights, for her nemesis to catch up with her, but all the day brought was a gradual increase in traffic. If Gary had told them about the gun the traffic would have ceased while armed police gathered up ahead; someone with a gun would surely be taken seriously. She considered chucking it, but didn't want to lose the feeling of safety it gave her, nestling like her own personal bodyguard in her pocket.

No, if he'd called the police she'd know by now.

She awarded herself a grim smile.

Things were going to work out.

The rain had almost ceased, and as dawn opened into day the artificial glow of the city disappeared. She listened for the sound of cars slowing down as she trudged along. It was rush hour, people zooming to where they had to be. It was unlikely that someone would simply stop and ask her if she wanted a lift. And if they did, one look at her would have them zooming off again.

She knew she was a mess. Dirty, bloody, and dressed

35

like a whore, which wasn't surprising. Her clothes had been given to her by Vince, and hadn't been chosen for the designer labels.

She was an outcast, now, well and truly.

She'd choose that any day in preference to the alternatives offered by society; that or death. She'd almost achieved that, once, too, and it hadn't scared her. Suicide hadn't felt like giving up, it had felt positive, like making your own decision in a world where decisions were made by others; like sticking your finger up at the world. But now she was glad she hadn't succeeded. A new start, a new life, things were going to change for the better.

She trudged on, fighting tiredness and the increasing nausea brought on by pain and withdrawal, until sprawling toy-town suburbia finally gave way to shops. Steering away from the main thoroughfare, she found a public toilet, and washed the blood from her face and hands. She took out some of Vince's money and bought a comb. Even with nothing more than her hair tidied she became less noticeable. Then she changed her clothes for something a bit more presentable, and bought something to eat, her first meal in at least forty-eight hours. She also bought a tub of painkillers and downed three times the recommended dose.

As she sat in the middle of Southampton the fire in her arm gradually receded to a dull ache. First, she had to get her arm fixed. She'd heard about doctors who'd do stuff for cash, but how did you find them? She grimaced, knowing the answer: you found the kind of person who would know.

She felt strangely light headed and nagging pains in her legs forced her to hug herself for a moment, striving to keep it under control. She urged to bring up the sandwiches she'd just eaten, and after a few moments, to the disgust of the passers-by, did so. Dismay trickled through the euphoria of freedom. She'd been away less than twenty-four hours.

The withdrawal was bad but would get worse.

How had she ever thought she could simply walk away?

That's why they did it, Vince, and his like. The smack wasn't wasted if it became a ball and chain that kept the most reluctant tom from running.

The honest citizens gave her a wide berth, not seeing was easier than having to do something, yet when one woman hesitatingly stepped closer her lips almost forming words, Jessie lifted eyes that burned with hatred, and the woman winced, stepped back, and disappeared.

She finally got up from the soiled seat, and limped away. You didn't sit still too long; she'd learned that in London, because sooner or later the police would come.

Her vision was doubling, and pain washed through her body with increasing urgency. She wandered around for most of the day, until the shop assistants began to yawn, until the thick swathe of shoppers began to thin. There was a crazy time when people ran from shop to shop, panicked into last minute purchases before the tills stilled. Then the lights went on: dirty yellow lights outside, cheerful, white lights inside. A faint mist descended and hung damply on her hair.

She shivered, her nerve ends screaming.

She hugged her good arm around her chest, and waited some more. She should have bought a sleeping bag or something, but it was too late, now. With the money she'd stolen, she could have afforded a room, too, but it wouldn't take someone with a lot of savvy to realise there was something wrong with her. She couldn't risk some do-gooder calling the police or the social workers. When the last of the shoppers were ejected and the doors locked, the night closed in. She chose a sheltered doorway and waited.

The window dressings stayed brightly lit, false cheer in the grim onset of an English autumn evening. Without the shoppers lining the streets, the pavements displayed their filth to her penetrating gaze

37

Her arm was now a swollen balloon. Muscles were contracting, grinding the broken ends of the bone, and every shiver was laced with pain. It would be easy not to act, but she had to save herself. No Superman of her childhood dreams was going to appear before her and solve all her problems.

She gritted her teeth and waited, scrunched into the doorway, knees to her chest, trying to control the involuntary shivers. Night moved slowly. It was the time when working people had eaten dinners and were curled up in front of the telly; when toms were uncurling from exhausted, drugged hangovers and gearing themselves up to face another long night to earn just enough to buffer reality with another hit.

With the instinct of one who had been there before, Jessie finally eased herself from the doorway, and began to walk. She wandered towards the older residential areas, the seedy streets by old men's pubs where the toms would hang out; roads that passed by old warehouses, alongside parks.

She crossed a bridge over a dark river that roiled away towards the sea. This looked more promising: a maze of terraced housing; old, mellow, on narrow streets. A pub, once brightly painted, now pitted by the salt breeze, its picture of a pirate hanging askew. Now she was searching with her eyes carefully averted, shoulders bowed. The smell of fish was on the air, a smell that permeated the buildings from centuries of gutting. A couple of youths stumbled out of a door, drunk already.

'Want a good time, darling?'

'Fuck off,' she spat.

They followed her hopefully for a bit, their overt suggestions gradually turning to abuse. Jessie fingered the gun in her pocket, her lips bared in a humourless smile. If they only knew how she itched to turn, wipe the sarcasm from their faces, shoot the silly fucks. As the youths finally lost interest, Jessie took a deep breath, and let go of the gun.

Finally, she came to a crossroads, and discovered what she was looking for. Under a street lamp, diagonally opposite, two women stood watching, whispering to each other. Across the street in the shadows, a darker shadow lurked: wary customer or pimp? There was only one way to find out. A man walked towards her, eyes firmly fixed on some other horizon. A city type, he wore a long coat, and was definitely not shopping. She stepped in front of him, invading his personal space to hell.

'Want a good time, mister?'

He halted so quickly, he rocked on his heels.

His lip curled distastefully as he stepped hastily aside, pace increasing to put distance between them. Even if he'd been shopping he wouldn't have wanted a street girl.

Besides, she probably stank of vomit.

Recalling that, her gut spasmed, and she gasped as the movement grated the bones in her arm. Blackness hovered, she fought it back. Hang in there, kid, she told herself. Just hang in there.

One of the women walked across the street, high heels clacking, the other followed close behind.

'You can't work here. This is our patch.'

'Says who?'

Jessie assessed the hard blue eyes shining from a plaster-mould of make-up. She shrugged disdainfully, her turned shoulder insolence itself.

The shrill voice leapt an octave and echoed in the descending fog. 'You hear me, bitch? Fuck off. This is our patch. You can't work here.'

'Fuck you.'

The other woman took a step closer. Two to one. They were brave in the face of such odds. Jessie snarled, braced herself. If they attacked her, she'd put one of them down, for sure, broken arm and all; dent their pretty noses for them.

A rich voice spilled out of the darkness.

'Solly! Kit! Back off! Get your tails out there by the

39

light where the punters can get an eyeful, you lazy pieces of shit. You! Come here.'

Jessie jumped, as she was supposed to, and sidled over, cowed into obedience, but with just the right combination of reluctance and defiance. He was big, early thirties possibly, easy with his expensive clothing and gold rings.

'New here are you, darling?' he said pleasantly, arms crossing his chest.

'Nothin' to do with you,' she muttered, glaring, knowing the bruises now ripening on her face probably lent the air of a woman who has already been beaten. But he didn't know Vince was dead. Macho, vibrant, sadistic Vince, a splash on the pavement, and she had his gun. She made to sidle past, and he stepped quickly before her so that she'd to stop short to avoid slamming into his chest. Eyes filled with a wide breadth of shoulder, she recoiled fractionally, enough to see the satisfaction on his face.

'Intending to work around here, darling?'

'I'm going to get a job in the local supermarket, shit-for-brains,' she snarled, trying to side step.

He moved quickly, echoing her movement.

The two women had backed off, but were watching the show from beneath a street lamp. A car slowed, the occupant peering. The two girls straightened, walked forward hopefully, but the car accelerated away. The pimp was watching this while talking to her, one eye on business as usual, the other on an opportunity.

'Didn't have you pegged for a cash-cunt, Blondie. Had you pegged for something quite different.'

'Get out of my fucking way.'

'Who d'you work for?'

That last was snapped in a low whisper; testing the water for sharks before reeling in the fish.

'I don't work for no one,' she hissed back. 'And I don't fucking intend to. Not no more.'

He reached out, grabbed a shoulder, and turned her face to the light. She saw calculation in his gaze; saw

40

the pound signs light up at her youth. 'Where're you from, bitch? You're not from around here, are you?'

'Never you fucking mind where I'm from.'

A small groan escaped, and she cramped visibly. He darted a triumphant glance, and put his arm around her.

'I can get you something for that, you know.'

She didn't move.

He shrugged, made to walk away. 'Up to you, darling.'

She stepped forward fractionally, a woman grasping reluctantly at a lifeline; hasty so as not to lose the ticket, even though the ticket wasn't appreciated. A faint whine crept into her voice.

'Just arrived a couple of days ago. Need a fix real bad.'

His satisfaction was complete.

He led her to a car in the next street. 'Get in.'

'I need a doctor first.'

He hesitated, half in, half out of the car, a caricature of his previous confidence. 'Why?'

'Broken arm.'

He looked relieved, but his voice was business-like. 'How?'

'Hitching. The bastard nearly killed me.'

Now his eyes narrowed.

'I get you fixed up, you owe me. Know what I mean?'

She hunched into her coat, gave him a sidelong, weary glance. She knew when she was beaten.

'You got meth?'

'Got crack, darlin'. It'll to the trick.'

Jessie realised he was enjoying himself. It wasn't every day a working tom walked into your area, not under anyone's protection, ripe for the plucking. He must think his luck's in. Then the street seemed to close in, the pavement rolled under her feet.

She was going to pass out, and hung on to her bag as though her life depended on it.

Suddenly he was there, supporting, helping, as if he

cared. He pulled at the bag, and she grabbed it to her chest. He didn't argue, he probably reckoned he'd have it off her later, see what crap she was toting. She found herself sitting in the passenger seat, doubled over. She tripped into a warped sense of time and space, and nothing made any sense.

She'd heard of that. A trip without a pip, a free one, what d'you know? When she opened her eyes, the red brick houses seemed to bow in above her head, trapping her into a bubble of city. They were on the move, driving through a kaleidoscopic tunnel, each scene changing, moving out of perspective, and receding behind them. She wasn't happy with the timing, but it was strangely comforting; she'd been there only once before.

'You hanging in, there, sugar?'

'Playback,' she muttered slackly, her tongue having difficulty with the words.

'Happens,' her rescuer offered knowledgeably. 'Don't worry; I'll get you a shot soon.'

Her head rolled on the seat, her eyes flicking out of focus. Then a pain ripped through her gut, and she folded double as the cramps began to flay her with renewed vigour. Pain forced her back to reality, and as attention began to return she realised that the city was gone. In its place were wide open spaces, tracks, and beyond that, trees.

'Where are we? Where are you taking me? Where's the fucking doctor?'

The man smiled at her, his sidelong glance cold and calculating. 'I'm going to see what you're made of, darling. You're going to give me something on account. How old are you? Fifteen? Sixteen? His shadowed eyes assessed her. 'Got a nice mouth too. Show me what you can do with it, then I'll pay the cunt quack to fix your arm.'

As he spoke of the backstreet abortionist who presumably set bones, too, he began to work the zipper on his trousers. Jessie stared at him.

42

What the hell was she doing?

Was getting a doctor worth all this?

Was she going to blow this low life fuck?

A moment ago she hadn't minded, damn it, she'd known what he would do. Inexplicably, rage welled. She didn't know what she wanted anymore, but it wasn't this.

'Stop the car, I want out,' she hissed from between clenched teeth.

'I'm not wasting all that petrol and effort so you can back out on me, darling. You get sucking, and I'll stop the fucking car when I come.'

Jessie stared. There was a hard look on his handsome face; she'd seen it so many times before.

'Fuck you,' she said. She opened the door and fell out.

She heard the pimp's cry of annoyance as she hit the ground hard, tumbling like a rag doll over her kitbag, bruises and broken bones. As consciousness faded, she heard the car speed away in an angry burst of acceleration. He probably thought she was dead meat, and wasn't about to stop and find out.

Sometime later she woke to a kind of stunned comprehension that morning had arrived. She lay beneath a hedge, her broken arm beneath her. She tried to move, but the pain sledge-hammered her skull, so she relaxed, knowing that the pains would soon be gone.

Once before, she'd looked death in the face. She'd chosen it. It hadn't scared her, and now was no different. Except this time there was no doctor to perform frantic first aid and pull her back into the nightmare of living, no psychiatrist waiting in the wings to be lied to. This was it. She looked for death now with a kind of relief.

Life wasn't good, never had been.

Anyone who said it was, lied.

There were intermittent periods of consciousness where she gradually saw the day rise and fade. Cars

43

passed like phantoms, unseen, and she wondered why she'd thought fate would change its mind and be kind to her, after all. Vince had told her she would die if she left him, and he was right. He'd killed her in the end. The money hadn't helped at all. She smiled faintly, because the bag of money lay beneath her feet. She was probably the richest dead tom in the world right now.

Christ, the fates could be cruel.

What was it Gill used to say? Life's a bitch and then you die. She used to laugh, and say you made your own luck. As if you could change anything. She'd miss Gill's brand of earthy sanity.

When she'd run from the hospital after the abortion it had been without conscious thought, just a need to escape, and Vince had unexpectedly provided a place to hide while she sorted out the mess in her mind.

But time had just kind of rolled on by and nothing had come clear. The theft of the money had accidentally provided the spur she needed to leave. Money meant freedom. In some secret way she'd hoped life held something better for her, and the money had given her the opportunity to find out.

Now she realised she'd been wrong all along. Seemed life was a bitch and then you died, after all. She'd simply found a different place to die.

Chapter 4

The police picked up Gill a couple of days later as she was making her way back to Vince's house. It appeared she hadn't seen the news, having spent some time in a motel with a man she couldn't or wouldn't identify, and had no idea Vince was dead.

Gill was no schoolgirl.

She was dressed in a subdued, mainstream fashion, and wouldn't have made a splash on the streets of shoppers. She was, at this time, without make-up. She'd a faintly motherly appeal and actually looked upset when she learned of Vince's demise.

'I'm sorry,' Redwall added belatedly.

She chuckled, and he understood. She wasn't upset about Vince. She, too, was simply wondering what was going to happen now. The devil you knew even if he beat up on you was better than the devil you didn't know.

'We can find you a place to stay,' he said.

'Rehab? Tried that before. It didn't work out.'

'You want to try again?'

She shrugged. 'Couldn't handle it. Needed a trip, know what I mean? What now? I get banged up or something?'

'What for?'

'I dunno. You tell me.'

'Murder?'

That shocked her rigid, then she relaxed.

'Shit. Someone did him in, then? I'm not surprised. The little punk didn't have a clue, really.'

'Didn't have a clue about what in particular?'

'Anything. He was getting in with a load of real bad-news guys from up Birmingham way, but hell, they wouldn't have whacked him. He was useful, even if he was gullible and too stupid to realise it.'

And you're not, he thought. So why are you on the bloody game?

'Can you give me names?'

'Not me. I want to live a bit longer. You think of any low life scumbags out there, and he was pals with them. He was into all kinds of shit.'

'Like what?'

'Just shit. You know.'

He thought he probably did. She rubbed her arms, shivered. 'Where are the others?'

'Sandy and Alice said they had a place to go, by the Acer Development.'

She froze for an infinitesimal moment, then gave a half shrug. 'They're fools. You can't go it alone in this game, you know. One of the other pimps'll find 'em, blacken their eyes. It's best to choose.'

'And Jessie?'

'What about her?'

'Do you know where she is? Where she was working last night?'

'I don't keep tabs on her. She tended to be worked in the house, upstairs, but I don't know for sure. Vince used her himself and his mates, when he was around.'

There it was again, that indefinable *something*.

'Tell me about Jessie. What made her special?'

'Special? Christ, she's just a kid he picked up, like the others.'

She seemed reticent to add to what she'd said, so he dug deeper.

'She was a tom, though?'

'What d'you think? Vince didn't keep anyone on charity. But she was like, a natural, if you know what I mean.'

'Explain.'

He read it on her face; there came a point where you

had said so much there was no reason to hide the rest.

'She's a hard one, Jessie. He picked her up at the station, gave her the spiel, but she wasn't taken in for a moment, didn't blink an eye when he put her on the game, like she'd been somewhere already, like the childhood was already pumped out of her.'

'Experienced, do you mean?'

'Not on the game, I think, but no sucker. Couldn't have been more than fifteen, if that. But she wasn't like the other kids. She knew what he was about from the start. I could see that, Vince couldn't. It was as if she chose him, rather than the other way round. But he still gave it the old sugar daddy spiel for the first couple of days, and she was kind of smiling, like she was just enjoying her moment of freedom before the work kicked in.'

She thought a bit, then carried on. 'What I mean is, when we're kids none of us think the game is what we'll do with our lives when we grow up, and when it happens, well, you care a bit at first. About what people think, you know? Well he brought her home just like the others, did the softening up bit, but you could see it in her eyes. She knew already what he was about, and didn't seem to give a damn.'

'You don't like her?'

He could see her musing. 'No; I do like her. I don't know what made her like she is, but ten to one some bloke's at the back of it, so it's not her fault. But she isn't a victim, know what I mean?. She did what she was told, but it was like she was her own boss. She stood up to him, once, said she could walk out any time she liked. He beat up on her, swore he owned her, but she just laughed at him and took it. She could do that. Make you feel small. Just with her eyes. What could do that to a young-un, eh?'

What indeed? Redwall felt a chill creep up his spine.

'So if she was that strong-minded why did she stay?'

'Christ knows. I guess she needed the roof over her head just like the rest of us, and the crack.'

47

'She was addicted?'

'She was in the end. That's what they do. What else is there?'

'Was she there that Sunday night?'

'I dunno, I wasn't, remember? But if someone killed him, she was capable of it.'

That was the second time someone had said that.

'Can you tell me what she looked like, Gill?'

'Jeez. Tall, skinny, blonde. How d'you describe someone? Not pretty, but striking, somehow. If she was done up, you'd notice her all right. And she's bright enough to not be working. Men seem to think she's got something special, but I can't see it. All you really notice is first glance she seems innocent, like, then you look again and just know she 'aint. I told Vince right from the start, she's trouble, with that accent, mark my words. The silly sod should have listened, but he didn't listen to anyone but himself.'

'What accent?'

'Kind of posh. She tried to hide it, talk like us, but wherever she came from they didn't use plastic plates, if you know what I mean.'

'You've been very helpful, thanks. If you see Jessie around, can you let me know, not spook her?'

Her smile was sardonic. 'Sure.'

'It's likely she had nothing to do with Vince's death. We might be able to help her.'

'You're too late for her, trust me.'

His eyes softened. 'And you, Gill. Is there anything we can do to help you?'

She was intelligent enough to see what she'd become. And if she wasn't quite sure where she was going, she had a rough idea.

'Buy me a dinner, and I'll be on my way.'

'When you find a place to stay, let me know. I might need to talk to you again.'

'Yeah, right.'

He handed her some cash. She gave a lopsided smile as she took it, guessing it was from his own pocket. For that brief moment they communicated, then the shutters went down, and she was gone.

It was past seven in the evening when Redwall got out. His long-suffering wife would be waiting with a dried-up dinner in the oven, and his children would be out and about in the streets doing Lord knew what. Christ, it scared him, thinking of his children out there, but you couldn't just lock them up. You had to let them grow up and away from you.

But no one ever told him it would be this hard.

Jim walked with him to the car park.

'Do you think Vince was set up, by this Jessie, perhaps? A contract? Did he jump or was he pushed?'

He thought on that for a moment as he hugged his coat closer around him in the chill air.

'No. I still think it was H&R. There was that pile of vomit, remember? Someone saw Vince and brought their guts up, and whoever did that wasn't a hit-man. No, I reckon it really was an accident. Why he was there, I have no idea, and maybe there was some kind of a deal going down, but everything points to his death being accidental. A real hit and run. Someone too scared to stop.'

'A hit and run that coincidentally took out a known dealer? Perhaps God's on the side of the righteous after all.'

Redwall grinned as he slumped into his car.

'Before deciding whether the car hit the biggest scumbag running around that night, it would be a good idea to discover what *was* going down. Go home Jim. It's going to be a long day tomorrow.
'

Chapter 5

Ben awoke, instantly alert. He had no idea why.

He lay in the dark, listening.

The clock ticked. The cat snored.

He climbed out of bed with a sigh. Something had woken him and he wouldn't sleep until he knew what it was. His bare feet made no noise as he crossed the floorboards; his feet knew the floor; every lump in the carpet and every crack in the floorboard.

The cat looked up, eyes yellow in the half light, but didn't move from the comfort of the bed. It wasn't dinner time, and it had done its instinctive hunting earlier for food it toyed with but didn't eat.

Ben scratched at the stubble on his chin, glanced over at the clock; nearly six. He didn't rise early these days, and resented the early start. Long gone were the days of rising to a klaxon at four-thirty and getting breakfast in the mess after drill when it seemed the day should be already half over.

He swung the bedroom door open silently.

Something had spooked him.

Sneaking downstairs toes first, hands loosely ready at his sides, he listened again. He was puzzled. Maybe it had been something outside, a tractor passing, a car horn? What Ben didn't consider was that he might be mistaken. His instinct was second nature to him, a legacy from a past that would be better forgotten but could never be. Maybe someone had tried to break in? There was a bang in the kitchen.

He swivelled in a blur of fists.

The second cat stalked in, tail flying high as the catflap shut behind it. He relaxed as she rubbed herself around his legs. He didn't know what had put the wind up him, but whatever it was hadn't bothered his animals. The buzzing in his head levelled, and the tension was exhaled slowly and evenly from his body. He bent down and stroked the cat. She nearly disappeared under his vast hand, then let out an earth-shattering yowl.

'O.K, O.K, I get the message.'

He reached for a tin of cat food, and there was a thump from upstairs as the other cat responded to the signal, and came haring to the kitchen meowing piteously until the food was scraped into the dented mess tin. In spite of the old adage *there's no pride in a cat* he thought they were pretty much like humans, existing with as little effort as possible. Perhaps that was why they cohabited so well.

There was a busy yapping as the cats snatched at the early breakfast, and although his inner sense of alarm had diminished to a faint feeling of irritation, he carried on and inspected his house for intruders. The training of years didn't simply vanish on retirement.

This wasn't the first time he'd been unsettled by things going on around him, He had wondered several times whether he should go back to the island of his birth to die; some sort of homing instinct maybe. England was just too damned crowded, but then again, he supposed Japan would be, too, and he'd been gone from there so long he would feel like an alien.

Even here, in the New Forest, there were too many people, too many houses. You couldn't step outside without hearing evidence of others: a shrill cry on the air, the sound of a plane in the sky, the distant rumble of the motorway, a yammering car alarm. It was just as well his time was nearly done. He no longer fitted in this busy world, and it seemed that all the things he'd done in his life with the intention of making the world a better place for the future had changed nothing.

Reassured, or as reassured as he could be, Ben went

into the room that had once been a dining room, and put his body through the routine that had been the mainstay of his life for the forty years since fighting for that same life in a U.S. hospital; that year of desolation and desperation when the paralysis of his mind was worse than the horrendous damage to his body. His doctors would have marvelled to see how fit he looked now, even with the wastage of age setting in. The burned and broken body they had worked on with such desperation had hardly seemed likely to carry him through his middle years, let alone take him to a ripe old age.

Ben had accepted disability discharge without hesitation. He'd come close to death many times, but when those he loved had been snatched violently from him in the same year, something inside him had changed forever. What was the point in trying to save the world when he couldn't even save his own family.

He'd worked through the pain of his injuries, the pain of his losses, and the mental dilemma of still being alive. Then, after he'd got used to being alive when others, more worthy, were dead, he had been offered a job that suited the man he'd become. He had refused at first, but Godfrey, the retired General who ran Mayday, and was a personal friend had pretty much lifted him from the depths of apathy with a single sentence. You can't save the world, he had said. But if you save one person, you will save yourself.

He didn't think of England as home, but he no longer thought of the States or Japan or the Middle East as home, either. He was exiled by his own inability to face the flood of memories that would be unleashed by returning to any of those places,, so England was as good as anywhere.

When he'd exercised, training his muscles, honing his reflexes, he meditated. He could bring himself to that lonely place inside his consciousness within minutes, and remain there for a while to emerge cleansed and alert. Sometimes he wouldn't be conscious of thought or existence while he was there, he didn't really know which realms he travelled, but wherever it was, it was a place of peace.

But even in meditation he was never totally unaware of reality. If anything entered within his sphere, he would have snapped out of his trance-like state within a second. Now, however, he was alone, and exited slowly, in control of his inner and outer self, only to find himself irritated that whatever had wormed its way into his subconscious in the early morning was still lurking there.

He uncrossed his legs, stood up and remained ill at ease for the rest of the day. The next morning he dressed in the faded denims and the checked shirt by which the neighbours knew him, and went to fetch some groceries from the shop a mile down the road. The walk, he thought, would clear his head. It was only as he exited his property that he discovered what had woken him the previous morning.

The woman lay sprawled in the hedge that bounded his property, almost hidden by the dense undergrowth. He wouldn't have seen her had he been driving. With pursed lips, he viewed her where she lay, face up, her body bruised, broken, and to all appearances, dead. He glanced up and down the road. She would have been invisible to all except a passing pedestrian, and this wasn't a stretch of road used by dog walkers, or joggers. From the unnatural position of her body he thought it likely she'd fallen or been thrown from a car.

Bending down, he felt for a pulse at the neck.

He'd been left for dead once, surviving only because a friend came back for his body. When his fingers unexpectedly caught the faint, erratic flutter of life, he ran his hands gently down her back and legs checking for major injury before heaving her bodily from under the hedge. Never mind waiting for an ambulance, she was too cold. She flopped in his arms like a puppet, and breath caught raggedly from parted lips.

Girl, not woman, he corrected himself, a lot younger

than he'd supposed, and bigger trouble. They always were. He sighed. Her eyes opened for a moment, but there was no awareness in them. He supposed he would have to call an ambulance and the police. That might mean all sorts of complications he didn't really want; he valued his privacy. But before making the call, he knew that he would have to deal with the girl first, it wouldn't be a lot of good if she'd lasted this long, only to die of hypothermia while he ran to the phone.

Though she stank of vomit, he carried her into the living room and lay her carefully on a futon. As he did, a gun fell from the pocket of her coat. He sighed again.

Hell, he didn't need this.

He turned the fires on full, and removed her sodden clothes. Her body was like an iceberg, long past the stage of shivering. He briskly rubbed her torso and limbs, avoiding the arm that was swollen and angry, towelling until her skin reddened under his hands. Then he wrapped her in clean bedding, but not enough to stop the heat of the fire reaching her body. She seemed to settle a bit as the warmth reached her, and her breathing eased.

He sat back, chin on hand for a moment, and perused her intently. She either had the constitution of an ox or a deep capacity for survival. He knew from his army years that you could never tell from appearances who would survive and who wouldn't, it was more a question of will- power than stamina.

He gently brushed the lank hair from her face and tried to assess her age, willing himself to understand what she'd been through to bring her to this place at this time, and in this state. She wasn't very old at all. In her teens, maybe, or early twenties; it was hard to tell she was so pale and wasted.

He was still wondering what was stopping him from making that phone call, when the girl began to move. Her eyes shot open in vivid green panic, and she began to talk; not that she was cognisant in any way. He listened intently as she made incoherent argument with people outside his sight, trying to hear a single word that might make sense of her predicament. She fought angrily in her own personal nightmare, but the dimension was locked to Ben's understanding. Who she was, where she'd come from, even her name, remained a mystery.

As he listened, the one thing that intrigued him most, however, was that she didn't cry. Not once. Not from pain, not from anger, not from loss. That, more than anything, gave him cause for concern, for what child of this age wouldn't cry for a mother, a father, someone, anyone, unless they had cried before and discovered it to be a futile exercise?

Without even knowing why, he knew what he was going to do.

Tight-lipped, he injected her with one of the painkillers that had brought him through his own personal nightmare, and waited for it to take effect. As he sat on the floor, Ben thought of his own pampered childhood. He stroked her head, mumbling words of comfort. It didn't matter whether she understood; she was simply an animal in need of the wordless crooning noises he was making. So young, yet so scarred by life already; the emaciated condition of her musculature, the old bruises, and the lank condition of skin and hair told its own story.

The lacerations and broken bones beneath shop-new clothes told another. Wherever she'd been before, she'd been trying to escape it, to move on.

When the massive dose of pain-killer took affect she lapsed into a state verging on unconsciousness and, he dealt swiftly with the broken arm. He wrapped a length of wood with padding, then bound it firmly under her shoulder before pulling her elbow down with gentle but insistent pressure, until the two ends of broken bone slid apart beneath the swollen muscle, and the odd lump disappeared. As he did so, a scream rose from her white lips, seeming to erupt from far deeper than her lungs.

He then bound the arm to the wood firmly with a thick layer of bandage. As a field dressing it couldn't have been surpassed, but a nagging doubt in the back of his mind told him that a doctor would certainly have made a better job of it, and would have X-rayed the bone to make sure the ends met properly, and that there were no splinters left lying in the flesh to cause infection.

She moaned throughout, a deep and heartfelt agony, but he ignored it. She would have no recollections of this particular torture when she came to. He then gave her a shot of antibiotics and a massive dose of vitamins to bulk up her depleted store. The sell-by date was long gone, but what the hell. He had them all, sealed up, leftover from the days when he'd had to inject his own body before he could even rise in the morning.

As Ben cleared junk from an unused attic room, he tried to come to terms with his own actions.

Why was he doing it?

He didn't know.

He cleaned down the cobweb-hung walls, fixed the broken door, and nailed the tiny window shut. He had little lingering regard for the mass of humanity he'd once pledged to serve, but this girl was different. She hadn't asked for his help. She'd fallen onto his property like a winged hawk. He would fix her up as he would any wounded animal that strayed into his territory, and when she was strong enough, she would at least have the strength to choose where to run to.

That would be that.

Yet what had she been running from, and were they still hunting her? That was the reason he had no intention of calling the police, or letting the powers that be know she was here. With the best will in the world they'd take her in, look after her, fix her up, and probably send her straight back to the place and people that had made her like this.

Here, for just a moment in time, she was in a safe haven.

Someone, a long time ago, had given him a second chance, and it felt as though the debt was being called in. If you hear me up there, he thought, Dan Johnson, this is for you. He knew what he was doing was illegal, and if she was under eighteen, which he suspected, she could be big trouble. But he'd lived outside and beyond authority for most of his life and wasn't about to change. He pursed his lips as he looked at her.

'You want to live or die, girl?

Your choice, now.'

Chapter 6

Chalmers didn't give a damn that Vince Bertini was dead, except that his timing could have been better.

Vince was, or had been, he amended, an idiot. He'd just happened to have the required warehouse at the right time in the right area, and possess the correct social awareness for the task in hand.

He was a criminal; but to be a successful criminal, you also needed to be fairly bright, and that was something the big man couldn't have accused Vince of being. In hindsight, using Vince seemed like a totally stupid thing to have done, but you made decisions, and sometimes they backfired.

Vince hadn't had any idea that Chalmers intended to terminate this somewhat undesirable association, and possibly terminate Vince, too, when someone with more long-term reliability could be found.

Now someone had done the job for him.

The problem was, why?

He had a man in mind to replace Vince, and wondered whether now was a good time to sound him out. However, a faint niggle of doubt remained, and he held back.

No more hasty decisions.

So, though Vince's early demise hadn't only been anticipated, but planned, the untimely execution of that plan by person or persons unknown stuck like debris in his teeth, leaving a very bad taste.

Vince's death, by its unexpected nature, irritated him. He didn't like surprises, even though it seemed that the integrity of the current shipment was intact.

What really shook him, though, was that the thick bastard actually managed to hide several million pounds of his cash before getting wasted, and that was unforgivable. He'd had to fish in his own pocket for the money just to keep the suppliers unaware of the problem. No way was he going to have this present pipeline, which was working very nicely, interrupted by the suppliers getting cold feet.

Though getting the money back wasn't as immediately important as keeping a lid on things, resentment smouldered in his chest every time he thought about it. Credibility was at stake. He would find the money eventually, of that there was no doubt. He flexed his hands until the knuckles cracked, then squeezed them into tight fists, reflecting how much happier he would have been if Vince was alive, and his balls were in them.

As he waited, another car pulled in and parked neatly beside him, the doors opening immediately, spilling three men and a woman onto the concrete. The men wore dark suits and blue shirts, the severity relieved by bright silk ties sporting, respectively, Mickey Mouse, leaping frogs, and psychedelic colours that defied logic.

He didn't like this new business mode of dress, this descent into levity. It was almost insulting to their trade. In his day, you wore black ties with your black suits, and sticking to that dress code without fail had done his business no harm.

Cary leapt out and opened the door for him, and Thomas of the psychedelic tie indicated a small door set in the side of the warehouse.

'After you, Mr Porter, Sir.'

'Let's do it.'

These men, too, were tools, albeit of a slightly higher calibre than Vince. All hired hands, but with a good track record, and their respect was palpable; he liked that.

His name wasn't Porter, of course, but it was the

handle everyone used when he was out and about. It was a tag designed to retain anonymity in the event of curious ears. He would have liked something a bit more original, a bit classy, but the name had simply happened one day, and it had been easier to let it stand.

He followed them into the warehouse, his chauffeur scuttling eagerly alongside, anticipation lighting his beady eyes.

Vince's whore, propelled before him in high-heeled sandals and cheap clothes, glanced nervously at him, and gave a hesitant come-on smile, as if he would be interested in a diseased piece of tail. He glanced at his watch, hoping this wasn't going to take too much time. He had a business meeting at two.

The whore must have realised she was in trouble from the moment they picked her up, but she went along quietly, as they always did. He could never understand how women could be that stupid, just hoping things would work out, not bothering to arm themselves or anything.

They deserved everything that came their way.

He didn't like women on the whole, but there were a few he respected to an extent; women who didn't allow themselves to be pushed around, and who defended their territory against their male counterparts with whatever cunning and guile was required.

In the huge empty space, two of the men pulled the whore to face him, hands jammed under her armpits and around her wrists. He walked up to her, drew his hand back, and slapped her hard around the face with his open hand.

Her head rocked.

She gasped, but didn't cry out. She'd been hit before.

He gave a small smile to show there was no malice involved, it was just business.

'That was just a little teaser, Gill, darling. The real stuff can happen, or not, depending on how much you want to help me. Tell me about Vince. About how he died, who was with him, and where the money went.'

'I was out working when someone topped him, I didn't know till the next day, when I got picked up by the cops.'

'And the money?'

'I don't know about any money.'

He stood back and flicked his finger.

In silence, the men tied her wrists, threw the rope over a beam and hoisted until her feet were just off the floor. They ripped the clothes off her. She struggled as they worked, but almost a token gesture, and still she made no outcry. There was a look of stunned panic on her face as they stood back. Now she was in absolutely no doubt as to what was going to happen.

'Recall anything, yet?' he asked.

She was whimpering from the pain in her wrists, her hands were already turning a dull red. 'I don't know about any money. I'd tell you if I did. You know I would.'

The big man turned to his chauffeur. 'Do it.'

Her alarmed protestations were cut off mid-word as the little man stuffed a rag in her mouth. The suits bent down, tied ropes to the woman's ankles, then pulled her legs apart and stood on the ropes. Eyes popping over the top of the gag, she stared in horror as the chauffeur lit a cigarette, and sucked on it until the tip glowed.

She struggled, making incoherent, panicked noises.

Chalmers watched impassively as his chauffeur got through a couple of cigarettes. Amused, he realised the man was rampantly aroused as the whore's flesh shrank before the glowing tip, and could have sworn the little shit almost orgasmed once as he dabbed it almost tenderly, like a lover, into the sensitive parts of her body: her nipples, between her legs.

The scent, combined with the faint hissing of fat, reminded him of pork crackling. She even made grunting piggy noises as she was cooking.

'Enough,' he said.

The gag was removed from her mouth, and she

panted in long, indrawn rasping breaths, but didn't scream.

'Good girl. Screams are so distracting and quite pointless. Now, take your time. Is there anything you'd like to tell me?'

His voice was mellow, charming, and had a faintly upper class drawl, an affectation he'd practised assiduously during his youth, along with the other things calculated to turn him into the rich man he was now.

She spoke between gasps.

Hanging like that wasn't doing her breathing any good.

'I don't know. I'd tell you if I did. I didn't see any money. I was out working.'

They tried again, two or three times.

He was finally sure the smattering of information he ended up with was all she knew, the most interesting of which was how keen the police were in finding the tom called Jessie who might or might not have been with Vince when he died.

If they were interested, perhaps he should be too.

'Very well,' he said to the men, glancing at his watch again. 'I've got a meeting to get to. I want to see the rest of Vince's stable. All of them, one at a time. I'll wait for your call.'

The woman hung, silent now, breathing in tiny, panicked breaths. His men cut the rope. She fell into a huddle on the floor, convulsively curling around her pain. In spite of appearances, the damage wasn't life threatening, but it wasn't a good idea to leave her alive.

Not when she'd seen his face.

'Cary. Take me into the city, and come back for these two when you've dropped me off.'

As he walked away he saw one of the men drop his trousers and punch the woman into obedience before pulling her face into his crotch while another took her from behind. He was fine about that. Such sessions always left men sexually charged, so they might as well not waste the opportunity, put their libidos back on an even keel before getting on with business.

He settled back down in the plush upholstery of his car, and forgot about Gill instantly.

Over the following days they discovered three other girls from Vince's stable, but he didn't bother to let Cary loose on them, much to the little man's disgust. It was obvious the bimbos didn't even know the time of day. He passed them onto a contact up north. It would be stupid to throw away experienced pieces of tail when they still had some good earning capacity; that would be like chucking dough on the fire. They would never be found by the London cops, and would never talk, especially after being shown images of Gill's last moments.

He'd made himself Vince's self-appointed executor and who was going to argue?

All in all, it was beginning to seem like Vince hadn't blabbed to anyone after all. But the fact remained, he'd been holding the money for just one stupid fucking day because the goods were late, and he'd lost it.

The other fact which concerned him was that the Jessie bint was still missing, and until he learned otherwise, two and two made four. Actually they made a lot more than four, because one of the other tails had mentioned, in the middle of a very convoluted and terrified babble, that Jessie had a big nob father who worked in London; a somebody, by all accounts.

How in hell did Vince end up with a rich bitch in his stable? But he decided not to let his little weasel of a chauffeur try to dig further information out of her, because it was his educated guess she knew nothing more, and he didn't want any more of Vince's toms iced.

One dead tom could simply have been a bad trick – if they found her - but more was a coincidence that might have stimulated the pigs into frenzied activity. Though, why they'd bother when it was only toms, he couldn't fathom.

It took three days to discover who the missing tom's father was.

Chapter 7

Edward Stowleigh was picked up as he walked out of the off-licence one evening. He knew a professional job when he saw it, and one small part of his mind appreciated this fact, even as the bottle of whiskey he'd just purchased at the offie was taken out of his hand.

He was hustled, startled, into the back seat of a large black car, before the merest hint of a protest could issue from his lips. He found himself seated between two grim-faced young men with expressionless eyes, while a third skinny one in the front drove the car away with due consideration for a young couple who were smooching at the side of the road in the semi-darkness, and who wouldn't have noticed a pig flying past.

'Hands behind your back.'

Even now he didn't open his mouth and make a fuss because there was a silenced handgun digging into the fleshy part of his thigh. The man who held it simply stared at him, daring him, turning his guts to water.

He leaned forward obligingly and let the men secure his wrists. Fear lends a strange kind of courage, even if that simply meant going to his death without screaming.

The gun was secreted away beneath the immaculate lapels of a dark suit jacket at that point. Having never been subjected to anything like this in his life, Edward was cowed into obedience, and just looked at them with stunned lack of comprehension as they drove on.

All sorts of things popped through his mind, like asking them what they wanted and where they were taking him, but, terrified of the answer he might get, he bit back the words. He couldn't think who, in all his business dealings, would have the capacity to pull off a stunt like this. Mentally he was persuading himself there were all sorts of scenarios that didn't involve him getting a hole in his thigh or his head blown off.

As they drove out of the residential area, and onto a dual carriageway, a black bag was put over his head, the drawstrings of which were tied off around his neck. Although this engendered the instant panic of claustrophobia, he forced himself to take struggling lungsful of dusty air, telling himself this was good, because if they were taking care to prevent him seeing a certain somebody or something, whoever these frighteningly silent men were, they were intending to let him go again. He desperately wanted to urinate, and clenched his muscles tight.

Eventually the car slowed, turned, bumped over an uneven surface, and stopped. The fabric over his face was thick, impenetrable, hardly allowing the difference of light and dark to enter, but his eyes strained, as if by willpower alone he would be able to see through it.

Nudged by a hard finger, he slid out of the car, and was manoeuvred along with hands on his upper arms, both directing and stopping him from falling when he stumbled.

He let just one small whimper of fear escape, then gritted his teeth tightly. It was part of the accepted tradition, and his background was rooted in tradition, that men did *not* show fear. Men did *not* cry.

The manipulating hands deserted him, and he was filled with a nauseous vulnerability. Was this it? Were they standing back, levelling guns? Were they going to shoot him now?

How he held his water, he didn't know.

'You may call me Mr Porter,' a voice said out of the darkness.

Edward jumped, turning towards the sound.

Did he know that voice? Did it belong to one of his colleagues? Was it some kind of joke in bad taste?

'Who are you? What do you want?' he demanded.

Someone punched him in his middle. Not expecting it, he half folded, retching dryly. When he could breathe again, he was hauled up by disembodied, unsympathetic hands.

'Don't you dare talk to me in that tone of voice, you pompous prick,' his captor said in a low, venomous tone. 'You're in no position to dictate, not this time, in spite of your blue fucking blood. Do you understand?'

'Yes,' he gasped into the expectant silence.

'Mr Porter, Sir, to you.'

'Yes, Mr Porter, Sir,' he echoed, realising that whatever else was required off him, at the moment humiliation and submission were sufficient.

'That's better. Now, what are you worth? In real terms, I mean?'

'I don't know,' he said hoarsely, still struggling to contain the sickness that was threatening. In spite of the severity of his predicament, he felt vaguely foolish talking through the suffocating folds of a boot bag.

'Humour me.'

'The house is worth about five million. I've got another million tied up in shares, but my overdraft is about a million and a half. It looks like I'm rich, but I'm not, really, it would take a while to – '

'Shut the fuck up! I asked for facts, not opinions. Your opinions aren't worth shit.'

Edward tensed his muscles at the snapped words, half bending, ready for another blow that didn't come.

He rapidly tallied figures in the darkness of his hood. They were after money, as he'd partially suspected, but who had ready cash these days? Christ, were they going to try to intimidate him into disposing of his assets? In the short term they'd end up with a much deflated value of his assets' current worth which was, in fact, a lot more than he'd just told them. He turned his head about, seeking in the darkness for enlightenment, realising as he did so that these men must be pretty stupid, because they had no hold on him that would stop him instantly from going to the police.

Unexpectedly, hands took hold of him. Before he realised quite what was happening, the button was flipped open, and his trousers and underpants were yanked down past his knees.

'Oh, Jesus, no. Please.'

He stumbled a couple of steps, wrists pulling against the bonds, the rumpled clothes further hampering his movements, nearly tripping him up. He managed to keep upright, but the sudden exposure panicked him. He began to try to back away from whatever they were going to do, his mind filling with icy fear.

'Stand still!'

The words were a command that he obeyed, and he felt the unseen presence loom towards him, huge and terrifying. He made a strangled noise, the importance of his financial investments minimised by an acute reassessment of the worth of his private parts.

'Are you scared, Edward? Do you know what I could do to you here?'

The time for bravery was long gone.

'Yes,' he whispered.

'Now that I've got your undivided attention, listen. You've got a daughter who ran away a year or so ago. You might be amused to know she's been living as a prostitute in London, right under your nose the whole time. I suspect you didn't care much care about her, but you're about to discover some profound paternal feelings.'

The news surprised and shocked him. 'Of course I care! I've had a private detective...'

Hands took hold of his lapels, pulled him upward, proving that the man behind the voice was no lightweight. 'You were a shitty father, and you're an ineffectual human being. Perhaps I should cut it off anyway, make sure you never have any more children to abuse.'

With true indignation, he blurted, 'I never abused her! Never! If that's what this is all about.'

'Shut up! As it happens, I don't give a shit what you did or didn't do to your upper-class spawn, but if you'd been a better father, I wouldn't have lost my money, and you wouldn't be in this predicament.'

'What money?'

Edward's tone reflected genuine confusion.

'The whole crux of the matter is money, which it usually is, don't you think? It may surprise you to know that your daughter has possibly run off with some of my money; quite a lot, actually. Nearly as much as the sum total of your disposable assets, including the house in Scotland, the Costa-del-Sol investment, and the other things you chose not to mention. Now I want my money back, and if I don't get it I intend to have yours. But I'm going to give you a chance to keep your money, because more than your money, I want your daughter.'

Edward could hear true anger in the tone.

'No one steals from me and gets away with it. All you have to realise right now is that you want to find her more than you wanted anything in your life. You're going to help the police nicely with their enquiries, but you're also going to hire a private eye, and you're going to find her, and do you want to know why?'

The voice dropped low with promise. 'Because if you don't, Edward, I'm going to do to you what you thought I was going to do just now, but it won't be all at once. I will hurt you so much that you'll beg to die. I'll get my friend, here, to peel it, inch by tiny inch, layer by layer, then I'll cut it off and stick it in your mouth so you can suck on it while you bleed to death. Do I make myself clear?'

Edward stood, stunned for a moment.

He sensed movement, and let out a faint yelp.

'Yes! I understand! I'll find her. But how will I get in contact with you?'

'I notice you didn't ask what I intend to do with her,' the voice said dryly. 'I wonder if she's got the same regard for her daddy? But as to your last question, you won't need to reach me. I'm going to be monitoring your progress. You will never know who my men are, or who is watching you. But be assured, they will be there. You'll spend whatever is necessary, and if I don't see enough enthusiasm on your part, I'll have you brought here again, and I'll have my man, here, give you a rather basic circumcision painful but not life threatening to impress you about the urgency of my request. Oh, and one last thing. If you tell anyone at all about our little conversation, then you can kiss goodbye to little Johnny-dongle from the moment you open your mouth, because I will know.'

Edward jumped as hands reached for him, and a small noise escaped his tight throat, but they simply pulled up his clothes, packed him away neatly, tucked his shirt in and zipped him up.

He almost felt more violated by this than he had at the sudden exposure. It was a measure of their control over him that he was obliged to stand there like a child as he could do nothing to help himself. Without another word, he was bundled back into the car, driven away and eventually transferred to the back of another car. His head was thrust between his knees and the rope cut from his wrists. He heard the car doors slam.

After a second of silence, of wondering if they really had gone, he picked in panic at the cords of the hood, ripping it off to find himself seated in the back seat of his own car at the off licence. The black car was no more than a fading tail light that turned a corner and was gone.

The terror of the last hour released, he burst instantly into gasping dry sobs of frustration and helplessness, slamming all the locks shut with desperate, belated haste.

Then, with shaking limbs he clambered over into the driver's seat, put the car into gear and drove on.

He didn't make it home before he wet himself.

Chapter 8

More than a week down the line, and there was no movement at all in the Bertini case. Redwall knew that the car that killed Vince had been pinpointed specifically to a Volvo by virtue of a single, tiny shard of painted metal adhering to the dead man's skull. With morgue humour, the pathologist commented there would be a larger proportion of the man's skull on the car, but there was no way every Volvo in England in that particular, common shade of silver could be scrutinised at forensic level for bits of blood and gore for by now the car would have been scrubbed superficially clean, if not already professionally fixed.

Even so, it was probable that the car had been dented in the impact, so a request for information had been broadcast, but he didn't hold his breath. If Vince had been a child or a pillar of society, his plea for information would have let loose a flood of sightings, but the dead man was a pimp and a dealer. It was more probable the garage doing the repairs would give the driver a competitive rate for the work rather than shop him. Maybe they even thought of him as some kind of hero who had rid the world of one of its more undesirable elements.

Maybe they were right.

If that caught no fishes, Redwall knew he would have to widen the net, but to do so would mean crossing county boundaries, stepping into the boggy mire of police politics, and that was something he was reluctant to do at this stage. Keep it nice and simple, in house, and in perspective. If he made a hooey out of his continuing search, the press would do a lot of screeching about the force wasting the tax-payers' money, when it was clear justice had already, if accidentally, been served.

But although he could see their point, a man had died, and he felt it was incumbent upon him to try to find out who did it. The hit and run driver, after all, didn't know who he had run over, and it *was* against the law to leave the scene of a crime. Where were democracy, fair play and equality, if the judgement was made beforehand? It wasn't always easy to remain impartial, but it was all too easy to tweak public response one way or the other depending on circumstances and the quality of the man behind the investigation. Contrary to public belief, it took donkey-work to prove an identified suspect was indeed guilty, rather than the proof turning up first and pointing an unerring finger at the culprit.

He'd learned, by virtue of a near disaster a long time ago (which could have fully grounded his budding career), that once you were gunning for someone, you had to keep a very firm hold on your ideals and prejudices just in case you ignored evidence that pointed irritatingly to your suspect's innocence. The memory of that potentially huge blunder sent chill waves flooding his spine. How was it that bad memories returned with startling clarity, accompanied by full-blown replication of past embarrassment and pounding heart, while memories of good times drifted past the consciousness like a distant mist?

His present irritation was compounded by lack of time and too much to do, as usual. It was all very well for his superiors to yell about prioritising, that was just a buzz-word for what they'd always done. Giving it a fancy handle and making everyone aware of what was happening really didn't help in the least bit. The fact was, there were just not enough resources to do anything else.

Lesser crimes were crowded out of importance

unless there was a high profile personage involved, and as the present explosion of minor crimes were mostly committed by under-age offenders, there was little incentive to apprehend them. You spent one hell of a lot of time and money tracing them, a whole bundle of red tape and social worker interference trying to get them to Court, and even when found guilty, they would, in all likelihood be given a day or so of community service, then told not to be naughty again. The little bastards ran off with their fingers in the air at the police and practised until they attained perfection.

Hell, there was no incentive at all.

He shuffled some files on his desk as Jim came in, wondering why he needed to pretend to *look* busy when his mind was working in overdrive. Jim threw another file onto the pile.

'That's the files for the Julie Barnett case. This one's a doddle. We've got a good likeness of the rapist.'

He flicked it open saw an artist's impression.

'Christ, Frankenstein did it. Have you gone through the files with her?'

'Started. It's going to take a while. She's not in much of a fit state, and any identification she makes is going to be suspect, anyway. He whacked her around the head with a brick a few times before raping her. It's my guess she hasn't a clue, except she thought he was white.'

'Thought?'

Jim gave a sardonic glance as he left. 'Uh-huh. It'll sound real good in court, but because she's black the Guv wants us to pull out the stops.'

'We could just be honest and say we haven't a hope in hell of finding him.'

Jim raised a brow. 'I'll pull out the usual suspects.'

Redwall hated sex cases more than anything else, not least through a sense of disgust against his fellow man, but also because working the case left him feeling grubby, as though some of the dirt had rubbed off on his hands.

73

He hated the questions he'd have to ask and the subsequent report he'd have to write up. Unless he was careful it would read with the fulsome detail of a wank-mag.

These cases pointed a permanent finger at a targeted group, too, the same people being brought in again and again just because they had once been convicted. There was no such thing as starting off with a clean slate, not for them.

It was a fact that a lot of convicted sex offenders did re-offend. It was just an unfortunate side effect that those few who erred once, or even unjustly accused, were never allowed to put it behind them. But then, the victims couldn't ever put it behind them, either, so perhaps it was poetic justice of a kind, at least in the cases where the bloke really had done it.

Poetic justice?

Christ, what was he thinking? Justice was a word with a multitude of interpretations that, in reality, had nothing to do with his early, naive belief that it was something police dispensed, like bounty or sweets.

The door burst open. 'Sir?'

'Well?' Redwall snapped at the young constable with all the annoyance his pensive thoughts had generated.

'I'm sorry to intrude,' she said, not looking sorry at all. 'It's just that I found her and thought you'd like to know.'

'Found who?'

'Jessie. Well, not exactly found her but found out who she is, at least.'

'Jessie?'

'That girl-prostitute you were looking for in the Bertini case?'

Redwall stilled, forgetting his irritation.

'Well? Who is she?'

Wainright looked down at her sheet.

'Elizabeth Jessica Stowleigh, the politician's daughter who disappeared from the hospital a year ago. She's still on the missing children list. I've requested the file.'

'Are you sure?'

Something dropped in the pit of his stomach. His question was vaguely hopeful that she was wrong, rather than the other way around.

'No, not for sure, but she's blonde, about the right height and age from the descriptions, and the name is too much to be coincidence, don't you think?'

He frowned, dredged his mind for detail.

'I thought she was traced up to Bristol?'

'Apparently she bought a ticket to Bristol, but maybe she didn't use it.'

'Which would also mean she didn't want to be found, otherwise why the deception?'

He shared brief, acknowledging eye contact with Jim, then stood up and grabbed his jacket, trusting to the instinct of the constable. A short while ago he'd been wishing he knew who she was, but now realised he would rather not.

'Wainright, as well as the file on the girl, get moving on a total overview of Edward Stowleigh, everything, including what colour undies he wears and his financial situation. I want to know if there's any reason why his daughter would choose prostitution rather than private schools and a Maserati for her eighteenth birthday.'

As Jim drove, Redwall was reading the file, and none of it made an awful lot of sense.

'Edward Stowleigh's wife left him when Elizabeth was five. It seemed she ran off with a Greek entrepreneur, leaving her two children with their father. The other sister, Catherine, is three years older than Jessie. According to the file the mother is still with her Greek. She was informed when Jessie disappeared, but she didn't return to the country. Apparently she never came back to visit her first two babies. Nice mummy.'

'Perhaps she wouldn't have exactly been welcomed with open arms.'

Redwall felt his lips thin with disapproval.

'She didn't challenge guardianship?'

Jim shrugged. 'Not all women are maternal, and the law might very well not have come down on her side anyway as she was the one who ran off and left them. Added to which her husband did have financial clout, was loyal to his kids, and could give them a stable upbringing etc. If he'd pointed all that out at the time and informed her about the costs if she lost the case, he could very well have frightened her off right from the start.'

Jim knocked the car down to second, peering both ways several times before pulling carefully out of a junction. He drove with the same methodical care which permeated every other aspect of his life. He wouldn't be much use in a chase, Redwall thought.

Jim added, 'And perhaps she really didn't care. They all play tootsie, these rich bastards. Mix and match marriages, pick-a-partner dinner parties.'

'Tut, tut, prejudice,' Redwall said. 'The working class aren't known for long term commitment to marriage these days, either.'

'Yeah, but, I mean, can you feel sorry for them, with their mansions and their jewels and their jetting about? Give me a chance to try it, that's all.'

Redwall was surprised. He'd never heard Jim speak like that before, but he understood.

When you went in some poor homes the dirt and squalor hit you, but what got to you most of all was the underlying apathy. It seeped out of the very pores of the buildings, infecting the people who inhabited them with the knowledge that this was their one chance at life, with no parole for good behaviour.

It was no wonder women read Mills and Boon, men got blotto on Saturday night, and the kids sneaked out to wreak havoc on anyone who had more than they did. But the rich, what excuse did they have to be unhappy? And even if they were, it was cushioned by comfort. The only thing that seeped out of their walls was an unhealthy discontent. He shook his head. In spite of logic the unfairness of it all was tangible.

The phone went. It was Wainright. 'Yes?'

'The father's been pulled out of some meeting in the city. He said he'll meet you at his home rather than his office.'

Overhearing, Jim did a full circle of the roundabout, and went back the way they'd come.

'What did you tell him?'

'Nothing. Only that you were still looking at the case and needed to ask a few questions.'

'And that brought him out of a meeting, post-haste?'

'He's her father, after all. Perhaps he cares.'

Did he detect a note of censure? WPC Wainright was still a little wet behind the ears, a little sentimental for a policewoman, but perhaps it wasn't such a bad thing to be. She lent a touch of humanity to the station. He reflected wryly that when she'd seen some of the things a parent could do to his or her offspring her naiveté would all too soon disappear. Time hardened you in this job.

Redwall settled himself back, resigned to the slow but frenetic passage through London, and a brief smile of recollection touched his lips.

Pressurised by a political campaign strategy, the Chief of Police had once issued the directive for the police to set a good example and make more use of public transport, unless responding to emergency calls.

The resultant mayhem had given the taxpayer greater cause to complain than the waste of public funds on police vehicles, and had done little to aid the political vehicle.

Following instructions, Jim finally turned into a private drive blocked by a wrought iron gate. He leaned out and pressed the buzzer. Somewhere there was a faint movement as a camera panned the car.

'Detective Inspector Redwall and Detective Stevens to see Edward Stowleigh,' he said into the grill.

There was a moment's pause, then the gates swung silently open, and they drove on in.

Redwall stared at the sweeping lawn, the rows of orderly flowers, and although he was trying to keep an open mind, he was all set to loathe Edward Stowleigh on sight, mostly because he owned more just by being born than most people earned in a lifetime.

He was trying to rationalise his thoughts, when the drive swept into a tight curve before the house. He hadn't worked the case when Elizabeth Stowleigh had vanished, so this was all new to him. The building wasn't quite as ostentatious as he'd been expecting.

It was a low, mellow house, possibly Elizabethan in origin, judging from the height of the doors and the stone windows, and was almost monastic in style. Age and history dripped from the walls in the form of thick branches of Wisteria with a warm undercoat of ivy, and its proximity to the City was indication enough of the value of the property, but overall, he had to admit it was pleasing to the eye.

Edward Stowleigh was already there. A silver Jaguar stood by the door, clean and spotless as though it had never been subjected to English roads. The bonnet steamed in the slight drizzle.

As they climbed out of the unmarked car, the front door was opened by Stowleigh himself. What had he expected, a butler in full uniform?

Redwall stared at the man for a moment and thought, illogically, that he looked just like his pictures in the paper. Clean-cut, mid-forties, but unlined, and sporting a slightly orange health-club tan. Just now he wore a worried expression, concern mingling with apprehension.

'Come in, come in,' he said hastily as they climbed from the car, ushering them out of the rain through a modern porch, and straight into a large reception room tastefully and warmly furnished in greens and golds.

'Please take a seat. Can I get you a drink, or anything?'

'No, nothing, thank you.'

They perched uncomfortably on the edges of a pair

of velour-covered chairs fringed with tassels.

Edward Stowleigh began to follow suit, got half way down before popping up again and pacing four steps towards a fireplace adorned with a huge display of dried flowers, where he swivelled to face them.

'Have you found her?' he asked abruptly.

So much for politicians beating about the bush, Redwall thought. His reply was equally to the point, knowing that nothing would change the shock of understanding. As with death, it was better to simply say it than prevaricate.

'We're not entirely sure, but a girl was seen a few weeks ago who may be your daughter.'

Edward's face turned a shade of grey as Redwall detailed the accident.

'All we know for sure is a girl was seen fleeing from the scene, but from subsequent talks to the other ladies under Vince's protection, it could very well have been Elizabeth. The description, the time-scale, and her age all fit.'

'Other ladies? You mean whores.'

'Plainly speaking, yes.'

'And you think Lizzie was one.'

His voice was flat, neither challenging nor outraged.

'Was she under any kind of duress, do you think?'

'It seems not. Of course, we're not absolutely sure Jessie is your daughter, it's just a possibility.'

'You called her Jessie?'

'It's what she was calling herself.'

'I see. Yes. Possibly.' He took another turn up and down the room. 'But you have no idea where she is now?'

'No, but we're working on it.'

Redwall tried to keep an expression of sympathy from his face. 'Mr Stowleigh. The girl in question had been working as a prostitute the last year. If this was your daughter, can you think of any reason at all why she would have done this, and not come back, or asked for help from someone?'

79

Edward seemed to jolt, then steeled himself.

'We never got on very well. She was a problem child from the word go. I thought children were the product of genes and parenting and education, but I was wrong. But if she was difficult before, she became impossible when her mother ran off. Nothing I did could ever make up for that, not the things I bought her, the horse, or the holidays. Yet I find it hard to believe she would choose to... Christ, what the hell else could I have done?'

'It's never as simple as that, Sir. Many girls get picked up from the station, given food and shelter, and discover it comes with a payback price. I'd imagine that's what happened to Jessie. The man who picked her up probably seemed like her saviour, a hero, for a short while before reality cut in. By then she would have become too deeply enmeshed; intimidated, in debt for drugs, afraid to go home and see hatred and loathing on the faces of people she loved. It's a vicious cycle.'

Edward Stowleigh stared out of the window for a moment, and the electric magnetism of his personality seemed to drain out of his body even as they watched.

'Was she... Did he hurt her?'

Redwall's voice was dry. 'I doubt Vince was nice. Pimps usually aren't, but the other women who worked for him said he wasn't the worst, and it seemed the girl was fairly self-sufficient. I even got the feeling they resented her because she wasn't scared of him in the way they were.'

Edward gave a faint, almost hysterical laugh, but when he spoke his voice was brittle.

'That sounds like Lizzie. She wouldn't listen to anyone, ever. She went her own way. No one could control her, not the nannies, not the school, not me. And yet, Catherine...'

He swallowed, was silent for a moment, then continued.

'I just don't know where I went wrong with Lizzie.'

He stood for a moment, looking out of the low window, shoulders slumped, hands stuffed in his trouser pockets, and spoke without turning.

'Do you ever stop in life and turn around to see that something has gone badly wrong, and you didn't have a clue how it happened? Perhaps I should have married again, provided the girls with a mother, but when you've had one marriage go belly-up you don't go leaping into another, do you?'

He paced a couple of steps, as if he wanted to get somewhere fast, then stopped abruptly.

'Christ, if I'd known... She was a wild card, Lizzie was. Always made things difficult for me and her sister. It didn't matter what I did, it was wrong. When I sent her to private school she hated it, when I took her out, she hated it. Even when she tried to commit suicide they said it was a cry for help. But for what? What else did she expect me to give her? What could I do that I wasn't doing already?'

His face betrayed genuine pain.

Redwall empathised. What parent ever really knew the ropes? You made it up as you went along, and hoped you got it right. Having two children himself, he knew how difficult it could be; the frustration of misdirected anger, personalities clashing. People assured him it would get better when the kids left home and came back to visit on their own terms.

He really hoped they were right.

'Is Catherine still with you?'

'She's turned eighteen now. She's gone over to the States to be a nanny for a while. There's a couple I know, friends of the family. They'll look out for her, show her the ropes. She'll do all right, I know.'

Redwall thought he knew, too.

She was probably into the mating game, Hollywood style. Swimming pool in the garden, nanny looks after the children between swims, and gets presented to the American equivalent of her own social bracket. Even across the pond the class act was still strong, and they'd

81

love her aristocratic ties and her accent. She'd be engaged before long.

'How did Catherine get on after Elizabeth disappeared? Did it affect her badly?'

Edward seemed almost embarrassed.

'They never really got on. Maybe they'd have grown together a bit when they got older, but, well, it was kind of quieter, calmer, once Lizzie left. I shouldn't have said that.'

Redwall understood.

With the disruptive influence out of the way, father and daughter had probably enjoyed a few months of guilty peace. He sighed, feeling strangely in sympathy with this man he'd been determined to dislike. The public persona of *nice guy* wasn't so far from the private reality. The man had made some mistakes – everyone did. But he was hurting, flagellating himself mentally for getting it all so wrong.

It was easy to make mistakes with children. They didn't come with instruction manuals, and their reactions could be vastly out of proportion to the parent's perceived crime.

He had a sneaking feeling of sympathy for the absent child, too. Abandoned by her mother, looked after by a series of nannies, the father jetting about on important government business thinking he was doing everything a father could do, but not really being there for her.

He could see how it could happen.

'When she tried to commit suicide,' he asked, 'did you have any idea things had got that bad?'

'No, none at all. She'd got really good grades at school, you know. She wasn't stupid in spite of all that anger of hers, and I thought for a while it was all going OK. It seemed as if she was settling down a bit. Her school said she'd decided to work in the fashion trade, as a model, or a designer or something, I don't think she really knew herself; but whatever she wanted to do, I think she would have achieved it, simply because she had the strength, the will-power and, let's face it, the looks. I just couldn't believe it when she tried to kill herself. I just don't know what was going through her mind. And as for becoming a prostitute, I really can't... She could have come back any time rather than that. Why? Can you tell me why my daughter would do that?'

More used to the idea now, his tone rose, the original astonishment laced with anger.

Redwall turned the conversation. It was easy to see why girls didn't want to face their parents afterwards. You could choose to forgive, but it would always be there, lurking under the surface.

'Was she happy at her last school, Mr Stowleigh?'

'I went through all this at the time,' he said, glancing absently at his watch.

Business beckoned.

'It was a new school, her fourth in four years, not that she spent much time in any of them. She was always absconding. I don't think she had many friends. Not real friends. Everyone said she wasn't an easy child to like. The teachers kept telling me how she kept her distance from everyone, wouldn't allow people to get close with her at all. They tried to help, but she rejected any overtures of friendship. One of the schools tried to get counselling for her, but she resented intrusion in any form. Then, when she tried to commit suicide, and they were all there, trying to help, she ran from the hospital. If it was a cry for help, why did she run? She just walked out when they weren't looking. And now you tell me she became a prostitute?'

He was genuinely bewildered.

'I should just remind you that the Jessie we're looking for might not be Elizabeth. We might all be barking up the wrong tree.'

There was a silence, then Edward gave a brief sigh, saying with intense honesty, 'But she might be. Any news is better than endless silence, Inspector; any news at all. You will keep me informed, won't you?'

Redwall left the building his head echoing with all

83

the rage and sadness of the father who, with all his money, had been unable to change his child's self-destructive downward slide. But wherever he'd gone wrong, it was obvious he cared deeply.

Chapter 9

Ben lost count of the days for a while. Life became a routine of looking after the girl, and the cats slunk up to the attic with him, confused at his rejection. It hadn't taken him long to realise the girl was experiencing withdrawal symptoms amongst other things, and though now and again lucidity shone in the pure venom in her eyes, usually they were blank with pain and the sheer exhaustion of simply surviving.

He cleaned her when she soiled herself, massaged her limbs when she cramped, fed her, and cleaned her again when she brought it all up. Now and then he resorted to physically restraining her, tying her to the old bedstead to stop her from hurting herself.

Then on top of everything, secondary infection set in. Her lungs bubbled, and her lips blued as she struggled to bring oxygen into her system. When she lapsed into near-coma, Ben thought there wouldn't be enough fight left in that fragile frame to survive the trauma. At that moment he resigned himself to her eventual death.

And if she died, so be it. He would call on Godfrey for help. His ex-boss would cuss him every which way to hell, but would still send in a team of cleaners, and in less than no time at all it would be as if the girl had never existed. Godfrey owed him that much.

He thought of the anonymous black van, the men's dark overalls and dark glasses, and looked down at the girl with more gentleness than he'd allowed himself to date.

No, he wouldn't do that.

When she died, he would dig a grave out in the New Forest where she could be at peace, where people couldn't hurt her any more.

Even as the thought crossed his mind, she seemed to stop breathing. With grim determination he all but crushed her ribs as he belted the life back into her, and to his surprise she rallied once more, drawing shallow, ragged breaths. Ben shrugged at the setback, and carried on, his own face stubbled from lack of attention. He was used to seeing people stitched up and sent back out into battle. This was no different to Ben, a man lost in time. He was almost surprised she didn't die. When he was convinced she'd given up the fight, she turned the corner, and began to rally.

Chapter 10

The body of a woman was found by workmen who had gone in to demolish the sagging red brickwork of a derelict wharf-side warehouse in preparation for transforming it into a unique and desirable residential area. Redwall had seen the architect's impressions and the advertising.

The site didn't look desirable at the moment.

The workmen were articulating excitedly to press and onlookers when he got there, already explaining in graphic detail how they had found the body hanging from the rusted structure of a rotting pontoon, and how it must have been there for quite a while because it was all grey and bloated.

The reporters babbled questions.

Yes, it was definitely a woman, she was naked. That much was clearly visible. But the warm weather and rats hadn't helped.

Redwall decided they'd had been lucky to find the body so soon. If the men who had thrown her in had got it right, the chains would have dragged the body down and it wouldn't have surfaced for months, and by then identification would have been all but impossible.

As it was, even in the state she was in, once she was on the trolley, he had been able to identify the woman, himself. It was always hard to comprehend the death of someone you had been speaking to recently, and he deliberately tried to distance himself from this thing which had been rocking gently to and fro under the pontoon as Gill. She had been a vital person, a kind person, he sensed, and whatever had happened in life to drive her into the age-old profession, she hadn't deserved this end.

A day later he was studying the photographs with reluctant attention to detail, closely following the accompanying report. The gloating workmen had had no idea the story was even juicer than they supposed, for it had become evident to the police as soon as they pulled the body out, that Gill had been tortured. The rope around her neck provided easy proof of her final moments. The ligature marks and the dislocation of her wrists suggested she'd been hanging from her arms while she was worked over, but because of the time that had elapsed before the body was discovered, they had been unable to assess whether she'd been sexually assaulted.

That particular bit of information would have done them no good, anyway, he realised, taking her profession into account; but no one should have to die like that, whatever their station in life.

The question which bothered him was: had she been tortured for information or for some pervert's sexual gratification?

He turned his face to another photograph; the missing girl, Elizabeth Jessica Stowleigh. Was she Vince's Jessie? Could Gill's last and traumatic experience of life be to do with her in some way? The photograph had been enlarged to the point of pixilation, but even like that, it was something concrete, proof that she actually existed. Or had existed. The sallow-faced child with blonde plaits stared back with the type of expression teenagers produce so readily; a warring mixture of superiority, self-doubt, self-importance, and dissatisfaction with the whole caboodle.

He knew from experience that the more you gave, the more they wanted, and little was given in return, but one thing you could never do was shield them. Life still slapped them round the face when they weren't looking.

'Tell me what happened,' he whispered, but Elizabeth stared back, saying nothing.

Christ, he felt old, sometimes, particularly when he picked his daughter up from school. The girls came out looking so sophisticated, like hoards of little tarts lining up for a taste of life, positively begging for it. He could see how it would be hard for a red-blooded man to keep in perspective the fact that they had no idea what they were asking for, or that they were in danger of getting it. It was all a big show, and they did it so well – until they opened their mouths.

Elizabeth Stowleigh, at thirteen looked sixteen, but her particular brand of arrogance was immersed in history. She didn't think she was superior; she knew she was. There wasn't anything in this image he could find to like. Her disdain for the cameraman, her expensive riding clothes, and the horse whose reins she clutched, were far out of his experience. Yet the hard eyes in that pinched, narrow face, were daring him to like her because she already hated herself more than he ever could.

Why?

He'd been going to ask Gill if Jessie could be recognised from this likeness, but he was too late. He was half convinced someone else had been asking questions before him. The burns on her body were consistent with cold and calculated infliction of pain; associated more with torture for information than sexual gratification.

But had the questions revealed the answers the torturer had wanted? And did they involve Elizabeth, or Jessie, or whatever she called herself now? What could Gill, or the other women who had worked for Vince, possibly know that deserved such premeditated, cold violence?

And Vince's other women had disappeared off the face of the earth. Were they lying in shallow graves somewhere, too? That Gill came to light was down to the laziness of the perpetrators; they hadn't bothered to drive away from the scene of the crime, but had simply disposed of her in the quickest and easiest manner possible.

But Gill's fate could only be tied to Vince's death or Jessie's disappearance by a leap of faith. It could simply be coincidence. She could have offered her services to a man with a lust for the darker side of sex. However, there were too many imponderables around Vince's death. There was more to it than he had yet discovered.

Had it really been Elizabeth Jessica Stowleigh, aka Jessie, on the dual carriageway the night Vince had been killed? Except for the fact that Jessie had been wafted away into thin air, and their only witness said the woman might have been blonde, that also was a stretch of the imagination, a leap of faith that didn't hold up under scrutiny.

In reality, the whole investigation had disintegrated underneath him. As far as the Guv was concerned he had no case and was to get on with his other assignments and stop wasting time. The truth was, no one really cared too much if Vince's killer got his just deserts, and this new murder was that of a whore not some respectable citizen, and didn't they ask for it, doing what they were doing?

So Redwall reluctantly let others look superficially into Gill's death over the next week, and watched Vince's estate being distributed by one legal crook to other crooks, with the irritating knowledge that not a penny of that wealth had been earned legally, or taxed, and there wasn't a thing he could do about it.

But the child's insolent face haunted him, for behind it there was intelligence. Why had she not gone home? What could have waited there for her that was worse than being a prostitute? Had the loving father actually been molesting her?

It was eating at his peace of mind, probably because he was a father. But of one thing he was sure. The girl in the picture had needed help, but hadn't found it at home.

Chapter 11

The day came when Ben realised she was watching his every move. Her iron gaze followed him warily, with total lucidity. And when he approached the bed, the sight of his ugly mug didn't bother her, so he realised with some amusement she must have been lucid before, feigning unconsciousness when he was around.

It's what he would have done. Assess the situation, gain the advantage. He carried on waiting on her, knowing she would speak when she was ready, but carried her down to the bathroom so that she could perform her most basic functions in privacy. He realised she was angry at her weakness, and hated to be carried, tolerating his touch only because she couldn't do it for herself.

He knew, in her head, she was planning escape.

Well, this wasn't a prison.

If she wanted to go, he wouldn't stop her.

When she eventually spoke he was clearing the uneaten dinner from her room. She'd been with him for nearly four weeks, and was even thinner than she'd been when she arrived, but there was a new vitality behind the startlingly green eyes.

'Did you do this?'

He glanced over. She indicated her arm, immobilised under the plaster sheath that had replaced his initial field dressing once the swelling had died down.

'Yes. It was broken.'

Hardness had crept onto his patient's face with the

return to conscious thought. A hardness that had been absent as she'd nearly died, fighting for breath, fighting for life, unaware that nature had instilled within her the deep capacity for survival. He counted it a blessing in some respects that she'd been so ill, for she had lapsed into unconsciousness throughout the worst of her withdrawal. She was now fighting the residual effects of pneumonia and the mental readjustment of not being dependant – if she did readjust. She could go back to it as easy as not.

That was up to her, and up to fate.

He picked her up easily, there was no weight to her at all, and placed her in the old chair while he changed the sheets. She stared at him, making no contribution to her own well-being, calculation obvious in her assessment. Why was he helping her? What did he stand to gain? He guessed she'd learned a long time ago that nobody did something for nothing.

He found it slightly unnerving as her eyes followed his every move. He was unused to being looked at. Usually strangers would glance, double-take as though they couldn't believe such ugliness could exist, then look away quickly, embarrassed, even while these actions made their thoughts transparent.

But the girl didn't do that.

She was openly searching for the character that lay beneath his mask of melted flesh, trying to decide what he was doing, and why. She had her own reasons for not trying to walk out at the moment. She knew she wouldn't survive long without help, and presently he was doing nothing to alarm her into flight. That was good, because if she was assessing the situation it meant she had a good will to live, and that gave her a better chance for survival out there in the cold world when she did take to her heels.

In the isolation of the old attic, she became curious. That too was good. He could see questions burning, and waited for her to voice them. Not that he could really say why he'd kept her alive, in this house, why he

92

hadn't called the police, got her to a hospital, because he didn't really know. She'd simply struck a chord inside him. There were many times over the next months he regretted his action, but in his own bull-headed fashion, having once made the decision he would see it through.

She began to get restless, and he guessed his silence was more unnerving to her than hers was to him. When she spoke once more it was, again, accusatory.

'Where's my bag?'

He indicated a cupboard.

'Did you look in it? Is my stuff still there?'

'You can check any time you want,' he said.

But he'd looked in her bag, of course. He'd gone back out to collect it later, where it lay under the hedge, covered in dew. He'd been expecting to find drugs, instead, he found wealth. Cash, and some things that passed for currency in a world where taxes didn't exist. Untraceable drafts and bonds that had no right being outside of a bank vault, and certainly no place in the carry-all of a scruffy girl-child.

He'd put the gun in there, too, unable to think of anything else to do with it. Noticing the safety was off, he had checked. It had been fired, once. He sniffed. Not so long ago; all bad news. He put the safety on

When he left the room he heard her take her first independent action. She climbed out of bed and, unable to stand, crawled with determination towards the cupboard. For a while there was silence. When he went up she was slumped beside the door, an angry scowl marring her face. She hadn't managed to open the cupboard; she couldn't reach the handle.

He pressed the lever, and walked away again. When he came back later she was back in bed, and the cupboard door was closed. Later he picked her up and carried her down to the bathroom once more. She went rigid, as she did these days at the contact, but he sat her on the wicker linen basket and left her there.

'Call me when you're finished.'

93

'Why?'

He turned in the doorway, brows raised in query.

Her voice was brittle.

'Why are you doing this? Helping me.'

'Are you sure that's what I'm doing?'

'You haven't called the police. You fixed my arm. 'What do you want from me?'

For the first time confusion must have shown in his face. When he finally answered, his voice sounded old, less sure.

'I truly don't know why I'm doing this. I have no idea.'

He felt in some ways he would be glad when he did go up to the attic room one day to find her and her sports bag full of bad news departed for pastures new.

'What do I call you?'

'Ben.'

After a long pause, she said, 'I'm Jessie.'

He realised that in her own way she was thanking him. It was probably the only thanks he would get, but he understood that. It was a tentative feeler, an almost grudging contact, but one that gave hope.

Over the next few days he saw a new resolve fill her hard face. He knew from the creaking floorboards that she was pushing herself, standing and walking when she thought he couldn't hear.

She forced food down and took his vitamins without complaining. The bloom of youth finally reached her haggard cheeks, but along with the light of determination, a raging anger also blossomed. He'd seen that look before, and it didn't make him happy. She had vengeance in her heart. Against who and for what, he didn't know, and didn't want to know.

As she recovered, he gave her books to look at, to focus her mind on something other than herself, and they embarked on a tentative communication based around a game of not giving anything away. Ben knew she was considering every word she spoke, lying, stalling, terrified of giving him any leverage, any real information, but then, so was he.

It was second nature to him.

There were times she inadvertently communicated an avid interest in life outside of her own narrow confines. When she looked at the faded photographs of his early childhood in Japan, his teens in America, his US army days, and his tour of duty, she asked, where, how, who, and why, until Ben became tangled up in a past he'd long ago ceased to mourn, and found she'd wangled out of him emotions that had long been dormant.

At the same time she betrayed more of herself than she realised: a fertile brain, an astonishing interest and knowledge of politics and current affairs, and a frighteningly personal experience of a much different strata of life from his own humble origins.

At those times he resented her intrusion in his life, but the nearer she came to getting fit, to walking out of his life, the more Ben became dismayed by the idea. He realised he would actually miss her, that his carefully ordered life had gone through yet another transformation. This stray waif had woven another strand into the rich tapestry of his eventful life. Even this near his end, he hadn't been able to put society aside; it had crept into his home.

There were times he cursed the impulse that fateful morning that had stopped rational thought. He should simply have phoned the police, and she would have disappeared out of his life the instant she came into it. Yet now, with a degree of self-derision he realised that her departure would leave an empty hole in his life; that his cherished solitary existence now stretched ahead in a rather hollow manner.

It dawned on him, finally, that he had taken her in, not for her, but for him.

Chapter 12

Just when the investigation dead end had solidified, Redwall was startled by an unexpected upturn. Throwing his other work aside, he yelled to Jim to come in and see what had turned up. The garage in question had simply made a curt telephone call to say they had received a car in the sort of condition that the police had mentioned on the TV a while back, and were stalling repairs so that the police could take a gander.

The Volvo had been damaged weeks ago, but had been cleaned and touched up, which the garage owner thought was suspicious as it was a simple insurance job. The owner said he'd driven by accident into a pile of earth but hadn't brought the car in for repair as he'd needed it. That was a crock, of course, because they always gave out a courtesy car for repairs on insurance jobs, especially those that were company-leased rather than owned.

Jim ran the car through the system.

It was leased to BondStock, a company dealing in finance and insurance, and presently used by a company rep. by the name of Gary Bryant. A forensics team was on their way within an hour while enquiries were being made by the Southampton force as to the whereabouts of Mr Bryant himself.

Chapter 13

Ben heard Jessie push open the wooden door and make her way down the flights of steps and into the house below.

He strove for a calm he didn't feel. He heard her pass into the hallway, and knew exactly what she would be seeing: darkness, with a shaft of light breaking from the quarter-light above the front door. Would she go, now? It was unlikely she'd get far. He heard her hesitate, backtrack to the kitchen. Another private place, up to now invaded by no one but himself and his personal belongings. Old pans, dented and discoloured with age, old chairs, wooden and functional, work-tops that were chipped and stained with use, and cupboards with doors that no longer fitted into the frames. For him it was a homely room, filled with light. He didn't need new work tops and stainless steel cutlery to make him content.

Would she go via the back door?

He heard her tread softly back to the hall, towards the room in which he knelt. He sensed her presence behind him, her confusion at what she now saw: a wide, empty expanse of polished wood flooring, no longer new, but not of the age of the rest of the house. The walls down the length of the room were bare save two flags that hung on either side of the photograph of an old man; and at the far end of the wall a long, slightly curved sword hung on a carved wooden rack, dominating the large empty space like an altar.

It would be a culture-shock to anyone seeing it for the first time, and there hadn't been many, yet she let no gasp of surprise escape her. The windows had been filled in with a trellis-work of fine wooden slats that cut the invading sunlight into harsh patterns on the wooden floor; all part of the calculated décor that made this place his sanctuary.

He knelt, facing away from her, towards the wall with the sword, but sensed her presence as clearly as if he were staring at her. The light from a speckled sun cast a network of shadows over one side of his body.

He was dressed in a suit of loose cotton, so old the edges had worn away, leaving a frayed edge of warp revealed; and the belt, once black, was now a faded grey.

He tried to imagine himself as she saw him, and wondered what she made of the room. Both were the remnants of a time long gone; a romantic notion born several centuries past in another land. This room, and his presence in it, were something alien to this place and this time. Perhaps she saw it as something archaic, slightly sad.

He listened to her, waiting for her to go, but she didn't. She slid down the wall behind her and came to rest. Eventually he moved. His breathing simply deepened in anticipation, and he stood, turned in a single fluid motion, one minute kneeling, the next standing, facing her. Contrary to expectation there was no hard derision on her face, no amusement, just curiosity.

A small thrill of happiness filled him knowing she sensed the peace of this room. To his own surprise, Ben bowed slightly towards her, an acknowledgement of what, he wasn't sure, then turned away again, and bowed not to the photograph of his Sensei on the wall as Jessie might be supposing, but to something deeper: respect for the age and honour of his calling. The photograph of his sensei was simply a point of focus. He could no more start his practice without this token of respect than he could fly.

'Honoured Master,' he whispered in Japanese.

Then he began the controlled movements that made a shape on the wooden floor with his bare feet, like a ballet in their decisiveness, At the same time his clenched fists moved in a precision of detail, the actions between the patterns of stillness so fast it blurred; and yet, when he stopped, the movement was finished, absolutely.

There was no momentary steadying of the hands; no casual re-alignment of the feet. He'd done this too many times, for so long now, his understanding was total. And as he practised he discovered a small part of his inner self standing outside, watching as he sensed she was watching.

First he performed an easy Kata, then moved on to the slightly more difficult. It was simply the process. In all things was a purpose, a reason, a progression. As he moved through the age-long patterns his battered body was no longer old. It was a machine, a thing of power and beauty: step right, arm block the opponent's fist, forward Kochoki, step behind, swivel left, block, and counter-attack.

The Kata was a dance with time; his self-containment absolute. He was at peace with himself. The world outside didn't exist. And yet, had he the need to kill, the old skill would surface without thought as it had in the past, courtesy of the hours of practice. This skill was primarily defensive, though its secondary effect was to mould a killing machine of the person who mastered it. That would be frightening, except that he radiated an inner peace that came only of the knowledge that he didn't have to prove his mastery to anyone but himself. Even as his thoughts tumbled, he was aware of Jessie, watching.

He stopped long before he was ready to stop. It seemed that she wasn't going to leave until he did so. He made his final obeisance to tradition then turned, a normal man again.

Her expression had softened.

'This is what keeps me out of mischief as I wait for

death,' he said, his arm indicating the room.

'You're dying?' she asked, startled.

'I'm old. Death isn't something to be afraid of; it's simply the correct end to life, which is infinitely harder.'

She made a convulsive movement. He realised she'd been sitting for too long on the hard floor, and was unable to stand. He leaned down, picked her up, carried her into the kitchen, and sat her in the cushioned rocking chair. The tabby cat came and jumped immediately onto her lap. She began to stroke it.

After Ben had showered and changed back into his normal clothes, he returned to make some lunch to find she'd fallen asleep with the cat on her lap. Her fair hair was tousled, and she wore an expression of contentment on her face which betrayed the girl she might have become, had circumstances been different.

When she was rested and had eaten, he took her outside for the first time since her unexpected arrival.

The garden was surrounded by a red brick wall. The far end was an orchard, under which grass grew, and in the summer, bluebells rioted, but near the house Ben had built a small, perfect little garden where the precision of the plants was an art-form. The paths were small, filled with gravel, and wove around the artificial landscape in a never ending ribbon, a maze of choices.

'It's nice here,' Jessie said finally, her voice unknowingly betraying regret that she wouldn't stay.

Chapter 14

Detective Inspector Redwall and Jim were in their car on their way south.

They found Gary's house easily, a semi in an upmarket estate on the Romsey side of Southampton. Gary opened the door himself. He was a skinny man with a receding hairline and that suave style of dressing that reps thought passed for quality.

'Detective Inspector Redwall,' he introduced himself, flapping his badge at Mr Bryant. 'We'd like to talk to you about the damage on your car. May we come in?'

Gary's face drained of colour as Redwall's eyes met his, and they both knew it was too late for lies. Swallowing, he stood back and showed the officers through to the immaculate living room with the regulation three-piece, chintz curtains, and large reproduction of an old master on one wall. No kids, Redwall thought.

A sharp-faced woman wearing clothes designed for someone younger and thinner, made her presence known at another door, glaring at them in silence. Gary looked over at her and seemed to diminish fractionally, then gave a faint shrug.

'I should have reported it at the time,' he said simply, with the air of a man who was, perhaps, quite glad to have been found out.

From the look on his wife's face Redwall realised the grilling they were about to give him wouldn't even come near the one she was going to give him, later. He felt faintly sorry for Gary, but listened with astonishment to the tale the man now told.

'So the fact that you were there at that time was purely accidental? You had no idea they were going to be there?'

'I didn't know who they were, and I still don't,' Gary said. He shuddered. 'I've never seen anything like that body, I've dreamed about it every night since it happened, but the girl, Christ, she spooked me. She would have killed me, I know.'

'Did she look afraid at all?'

'Afraid? That bitch wouldn't have known what the word meant.'

'But you said it looked as if she was running from the man?'

'I dunno. I thought he was chasing her, I thought it might be some punter she'd robbed, or something, but she kicked him, afterwards. After she'd robbed him, I mean. She said she'd have killed the bastard if I hadn't, or something like that.'

Eventually they had a statement drafted, and he could think of no more questions to ask. The man had poured out his story without a break, and Redwall was convinced of its truth. He even felt a little sorry for the poor sod as they got up to leave.

'Are you going to do me for hit and run?'

'I'm afraid we haven't got any choice,' Redwall said as they rose to leave. 'But in the circumstances I'm not going to haul you away in handcuffs. Just don't leave the area, in fact, stay at your house for a few days, I might want to ask you a few more questions. But you should get yourself sorted out with a good lawyer. If it can be proved you were kidnapped and in fear of your life, and if you forget to mention you'd been drinking, you might just get off with a suspended sentence.'

'Thank you,' he said sincerely, but as they left they heard the shrill voice of his wife, and Redwall wondered if it might not have been kinder to have put him in the lock-up.

'Did you believe him?' Jim asked, changing gears

rapidly on the motorway.

'It's too implausible a story to have been made up. And his description certainly fits that of Jessie. I think he has proved quite conclusively that she was the one with Vince, even if we don't know why.'

'He wasn't sure about the picture you showed him.'

'It was night time. He was scared. She's grown up a bit since that was taken.'

'She'd still only be fifteen, but her actions didn't sound like those of a terrified child.'

'No, you're right. It sounds like she's taken the underworld to her bosom. But why were they racing about on a dual carriageway at night?'

'He said she was carrying a heavy bag,' Jim said. 'If she had her stuff with her, perhaps she was simply running away. Pimps, as a rule, don't like their girls running away.'

'It's a possibility, but toms don't usually have that much stuff.'

'And she took something else, off Vince, after he was dead. And maybe the gun, too.'

'At least Gary confirmed there was a gun, and the shot we heard was fired into the air.'

The lack of a cartridge remained a mystery, though.

'H'm. What could she have taken off him? It had to be something important to her. Gary said it was something small, like a notebook, or a mobile.'

'She didn't take his wallet, though, and there was cash in it, which, strangely, suggests she had money enough.'

Redwall was silent for a moment, watching the countryside flash past. 'But whatever it was she took, perhaps that was what Gill was tortured for. And if so, it was important to someone else, too.'

'Where do we go from here, I wonder? We still haven't proved conclusively this girl is Elizabeth Stowleigh.'

'That doesn't matter. We still need to find her. Whoever she is, she's either trouble, or is in trouble.'

103

'If we're not too late, of course.'

Jessie's photograph was plastered around Southampton for a bit, with a plea for information. They checked through the hospital records to see if anyone had been treated for a broken arm at the time, and the local force checked out the face of every hooker on the streets for a while, but got nothing in return for their pains except a single possible sighting in town the day after Vince's death, which couldn't be confirmed.

Once more, Jessie had disappeared into thin air.

The Southampton force were convinced that if the girl was running scared, she wouldn't have stayed in Southampton, but would have hitched onward to some other destination to lose herself further, and Redwall was inclined to believe them.

If she'd still been there, she would surely have been sighted by now. He contacted various other hospitals in the South over the next couple of days, but, the Guv said sarcastically, she could have used any name, and he didn't have time to chase after wild hunches. So he was obliged, once more, to turn his mind to other matters.

He reluctantly called on Edward Stowleigh to update him and admit that they had lost all trace of the girl who might or might not be his daughter, but assured him that cases of missing children were never closed, and that if anything new turned up they'd contact him instantly.

Chapter 15

Jessie watched Ben train every day. It became a routine, and Ben kidded himself Jessie would stay with him, because in the deepest part of his heart he needed her to.

He was slightly surprised at himself for discovering again, at his time of life, the meaning of loneliness, when he'd assumed himself to be long cured of the need for other humans. But as each day passed, he became sure he would wake up one morning to find her gone.

It wasn't love he felt for her, he knew, but a kind of mutual need, as though by healing her he would also be healing himself. He shook his head in amazement. All those years, kidding himself he didn't need anyone else, and all it took was one stray waif, a damaged child to prove him wrong.

And yet theirs was a strange relationship, for they hardly spoke.

There were a hundred ways around the maze of paths in the garden, and each day they walked a different way around. Ben took Jessie's arm, at first to assist her, then because he liked the comfort of touch, and he sensed her grudging acceptance; for once he'd stopped tending to Jessie's needs, that was the only time he ever touched her.

He recognised the change in status: she was no longer a patient and he was no longer the nurse. However, a new and almost indefinable status quo existed between them: a mutual realisation of his worldliness, and of Jessie's need to learn.

He woke up every morning to the sound of bird-song, and the touch of sun on the window expecting to find her gone. It disturbed his sleep to the point he awoke late one morning to find her room empty.

Tense with the knowledge that she'd finally gone, he made his way to the dojo to work the strange emptiness out of his mind, and heard movement.

Padding silently forward he was astonished to see Jessie clumsily trying to emulate some of his movements. She made her hand into a tight fist, and her actions were gauche and clumsy.

He hesitated, knowing he was watching a private moment, but it was too late, something told her of his presence. She spun around guiltily, flushing with embarrassment.

For a moment neither knew how to react.

Then Ben went behind her and pushed her left hand forward with his own. She went rigid for a second, then realised what he was about.

'Keep your hips straight,' he said gently.

'In line with your body, like so. Spread your feet apart just a bit more, and relax the knees slightly to take away the strain. Keep your shoulders in line with your hips. Loosen the fist. Tighten it only when you make contact or the muscles will be permanently stressed. The other hand counterbalances the movement, always.'

He then brought her right hand up, and placed it on her hip, turning it upwards and folding it into a loose fist. 'Does that feel better?'

She nodded fractionally.

He then went and stood beside her, and slightly forward so that she could watch.

'Now, pull the left fist back, push the right fist out, and when they reach half way, twist them. Like so.'

In slow motion he showed her, his fists moving, left, right, left, right, slowly and surely from hip to punch, swivelling from the punch position into the hip position and back again.

'With me.'

She tried, and her fists ended up the wrong way up on her hip, and wouldn't swivel at the middle of the movement. The inability to perform this seemingly simple action tightened her features into a mask of irritation.

'No anger. Learn slowly, learn calmly, and the body will remember when you need to move fast. Forget I'm here. Concentrate on what you're doing, nothing else.'

There was silence for a moment, and after a while Jessie relaxed, her body beginning to respond to these new, strange commands. Her fists began to swivel.

Ben smiled, and placed himself before her.

He pointed at the hollow beneath the centre of his ribs.

'If you want to kill me, that's your target,' he said, taking her fist and pushing it hard against him. 'Aim for that spot in your mind's eye. With each punch you must want to kill me. And each punch should be aimed not at that point, but a hand length beyond it. You don't punch *at* your enemy, you punch *through* him. That's where your power comes from.'

He knew she felt inadequate, ridiculous.

He'd felt the same way once, a lifetime ago. But it was worse for her, a woman who had, presumably, felt the rage of a man's body.

'A woman can defeat a man if she's trained,' he said. 'It's about reacting before the aggressor's muscles are tightened. It's about being strong mentally, and about being quicker. It's about practice, practice, practice. Then you can overcome any thug who tries to overpower you.'

'And if I meet someone like you?'

'You won't; but if you do, run.'

He caught the hint of a smile.

'Now. again.'

As she practised, he walked out of her sight.

'For now you punch the air, but keep that place on my body in your mind's eye. It's my weak spot. For this practice it's your focus point. If you don't focus, your mind will wander.'

Jessie carried on until her biceps complained, and her arms began to drop. That was when Ben raised his voice.

'Punch!' he snapped. 'Left, right, left!'

The sheer volume of the tone made Jessie's hands go back up as if she'd been threatened.

'Don't think weak thoughts, think strong ones! You can be as strong as you want to be, Jessie. No man need rule you ever again. You're not weak as people would like you to believe. You are strong! Punch! Punch! Punch!'

Almost as if he was a puppet master and she the puppet, her hands shot out with more force than precision, tired muscles bypassing thought, to obey his biting commands.

Chapter 16

Redwall made his way down the small crazy-paved path with care. It was exceedingly slippery and he was loathe to lose his dignity by landing on his backside. A first glance revealed a garden that seemed wild and untended, but he was, by the very nature of his job, observant. The careless abandon of wild flowers that bordered the path, and even the thyme that mortared the stones beneath his feet, were part of a calculated design. The cottage he was picking his way towards bore the same comfortable, homely appearance: floral curtains at the windows, climbing roses, and not a net curtain in sight.

He wasn't sure this visit, outside of his official capacity, was going to be of any benefit at all, but there was something in him that just wouldn't allow him to abandon Jessie without at least trying.

The bright red door opened. Miss McPherson, he guessed, smiled and beckoned him forward.

'Come on in, Inspector. I've been looking out for you this past hour. I do hope it wasn't a bad journey?'

'Appalling,' he said, but the brevity was accompanied by a smile: he liked her immediately.

She was a small woman, spare and angular in age, her pure white, wispy hair gathered into an elastic band, but her eyes were bright and her manner perky. Her clothes were threadbare, but neat. Thrifty, not broke, he thought. He started to get out his badge, but she waved it away. He followed into a small living room filled with treasures probably collected at jumble sales and charity shops.

'I recognised your voice, Inspector, from the phone. I'm sure you could do with a cup of tea. That road can be foul. Do come in. I forgot to mention they always dig up the roads in the summer holidays. It seems to be a tradition.'

She made tea in a tiny but functional kitchen just off the living room. He was standing at the window looking out over Lyme bay as she walked in carrying a battered tray.

'Lovely view, isn't it? I always wanted to retire to a cottage by the sea, but there were many times I thought it would never happen. I've been here six years now, and I never tire of it. I often just sit and look at the water, the seagulls, and the boats and wish I'd been the sort of person who could just sail off into the sunset. And when the storms are down, it's something else. If I died tomorrow I think I would go content.'

Redwall smiled. 'I do hope you have many more years yet, Miss McPherson.'

'Betty, please, Inspector. I do hope you don't mind mugs. Cups are so fiddly, especially when you tend to lug them around the garden as I do.'

Redwall eased himself into a cottage chair opposite her. 'Mugs are fine. Thank you.'

She put them directly on the rough wooden table before him. There were no fancy little cup mats to soak up the spills.

'I understand you're here to talk about Elizabeth Stowleigh,' she said. 'What exactly did you want to know, Inspector? It was a long time ago.'

'Have you heard anything about her over the last few years?'

'I'm still in touch with some of my ex-colleagues, as you know. I heard stories, of course, but they seem rather far-fetched. Tell me what I've heard is wrong.'

'You liked her, then?'

'Don't sound so surprised, Inspector. Most children are likeable, when they're little. They're so keen and fresh and excited by life. There are exceptions, but

110

Elizabeth wasn't one of them. I remember her well, a charming child, bubbly and full of mischief, unlike her sister who was so sure of her superiority, even at five. Lizzie wanted to be a ballerina back then. I recall her coming in to school with a pink net dress and some new ballet shoes, because she was starting real classes that day, after school, so she informed me. That was just before her mother left.'

Redwall saw her eyes mist with memory, then she focused on him. 'Tell me what could have happened to change all that so very, very much.'

'I was hoping you could tell me. I wondered, perhaps, if her mother leaving had been the cause of the change.'

'It might have been, you can't really tell. It changes from child to child. It certainly affected her badly for a while, as one would expect, but she rallied round well enough. Children are resilient. You'd be surprised what they can cope with, if the first few years have been stable. I taught her for the year *after* her mother left, so whatever happened to change her happened after she left my class.'

'You're adamant about that?'

'I would swear it in Court, Inspector.'

'Did you know much about the problems between the Stowleighs? The parents, I mean.'

'Not really. People like that don't air their problems in public. But I had the feeling Mr Stowleigh ruled the house. In spite of his very charming manner, he was, perhaps still is, a very inflexible character. When Mrs Stowleigh made it clear she was going to leave him, I was told he didn't take it so well. He was instantly hostile to his wife and took over all the school runs. Sometimes people take rejection of that kind as a personal slight.'

'Which it is, surely?'

'Not at all, Inspector, it's just incompatibility. You, of all people, should know that. As a teacher I saw both ends of the spectrum. People like Mr Stowleigh, and those who fought their own prejudices to maintain a working relationship for the children's sake.'

He felt suitably reprimanded.

I was told there were a few ructions at first, when she tried to collect the children. I didn't see that, though, it's all hear-say. Then, of course, she left for pastures new.'

'But she didn't try to take the children with her?'

'I used to think she was too wrapped up in her own unhappiness to recognise the children's, but now I wonder if he simply didn't let her. She married very young, and hadn't known what she was letting herself in for. Being the wife of someone in his position must have been a very difficult garment to wear. She was a very homey kind of person. I don't think she fitted very well into his social strata, and I doubt she saw as much of her children as you and I might have. They had nannies from the word go, and chauffeurs, and gardeners. The children were simply part of the estate, and were managed with the same attention to detail Mr Stowleigh gave to all his holdings.'

'I gather you don't hold him in a great deal of affection?'

'Don't get me wrong. In the years his children were in my class he never once gave me reason to dislike him. He called often to ask how was Lizzie doing, was she happy, was she good... Things any concerned parent would ask.'

Redwall cleared his throat. 'I have to ask, do you think the children were, ah, interfered with in any way?'

'No, I don't believe he molested them, if that's what you mean. Do call a spade a spade, Inspector. I've seen children who've been molested, and Stowleigh's weren't like that, neither of them. I'm rather afraid to ask why you're here. Is Lizzie dead?'

'Dead? No, I don't think so.'

Bright eyes questioned.

'I can't tell you the whole story, because a lot of what

I think is pure supposition, but she ran away and I believe she became involved with some rather unsavoury people. I'd hazard a guess she needs help. Whether she will accept it or not is another matter. Right now I don't even know where she is.'

She gave a small *shush* of irritation.

'Was it true about her pregnancy? I heard rumours of a forced termination, but you never do hear the truth of it.'

He sat upright. 'Termination?'

'I heard that by the time she reached her early teens she was wildly promiscuous. That was according to her last nanny, who was a friend of a colleague, so it might not be so very outrageous to suppose she got pregnant. If she'd been forcibly terminated, and Edward Stowleigh would have been entitled to do so because of her age, it might explain why she tried to kill herself, poor child.'

'Poor child, indeed.'

Redwall recognised the implication of hormonal, teenage angst that would have followed the trauma of an enforced termination.

The hospital wouldn't have mentioned any of this stuff without the father's consent, but in the light of her disappearance, he wondered why Edward Stowleigh hadn't thought to inform him.

He warmed even more to the spinster before him.

The teachers at the school had been a bit scathing about the old dear (she devoted herself to other people's children, you know; probably never had a man in her life), but he liked her immediately. She was the first person he'd met who actually cared about Jessie as a person rather than being titillated by the gossip that surrounded her. It had been worth the journey just to know someone did.

However, he drove away feeling more confused than before.

He flattered himself that he knew a bit about psychology, it was the one thing a detective couldn't

113

avoid if he wanted to do his job properly, and he was convinced Miss McPherson was right.

Something must have happened to Jessie, but a year or so *after* her mother left, something she was unable to share with anyone. Perhaps her father should have provided the children with another mother, but hell, you couldn't just whip one out of the air, and that milk was too long ago spilled to be mopped up by wishes.

It was a long and frustrating drive back to London, most of his Sunday gone. He knew he was flying in the face of opposition from his superiors, but if they made noises, it was his own time he was wasting.

Except that he didn't feel it was wasted, entirely.

Chapter 17

As the days went by Ben took it for granted Jessie would accompany him to the dojo. It gave him new purpose in life to teach her, and she was an apt pupil.

He hadn't had a pupil with true talent, since Michael, but that was a door best left closed.

Jessie learned the Taikyoku Shodan Kata easily, and practised the basic movements without being prompted. Either she was a natural, he though cynically, or she was just bored enough to keep at it.

Then, as her strength increased he set her to trotting around the boundaries of the large garden and squeezing press-ups out of reluctant muscles until gradually her body started to fill out. Even the arm that had been broken began to lose the hard lump of muscle that had contracted around the damage.

Ben ceased to remind himself of what it would be like if she left him. She had become his purpose in life and he couldn't imagine living without her. No matter where she'd come from, or what her problem had been, they were a team now, as close as he'd ever been to a person since his wife had died, all those years ago.

In the back of his mind Ben knew this time of idyll would come to an end, but how and why, he refused to contemplate. It was as if fate had dumped upon him a grown up child to replace the one he'd lost so long ago.

No, he amended, never replace.

This new child stood side by side with his own, a grown up sister to the one who would remain forever five.

Chapter 18

Redwall's house was filled with the smell of the Sunday roast and the sound of Beethoven. His wife was at the sewing machine making yet another patchwork quilt. He wondered how many quilts a house actually needed. He pecked her on the cheek.

'That's looking damn good. Where are the kids?'

'Sally's at a friend's, she'll be back for dinner, and Alex is out and about, you know.'

He knew, all right. Hanging out, they called it these days; standing on street corners looking cool, without any constructive thought behind it. He knew he'd be much happier when this teenage phase was over, and Alex developed some sense of responsibility, even some interests, for goodness' sake. Neither of his children had any clear idea of where they wanted to go in the future, as he'd fondly supposed by now they should have, but he'd learned the hard way that children don't do things to please their parents.

It was always the other way around.

'You're brooding about that girl, dear, aren't you?'

He looked up to find her staring at him with concern.

'I suppose I am. Her name's Jessie. It just seems such a shame, you know. I can't help comparing her to Sally. When she ran away she'd be the age Sally is now. Imagine.'

'I'd rather not. Did you have any luck?'

'I discovered something I didn't know, whether it will help or not, I have no idea. Betty McPherson seemed to think she'd had a pregnancy terminated

116

before she absconded. Her father never mentioned that, which is understandable, I suppose, but not helpful. I think I'd better try to verify it before tackling him again.'

'Not the kind of thing to get wrong, I suppose. Then what?'

'I've traced the last nanny, but she's now working in Scotland. I'd like to talk to the sister, but she's in the States, and I'd like to talk to the ex-wife...'

'But she's in Greece.' She smiled. 'Have you tried to contact her?'

'I have, but it's strange, you know. The person who answers the phone doesn't speak English. I thought at one stage I'd been put through to Mr Alexopoulos, but I didn't get a couple of sentences out before I was cut off. Either that or he put the phone down on me. I've got someone at the office trying. I'm hoping I'll be able to speak to Stowleigh's other daughter, Catherine. She might shed some light on her sister's character.'

'The force won't pay for you to go out to the States, surely?'

'You've always said you'd like to go there for a holiday.'

She chuckled, and he thought again what a wonderfully normal woman his wife was, and what a lucky man he was to have found her.

But, next morning, at work, the need for a holiday in America was pre-empted by an unexpected call from Edward Stowleigh himself. His tinny voice on the end of the phone held a mere hint of censure.

'My secretary tells me you want to talk to Catherine. I've spoken to her, and she'll see you when she visits before Christmas. But I want to make it quite clear I'm not happy about you upsetting her. She's gone through a lot, with her mother, and now Lizzie.'

'I'll try not to upset her,' Redwall said mildly. 'I simply thought it possible that Catherine might be able to offer some insight into her sibling's character.'

'I doubt it. They were never close. They fought like

117

cat and dog; total opposites. Anyway, for what good it'll do, my secretary will call and make an appointment with you when Catherine is home.'

He put the phone down without a closing statement, and Redwall was left holding the buzzing receiver to his ear. He stared at it thoughtfully as he put it down.

Edward the politician was manoeuvring him.

Catherine's visit had been engineered.

But he was left little time to ponder why.

Jim crashed in and slammed the door behind him. His buzzing excitement sent an echoing adrenaline-rush through Redwall's spine, but he buried it beneath his normal brusqueness.

'What?'

'Gill was murdered for info, and I know what they're bloody-well after.'

'Do tell.'

Redwall's voice was almost toneless in its sarcasm.

The young detective grinned. 'You don't believe me, but it's true. You know Vince was handling drugs...'

'We guessed.'

'But did you know they were coming down from Birmingham in a consignment of cheeses imported from Holland, and that he was part of the supply chain?'

'Go on.'

Redwall leaned forward, his false air of nonchalance eradicated.

Pleased with the response his news elicited, Jim bubbled on. 'News is on the street that Vince was holding a wad of cash to pay for the consignment, but the night he was killed, and Jessie disappeared, so did the cash.'

'Can we verify this?'

Jim shook his head. 'I shouldn't think so for a moment. A little bird heard the noise on the street, and he sure as hell won't sing to us again, he'd be too scared. But apparently everyone in the underworld is looking for the money. Some guy, I couldn't get a name, has posted a big reward. You only have to see the activity down there to know that something big went down. I found a tom who'd talked to one of Vince's girls before they disappeared. Apparently they were questioned about the same time as Gill, but they got off with just a few bruises. She heard rumours they were packed off to somewhere up north to work. Presumably so they couldn't tattle. Sounds plausible, doesn't it?'

'How much money are we talking about?'

'The word is that it's millions.'

'Shit,' Redwall said, mildly

'Yes, quite. If Jessie stole the money, whether planned or not, and just scarpered, it could be that Vince was chasing her. That makes sense. How big would a few million pounds be in a bag?'

'Too much for the bag Gary Bryant described. Maybe they're exaggerating to get people moving.'

'What if it wasn't cash, but bonds, or something?'

'Feasible, I suppose. It would rather explain why there was a huge activity around the Southampton area after we traced the girl there, too.

Strangely, too, Edward Stowleigh seems to be trying harder to find the girl now than he did when she first disappeared. I wonder if he's being leaned on? Of course, it might be totally paternal, and he simply now has something to follow, which he didn't have before, but...'

Frustratingly, it was all supposition.

'If he's being threatened, wouldn't he ask us for help, on the quiet?'

'Not if he's being blackmailed. Who knows what skeletons he's got in his cupboard. He's a politician. With people like him it's not just money. It's credence, social standing, career; his whole life could go down the pan.'

Redwall leaned his forehead on his hands for a moment, then looked up.

'You do realise what this means, don't you? If this is true, and if Luther, Edward Stowleigh's private eye, actually finds her, you can bet whoever is looking for the money will know. That doesn't bode well for Jessie's chances.'

'We could always talk to the P.I. quietly, explain the situation. If he knows he's getting into drugs money, he might just quit on this one.'

'Or he might be even keener for a bit of the action. You have to ask yourself who's paying him most, Stowleigh or one of the dealers? Get me a profile on him. See if he's got a record.'

Redwall spoke as Jim was exiting, 'By the way, well done.'

But they found nothing on Luther McCormack to suggest he was anything other than good at his job, which was, apparently, tracing missing people.

A short while later he learned that Edward Stowleigh had also posted a sizeable reward for information leading to his daughter's whereabouts.

Though he was worried about the outcome should Jessie and Lizzie turn out to be one and the same, Redwall genuinely hoped that the PI had more luck than him, if only for Edward's sake. It was possible he would come up with something simply because he had the time to do so.

As a father, he was moved by Edward's paternal dedication, knowing he would never have let it lie if it had been his own daughter who was missing; not knowing what had happened to his daughter must be killing the man by inches. The uncharitable thought that Edward might have been molesting his daughter seemed to be a million miles from the truth at that moment.

Chapter 19

Ben finally decided he could no longer stand not knowing if she would be there when he woke up in the morning. A cold sun shimmered on Jessie's fair hair as she sat in meditation before practice, and he broke the peace with a single sentence.

'Are you going to leave, Jessie?'

Where she'd been relaxed, now her body hardened almost imperceptibly, and when her eyes rose, she wore the stony mask that had nearly ceased to exist.

He hadn't known quite what to expect, but she rose silently without a word, and walked upstairs.

He heard her packing.

She was well now, in body if not in mind.

His own face hardened. If she walked out, he wouldn't stop her. Her arrival had been accidental, his acceptance complete; but the decision of whether she should stay or go was hers alone, and she was now well enough to make it.

He changed into his gi, the loose cotton garments he wore for practise, and worked hard until the sweat ran from his body and his mind was under control. Then he sat and meditated, subconsciously choosing the same place she'd used. The low sun shone coldly through the latticed windows, and he blanked his mind from the expectation of loneliness so that he wouldn't affect her actions by his overwhelming mental grief, for emotions gathered on the air like dust motes, and affected a person's psyche.

Time passed. He waited.

Finally he heard the soft pad of steps behind him,

and he felt a relief out of proportion to his expectation.

Jessie came and knelt by him. He brought himself to awareness.

She took several breaths before asking, 'Do you want me to leave?'

'No.'

'Then may I stay?'

She spoke in a very small voice, and he was sure this was the first time he was really privy to the person she was hiding deep within herself.

The corners of his eyes were slightly damp as he gave a single brisk nod.

'I have something for you.'

Rising with his normal grace, he walked soft-footed across the dojo to the window sill, and came back with a small paper parcel.

She opened the package without comment.

Inside, there was a brand new gi of white cotton.

Chapter 20

December arrived, and with it came Catherine Stowleigh.

It was over a year to the date of Vince's death, Redwall realised, and Jessie remained stubbornly missing. As he made his way to the interview room, her possible fate loomed darkly in his mind. He just hoped she was actually still alive, that he wasn't chasing moonbeams.

Deep inside, he feared the worst.

He held out his hand and introduced himself, assessing her as he did so. There was a subtle hint of Edward Stowleigh's media profile in her superficially pretty face, but she, too, was tall and blonde, and it was easy to imagine how Jessie might look now, seeing the sister in real life.

'Inspector.'

'Miss Stowleigh, pleased to meet you. Did you have a good flight?'

Catherine took his hand briefly, but the flinty look in her eye and the tight lipped greeting were indication enough of her true feelings. She spoke with that upper-class strangulation of vowels that set his teeth on edge.

'Let's cut the crap, Inspector. I'm here because you want me to be, not because I see any real value in it. Let's just get on with it, shall we?'

Just here to get a smelly job out of the way and get on with life, he thought; true sibling devotion.

'Do you care that your sister has disappeared?' he asked frankly.

The green eyes she levelled at him were like chips of

glass. 'Yes, I care. It's having repercussions on Daddy's work, and it's involving me again. She always was a selfish cow, and this is just her way of hurting us both.'

'So you think she's just staying away to cause trouble?'

'She's done it before. She ran away from school more than once, and didn't ever let anyone know where she went. She was probably in some guy's trousers, like always.'

'How old was she, then? When she ran away from school?'

She shrugged. 'The first time? Thirteen.'

'And you think she was having sex with men at thirteen?'

'It's not what I *thought*. It was common knowledge.'

'How long was she gone, on average?'

'A few days. She always came crawling back when the money she stole ran out.'

'Except this time. She's been gone for well over a year. Did it occur to you something bad might have happened to her?'

Her reply was defensive, now. He didn't doubt she hoped Jessie would remain lost.

'Of course it did. Daddy told me yesterday she'd been working as a prostitute all the time he'd been looking for her. That's obviously what she's doing now. It doesn't surprise me, in fact it's probably – ' She bit the words off, but Redwall could have finished the line: it was probably exactly what Catherine would have expected of, if not recommended for, her sister.

'Anyway, if something has happened to her, she brought it on herself. She never tried to hide that she went out with men all the time. Hell, no, she boasted about it because she knew it would hurt Daddy. And when she got – '

She stopped short, and a shuttered look came down. She didn't have the manipulative skills of her father, that was for sure.

'And when she got pregnant?' Redwall prompted

124

softly.

'Well, she did. I didn't tell you that, though, Daddy would kill me. He kept it quiet because it would have been all over the papers when he was just starting his new office.'

'So he had it terminated?'

'Yes.'

Her muttered assent to his guess was barely audible, but she took a breath, and carried on, vitriolic in her condemnation.

'What else was he supposed to do? She got up the spout on purpose. She told me afterwards. She wanted Daddy humiliated, she wanted him to lose his job, she wanted to pay him back. She even had our gardener, lost him his job. Christ, he was nearly thirty and she was fourteen! How could she?'

'And your father never took that to the police?'

She flushed. 'Of course not. It would have harmed his career, and that would have been exactly what she wanted.'

'So her promiscuity wasn't because she was a raging nymphomaniac, or that her hormones were out of control. It was a calculated move because she wanted to get back at her father?'

'Pretty much. And you should have heard her boasting about how many, how big they were, and how she'd had it. Christ, it made me sick!'

'So what was she getting him back for?'

She stopped short. 'What do you mean?'

'You said she was *getting back* at your father. That means he did something to upset her in the first place. What did he do?'

Catherine flushed slightly. 'I didn't mean that at all. That wasn't what I said. You're twisting my words. I don't know why she wanted to ruin him, but that's what she wanted.'

'Since when?'

A look of bewilderment crossed her face. 'Always.'

'You're three years older than Elizabeth. When you

were little, I've been told you got on very well together. What changed that? When did you stop being friends?'

For the first time, she seemed to really ponder the answer. 'I do remember playing with her, you know, but it just changed as we got older. We began to fight all the time. Children do that, it wasn't just us.'

Tell me about it, Redwall thought. His own house was like a war zone, sometimes, usually over a lost pair of shoes or something equally stupid.

'So you don't recall any particular time in your life when Elizabeth changed towards you or her father. There was no particular event that could have sparked it? Your mother visiting, your grandmother dying, being taken away from a school where she was happy anything at all that might conceivably have seemed big in a child's eyes?'

'Dad's parents died before we were born; they were quite old when they had him. That's why we've had the house since forever. Then Mum's mother died, when we were still little. Of course, that's why she ran off. She never did come back to see us.'

'Pardon?'

'I said she never came to see us.'

'No, before that. You said of course your mother ran off when her mother died? Why *of course*?'

'It was the money,' she said, as if it was obvious. 'Gran left all her money to Mum, so she just took it and ran. Daddy needed that money for his career, and she knew it. All he'd done for her, and she ran off to that Greek bastard with the lot. Some of that should have come to us.'

A look of profound dissatisfaction crossed her brow, and Redwall realised Catherine was pretty miffed at losing out on an inheritance she felt was owed to her.

'Did it occur to you she might have fallen out of love with your father and into love with someone else? It happens.'

'George was a money-grubbing dago. I never met him. Don't want to. Anyway, Elizabeth won't recall any

126

of that, she was too young. I don't really remember Mum myself, only from the photographs.'

The phrase 'money-grubbing dago' somehow didn't seem like the sort of phrase Catherine would have invented; but somehow it wasn't difficult to imagine it falling from Edward Stowleigh's lips.

He was also under the impression Annie Stowleigh had run off with an entrepreneur millionaire, so why paint him as a fortune hunter? Additionally, with a large inheritance under consideration, a huge rift between husband and wife was equally as difficult to visualise. If he *needed* the money he would have tried to hang on to her, surely?

After he got his hands on the money, maybe he wouldn't care, but his lifestyle and ambition would have demanded a large cash input, so would he have thrown away that possibility? The anticipated inheritance might even have been the reason why Edward married a woman who appeared to have been less than the ideal politician's wife.

It would be worth finding out exactly how much that inheritance was.

'So after leaving, she never visited you, not even once?'

'She wasn't wanted. She abandoned us, remember?'

A bit more parental guidance going on there, he thought. Instil hatred into the young, why not? He was beginning to doubt his own assessment of Edward Stowleigh.

'Did Elizabeth have any friends that you recall?'

'I don't think she ever had any. She scared all the other kids off. She was dangerous to be around, off her head, cuckoo.'

'In what way?'

'It was like she had a death wish. She'd dare kids to do things dangerous, silly things, like run across the road in front of cars, jump from high walls. She'd do it herself, then have a go at me and the other kids, because we wouldn't follow. After that Dad sent us to

127

different schools because she was stopping me from learning; holding me back. That was when she started going out with men. Sick psycho.'

She shuddered dramatically.

'Did you ever wonder why she got like that?'

'Of course I did. I didn't like having a fruitcake for a sister. It rebounded on me. And I'll tell you something else: she doesn't believe Mum left of her own accord, she believes Daddy kicked her out because she didn't turn out to be the kind of wife he needed, but that's not true. She was vindictive. She wouldn't even divorce him, and that's the truth of the matter. Daddy couldn't divorce her for years because she refused, and when he managed it, it was without her consent. She probably hoped he'd die in the meantime, and she'd inherit his money, too.'

That would explain why he didn't re-marry. And once he had freed himself legally, it could have made him shy off making the same mistake again.

'And another thing, our precious Mum was a bit of a whore on the side. She'd been with other men before she ran off with the Greek, Daddy knew that. And that's probably why Lizzie went off with all those men. She's just like her mother. So you can stop doing the psychoanalysis bit. Bad blood will out, you know.'

'And what about your blood?' Redwall said gently, knocking the smugness from her face. 'Isn't that from the same source?'

Catherine Stowleigh left Redwall with a sour taste in his mouth. He wondered whether the holier-than-thou Edward, who apparently told his daughters their mother was a whore, had sexually abused those same daughters, despite what Betty McPherson thought. That would certainly account for Jessie's problems, but the psychological profile just didn't pan out.

If he was going to abuse one, he would have abused both, starting with Catherine simply because she was the oldest; yet she bore all the hallmarks of a spoilt rich

128

kid, and none of those of an abused child.

In Catherine's eyes, her father truly was the paragon of virtue he appeared in the media. Yet he was still left with a totally disturbed second child. Why?

What if Catherine was right in saying Jessie was simply *bad blood*.

Was he blinding himself to the obvious?

What if she was giving him the unadulterated truth? What if the mother had slept around, and the other daughter simply had followed in the mother's footsteps through some inherited gene? What if he was trying to save a kid from something she couldn't be saved from, something that was in her very make-up?

Was he simply wasting his time, as his superiors believed?

He guessed he might find a little more of the truth in Greece, if he could afford the time to get out there; not to mention the cost.

The fact was, Mrs Stowleigh really had run off with a Greek entrepreneur called Georgiou Alexopoulos, because her affair with him had been well covered by the press – if that was anything to go by.

It would be useful to hear the story from their side at some stage. The only problem was, the way it was going, he wasn't going to get anything from that source unless he went out there in person, with the Greek police in tow. Mr Alexopoulos at present didn't seem the least bit interested in communicating of his own free will.

Chapter 22

Edward Stowleigh was losing the plot.

He was being broken mentally, and if he couldn't keep at the front edge of politics, he would be broken financially, too. Becoming paranoid, he was seeing Mr Porter everywhere, in everyone, and the veneer of sophistication that carried him through the day was beginning to crack.

It was driving him mad because he was always looking for the man he hadn't seen, the man who had made his blood run cold with those softly uttered threats. Every man he spoke to or bumped into was assessed for the potential to be that man, and unfortunately many of them made the grade.

If he didn't find the stupid bitch soon, he didn't doubt they'd follow through, and circumcise or castrate him, or whatever else it was they had promised. Or kill him. Or all of it, one after the other. He should have had her incarcerated years ago, locked in a straitjacket of drugs, where she couldn't do him any more harm.

Over the year he'd been in constant communication with that Inspector Redwall, slovenly great lump of a man that he was, and had continued to throw money down the drain at the gumshoe, Luther McCormack, who was supposedly trying to trace his daughter.

The fellow had been looking, that was certain, but had come to a grinding halt in Southampton, just as the police had, in spite of all of his underhand sneaking and prying. If Edward hadn't had this threat hanging over his head, he would have sacked the bastard months ago.

During the day he laughed, joked, and plied his business in Government with the same passion that had become his trade-mark over the previous years. It was continually said if there were more people like him in Government, England wouldn't be in such a sorry state.

He was the people's hero, the whiter-than-white promoter of ordinary citizens' rights, and both his wife's desertion and his passionate search for the missing daughter had now given him a kind of martyred appeal that, rather than being detrimental to his career, was improving it. He was, in short, a human being, and people could associate with his misfortunes.

But, though he probably looked the same to everyone else, he was slowly losing self-control. When he looked in the mirror he glimpsed the furtive, hunted man within, and wondered when it was going to start to show.

That was why he drank himself blotto every night; being unconscious was the nearest thing he could get to sleep.

Chapter 23

Godfrey Kyam looked down at the latest note sent in by Ben, and felt a twinge of alarm.

> *'...but finally, my dear friend, I would ask a favour. I have never worried about dying, I am an old man, after all, and though I might have a few more years left to me, I need to know that when I die, someone will care for Jessie. I am leaving my property to her, as she needs sanctuary, but she has been badly damaged and needs a mentor and protector more than she knows. I would ask you to please be that person.'*

Ben had told him a long time ago that he didn't know what to do with the property, but to leave it to a girl who had crawled out from the under-belly of society?

Did she know he'd left the property to her?

God knows, people had killed for less.

And how could he be mentor to someone he didn't know, didn't trust, and probably wouldn't like?

When Ben had first mentioned Jessie's arrival at his home, Godfrey had been dubious about the wisdom of her being there, especially as he suspected she was still a minor.

Where she'd come from, and what kind of trauma she'd run from, he had no idea, but the girl was obviously trouble for so many reasons he could hardly list them. He'd just hoped she would scarper, as Ben suspected she would.

He'd been surprised a year later to find she was still there, and that had prompted him to visit Ben since he had retired.

He'd been glad to do so.

Time passed him by, and somehow many of the things he meant to do simply didn't happen until they were forced on him, so he'd enjoyed the visit.

And, by God, what a stunner the girl was, if you could ignore the antipathy that hit you from forty paces.

But, he conceded in his own mind, he had never seen Ben radiate such contentment. That, more than anything, was why he left them alone, for of all the people Godfrey knew, Ben was a man who deserved at least some happiness in his twilight years.

So he'd walked away, hoping that Ben knew what he was doing, but that didn't stop the odd niggle of worry hitting him at various times, when he should have been concentrating on other things.

Chapter 24

Jessie sat in the lotus position in the dojo. An early spring sun cut through the trellis, and motes of dust danced in front of her shadow on the polished wooden floor.

If she had ever been content in her life, it was now. She had been sitting like that for more than an hour, the left hand cupped inside the right, and her awareness of self passing through them in a continual circle within the confines of her physical body, as Ben had taught her. She was neither thinking nor dreaming, but somewhere beyond both.

She had realised a while back that Ben's own loneliness had reached in to pluck her from self-destruction, but that didn't matter. Everyone had a private agenda, and theirs had met in accidental harmony. It was where agendas collided with opposing force that lives exploded off at tangents; like hers and her father's.

No, bury it.

As the years went by she felt something grow inside herself for Ben, a feeling she'd never known for any person. Perhaps it was love, she didn't know.

She did know she took to the martial arts as easily as breathing, that hers was a natural talent. No man would ever again be allowed to touch that secret place inside her that was filled with hurt.

She sensed, rather than saw Ben come into the Dojo.

Knowing that the presence was benign, she didn't acknowledge it, although her heartbeat increased by an imperceptible amount to accommodate an awareness outside of self.

He knelt beside her and waited. In spite of the sun the room felt slightly chill, for although the April morning had dawned bright and clear, the sun didn't yet have the power to warm the earth.

She knew Ben remembered the warmth of his childhood with a mild longing now that he was in his twilight years. He spoke rarely of his childhood, but from the few times he'd mentioned incidents, she drew an image of privilege and tight family unity.

The English weather hadn't been kind to his joints, and they became increasingly stiff and painful as the years went by. He'd told her little of his past, but probably more than he realised, and there were times she hinted of hers. The day would come, she knew, when it would all come pouring out onto the floor like vomit.

One day, but not yet.

There were also times when she knew Ben resented her intrusion into the privacy of his retirement. When she sensed that mood on him, she slipped out and ran in the New Forest, leaving him to work it through in his own way, and when she returned, everything was all right again.

She wondered what she would do if it wasn't.

The world beyond her present narrow confines had never been kind, and she doubted it had softened in the intervening years, any more than the knot of hatred towards society had that burned in her breast.

Ben enjoyed the challenge and the company.

She'd become his daughter, his life-blood, his reason for continued existence in a world that he thought he'd left behind. She was pleased, but concerned; caring about another human being was to become vulnerable.

Finally she stirred. She brought herself back to the present, brought herself to her knees alongside him. In unspoken accord, they rose together to the feet without the aid of hands. The single fluid movement was a graceful legacy dating back a couple of thousand years, when the Samurai would have needed the hands free for drawing a sword as they rose, right hand drawing from the left hip, or left hand drawing from over the right shoulder or, for a trained warrior, sometimes both at once. She knew this, because Ben lectured morning, noon and night; a word here, a gesture there.

She never questioned the concept of immersing herself in the traditions of a past era and a different culture. It simply happened because it was an integral part of Ben's character, and it was also her salvation.

The creed became a lifeline in a world that had previously held little meaning. Without the nuances and small gestures that made up the code of practice, Ben said, Karate was just a thing of destruction, but with them it was respect for life, a way of understanding her *self*, a way of tuning her awareness, to make full use of her own capabilities.

Though it was a martial art, and without doubt could be used to kill, it was more truly about knowing one's inner self and protecting one's ideals. Flower arranging, he told her, was also a martial art.

Chapter 25

When the men in the tacky suits finally arrived for Edward Stowleigh, they simply walked into his house one evening through the back door. He was sitting in his living room with the ever-present tumbler of whiskey in his hand.

His mouth dropped open.

With almost detached interest he wondered why he'd thought himself safe in his own home. Yet even the numbness of whiskey couldn't dispel the terror of their arrival.

'There's no point in all this,' he informed them hysterically, his voice slightly slurred, lacking the conviction his plea was going to bear results. 'I've looked for her. The police have looked for her. My gumshoe has looked for her. I don't know where she is. No one knows where she is.'

'Mr Porter would like to talk to you, however,' one of the men said politely. 'Please come with us.'

To be fair, he tried.

'He's drunk as a coot,' one of the men said, picking up the whiskey bottle and assessing it as though it would tell him just how much Edward had consumed.

'OK. Let's do it.'

Edward moaned faintly at the words, and flapped his hands at the men as they heaved him out of the chair, but 'do it' obviously meant a belt in the solar plexus rather than a gun to the head.

He gasped, folded, and brought up his guts all over the Persian carpet. Then as he was on his knees, still trying to gasp air into his lungs, his hands were tied behind his back and he was dragged roughly to his feet.

'Mr Porter likes people to be sober when he talks to them,' he was informed.

'Fuck Mr Porter,' he said hoarsely.

For some reason they found that extremely funny, but even whilst recovering from whoops of laugher, they dragged him to his own bathroom and threw him face down into the bath, clothes and all. The plug was put in, and water began to run. He gasped with shock as cold water flooded through his clothes.

He tried to pull himself back, but one man stood at the foot of the bath, holding him firmly by the ankles so that he remained face down, his chest glued to the bottom of the forget-me-not blue ceramic despite his struggles. As the water began to fill the tub, the chill and the fear of drowning made him verbal.

'Please, no, please don't do this, no please.'

The water was only a few inches deep, yet already it was lapping at his chin as he pulled his head back to keep his face from the water. The second man grabbed a handful of his hair and pushed down.

'Drink,' he advised.

The cold water had the required sobering effect, and after a couple of seconds Edward's now silent struggles became more frenzied, more desperate. But the man held his face under water until he was reaching for breath, and involuntarily drew in a belly-full of water.

His head was pulled back up.

He retched, coughed, choked, and they did it over until he was well and truly sober.

He was eventually pulled from the bath and dumped on the floor, shivering uncontrollably, trying not to cry. The realisation that they really did want him sober and not drowned wasn't comforting. Some things were better handled with a jug-full of whiskey in you, and to Edward's terrified mind, emasculation was probably one of them.

He was kicked in the kidneys.

'Stop blubbering or I'll put your head in the fucking

138

toilet.'

He took a deep, shuddering breath, resignation reasserting itself.

'What are you going to do with me?'

'You'll find out.'

'Can I get changed? I'm cold.'

One of the thugs bent down and pulled him effortlessly to his feet. They were so incredibly strong, these men. Stronger than the sort of people he normally dealt with. As he shuddered uncontrollably, they cut the cord from his wrists. He surveyed his blue, stiff fingers.

Was that what they'd look like when he was dead?

'Where's your bedroom?'

'My dressing room's through there.'

'Dressing room? Fuck.'

Cold eyes watched impassively as he towelled and dressed in dry clothes, and he followed them nicely out to the car when told. Not a black car, but maroon. He thought about all the black cars his eyes had followed in the last year.

When they put the hood over his face his hands remained clasped in his lap. They hadn't even bothered to restrain him. He realised with self-loathing that he was going to do nothing to try to escape this fate, and they knew it, too. When it came to the crunch, the people's hero was a big woosie.

They seemed to drive for a long time, it might have been twenty minutes or a couple of hours, time had no meaning any more. When he climbed out, he recoiled fractionally as the damp air of the warehouse hit him, recalling the smell as if it was yesterday.

There was also another faint odour, and he knew Mr Porter was waiting there for him, his own particular brand of aftershave hanging on the chill air. The hands on his arms receded, leaving him standing on his own in the dark, his senses swimming with overload.

'Walk forward, two paces.'

It was him. That voice!

Putting his hands out before him, Edward shuffled forward, feeling tentatively with his foot for chasms in the floor. There was no temptation at all to rip the hood from his face. He had no desire to look fate in the eye. His left hand hit something metal; his fingertips explored of their own volition, finding an upright iron girder.

'There's another pillar by your right hand. Check it out.'

He did, and stood there in a self-imposed cruciform, now realising that he could also feel chains attached to the pillars of metal, but he was mentally chilled from the enforced sobering, and panic had levelled out to blank despair.

This was it.

End of the line.

If this man told him to do up the manacles himself, he would do what he was told because he'd no free thoughts of his own any more. He was drained of the will to fight them, mentally or otherwise. The darkness made him lose balance for a moment, and he clutched at the chains for support.

'I'm really disappointed in you, Mr Stowleigh.'

'I'm sorry. I tried.'

Even his voice was toneless.

'So, Mr Stowleigh, what shall I do with you?'

'I don't know.'

'It was a rhetorical question. You remember what I promised, don't you?'

'Yes.'

Oh, yes, he remembered. A small spark of self-preservation rose, a desire to vindicate himself.

'But I did try to find her. Really, I did.'

'And that, my dear fellow, is why you're not dead. You really did try. It was quite impressive. The grief-stricken father came over quite well on the media, you know. After a while you really even began to look the part; haggard, even.'

Edward heard footsteps walking around, and tried

to follow the direction. When the voice came again, it was from behind him.

'Ah, now, I gave you two options, didn't I? Your daughter or your money, and as I don't seem to have your daughter I was thinking it was time you liquidised your assets, if only to pay off the interest. But you know what? I had another thought while I was watching you on TV. I thought what a nice man you were, and I decided to be lenient.'

For a brief second hope rose in Edward's chest, then died with the realisation that this man would never be lenient.

'I had a better idea. Edward, you'll be pleased to know you're in just the right place to be of help to me. So rather than cut off your pecker, I've decided to let you join my little syndicate. I expect you can guess what we import.'

Edward groaned.

'And to facilitate our new relationship I've had half a mil put into a bank account in your name, in the Cayman Islands. Isn't that nice? And there will be more to follow, if you're a good boy and do as you're told.'

Edward went cold.

Who would believe he hadn't done anything to earn it and hadn't known about it? And following on from that was the realisation that you got nothing for nothing.

Life, which, a few moments ago hadn't seemed like too long a prospect, now tumbled ahead out of control. With dawning awareness that he might yet live, albeit in a different kind of world, anger began to creep into his mind; anger towards Lizzie, or whatever she called herself now.

It was all her fault.

His arms ached. He began to lower them.

An elbow or something drove in the small of his back.

'I didn't say you could move.'

He squealed as the force of the blow propelled him

into the unknown, and he tripped and skidded on hands and knees, coming to rest in a pile of debris. His hands were scraped and stinging, and his spine felt as though there was a nail through it. Mr Porter's voice flayed his mind like knives as he nursed his pain, trying to stand.

'No, don't move. Stay on all fours, you pussy, right where you belong. From now on you belong to me, Stowleigh. I'll send instructions by one of my men, and you'll be addressed as Mr Yellow. No, Yellow Streak. Yes, I like that, Yellow Streak.'

Yellow Streak? That was something out of a comic. But he wasn't kidding.

'You'll follow any instructions to the letter, arranging money transfers, purchases and disposals of stocks, shares, or goods. You'll keep records of all transactions, and will receive a fee upon completion of every transaction. Needless to say, I'm not going to write out a contract. I'll just add that you will either do as you're told and become the very rich person you're presently pretending to be, or you'll become slowly and painfully dead; your choice.'

Edward knelt on the floor in the dark knowing that life as it had been was gone. He was destined to become a money-launderer for a bunch of drug dealers.

He wanted to cry, because he knew he would do it.

He wished he'd found the courage to go to the police before it was too late, even though he didn't know what Mr Porter looked like or where he came from. Yet a little voice inside told him that if he'd done that he would already be dead – slowly and painfully dead.

Things could get no worse.

'And now, Yellow Streak, I'm going to prove to you with absolute certainty just how much I control you. Drop your pants.'

'Ah, no. Please, I thought you – '

'Shut up. Just do it.'

Edward was dropped off at home knowing he was no

142

longer his own man. He was a chattel, a thing, a tool to some unknown criminal, and he would never escape the shame of that sealed bargain until the day he died.

Yellow Streak was the right name for him.

Cowed into submission by words alone, he'd knelt there on the hard concrete, a black bag over his head, expecting some kind of punishment, but nothing had prepared him for the reality.

The shock of feeling the man kneel behind him and drop his own pants had brought hot bile of understanding to his throat. He'd clenched his fists and tried not to cry as the man raped him, knowing it was his submission alone that gave his new boss the hard-on which burned his arse like fire. As his body was rammed into submission again and again, the annoyance he'd felt towards his younger daughter solidified into bitter hatred.

This was all her fault.

Chapter 26

Jessie knew Ben was surprised by her single-minded dedication. He had never expected her to become as proficient or as committed as she was. He gazed on her with the pride of father and teacher combined, and she knew that her eyes reflected some inner emotion of her own when they met his.

She was no longer the stray waif he'd nursed back to health. Her body had filled out, become rounded and curved as a woman's body should be, and when she looked in the mirror she saw that she was beautiful; not in the plastic, painted way of society, but in the way her skin was clear, her hair shone like corn, and her muscles were toned and hard. She was an animal at its peak performance.

She almost liked herself.

But this was an island of dreams, a temporary haven; her safety a mirage. She told herself not to care, for one day the outside world would come driving in.

They bowed to each other now, from the waist, hands at the sides, eyes in contact, then stood apart.

'Yoi!'

Ben commanded attention.

Jessie stepped back a pace, planted her feet a shoulder's width apart, knees slightly bent, crossed her softly fisted hands before her, then lowered them to her hips, ready. Ben, by her side, had performed the same ritual.

'Teikyoku Shodan!' he barked.

'Teikyoku Shodan!' Jessie echoed, and before the resonance of her mellow voice had faded, they moved independently, together, in the same precise pattern of movements that she'd first seen Ben perform alone in this very room.

Today they began with the most basic of the Katas. It was always good to remind yourself of your humble beginnings. The pace of their movements was tempered by the control of their bodies, each block or punch so full of grace and power it seemed as if they floated from stance to stance, pausing momentarily from time to time as the Kata dictated, before sweeping into a wide turn, brushing aside the invisible opponent along with the dancing motes of dust. Almost as soon as it started, it finished, the last lunge plunging into absolute stillness.

'Yamé,' Ben breathed, and they stepped back with the left foot, swivelling silently to the starting position.

'Heian Shodan!'

'Heian Shodan!'

In the early months, Jessie thought she knew the Katas, and it was only as she'd progressed into the realms of the master that she realised she hadn't. Now, each flick of the wrist or tensing of a muscle belonged to her alone, came from within her, and made the Kata of her.

The motions alone didn't make the Kata, it wasn't a dance to be learned and performed; it was a philosophy, a way of life, a deeper education than that which moved the body. Only when the harmony of body and mind gelled, had she really started to understand that which she had already learned. And just as the movements alone didn't make a Kata, nor did the Kata make Karate.

Only when she had learned them all, and practised them to the point of monotony, had her body awareness developed enough to pluck out from the vast store of movements in memory the particular one needed in each moment of action. Once learned, the body awareness developed beyond mere thought.

Now, as they practised the more complicated

145

routines, the speed and intensity of their movements became a pressure, a power, which, having been compressed, burst, like the fall of water from a dam.

'Kai!' they cried, the harsh and the mellow voice respectively blending as one, pushing the physical power of the punch into a deeper and more punishing penetration of the hidden enemy's guts.

'Yamé,' Ben said gently.

His breathing was quite normal though patches of sweat broke through to stain the white tunic under his armpits. He glanced sideways at Jessie. She was instantly aware of his displeasure.

'Kokyu!' he snapped, and she forced herself to still the tell-tale breaths that had shortened in her lungs. Weakness was human, but displaying it made you vulnerable.

Ben said her biggest weakness was in being born a woman. Never mind that she couldn't help it, the weakness must be overcome. She was a Karateka, a student with as much potential as the next man, except that she would have to be better than him to succeed, for he had strength on his side; or had once, he added, directing his amused comment to himself.

Conversely, he informed her that being a woman was also her biggest advantage, as her hidden ability would be initially unexpected. But once exposed she would have to rely on speed and guile to maintain distance from a stronger opponent.

And if he got too close, she had another fund of knowledge, a part of karate not generally seen. Similar to Aikido, the oldest forms of Karate could take an opponent's strength and turn it against him. Jessie was aware that Ben had turned away from the style of practice he preferred, in order to make his pupil proficient in a style that better suited her build and gender.

For the next hour they went back to basics, back to the punches, the blocks; the continuity of movement, and the internal strength that the practice pulled forth

146

to build body stamina. 'Each, ni, san, chi, go; mawatté!' Ben called. 'One, two, three, four, five, turn!'

Then, standing opposite each other they opposed movement for movement, forwards and backwards, one attacking, the other blocking and retaliating, the roles continually swapping. Although Ben commanded, they were so used to each other now that the actions were anticipated long before he barked the commands.

Because his own sensei had used Japanese, so now did Ben in his capacity as teacher to Jessie.

Somehow the actions born of an oriental mind were suited to the poetry of the oriental language. There was no real aggression in this type of practice, fists and feet would stop a mere inch from the target and although the blows had the power to maim, the blocks would sweep them aside with the most feather-light of touches.

Jessie knew she was living in a vacuum, that life would one day reach out and pluck her from her haven, but for now, she was content.

Chapter 27

For Redwall, the weeks that had rolled into months, now rolled into years. Jessie's trail, which had never been truly substantiated in the first place, was never regained.

He learned eventually that Edward Stowleigh had paid off his private investigator, and was busy getting on with a life in the public eye. It seemed he could do no wrong these days. Every time he turned the news on, there was Edward in his expensive suit gunning for the rights of the common man, or ploughing public money into worthy causes.

Jim told him that Vince's lost millions had become something of an urban legend, wistfully related by the kids on the street. There were rumours of a massive reward offered to anyone who could offer leads, but that in itself became an urban legend, because no-one knew who had posted such a reward, if it had ever happened.

Before contact could be made with Annie Stowleigh's Greek lover, the pressures of heavy workloads and popular opinion forced him to abandon his interest.

In any event, did it really matter what had sent Jessie off the rails, now? Did it matter that her mother had abandoned her 15 years ago? Did it matter whether Annie Stowleigh had left her Greek lover for another man?

He had wanted to know in order to help Jessie, but as she had disappeared of the face of the planet, either she had found a life for herself, or was dead.

But there was still one thing about Jessie's case that rankled, because of the inconsistency: Catherine's assertion that Annie's Greek lover had been a money grubbing dago, versus the reality that he was a wealthy man, an entrepreneur.

The biggest cause of crime, he had long ago learned, was when one person wanted what another person had, and he wondered what the truth was behind Annie Stowleigh's inheritance. He would love to get his hands on Edward's personal financial records.

But that was never going to happen.

Though hardly a day passed when Redwall didn't wonder whether Jessie was alive or dead, he gradually began to believe the latter. At least, he told himself quietly, he hoped she was, because the alternatives were simply too unkind to contemplate.

Chapter 28

Jessie brushed away the sudden and strange thought that she was in danger, and carried on practising until the drain of tiredness swept through her body.

'Yamé,' Ben said.

Jessie controlled her breathing; anticipating, wary, and the buzz of adrenaline forced the tiredness at bay. There was something not right. She searched her consciousness for whatever was worrying her: something outside, a car, the howl of an animal?

She knew, a fraction before Ben moved, that he was going to attack. He lunged in with a snap-kick to the chest, and she avoided it easily, side stepping, knocking his foot to the left, sweeping aside the lunge punch that followed through, and snapping her arm to a back-fist to his face, which he blocked before retreating.

The sequence took little more than a second, the blows tempered by distance, no blows reaching through the body to maim or kill.

Jessie swivelled slightly, sinking into Kokutsu Dachi, a stance that would present Ben with a smaller target.

There was an impasse for a moment, each waiting to see if the other would attack. Jessie feinted forward a fraction, but Ben wasn't deceived. He attacked again, open, callused hands blurring with a suddenness that would have floored the mind, but her body reacted, and she blocked and leapt out on the defensive again, before swinging full circle and clipping Ben's head with the edge of her foot in a roundhouse kick.

Inside she was elated for a second, for it was rare

that she got within Ben's defences, even now; but there was no congratulation from her Sensei. Ben just stared at her, then lowered his hands, and walked forward.

She was confused.

He'd never done that before, had he? Was the session ended? Her moment of indecision was her downfall. Ben reached out, grasped her wrist, twisted it painfully, and she found herself flat on her back, winded. She looked up balefully, annoyed that he'd tricked her.

But Ben's expression didn't change.

She rolled fast, anticipating the sudden movement; not fast enough to avoid the kick, but just enough to stop it from rupturing her kidney. She gasped as his bare foot thudded like a mallet into her side, and completed her roll, bounding cat-like to her feet, her back an angry knot of pain. Warily she backed slightly, hands ready, on the defensive. She couldn't allow herself to relax to assess the damage. Ben had never deliberately hurt her before. What was he doing?

Her eyes narrowed.

Ben attacked again, and his eyes blazed with the anger of a rabid dog, unfocussed and terrifying in its mindless rage. Jessie felt something drop in her belly with a thud.

She'd learned something of the trauma that had been part and parcel to making the character of this Sensei of hers. She'd heard snippets of the destruction he'd seen a lifetime ago in military conflict. She knew about the fire into which he had plunged, trying, but failing, to save his wife and child. She knew of the seven years of anger-lashed roving that followed. She knew he ended in a quiet backwater in Japan where a man with skills beyond his comprehension finally healed his mind. She had guessed that in some way Ben was repaying that act of compassion in the past, by trying to heal her now.

Was it possible that his mind had just blown the fuse that tempered his mental wounds, and that she had

151

caused it, merely by being here in this time and place?

Jessie wasn't afraid of dying, she had chosen to, once, but was more hurt than she would have believed possible by the thought that her death might be caused by Ben.

In that moment, she realised something else. Of all the people she'd ever crossed paths with, the only one she cared about was here.

She didn't want to hurt him.

Ben's regard for her had grown into something closer than that of teacher-pupil, too, and she knew that if he killed her because he was lost in some private hell from his past, once he realised what he'd done, his life also would be finished.

This whole understanding flashed through her brain in seconds, and no more than seconds had passed since she'd inadvertently brushed Ben's head with her bare foot.

She backed slightly, unsure of how to react.

His eyes now locked onto hers balefully like a missile homing in on a target, and she knew that it was real. Ben had somehow been cast back into his tangled past, into some place where enemies sought to destroy him. His only way out was in violence and death. He advanced, step after sliding step. His teeth bared in a death's-head grin as she backed.

He would kill her.

He had told her if she ever met anyone like him, to run, but that wasn't an option. He would kill her before she reached the door. She still backed, knowing that she was running out of floor. Was it down to a killing, me or him, pupil or teacher?

If so, Ben would advise her to kill him, because she was younger, and still had a life to live.

She didn't want to kill him.

She didn't know if she could.

She knew she had to try.

As she backed Ben followed, his body neither rising nor falling with his steps, but maintaining a strange

152

equilibrium, unfocused eyes firmly planted at her mid-bodyline. She knew him well, and moved an instant before he did, a scream of animal survival leaping out of her throat as her hand thrust at the base of his throat.

Her weakness was being a woman, and she couldn't hide it from the man who had taught her that truth. Her strength lay in that he wouldn't expect her to attack.

But Ben moved more quickly than she'd ever imagined a person could move, bringing his hand down on the side of her neck. She twisted desperately, avoiding the full brunt of force, and tumbled to an ungainly heap. It was only the speed of her own reaction that saved her from a broken neck, but she was still on the floor, where she should not be. Knowing it was too late, she rolled backwards desperately, presenting her left shoulder instead of her stomach to the dismembering kick that would maim or kill her.

It didn't come.

As she came out of the roll, almost in slow motion, and rose automatically to a straddled, defensive stance, Ben was standing there, watching her. His hands were on his hips, a smile lurking behind the bland mask of his face. She straightened, anger flooding her body at the deception.

'You're dead,' Ben said.

He bowed smartly, turned, and strode off.

'I scored first!' Jessie shouted after him, relief freeing her tongue.

Ben stopped and turned. His voice was cold.

'I'm sure that must provide great consolation.'

Jessie went to the shower and let the hot water wash the annoyance from her. She'd been taught another lesson: never take anything for granted, not even Ben.

He came in while she was towelling herself. He had stripped off his gi, and was simply wearing a pair of jogging trousers.

Now, he looked like the wizened old man he was.

The bones in his back had begun to warp and his seamed and patched hands were gnarled with arthritis. It was hard to equate that body with the one which had recently moved with such lethal strength. His whole upper torso commanded attention, ridged with pink, twisted flesh, and Jessie still couldn't view it without feeling a stirring of pity deep within. Not for the appearance, but for the old pain that that body had lived with. Those burns could never be disguised by plastic surgery, nor had anyone tried.

'Let me look at your side.'

She showed him the rapidly purpling bruise that had blossomed above her left buttock. She felt neither sexual arousal, nor fear, nor embarrassment as Ben viewed her body. He was father, teacher, God almost.

'Lie down.'

He took out his foul-smelling home-made liniment and rubbed it into her injury.

'No damage done,' he said, massaging the muscles, feeling the lie of the fibres with understanding fingers.

Despite it all, his deep-set, narrow eyes were filled with the breath of life, and held no hint of regret. They smiled at her now.

'The enemy is not always who you expect him to be, nor does he come from the most direct angle. I told you that.'

Jessie smiled ruefully. 'I didn't want to hurt you.'

'Best of my pupils, you will never make the same mistake again,' he said as he walked away.

Jessie glowed.

She had never received praise of that order before.

Then she realised the words could be taken more than one way. She shook her head, and laughed at herself, probably for the first time since childhood.

Chapter 29

As Godfrey read to the end of this latest missive from Ben, he cursed quietly. It proudly informed him that Ben, bless his cotton socks, had been teaching this girl – who had arrived out of nowhere hooked on drugs and packing a firearm – karate for five years, and she was now equivalent to a Master of the fifth dan.

'Christ,' he muttered under his breath.

Having discovered she was introverted, with an ingrained hatred of society, the crazy bastard had also set out to turn her into a lethal weapon, teaching her a code of morals that dated from the third century BC in a different culture? That, Godfrey admitted to himself, had come as a bolt out of the blue. All that aggression and antagonism coupled with a degree in killing?

And what else had the old goat taught her? It didn't bear thinking about. He reached into his filing cabinet and pulled out the previous notes, one a year, and re-read them in sequence. They contained little he didn't recall word for word, and were disquieting by their very lack of information.

How had he missed that important point?

Godfrey's analytical mind shuffled the data, and came up with the inevitable conclusion that it was time he took a keener interest in the girl. After all, where would she, could she even, fit into society now?

With her unknown background and newly acquired skills, it wasn't just conceivable that without mentoring, she would turn to crime, it was inevitable. And what a criminal she would make, with not only the capability to kill, but the ethics which would allow her to do it.

Godfrey whistled slowly between his teeth.

Ben wasn't seeking approval or asking for guidance, he was simply leaving a record of his actions with his previous boss, who also happened to be a friend.

And, without directly saying so, asking if he would take her under his wing.

He knew more about Ben than Ben probably realised. The traumas of Ben's past had served to diminish a strong social conscience, which characteristic had made him one of the best operatives Godfrey had ever worked with, despite his advancing years; but the independent streak that had made Ben a nightmare to manage, had now by-passed common sense.

In charge of the unit he'd never wanted to manage, Godfrey felt the responsibility of Ben's actions as though they were his own. The girl was an unknown quantity, a possible spanner in the works of society.

Although most of his operatives had been enlisted from the ranks of those who no longer fitted within society, for whatever reason, all worked within a sound conception of morality. That was the whole point of Mayday.

He needed to see Ben in person once more, get some stuff out on the table between them.

Chapter 30

Ben's house, was situated on the edge of the New forest, in a discrete section seldom visited by the swathes of tourists that came to enjoy the parks each summer. Jessie loved the privacy and isolation of it, an almost bizarre contradiction to the commercial world that raged around it.

His was a solitary residence surrounded by a tall red brick wall, each six-foot wide section supported by a built-in pillar, over which the trees of the forest leaned.

Here, in this oasis, outside life passed them by.

For Ben it was the place where he'd quite accidentally landed to end his years. For Jessie, who had blundered unwittingly into his twilight dreams, it was a new life, another in a series which were finite, each counted in years.

Her early years, when her mother had been the hub of her life she recalled as a few isolated memories; those sepia images lifted into daylight on rare occasions, then carefully packed away for another day; the confused years, when her mother had been snuffed out of their lives, never to be mentioned, taking joy with her; and the time with Vince, which she had deliberately embraced as a road to perdition.

And now this time with Ben, suspended in a serene world which had all the permanence of a dream. She had lived each of her lives as a different person, and in the dark reality of recurring nightmares, knew that this present life would one day break open and society would come blundering back in.

But for now, it was enough.

She whistled as she began the evening meal.

That she learned to cook, and actually began to enjoy doing it was another of Ben's little victories. For a long time she would do nothing but train, train, train, her thoughts too angry to direct anywhere else. But eventually something stirred within her, and she discovered there were other things worth knowing and doing. Understanding about food was a skill that assisted in the body's performance, so was a natural progression.

Picking locks, dismantling security alarms, and understanding electronic security were games to be played when the weather was bad, things which stretched the mind when she was all trained out. It never occurred to her to wonder why Ben knew these things. Maybe everyone did.

But she could not be interested in gardening.

She sought Ben out and watched him as he pulled the small weeds from the rockery, and raked the surrounding chippings into neat lines, pulling them into swirls and patterns that pleased the eye. His garden was his joy; she knew he used it to calm a mind that echoed with old pains.

'I don't know how you can do that,' she said petulantly. 'It's boring. I came to say dinner's ready.'

'You should try to grow things, Jessie, as opposed to wanting to kill them. It's good for the soul.'

He stood up, stretched, then shook his head.

'You'll break hearts, child. You should learn to love life, just a little.'

'I love life well enough, I just don't like people.'

'I know, and that's why I have a present for you.'

He handed her a full driving licence in the name of Anthea Gray.

'Where did you get this?'

'The people I used to work for can still provide little perks. Don't look a gift horse in the mouth. Just say thank you.'

She scowled, hating the empty slate where

158

information should be. Ben had told her of his early years, of his wife and child, and his years in the army, but would tell her nothing of how or why he came to England, or who he had worked for.

'All in good time,' he would say.

In return, she told him of her life with Vince, and some anecdotes from her school days, but betrayed nothing of her parentage, or what had made her dive headlong into the bowels of society. She had her secrets, so why did she mind so much that he kept his?

Jessie had no problem driving. After a few lessons from Ben, his car became another haven, for within it she felt safe. The outside world beckoned, and she was able to view it once removed, through the glass.

Less easy to cope with were the driving lessons Ben insisted she take. He chose a female instructor, a middle-aged Irish woman, Mairead, whose long experience had brought her into contact with many people. She took Jessie's aggression in her stride, but Jessie came in swearing after the first lesson. Who was that woman to tell her what to do?

She was never going to do that again.

Ben's response was simple.

He went to the dojo each day and meditated, ignoring her totally. After a week she slammed in, and said, OK, she would take his stupid lessons.

'You will not only take them, you will learn.'

'Ok, I'll learn.'

'Very well.'

He had the grace not to look smug as he began the morning's workout as if they had never stopped.

Leaving the illusion of safety to walk into a shop or onto a crowded pavement was an even greater challenge. She resisted for a long time, till Ben's refusal to buy her personal things or clothes, effectively forced her to do it for herself.

Jessie treated people as objects and purchases as a necessary evil. Women were wary of her, jealous of her sleek body and inherent self-assurance, and men eyed

159

her with lust for the same reason, but, maybe sensing the sleeping danger in her eyes, admired from a distance.

On her part, she swallowed the urge to kill them, because she knew she could. There was a kind of freedom in that knowledge.

But eventually it dawned on her that she didn't have to be worried. People had their own lives, their own agendas, and she had to do nothing but keep to herself and outwardly observe the dictates of society if she didn't want to be noticed.

Chapter 31

One summer's day, feeling a deep need for solitude, she exited via the back door, as Ben called it, running up the six-foot high wall, and vaulting over to land cat-like on all fours the other side. She was up and running before movement ceased. Sometimes she passed a solitary jogger plugged into ear-buds, as if the natural silence of the forest was too alien to cope with, but mostly she was on her own.

What she loved most, after training, was to run.

When she ran, she breathed new air, she felt vibrant and alive. The forest became an extension of Ben's garden, once she'd braved the boundary, and she loved the sense of peace it gave her.

She ran easily, her body loping fox-like over the miles, her eyes seeing the obstacles, her body reacting to them, while her mind covered many other miles.

Mostly she chose routes that avoided the scattered houses, and when she did pass someone, she was almost annoyed, as if they had no right to be there, invading her space. She guessed there was speculation about her relationship with Ben, but what the neighbours made of it, they kept to themselves.

Today, she passed the Cary children as they cantered across her path, staring curiously. The forestry warden waved a salute, but she didn't acknowledge it.

She didn't notice the adolescent youth on the path this morning until he stepped out in front of her. She recognised him as the son of someone in the estate just beyond the treeline, and knew this meeting wasn't an accident. She had distantly observed him mature from a gangly teenager to a young man.

If she had seen him she would have veered off, and she had before. He was there more often these days, looking out for her, she guessed. But this time, as she tried to avoid him, he stepped sideways so that she almost ran full tilt into him.

Her eyes met his.

She knew that look from old.

The moment her body touched his, the reactions of the last few years surfaced of their own accord, she grabbed an arm, twisted, and the youth flopped face down on the floor with a grunt of surprise. She twisted his arm further backward, hardly gripping his wrist, but her thumb was pressing on the nerve and he gave a muffled screech. Shocked at the efficacy of her move, she let go and stepped back.

'Don't ever do that again,' she said coldly.

The youth scrambled to his feet in blind panic.

'I only wanted to – '

'I know what you wanted.'

She could see it in his eyes and was glad she'd floored him, glad she'd made him scream. It was what she'd been waiting for, the chance to take care of herself.

'I only wanted to talk, to ask if you would...'

The boy backed slightly at her blast of animosity.

'Don't ever touch me again,' she hissed, 'or next time I'll break your fucking neck. Do you understand me?'

'Jesus,' he said, and turned and ran.

Jessie was still seething when she arrived back at the house. She stomped down to change into her gi, but Ben stopped her.

'You know better than to go to the dojo angry,' he said. 'What happened?'

To her surprise and further annoyance, Ben burst out laughing.

'What's wrong with a boy finding you attractive? Even I know how attractive you are. Oh, wake up, Jessie, my girl.'

Ben thumped her on the back, making her wince.

'You're a striking young woman, not a nun. You're very lovely, and of course men are going to say so. You can't go around throwing them all to the ground. You have to learn to be a bit subtle. As a woman, your tongue is your first weapon, so do yourself a favour and try using it first.'

'Yes, but I didn't think he should – '

'Your trouble is, you're reluctant to think at all. Whatever it was that hurt you in the past, I think it's time you sorted it, don't you? I hope you didn't hurt the boy, just because he fancied you?'

He looked relieved when she shook her head.

'I did scare him a bit, though,' she said guiltily.

'No matter; but in future, take it as a compliment that the boy wanted you. Sex is a perfectly normal thing. Not only that, it's enjoyable, as you will hopefully discover one day. How do you think I conceived my children? I fucked my wife, Jessie. I enjoyed fucking her, and she enjoyed it right back.'

Jessie was shocked. She'd never heard Ben use such words before. Then, to her surprise, and Ben's, she burst out laughing.

Ben hugged her, and laughed too.

'Jessie, hang in there, girl. You've got some big problem choking you, but you'll be OK. I know you will.'

Chapter 32

When the summer was at its height, Ben informed Jessie he was to have a visitor.

'Who? That old guy?' she asked, for in the five years she'd been with him, other than deliveries and salesmen, he'd only been visited twice: a tall, grey-haired gentleman in a suit who greeted Ben with a small, sharp nod of the head, equal to equal.

Ben chuckled. 'Godfrey would be most upset to hear himself described as *that old guy*, Jessie. He's rather particular about his appearance. But no, not him.'

'Then, who?'

'Someone I would prefer didn't know you were here,' Ben said enigmatically. 'Will you humour me and go out for a run in the forest?'

'But – '

'This is something I wish to handle alone.'

How could she refuse?

Sometimes when she ran her mind would free itself of all the ugliness that simply would not be erased, but not today. As she ran her curiosity regarding Ben's more recent past consumed and irritated her.

Godfrey featured somewhere in Ben's past, too, and was certainly a man Ben trusted. He'd arrived unexpectedly the first time, not staying more than an hour, and leaving with the same lack of ceremony, as if snatching an illicit moment with the enemy.

He and Ben had talked in hushed voices, and not even Jessie's keen hearing caught more than the odd word. The secrecy all seemed a bit childish, but also it was worrying. It smacked of secret organisations with funny handshakes, like the ones her father belonged to which purported to do things for charity, but were more to do with self-advancement.

She hoped Godfrey wasn't one of those.

Thinking of her father made anger boil inside her head. She did what Ben had taught her, and put him back into his box.

Preferably a coffin-shaped one she thought, viciously.

The second time, Godfrey had strayed longer, and Ben had asked her to meet him.

They had sized each other up, like combatants, and their dialogue had been a sparring of wits, each trying to find out about the other, while revealing little. For some reason she found Godfrey's calculated assessment unnerving, and was pleased when he left.

Ben had not even tried to hide his amusement.

The smell of the trees and the spring of turf, normally a balm to her mind, left her coldly uninterested today as she ran beneath the dawn-speckled canopy of the place that had cocooned her for a while in its scented embrace.

Normally at this time, she and Ben would begin the formal exercises, the muscle stretching and strengthening routines. They would then perform the Kata before going on to the kihon, the free-style fighting, and more recently, Kendo.

Despite her wonder at being presented with a real Japanese Katana, her very own sword, to keep, Ben had said, of all of it, Jessie still loved the Kata most of all.

At first, she'd seen them as a sequence of movements to be learned, getting harder and harder as you progressed through them, and had revelled most of all in the free fighting, giving rein to the need to lash out, to flex her newly discovered muscles; but now she knew better.

The Kata provided the blueprint for a considered ballet of deadly moves, performed to absolute precision and timing. They were the keystone upon which the

Martial Arts piled its load of lethal bricks higher and higher, and the more she understood this, the more keen became her desire to perform the Kata to perfection.

She could see Ben's bent body in her mind's eye, and understood now the control that was pulsing through every graceful and beautifully perfected action, and was aware that her own body could now shadow his, movement for movement, with scarcely less skill.

Her measured steps in the forest faltered to a halt.

Today, Ben had shut her out, totally.

It irritated her, but also left an aftertaste of concern in her mouth.

What was it about this visitor?

Was Ben worried for her safety, or his?

Almost of their own volition, her feet turned towards another path, and sped her on her way back. Hiding in the ancient oak above the brick wall that surrounded the property, she waited to see the visitor arrive.

In due course a sleek red car drew up the drive, and a man climbed out. He was mid-forties, maybe older. He had tidy brown hair and a brown suit, and a pleasant, open face. Some indefinable thing in the way he moved told her he was trained, like Ben, like herself.

Ben's greeting was formal, almost sentimental, with an underlying depth to the welcome, almost subservient, apologetic. That was not like Ben.

They didn't shake hands. Instead, Ben made oriental obeisance to the guest, who replied in kind; an ex-sparring partner or pupil?

Guilt filled her. Ben had asked to be alone, she shouldn't be watching. As they walked towards the house together, she dropped from the branches down to the forest floor and tried to rationalise her jealousy.

It was childish.

Surely Ben was allowed to have friends she didn't know?

Angry with herself for being nosy, suspicious, whatever it was, she ran longer and harder than she normally would have, knowing she was going to get back too late to perform the Kata with Ben, but she was still suffering from annoyance, so it would serve him right.

By the time she got back protocol would make her stand back and watch Ben practice alone, unless he invited her to join, but as she rhythmically thumped her way back to the house, her irritation had washed away.

She didn't mind missing out on the practice; she was just pleased to see the red car had gone.

She calmed her erratic breathing, took off her shoes, and made her way to the dojo to apologise, but to her surprise Ben wasn't there. She finally found him in the confines of his small ornamental garden, his ruined face holding a serenity that was beautiful.

He'd been shot at point blank range.

The bullet hole in his forehead was a tiny, dark circle, but the exit wound had obliterated the back of his head, smearing his memories over the intricate swirling designs in the gravel path. Either he hadn't seen death coming, or knowing, had accepted it.

Rage blossomed and poured like an erupting volcano towards the dead man. She took his shoulders and shook him as though she would shake the life back in, and cried out over and over, 'You bastard, you knew. You bastard!'

The browning stain where his life had puddled onto the stones burned into her brain like a canker. He'd let her down by his death. Her saviour, her enigmatic sensei had been human after all, vulnerable and undependable.

He had abandoned her.

She hated him for having anticipated his death, for not brushing it aside as easily as he brushed aside her attacks in practice. She screamed into the empty sky, but didn't know whether she'd actually formed the noise, or whether it echoed in the emptiness of her mind.

167

In that same, blinding moment, she knew she was angry for own selfish reasons. Once more loneliness reached out and clawed her into its grasp.

She was afraid, for the first time in years.

When her mother had disappeared out of her life, she had been unable to open herself to anyone, ever, until Ben had wormed his way past her defences. Now the emptiness of loss that followed was the loss of her mother magnified a thousand times; because she had allowed herself to *feel*.

It was her own fault.

Best of my pupils, his words echoed in her head, with underlying irony, you will never make that mistake again.

Ben's body, limp and warm, was a dead weight, despite the ravages of age, yet she managed to drag him into his dojo. The act of dressing him in his gi was a painful task that she performed with reverence, lying him in state with something akin to religious fervour. She covered the small hole in Ben's forehead, a hole hardly big enough to let out a man's life, with the embroidered headband that he'd revered, but had never worn in her presence. It had belonged, so she understood, to his own Sensei, somewhere in the mists of his past.

With the same practicality that had prompted her to take Vince's money in the first place, she collected the army kit-bag that had lain untouched for five years. She took the third white gi that Ben had provided her with – the first she'd grown out of, the second had long gone to rags – and some necessities to see her through the first few weeks.

Ben's antique sword, the Katana she took as her death gift, and cried as she wrapped it in a blanket. His sweat had darkened the bound leather handle. With that blade, in the fullness of time, she would kill his assassin. He would see death coming, and Ben would be avenged.

These things were all she took.

168

She searched Ben's papers for some clue as to how to find Godfrey, for instinct told her he would provide the key to Ben's murderer.

While she worked, thoughts ran riot in her mind. Had Ben really known that death had walked in that morning via a man he greeted with such familiarity? Had he sent Jessie away, knowing that it was a farewell for all time?

Once anger died, she found she couldn't believe that.

She wondered, later, if she would also be lying dead along with Ben if the assassin had known of her presence. But if she had been there, Ben wouldn't now be dead, she was sure of that. So what had gone wrong?

But she found nothing at all in his papers that related to anything save the property he'd lived and died in, and a will that left it all to Anthea Gray.

Shocked, she found he'd also obtained a birth certificate for her in that name which presumably would satisfy the legalities. If anyone discovered these, she'd be the first suspect in the murder enquiry. She probably was, anyway. But with that knowledge, she knew Ben hadn't anticipated his death. He would never knowingly have left her that legacy.

Yet what now?

She knelt by his body, seeing, but not seeing.

She couldn't trace the elusive Godfrey, but she did have an unfinished task from her past. Outside forces had determined it was time to move on, to settle some old scores.

It was time.

The new Katana that he'd expensively imported from Japan for her, and which she thought she would treasure above life, she placed in his hands to see him on his journey.

There she meditated, by his body; a long farewell.

Ben had lifted her from the gutter, given her reason to live, but now her whole future had been swept aside in that one tiny flash of metal. There, on the polished wooden floor, she watched the red loneliness of night

169

coming across the sky, and welcomed thoughts of vengeance because it was better than leaving an empty space where life should be. Ben had said revenge was futile, but it was all she had; there was nothing else. And if she died in the process, well, no-one would mourn.

As evening approached, she gathered wood from the forest and set it around Ben's body. She whispered her goodbyes as the flames took hold, and backed out in the face of intense heat as the wooden floor took hold. She sent the essence of the man that had been Ben drifting up into the freedom of the stars as he'd once told her would be his choice, rather than being entombed in the earth. That her action would be seen as illegal didn't enter her thoughts. His will was irrelevant, too. With Ben's death, no one would live here, not even her.

She leapt up onto the wall and ran along till she could leap over into the vast tree from which she'd seen Ben's murderer walk in. There the night washed over her, bringing with it the ululating sound of the fire engines that had no power to disturb Ben's rest.

Chapter 33

It took three days for Ben's death to filter through to Godfrey's office, via the internet and newspapers. Though Godfrey stared towards the tooled leather inlay of his large desk, he wasn't seeing it. He was filled with inadequate fury. Why had he not had his men pick the girl up before, never mind what Ben thought?

He had let Ben down by his inaction, and the guilt festered. Ben might have been blind as to Jessie's true character, but he hadn't been. Her basic nature had risen to the fore, as he had once said it would. He hadn't acted, and now Ben was dead. He'd also known she had a gun, Ben had told him so. Like a fool, he supposed Ben had taken the bloody thing off her. Like a fool, Ben had obviously not.

'Damn and blast you, Ben, you stupid old goat,' he said out loud, thumping his fist on the table in frustration, 'Your note said she was damaged goods. Why didn't you listen to yourself?'

When Ben had first informed him of Jessie's unorthodox arrival, he had done nothing, seeing in Ben's note something he hadn't seen for a long time: interest in life.

In fact, he'd wondered if saving the girl would give Ben something other than the past to think about. It hadn't occurred to even him that a stray waif taken in and nurtured out of kindness would turn and bite the hand that fed it. Hell, he should have known a leopard didn't change its spots.

He had been going to visit Ben, to ask what the hell he thought he was doing, but something urgent took precedence, as it always did, and the time passed.

And what he'd worried about, and hadn't acted on, had become fact. It was done, and the girl had scarpered. A faint sneer crossed his face. If the little fool had waited, she would have inherited a property that was vastly more valuable than it appeared, because of its location more than its size. Well, she shat out there, big time. When the fire department had arrived, the blaze had been too fierce, too far gone, for them to seek life within. They had only been able to do that once the fire was under control the following day.

Then they had found Ben's body.

Then the coroner had found the bullet hole in his skull, and knew they were dealing with murder.

And Jessie was nowhere to be found, alive or dead.

It was fairly easy to come to a conclusion.

Godfrey picked up the phone. He was used to throwing his weight around, and now did so to some effect. Minutes later he stood, tidied his suit which was already immaculate, and called to his aide.

Oscar, clean cut and smelling of aftershave, arrived within minutes. There was a familiarity about his attitude that wouldn't have been accepted in Godfrey's army days, when he'd truly held the rank of General. Several years into retirement, however, to his wife's relief, he'd begun to discard Army protocol from his daily existence, so was able to cope. He still was a general, of course, no one could take that from him, but the title was rarely used in his present position.

There were things he disliked about Mayday; the name for one, and the covert nature of the work for another. The underhandedness of it all went against everything he'd previously stood for. He'd been retired a couple of years when he'd been approached for the job. He hated spooks and spies, and had refused the position when it had first been offered, but the powers-that-be were right in thinking two years of retirement would have him climbing the walls.

As the ultimate overall commander of Mayday, he

172

didn't need to stoop to subterfuge himself, of course, but used his tactical knowledge and endless experience to direct Mayday's operatives towards some degree of success, keeping everything under the social radar.

There was a conspiracy theory that Mayday existed. His computer geek spent quite a few hours each week undermining that theory.

His catchphrase was: we go where rational methods have failed; ergo, we go in sane. He hadn't lost his love of subtlety. There were benefits, of course. It wasn't as lonely here as it had been in uniform, people were not afraid to talk to him. And here he was, decision-maker extraordinaire, with people's livelihoods, and even their lives, at his fingertips.

Yet he hadn't made the one decision that would have forestalled Ben's death. If Ben had been a fool, he had surely been a bigger one.

He gathered his coat and his case.

'Get the car, Oscar,' he said. 'We're going to Southampton.'

Oscar hated his present role of babysitter to Godfrey. It was a bit of a cliché, the white general with his limo and black chauffeur. He was no chauffeur, in truth, and though he admired and liked his boss, he wanted to get in with the action, get involved with a real mission.

The only perk was the limo.

The General had become used to being chauffeured around in comfort during his latter army years, and it was the only thing he'd insisted upon as a prerequisite when accepting the post. It was the one thing the powers that be hadn't liked, it being too visible. But they gave in. It wasn't all show, though, for the car was bullet-proof and could touch two hundred on a straight road.

That, Oscar liked.

They exited the premises past the security cameras and razor wire fences. The inauspicious concrete buildings receded quickly behind them.

Aside from being the headquarters for Mayday, this was a very real training establishment, and boasted a full field commando course, gym, range, everything that a seasoned soldier needed for re-training into the elite sections of the forces. It was no play-time, in this camp. The majority selected for trials dribbled back one after the other to their old units, for only those with something that took them beyond the realms of ordinary managed to stay the course.

The soldiers looked like little toy men behind the tall fencing, marching, running to the Sergeant's bellow, but Godfrey wasn't seeing them.

He was wondering if his time was done.

Only a handful of people knew that the building also housed Mayday, an organisation that had no existence in the public eye. They comprised a small, eclectic group of men and women who were trained to think beyond military protocols, and deal with things that undermined basic human rights. They worked outside law or constitution in order to preserve it.

It was apolitical in nature: vigilantes, crooks, kidnappers, monopoly, insider-trading, prostitution, self-seeking government employees, and child pornography had all seen its intervention. Anything, in fact, where direct action by civil servants contravened the very laws they were upholding.

Somewhere there had to be reason in all that madness.

They were a safety valve society didn't know it had.

Initially the unit had been intended as a group of covert fact-finders, gatherers of evidence, and where possible the police or army would then move in to break whatever situation had arisen, and though that was still believed, the reality was something other.

There were too many times when sanity vanished under the avalanche of protocol, and action was required in the heat of the moment, outside of the bounds of peace-time law. At those times a Mayday had

174

to sink underground. Save for the intensely philanthropic nature of its work, and the educated, calculated responses of its operatives, its very existence verged on the status of vigilante.

He could just imagine how the press would enjoy uncovering that story. And how, by so doing, destroy the very protection it had accorded them.

And now, the General mused, as the sleek limo rolled towards Southampton, one of those men who had put their lives on the line for him in the past had been murdered by the low-life scum of a girl the man had tried to rescue.

They all made mistakes, of course, but he felt personally responsible for this one simply because he had done nothing, which was unforgivable.

He should have found the time to see to it. Not just the time, the inclination. It had been so easy to decide it was an issue that could wait, because that was what had suited him, and because of that Ben was dead. What he would do, though, was make sure that they found the murderer, by whatever method, and make sure she never saw the light of day again.

But why had she done it?

What had prompted it now, after five years?

He sensed the first niggle of doubt and mentally chastised himself for this pre-judgement. He should at least give her a chance to explain. He had no proof it was her, after all. He was doing what he preached against: accusing and condemning in the same breath. He should wait and see what evidence was brought to light.

It was, without a doubt, someone Ben had known.

It could have been someone with a grudge from the past, though it seemed unlikely, for Ben had been out of the limelight for a while. Besides which, he was virtually untraceable; if he hadn't been so badly scarred, he would have been totally untraceable.

Despite all his own self-doubt, deep in his heart, he knew it was the girl. He chastised himself throughout

175

that long journey south.

In Southampton Station the Chief introduced him to Detective Inspector Allinson, who was leading the enquiry into Ben's murder.

In suspicious silence Allinson climbed into the limo and directed them to the charred remains of the bungalow.

It was late summer, a year since the arrival of Ben's last letter, and Godfrey viewed the remains of Ben's home with regret. He had been expecting a letter, not this. No stranger to violent death, he always experienced the same sense of insubstantial angst when someone he knew died, as if he should have been there, should have somehow known and stopped it. But he wasn't God, as his wife was pleased to remind him whenever he railed against this particular short-coming in himself.

It was the lack of any sense of occasion that hurt, the casualness of dying without choice in time or location or method. Here one minute, gone the next. No matter whether they died on the field, or in bed from old age, you could never anticipate the moment. You couldn't walk up, shake someone's hand and say, 'See you, old chap,' as if somehow that would have made it all right.

Allinson filled him in on the details, but he was only half listening. As it was obviously murder, forensics had done what they could, but knew little enough.

For his part, Godfrey had decided Jessie would pay the price, if he had to spend the rest of his life searching for her. Though it was too late for Ben, the girl wasn't going to get off scot-free; he would make sure of that.

He should have seen his friend more often.

Theirs had always been a strange relationship, though, for Ben had never been an easy man to know, or like, come to that. Ben had always been a free agent, not anyone's to command, at the end of the day. Only someone he trusted could have taken him out.

Yet why had he trusted the girl? What had there

176

been about her that caused Ben to take her under his wing, to adopt her.

What was he not seeing?

He imagined Ben spending his hours in the dojo that had been built onto the side of the house; he imagined the bent figure holding the past at bay behind the calm barrier of his art. He imagined Ben teaching the girl how to kill him, unaware that he was training her towards that end.

Godfrey climbed out of the car feeling as old as his years. Maybe it truly was time to be put out to grass.

The garden stretched out, blackened around the core of rubble. The fire engines had knocked down part of the surrounding wall, leaving the sunken Japanese garden on view to sight-seers.

'Why didn't all this go up?' The General indicated the rest of the summer-browned garden. The smell of charred wood filled their nostrils, and as they stood and assessed the ruins, damped now by a heavy downfall of rain.

'The fire department came out fairly promptly. The house had gone up like a torch – it had a wood frame between the bricks, a traditional method around here – but they were in time to make sure it didn't take the surrounding vegetation with it.'

'It was arson?'

'Not just arson: a funeral pyre. The old man was found there.'

He pointed to the remains of the dojo.

'From what we can gather, he'd been shot just hours before the fire. He'd been laid out in there, the arms were crossed, and he'd that curved sword on his chest.'

'It's called a Katana. Could he have been using it in the dojo when he was shot? Are you sure that someone put him in there?'

'He was shot in the garden, there, and dragged in.'

He indicated, again.

'It seems that whoever torched the house did it out of respect, though I can't quite understand how they came to that conclusion. I mean if you like someone you don't torch them, not in this day and age.'

Godfrey was confused.

If the girl had killed him, why lay him out, give him the send-off he'd always wanted, but not expected to have? Or did someone else do that?

'Where's the body?'

'Still in the morgue, we didn't know what to do with it until you came forward. No one knew who he was, who owned the house, or anything, until we started digging.'

'Can you release him?'

The detective nodded.

'I'll have him cremated, and deal with the ashes myself. I also have a copy of his will.' He said, over his shoulder, 'Oscar, get on the phone. Deal with it.'

As Oscar stood back and punched numbers into his mobile, they walked around the blackened timbers.

'What about the girl?'

The detective was startled for a moment, then grinned.

'I wasn't going to mention her, but as you know already... It's not known by the press, and we'd like to keep it that way for now. No doubt it will get out, but at the moment we don't want to start a witch hunt. There are certain reasons why we feel very much in need to question her; not least because she's disappeared. Did you know her?'

'I'd met her.'

'Well, the fire was pretty well established when the boys got here. When we started talking to the neighbours we thought we were going to find two bodies, but there's no sign of her.'

'Have you any reason to suppose she killed him?'

'Only circumstantial. But if she didn't do it, why scarper? We don't know how she left the area, though. She didn't take the old man's car, and as far as we can ascertain she didn't have one of her own.'

'She wasn't taken by foul play, herself, kidnapped by

the killer?'

He shrugged. 'We wouldn't know.'

'So you've got no lead at all?'

He shook his head. 'Disappeared into thin air. We're making enquiries around the locals to see if anyone ever spoke to her. So far we haven't even found her name, and no one knows when she came here or why.'

'She called herself Jessie.'

Allinson's brows rose in question.

'That's all I know,' he added. 'No surname, no background. Ben rescued her, got her off drugs. Treated her like his daughter.'

'And you think she then killed him?'

Godfrey was miles away, thinking.

Allinson was irritated.

'Exactly who are you, and why the interest in my case?'

Godfrey gave a dry smile. 'The title General is not honorary. I have a little clout in the army.'

'I meant no offense.'

'Of course. Ben used to work for me a long time ago. He retired here, and it's possible that one of his old contacts, for want of a better word, found out where he was. We'll look into that. You haven't found traces of anyone else visiting the property recently?'

He shook his head. 'But we did find a handgun on the premises.'

'The murder weapon?'

'No. From its position, we guess it was in one of the upstairs cupboards. It hadn't been fired for several years, and was the wrong calibre. The gun used to kill the old man had a silencer.'

He reassessed his instinctive thoughts. Ben hadn't owned a gun, but the girl had, and if it was her gun in the house, and it hadn't been used to kill Ben, then there was a chance she wasn't the killer, after all. Perhaps he'd been totally wrong.

'Do you mind if my man has a look around?'

'Forensics have finished,' he said. 'You can go where

you like. But he won't find anything.'

Oscar prowled around the ruins, for all the world like a dog sniffing the air, using some sense that Godfrey couldn't for the life of him, identify. He circled the garden, then disappeared over the wall in front of them. He moved like a predator, all grace and power.

Allinson said, 'He's no bloody chauffeur. What the hell are you guys?'

'I was Ben's friend. Whatever else I am is not important.'

He could see Allinson didn't like this.

'He was a strange fellow, by all accounts, he said. 'The neighbours say he used to practice Kung Foo out here, all on his own.'

'Karate and Kendo, mostly. And he was alone, till he took Jessie in. Did anyone find his cats?'

'Cats?'

'There were two, a tabby and a ginger. I'd be obliged if someone would rehome them. That's the least I can do for him.'

'I'll have someone look into it.'

There was a rustling, and Oscar popped back over the wall, grinning.

'Looks as if she was here the whole time the fire was burning, and longer, from what I can see,' he said smugly. 'Maybe days.'

The Detective was startled. 'We were searching the grounds before the fire was out. She couldn't have been.'

'Come and take a gander.'

He led them through the gate and to the far side of the wall where the branches of a huge oak towered over the garden. He climbed up onto the wall, jumped up onto a wide branch, and disappeared from view. His voice sounded muffled.

'Are you coming?'

Allinson took his dignity off with his jacket, and followed up into the tree. Godfrey heard him say, 'Shit!' and after a moment both men descended.

180

How the hell could she have been there? We had dogs, and everything.'

'If she accessed the tree from the wall the dogs wouldn't necessarily have followed her scent. And there are rags up there. Ten to one you'll find they're impregnated with something to disguise her scent.'

'But why would she hang around?'

'Yes, that doesn't make sense. If she was guilty she would have been long gone.'

'Information,' Godfrey said. 'She was listening.'

'What for?'

Oscar said, 'It's what I would have done if I wanted to learn what the police knew; if I wanted to get the murderer myself.'

'Jesus. That's a leap of a conclusion.'

'It's a supposition,' Godfrey said. 'But Jessie, as far as I know, wasn't your usual girl. Whatever went down, here, she needs to be found, and quickly. For her own sake, as much as anything, if she didn't do it herself.'

Allinson did a 360 visual sweep, turning to follow his eyes. 'I agree. This needs to be kept out of the papers. The hounds have lost interest for the moment, but if the murderer knows there was a possible witness, he might go after her. Have you any clue at all about her background?'

Godfrey shook his head. 'That we never knew, nor did Ben. She just turned up one day, needing help and a place to stay. She had a broken arm, as I understand, and was an addict, so I doubt she'd come too far.'

Allinson took out his mobile, and summoned the team back to check the surrounding area, and forensics to work the oak tree, while Oscar booked him and Godfrey into a local hotel.

Godfrey commandeered a room at the Station the next day, to work in, and demanded the files pertaining to the case. He was informed, later, that they had checked every tree within a thirty yard radius of the property boundaries, but had found nothing more.

He hadn't expected them to.

181

The rest of the staff went about its business around him, muttering and grumbling because they hadn't been told why, or at whose authority, he was able to have access to police files.

National Security, they were told.

The descriptions of the girl were good, and Godfrey asked if anyone had been asked to make up a computer image, but the only thing the locals could all agree on was that she'd been tall and blonde, pretty and fit, and kept herself to herself. They had 'learned' through the grapevine that Ben was her uncle, and that her parents had died, which was why she'd come to live with him. Misinformation from Ben, covering the gossip angle, Godfrey assumed.

Aside from the odd shop-keeper, only one man claimed to have ever spoken to her.

Godfrey called Allinson. 'I want to see this Alan Winscombe. Would it be possible for you to get him here?'

'Why him? He saw her, but couldn't give us anything, for all he said he spoke to her.'

'For someone who only spoke to her, how come he disliked her?' Godfrey asked.

'He didn't say that.'

'It's in every line of speech. To dislike someone you have to do more than say hello.'

'You think he's lying?'

'He's not saying something for sure, and whatever it is, it might be interesting.'

Just then a uniformed policeman knocked on the open door, cleared his throat, and stood waiting for permission to come in. The General's brows rose in question.

'I just heard you say the girl's name was Jessie, Sir. I didn't know that before, otherwise...'

'Yes? Well?'

'I recalled about four years ago a detective from London came here looking for a girl of that name. She would have been in her teens then. It seems that she was wanted for questioning over some sort of murder in London.'

Godfrey was still for a moment.

'Why did they suppose she'd come here?'

'The man who gave her a lift to Southampton was found, but everyone assumed she'd hitched further on, because she never turned up.'

'Well, well.' Godfrey mused. 'It seems that one little mystery has an answer, after all. Have you contacted this detective? Is he still based in London?'

'I wasn't sure if you or Detective Allinson would want me to, Sir.'

He was obviously confused as to whom he should direct his comments.

Allinson said wryly, 'Joe, I think you had better assume that we're working as a team, otherwise this could get complicated.'

Godfrey gave the merest hint of a smile.

'I think we would both like to speak to him. Can you arrange it? And get that Winscombe chap in.'

Chapter 34

Despite the clean-cut health of someone who cared about his appearance, Alan Winscombe's angry smear of acne betrayed his youth. His demeanour was sullen and, Godfrey thought, wary.

'What do you want me for? I told you everything last time.'

'Please sit down,' Godfrey said. 'We just need to clarify a couple of points from your statement.'

Reading between the lines in the file, he assumed Alan had come forward at the time because it seemed exciting to be a major witness in the hunt for an arsonist, rather than through some altruistic sense of responsibility.

He had apparently seen her jogging a few times, and had given the best description they had of the girl to date, but now sat on the edge of the seat, probably wishing he'd kept quiet.

'You didn't tell us about the incident with the girl. We want to know why,' Godfrey said, looking down at the file. 'It seems you molested her.'

Allinson was startled by the outrageous comment, but it bore fruit in a way he hadn't expected.

'I didn't touch her!' Alan blurted, shocked into leaning forward. 'If she said that she lied!'

'You do realise that misleading the police is an offence, don't you?'

Godfrey was rewarded by a faint greying of the young man's livid spots. He was shaking slightly, probably imagining himself being hauled away in handcuffs.

'I didn't mean to mislead, it was just I didn't think it mattered. It wasn't anything to do with the old man, or the fire, or anything.'

Allinson's comment was a little gentler.

'Perhaps you'd better tell us now, in your own words, quite what happened.'

'I just tried to talk to her, that's all,' he said in a small voice, his very words implying that it wasn't all.

'Where, at Ben's house?'

'No. She used to run in the woods. I watched her. Several times.'

'Fancied her, did you?'

He nodded guiltily. 'But I didn't touch her, honest I didn't, even if she said so!'

'But something happened.'

'She was always running. I tried to speak to her a couple of times, but she would always turn away if she saw you. She'd just run off the path, you'd never find her. Just didn't want to talk.'

'So what did you do?'

'I hid behind a tree,' he said in a small voice. 'I just wanted to stop her, that's all, tell her how I felt.'

'And how did you feel?'

Alan's cheeks went bright red.

Allinson was having trouble keeping a straight face; he wouldn't be of much use in Mayday, Godfrey thought.

'Being sexually aroused by a pretty girl isn't a crime. So what happened then,' he prompted.

'She just sort of grabbed my arm and there I was, sprawled on the floor. I still don't know how she did that. She got a nerve or something, it was days before I could use my arm properly again.'

'Perhaps she thought you were attacking her, trying to rape her.'

'I wasn't, honest. I fancied her, who wouldn't? She was real sexy, but I wouldn't rape anyone. Honest.' He glanced at both men as if looking for confirmation that they believed him.

185

'What happened next?'

He looked slightly confused.

'The thing is, I thought she was going to kill me. I mean, I think she could have if she'd wanted to. She was so quick, and so strong, it was kinda *wrong* for a girl to be able to do that.' He hesitated. 'She said next time I touched her she really would kill me, and I believed her. I never went near her again.'

Godfrey could see why he hadn't told the police of this episode. To be physically overpowered and intimidated by a girl wouldn't show him up in a good light with his peers. But whether it helped them at all he didn't know, apart from add credence to what he'd already seen himself, that she'd been a good pupil, and wasn't afraid to put what she'd learned from Ben into action.

Allinson put Alan out of his misery, and patted him on the shoulder as he showed him out. 'Don't be ashamed of being beaten by her, son. It's just as well you didn't try to retaliate; I think you were right when you said she was dangerous. But I'll tell you something else. You've kept this little secret to yourself this long, and I'd advise you to leave it that way. If I hear you've spoken a word about this to anyone, I'll throw the book at you.'

Quite which book, he wasn't sure, but the threat worked. Alan would have agreed to anything, just to get out of there.

He was at the door when Godfrey said, 'Oh, one last thing, Alan. What did she sound like? How did she speak?'

'I told you what she said.'

'I mean her voice, her accent. Did she come from round here, or London, or somewhere up north? Was she foreign? Did she have any speech mannerisms, like a stutter? Anything you can recall.'

'She wasn't foreign. Her voice was kind of low, and soft, even when she was threatening me. She spoke kind of posh, too, if you know what I mean. Classy, like.

But that's all I know.'

    'Thank you. You've been most helpful.'

Chapter 35

The next day Detective Inspector Redwall, from London, turned up. Godfrey's first impression wasn't flattering, which was surprising in the light of what he'd been told about the man's exemplary career. There was a sort of seedy air about him, as if life in general, let alone his job, was a burden he didn't want to be bothered with any more, but once they started talking about Jessie, he seemed to become animated.

'I was convinced she'd turn up sooner or later,' he said. 'Do you know where she is now?'

'No, I'm sorry, we've got no idea.'

He briefly put Redwall in the picture.

'So anything you can give us would be a help.'

Redwall put a file of his own on the table between them, and gave them a summary of the contents.

'So, you see, if this really is the Jessie I've been seeking, I'm pretty sure I know who she is, and where she came from, at least, as much as anyone can be sure. Why she went out on the streets in the first place, I never worked out. I believe she must have been traumatised at some stage during her childhood, but apart from the mother running off when the children were toddlers, there wasn't anything else I could discover.'

'Did the father seem a caring sort of person?'

'I don't think he molested her, if that's what you mean. He told me the mother didn't want the children, and her lack of interest in them seems to suggest he was right. The fact that the mother ran off with a Greek businessman was verified. And a year or so later, it seems she left *him* for someone else, so the sister's statement that her mother was a whore seems crude but understandable. I was unable to trace her after that last move from Greece. She could have gone anywhere in the world, and in all honesty, I didn't have justification to spend any time on it.'

Allinson commented. 'But you have no proof that she is, in fact, Elizabeth Stowleigh?'

'No,' Redwall agreed. 'But there's no such thing as coincidence, only evidence. It's a shame you haven't got a photo. Five years ago I was looking for a child, though she was five-foot-eight or thereabouts even then, but now it seems we must be looking for a young woman. A beautiful one, judging by what I'm hearing, if not a dangerous one.'

He pulled a photo from his file.

'That's the only picture I had of Jessie, or Lizzie, as her father called her.'

The men stared at the grainy picture of a girl, maybe ten years old, with a centre parting and two plaits of blonde hair, willing it to tell them a story. He lay another picture beside it, a girl with a fuller face. The similarity was obvious.

'And that's the older sister, Catherine as she was four years ago. Would it be possible for some computer whiz to make a likeness up from those two?'

'Probably. I saw the girl myself,' Godfrey said. 'Albeit three years ago, and very briefly, but I could probably tell if the likeness was a good one or not.'

'There were times I thought she was a figment of my imagination,' Redwall admitted, with a wry twist of his lips. 'It's nice to know someone here actually saw her.'

'I'll get someone on to it,' Oscar said. 'May I borrow them?'

'Of course, and I'd really like a copy, if I may. I'd also like to see where she's been living these last few years, if you've no objection? I spent so much time trying to find her, you see.'

Godfrey realised there was a lot he wasn't saying,

189

that his involvement with this case had got to him. He could understand that.

There was something rather sad about a child who went off the rails, and this one seemed to have touched Redwall's heartstrings on the way.

'My chauffeur will drive you out there, when he comes back,' he said.

When Redwall was gone, Godfrey stewed over the history in the new file, and also became, without realising it, intrigued.

'Reading between the lines, my view is there's a good chance she'll turn towards crime.'

'That fits the profile we came up with,' Allinson commented.

'Redwall's right about her background,' Godfrey mused. 'There really is something odd about it, if she *is* the missing Stowleigh girl. Everything's too nice and tidy: father a politician, expensive background and all that, long family history in politics, nothing shady in the press. I mean, who manages that these days? I've seen him on the television, too; very presentable. D'you know, I don't think we'd have a lot of trouble convincing Redwall to go take a further look into Stowleigh if I came up with the funds and the incentive.'

'What on earth do you think he's going to find now, after all these years?'

'I don't know; that's the point. But we do have a problem. It seems Ben has turned this girl into something I'd rather not contemplate letting loose in society. If we get her now, what are we going to do with her? Institutionalise her for the rest of her life? But if we could find out what actually went wrong, get a real psychological profile, there's just a chance we could help her.'

'Bit late, wouldn't you say?'

'Probably, but are you saying we shouldn't try?'

'Hell, no. She's a bit of an enigma. It would be nice to understand what went wrong, at least.'

190

'The missing drug money is a nasty little complication, if it's true,' Godfrey remarked. 'That kind never give up.'

'We'll try to keep it under wraps, but you can bet your bottom dollar this will leak out somehow, and then we'll have all kinds of unsavoury characters down here looking for her.'

'Which makes it all the more necessary for us to get her before they do,' Godfrey said. 'It's a shame none of us have a clue where to start.'

Chapter 36

It took Jessie two days to get to Birmingham via several bus changes; more to hide her trail than because there wasn't a direct link. She spent three days in cheap motels before she could find somewhere to rent. Most estate agents wouldn't rent anything to her without a reference, despite her forged driving licence and birth certificate, but eventually she found a woman who discreetly slipped the proffered pile of notes into her handbag, and asked with a bright smile which property she was interested in.

A small house took her fancy. End terrace, with two entrances, one onto the road, the other onto a back alley, and a third exit from the second storey onto the roof of another house.

Never let yourself be cornered, Ben had told her.

Never again.

When she'd stolen the money she'd been naive and stupid, seeing the money as a way towards a different life, but she knew now she'd stolen not just money, but trouble.

Without it, Vince wouldn't have bothered to come after her, the other dealers wouldn't have known or given a shit about her, and she would have simply disappeared once more. There was no point trying to give the money back, though. They'd take the money and still kill her, because anything else meant loss of face, especially as she'd eluded them for five years.

She deposited the money, and whatever those other papers were, under the floorboards, trusting no one, and opened Vince's notebook for the first time.

If the enemy is after you, your best form of defence is to attack, Ben had said.

Well, they were after her all right. She didn't need to see them to know they were still out there, waiting to catch up with her. Now she'd left the haven of Ben's home, she was vulnerable once more. If they found her they'd kill her, without a doubt, but not if she killed them first. Then she would be free to search for Ben's assassin. How, she had no idea, but she would find him, too.

She was disappointed.

There wasn't much of any use in Vince's book, except for several names that meant nothing on their own. Vince had boasted he was going to be big, like the Godfather, and everyone would look up to him, fear him; and the notebook had been the key, he'd said, shaking it under their noses.

His cunning plan had been simple.

When he'd discovered the names and addresses of all the people in the drug syndicate he'd been going to blackmail them, take a larger cut for himself, become the big I Am.

Fool, Jessie thought. They would have cut your fingers off one by one and fed them to you before that happened.

As big a fool as herself for taking the money.

That she'd been young, desperate, on drugs, and without a plan didn't mean anyone would forgive her. And for once fate had been kind, sending her a wanker in a Volvo, then Ben, to help her disappear.

So, first things first.

There were five names in the book, but she had no idea if that was the sum total, or which one was the boss, if any. Neither did she know if they were first names, surnames, or nicknames, but once she found one, the others would follow. As far as she could make out, and exactly as it was written in Vince's semi-literate scrawl, they were Porter, Jalmers, Smiley, Sharpie, and Blue. So, what Vince had managed to

193

discover about the Syndicate was pretty minimal. Five nick-names, and nothing else, save his belief that the consignments came down from Birmingham.

Well, if they were here, she'd find them.

Unlike Vince, she had no intention of trying to screw business or dosh out of them. If she wanted to ever be free, she had to find out who they were and kill the lot of them. And when she had killed the dealers, and killed the man who had murdered Ben, she was going to kill her father – clean the slate.

Jessie had considered leaving the kitbag of dirty money in Ben's house when she torched it, but reality intruded. There had been no point at all in throwing it away. It was still current tender, so she might as well make use of it, especially as she might end up dying for it whether she used it or not. There was a tidy sum in notes, and some other things she didn't understand, but they had large sums printed on them, and she didn't doubt someone would help her cash them in for a cut.

Chapter 37

Jessie had vaguely thought Birmingham would be like London, but it wasn't. It was big like London, but without the centralised historic charm. For the most part she found it characterless, dirty and squalid. There were miles and miles of roads, huge areas of factories, housing estates, parks with vandalised tress and swings, shopping centres that smelled of urine, and abandoned areas of old warehousing, blackened from some long-forgotten industrial era. Just the sort of place one would expect to be rife with a strata of dropouts looking for drugs.

She bought a map and began a routine and systematic dissection of the city, and got to work. She slept during the day, waking up late in the afternoon to search out the places where packs of youths hung out: parks, street corners, pubs. She made no contact at first, she simply walked on the edge of the underworld knowing that eventually that world would reach out and suck her in. If the guys she was looking for dealt in drugs, they'd eventually come to her. Then having found the street sellers, she would follow them, working her way up the chain until she found the suppliers.

After a while she began to get a feel for the place. She learned where the prostitutes hung out, she saw where dealers hung out on street corners. She knew the clubs and the parks, and she also sensed that people had started noticing her, wondering what she was doing there.

But she also became exhausted.

Every time she tried to sleep the nightmare came back, and tonight was no different: a brown-coated man was walking up the gravel path towards Ben. She was running, running, trying to get there in time. But she was running through treacle. In the dream, a hand lifted a gun in slow motion. It was always the sound of the shot that woke her, yet in reality she had heard no sound; she hadn't known Ben had died.

Once again, she lay for a moment, her heart thumping, her breath short, as if she really had been running, before climbing out of bed to check the time.

Consciousness brought the onset of frustrated anger that increased her heartbeat and wouldn't let her fall back into oblivion. Looking at her watch, swearing, she dressed and went out into the night, as she always did, not for any reason other than simply to run, to dispel the vast store of adrenaline that was choking her. Cavernous in the baleful amber glare of the overhead lights, the streets unwound under the paced thudding of her feet. It was the blackest part of the night when, once upon a time, before all- night stores and shift work, good people would be lying asleep before waking to face another day, and dealers and whores would be falling into bed after a heavy night.

Insomnia had been a gift from her father.

When she'd been younger fear and inadequacy had been so strong she'd been suicidal in those dark, wakeful hours, but now she refused to give in, and as she ran through the silent streets she piled the beasts from the nightmare back into the crack they had slipped through.

They wouldn't kill her, she would kill them.

As she ran, her mind took her through the various truths of the Bushido, truths that Ben had lived by. She chanted them; a litany to the pounding of her feet: justice, courage, mercy, politeness, honesty, honour, loyalty, self-control. Honour and loyalty she owed to Ben; justice she would dispense whether or not it was her place, because who else was going to do it? Courage she would find; self-control, sometimes; but mercy? No, mercy wasn't hers to give at this time.

The difference between good and evil, between right and wrong wasn't open to question. She knew the difference.

Revenge was a fool's errand, Ben said, but by whatever name, this was justice, plain and simple.

These thoughts of retribution fuelled her concentration, and thrust aside the dark demon of an empty, pointless future. She didn't see the cracked and uneven pavement; her feet guided her safely over the pock-marked surface.

She was awake, but refused to let in reality.

She would choose her own dreams, now.

A street light overhead flickered.

Awareness surfaced in that split second, and Jessie came back to the present with a surge of loneliness that washed through her like a tidal wave, dredging up the deep murky depths of anger.

Ben was dead. The words thumped into the pavement with her steps. Ben was dead. The empty space inside gradually filled with a consuming hatred that encompassed the people who surrounded her, known and unknown alike. Ben was dead.

The nightmare raised the image of the assassin, but he was burned into her brain. If asked to describe him, she wasn't sure she could do so. He was medium height, had medium brown hair and pleasant, open features; a normal, middle-of-the-road person. Yet there was something that was unique the way the man stood, walked, or existed, Jessie wasn't sure, but whatever it was, she would know him, and would kill him.

And here she was.

In the grimy centre of yet another city: vastly different in appearance to both London and Southampton, but with the same dark streets, the same greed, the same low-life scum floating on the surface of that dark amorphous mass of humanity. Yet this time she was not dependent, she was there for no man's taking, and she had a reason to live.

Barely realising she was doing it, Jessie scanned every car that went past, and every man, knowing that one day she would find Ben's killer. She knew now that the car he'd driven had been a Porsche, she'd seen one since, and her heartbeat had increased as she recognised it. She'd been pleased to add that knowledge to her minimal store, and also the knowledge that whoever drove it must be well-greased, but at the time she'd been dealt a blow of severe disappointment at the realisation that the driver had been neither the man she wanted to kill, nor the specific car she sought.

Now, in the false city light, in the darkest part of night, the last months dragged through her mind again like a film on continuous play. She couldn't stop it, and she knew it was driving her slowly but surely insane.

She didn't care where her feet were taking her, for unlike those who lived here, she knew no fear of the back streets, and when she needed to return to the house which wasn't a home, some internal map would send her back in the right direction. The last dying flicker of another street light jolted her into sudden awareness that she was once again by the canal. She didn't know why, but the cold water, the seediness of the blank-windowed warehouses, and the dying hulks of rusting metal attracted her.

Chapter 38

And now, in the encroaching blackness of a place not worthy to have lighting, something called to Jessie. Not in words, but as an animal cry of desolation. Small, muffled, terrified. She knew that sound, it drove its claws into a memory she wanted forgotten, and for a second she was lying naked under the body of a man who was pumping hard into her body, biting her, wanting her to cry out to feed his sexual needs. She didn't like the men who had used her, but she'd welcomed them to her body, for the pain they inflicted was penance for a sin she couldn't wash away.

Neither Vince, not the men who used her cared what strange things were running through her mind. To the one she was a source of income, to the other an instrument of pleasure.

Some men were animals. They liked to cause pain, so she had learned to whimper even if she wasn't hurting. Being passive didn't do anything for their egos. And when she wasn't hurting, she welcomed the odd hit that Vince threw her way to make her dependant, to keep her there. She could float for a moment in time, without thought. She hadn't needed the drugs to keep her there, just her guilt, but Vince had been too stupid to realise the difference.

Then one day something in her changed. When she looked up at the man who was hurting her, her dead mind had snapped into focus. What was she doing there, with him, with Vince? She'd been unable to stop the cry that had been wrenched from between clenched teeth at that moment, and the man's teeth had bared in a smile of satisfaction as he exploded into her.

Now, in the darkest part of the night, in the seediest part of the city, she recalled all that in a split second, for somewhere near here someone had cried out with the same hurt she'd known on that day.

Without conscious thought of the implications, Jessie turned her steps towards the sound, and increased her speed. Silence hovered on the straining ears.

Nothing.

Then again, no more than the hint of a moan, then gone, but she swerved to its point of origin. A grey warehouse loomed up before her, holding dark secrets that daylight wouldn't expose. It was a place where normal citizens didn't venture at night, a place the police would choose to forget in their nightly rounds.

The windows were barred, the doors were solid. She slowed her footsteps and trod noiselessly around the rubble which was housed by the dirty hollow of the path. Her senses were attuned now to the night, and her eyes picked out the faintest flicker of light. Not in the warehouse, but below her. There was a small bank, over which Jessie peered. In the near darkness, the internal light of a long, sleek car glowed, exposing writhing figures inside.

She slithered down the bank, wrenched open the back door, and smelled the familiar odour of sweat and semen. There were three bodies within, and three pairs of eyes turned instantly to focus on her as she glanced over them. Two older white men, partially clothed, and across their laps a naked black boy, his hands bound cruelly high between his shoulder blades. Raw cigarette burns littered his thighs and buttocks, like stars in the night sky.

She knew the score, instantly. They had already had sex once, and needed the stimulus of violence to stoke up their internal fires once more. Marks of abuse ran down the boy's legs, and blood smeared a face bloated from a beating or weeping, Jessie couldn't tell. In the same split second it took her to analyse the scene, the three occupants realised that she was just a woman.

The pain in the boy's eyes didn't change an iota, but the alarm on the men's faces turned to irritation.

'What the fuck?' one of the men asked. Then, his eyes adjusting to the dark, he advised, 'Butt out, bitch, unless you want to join in.'

Jessie bared her teeth in a smile. She bent down, picked up a broken brick, and scored a long line down the elongated side of the limo.

The man furthest from her was frozen into silence for just a second, then he screamed, 'My car! You fucking cunt, you – ' He spluttered in wordless rage as he thrust the boy from his lap, and fumbled for the door handle.

Jessie stood back. The man nearest to her had watched with some amusement as she'd vandalised the car and, casually doing up his open flies, slid out almost at the same time as his irate partner.

Jessie backed even more.

The angry man had no thoughts. His rage was beyond words, and he leapt around the car, still trying to hang on to his trousers, and ran at Jessie like a buffalo, head down, never stopping to wonder why she hadn't run at the first sign of retaliation.

His hand was out to grab, but Jessie walked into his embrace, turned, and with the full force of her inner energy, elbowed upwards into his face. There was a crunching sound, and her spin carried her round and out of reach as the man's momentum carried him forward. He piled into the brick wall behind her, and was still.

For the split second it had taken Jessie to disable the first man, the other had simply watched, probably expecting his mate to knock seven bells of shit out of the bitch that had damaged his car, but as the other man fell, so did his own complacency.

Crouching low into a fighter's stance, he sidled towards her with more caution. Jessie waited. The first

201

man had acted on rage alone, the damage to his car side-stepping the brains he might have been sensible to employ.

The second man was a different kettle of fish. Lithe, slim, and sure, he advanced, sizing up his opponent, his hands balled into fists.

Ben would have said now was the time for subtlety.

She backed hesitantly towards the wall, her expression registering dawning panic, fear, sincere regret that she'd interfered. She glanced behind her once, then back, indecision written on her face: should she run? Now that his eyes were accustomed to the darkness, her assailant saw her fear, and confidence radiated. In fact, he grinned with anticipation. He obviously thought he'd obtained a new plaything.

She stopped, just short of the wall. Her hands were now out in front of her, as if to ward him off. Gone were the fists and the arrogance. Her eyes were bright, and she breathed small, panicked breaths, her heaving chest straining within the dark jogging top. She invited his attentions with a wet pass of her tongue over her teeth, this betrayal of fear making him even more sure of himself.

Instead of punching her, as his first instinct had advised, he reached out to grab her hair, shielding the part of his body a woman would most likely go for. As he lunged Jessie instantly dropped the scared look.

Awareness sprang in his eyes. Too late danger signals lit in his face as she grabbed his wrist, plunging his fist directly into the stonework. She ducked under his arm as he screamed, then turned and smashed his head into the wall. She spun behind him as he fell, and kicked him hard in the groin from behind.

He spasmed uncontrollably, dropped to his knees in a near foetal position, and she followed through with a kick under his jaw as he fell onto his side. It had all taken about three seconds.

She stood still, breathing heavily for a moment, waiting, to make sure that he wasn't faking, but he didn't move. Bending down to assess the damage, she realised that he wouldn't move again. She'd broken his neck. Despite all the tuition, the practice, she hadn't realised it would be that easy.

The other man groaned faintly, but he wasn't going to bother her, with a broken jaw and a flattened nose. She ignored him, and went to the car. The youth stared at her from his contorted position on the plush carpeting of the floor seeing in her not a saviour, but something else to be afraid of, for he was helpless to protect himself. He winced as she closed in, fear in every fibre of his being, and gasped when she drew out a knife. She cut the knots that held his wrists behind him to his neck. He almost screamed as his arms were released, then after a second he rolled over awkwardly onto his burned backside, and tried to cover himself with hands that wouldn't function.

'Don't be silly,' Jessie said sharply. 'I've seen it already. Get some clothes on. We'd better get out of here before the police come.'

The boy struggled with numbed fingers, but she knew better than to help. She slammed the back door, walked around and climbed into the driver's seat. The keys were dangling in the ignition.

'Ready?'

The boy recovered his composure somewhat with his clothes, then sat there, bemused. Jessie saw his eyes slide towards the figures that lay on the dark rubble.

'Are they dead?' he whispered.

'One is. The one who presumably owns the car isn't, yet. Do you want me to finish him off?'

The boy was out of his depth. Jessie saw him shrink into the upholstery, and saw tears form.

'God's sake!' she said angrily. 'Would you rather I'd let them get on with it? You know they were going to kill you, don't you? I could see it in their eyes.'

The boy didn't answer, so she started the engine, and backed the sleek car angrily down the gap between the warehouse and the demolished building, and out

203

onto the road, scraping it along the side wall as she did so. She drove for a few moments.

'Well,' she said. 'Where shall I take you? Have you a home to go to? Or would you rather a hospital?'

The boy didn't answer, and Jessie could see him staring at her in the mirror as if wondering what planet she'd come from. She sighed, parked the car on a no-parking zone, and got out.

'Come on,' she said, opening the back door. 'Let's go before the cops see us.'

He moved at that, obviously not wanting the law to find him any more than Jessie wanted it to find her. She walked on, and the boy followed hesitantly, all the way back to her house, like a puppy who had been reprimanded: afraid to follow, afraid to trust, but unwilling to be left alone.

Inside the house she ran a lukewarm bath, and put salt in it. 'It's going to hurt, but you have to do that or get treatment,' she told him, and walked out. She found a jogging suit and threw it in through the door without looking to see whether he'd obeyed.

More than he could have guessed, she understood how much a simple bath could wash away the stains of memory. The night was dark and still, but Jessie sat in the empty living room without a light on, waiting. Finally she heard the hesitant sound of footsteps on the stairs, and went out to meet him.

Clean and tidy, she could see he was older than she'd supposed, but still no more than thirteen or fourteen. Her lips pursed.

'Come in the kitchen,' she said. 'I'll make us a drink.'

They sat at opposite ends of the scarred table, and wrapped their hands around steaming mugs. The boy didn't volunteer any information, and Jessie didn't ask. When she'd finished her own coffee, she said, 'There's a spare bedroom upstairs. First on the right, if you want to use it.'

Jessie didn't know whether he would go or stay, and in her own bed, she sank into a deep sleep for the first time in ages.

The boy stayed.

He rose and dressed in his borrowed clothes the next morning, and stood at the door of the one-time dining room watching while Jessie worked out. When she'd finished she made coffee, and passed a mug to the boy, along with a wad of money. 'If you are going to stay, nip out and fetch some bread and milk and stuff, we're totally out. If you want to go, that's fine, it's yours.'

When the boy had slipped out with the fist-full of money, she hadn't expected him to return, but when he did, she accepted it with equanimity.

'Don't you know better than to get in a car with two men?' she queried.

He shrugged. 'I just thought I'd get two lots of readies.'

'Men are animals. Singly they're vicious. In packs they kill.'

'Why did you help me?'

'I got mad.'

'I noticed,' the boy said.

They both smiled, and for some reason, Jessie felt good, she wasn't sure why. Maybe Ben had felt like that when he'd picked her up and put her back together.

'How long have you been prostituting yourself?' she asked. 'You don't look very old.'

'I'm fourteen, but I've been on the game for a few years. My dad and my granddad and my uncle all did it to me, since before I can remember. I just thought one day I might as well get paid, so I ran away.'

'And is it better?'

'Sometimes you get cold and hungry, but yes. The difference is I can choose not to sometimes.'

'Are you gay?'

'I don't know. I guess it's too late to worry about that, now. I don't know what else I could do.'

'Have you got a place to stay?'

'I've got a sort of shed no one's using. It's all right.'

205

'You can stay here. As long as you don't bring anyone back, and don't talk about me. I wouldn't like that. What's your name?'

'Jude.'

'You can call me Jessie.'

Chapter 39

As Redwall drove up towards Edward Stowleigh's Elizabethan mansion, he realised that the last time he'd visited he hadn't taken in just how exclusive the place was. It was now autumn, and the house was picture-postcard pretty, quaint, but at the same time reeking of age, money, and a lifestyle outside of his experience. The garage, probably a stable block, once, had four up-and-over doors, and renovated accommodation above it, for who? Chauffeurs, maids?

Strange that a child from a background like this should end up as a prostitute on the streets of London. Mind you, he'd heard of other rich kids rebelling in strange ways: marrying jobless drunken bums, become terrorists, whatever, as if being rich was a stigma that had to be obliterated at all costs. Was that what Jessie was doing? But being rich didn't seem to be her problem, not if she truly had stolen a bundle of drug money, as rumour suggested.

There was a new Rolls Royce on the drive, a rich, dark blue this time. Made a change from silver, he supposed, but with the personalised number plate it was hard to tell what year it was. Even so, it was worth more than his house. He wondered why he minded so much.

Edward Stowleigh opened the door, as he had all but five years ago. He'd grown a few grey hairs, and the little-boy charm that was still so very evident on the box seemed to have slipped a little more than one would have expected in five years. Edward now looked all his age, and more. But obviously unaware of the slightly unfavourable impression, Edward, blasted a professional welcoming smile, held out his hand, and drew Redwall into the house. Nothing much had changed here. The décor was the same, the furniture was the same, and the same ancestors stared from the walls.

'Can I get you a drink?' he asked, waving a hand at a tray of bottles and cut glass.

Redwall experienced a distinct sense of déjà vu, and answered as he had then, 'No, thanks.'

'On duty, officer?' Edward quipped.

'I'm on duty, but I don't drink.'

'I take it this is not a social visit?'

'No. As you obviously suspected, it's about Jessie.'

'It's been a few years, Inspector. You're not now telling me you've finally traced her?'

Edward Stowleigh turned, poured himself a whiskey, and Redwall had the distinct impression he was, in some way, hiding himself behind the light sarcasm and the rather generous glass of spirits.

'I only wish I did know where she was. We seem only ever to know where she's been. Your daughter has the McCavity syndrome.'

'McCavity?'

'Elliot: 'but when you reach the scene of the crime McCavity's not there,' etcetera.'

'Ah, yes; and then there was a bit about a monster of depravity, if I recall right?' Edward said.

Redwall flushed. 'I didn't mean to imply... Well, it's just that once more she has been put, possibly put, at the scene of a crime, but has, again, disappeared into thin air.'

'Frustrating, isn't it? What has she been up to this time, do tell.'

Redwall was slightly unnerved by the vitriol behind Edward's light-hearted words. The man who had, just a few years ago, thrown a lot of money and angst into trying to trace his much-loved daughter, now talked about her as though he wished she would crawl back beneath the stone she'd been hiding under all these years.

He said, mildly, 'I'm well aware of the amount of time and money you spent looking for her after she turned up that last time. I'm only sorry it bore no fruit.'

'Yes, well. We're all sorry about that.'

There it was again, that hint of aggression, that underlying feeling he wanted to say something entirely different.

The man's feelings had probably undergone some drastic changes over the years of his daughter's disappearance. Something like that could never leave a family without scars, and it took people in different ways.

He tried to show that he understood. 'I've always thought this kind of loss is worse than death. You have hope, but you also have hopelessness. At least when a person dies you bury them and get on with your life. This kind of thing leaves people in limbo. It's not easy.'

Edward took the initiative. 'Please, Inspector. Sit down. I apologise for my attitude. As you say, this has not been easy. It continues to be not easy.'

Redwall explained about the old man's murder in the New Forest, and about the possibility that Jessie had been living there for nearly five years.

'With this old man?' His brows were raised.

'Not in that way. I believe, from what we since learned, that he treated her like a daughter. As an ex-army man, it seems fairly likely he also taught her some survival skills.'

'Like what?'

'Ben was a Master in the oriental arts. A black belt, in at least three forms of self-defence, including Shotokan karate and Kendo, the one that uses a Katana, a Japanese sword. He's taught her something, but we have no idea what, or how far he went.'

'Christ! My angry little Lizzie with a sting in the tail? I wouldn't have recommended it. Meditation, maybe, or yoga. Aren't these forms of self-defence supposed to be about self-control? A thing that Lizzie, to my knowledge, never achieved. You say the old man was killed. How? Did she do it?'

'Ben was murdered. He was shot, but the police don't think she killed him. They have reason to believe she had developed a fondness for him.'

'That puts me in my place, doesn't it?' he commented bitterly, then sighed. 'It takes it out of you, all this emotional trauma. If she developed a bond with this old man, and if he helped her in some way, then I should be pleased, but it's painful, all the same.'

'I'm sorry. It must be hurtful, but it seems he kept her safe for five years, away from drugs and prostitution. So hope is not lost, and the police are actively seeking her again, mainly because it's likely she has information about Ben, or his death. They suspect she may have seen his murderer, or even gone off looking for him herself.'

'Christ. That's what I meant. She never could hold her temper. She'll end up in prison, yet.'

'Or dead; and that's what I would like to avoid, as I'm sure you would, too. A vigilante out on the streets isn't something that makes me happy, either. I'd rather justice was done in the proper way.'

'So do they have any idea where she went?'

'None, but as she's surfaced again, and is out on her own, I wondered whether you would be interested in helping us to find her. Run a plea on the television for sightings, for instance.'

Edward's lips pursed. 'Off the record?'

'No one's taking notes.'

'I don't know why, but Lizzie hates me. She ran away from here labouring under some vast sense of injustice that I still don't understand. A plea from me is going to do more harm than good, but she is still my daughter. I would very much prefer it if you could simply keep me informed of your actions, and if at some stage you find her, then I'll give you whatever help you need. Financial, or otherwise, but I would rather she didn't know it came from me. It would just make her go underground again.'

In spite of the new realisation that his earlier empathy for Edward Stowleigh had somehow dissipated, a hint of sympathy surfaced. Here was a father who didn't know where he'd gone wrong, and he'd a chance to put it right in the long term without her knowing, his philanthropic actions speaking louder than words.

Redwall now knew just how devastating it was to not have that chance. To have his child taken from him with no chance to redress whatever mix-ups had happened during the stresses of normal living.

'It's very brave of you to talk to me like this,' he said gently. 'We all make mistakes, God only knows. I'll remember what you said when we find her. Time has been known to heal such rifts.'

Edward shook his head as though he doubted it, but his next words were still positive.

'Would it help if I got that gumshoe onto it again?'

'I doubt it, but if it makes you feel better, do so.' He threw Edward a quizzical glance. 'You never know. They do sometimes discover things because they're not bound by some of our rather restricting codes of practice.'

That television smile went off like a flashbulb. 'Like ethics, honour, integrity, privacy that kind of thing?'

'Got it in one.' Redwall stood up and offered his hand. 'I really don't think there's anything else I can tell you, unless you have any questions?'

'None, Inspector. Thank you for coming, and please keep me informed. Any time of night or day, I'll make myself available for your call.'

Chapter 40

In Jude Jessie found a kindred spirit, and his presence gradually altered her perception, made her aware of the companionship that she'd lacked over the last months. She also found it an irritation, because he was always asking questions

'What did you come here for?'

'Looking for some people.'

'What for?'

'To kill them.'

'Why?'

'None of your goddam business.'

And later, 'Where did you come from?'

She glared at him, and he backed off, hands raised. Once out of reach, he asked, 'Will you teach me some of that kicking-shit?'

'I haven't got time.' She saw his crestfallen look, and relented. 'But I can teach you something that would help.'

But even if she didn't answer his questions, she couldn't stop his endless flow of information. About himself, the people he'd been with, his likes and dislikes, and what he really wanted to do when he got some dosh together.

'See, I want to be a chauffeur.'

'What for?' she asked blankly.

'I don't know, but I don't want to be on the streets all my life. It just seems like a nice thing to be. A smart uniform, smart car, learn how to drive fancy and do spins and things. You know.'

'You mean be a bodyguard?'

'Yeah, that, too.'

She learned of other women who had passed through his short life: his mother, who had allowed her boyfriends to use him; the scared social worker who had done more harm than good, earning Jude a whipping when she interfered; and a whore whose sympathy had given him the will to run.

Jessie found herself yanked a notch out of her depression by this new relationship. It wasn't as if Jude asked for anything from her, quite the opposite. He was pretty self-sufficient, obtaining money and goods with the ease of long practice. He never asked for money, or helped himself to any, despite the fact he'd found her stash of money. She respected his need for independence, but somehow his exuberance for life, and his ability to get into scrapes made her unwittingly take on the role of guardian.

He arrived back at the house one day on a motorbike, and proudly took her out to show it to her. Jessie, for the first time, lost her temper.

'If you have to steal,' she raged, 'Why the hell park it right outside my front door? Do you want to bring the pigs here? Have you got no bloody sense?'

He looked aggrieved, and sullenly tipped it from the stand, and threw a leg over the bench seat. The set of his thin shoulders betrayed defiance mingled with the anger of being caught in the wrong.

'Wait!' Jessie called.

He looked up from fastening the helmet under his chin.

'I've never been on one of those.'

It was only a small bike, for Jude hadn't yet reached his full height or maturity of stature. He was as tall as Jessie and would probably overtake her one day in both height and strength, but presently he was lanky and lacking in muscle, and had picked a bike to steal that suited that frame.

He grinned, never one to hold on to anger, and she climbed on. They rocketed off as he put the clutch in too quickly, nearly doing a wheelie down the slope towards a housing estate.

Jessie burst out laughing.

It was the first time she'd laughed since Ben died. By the time they abandoned the bike Jessie realised how stupid she'd been, going out without a helmet was asking to be stopped by the police, but she was also hooked.

She decided to get one herself, one with a bit more power and less flashy plastic-work. It would actually get her around the city faster than running, and was more versatile than a car in a city choked on cars. It was then Jude told her he knew where to get a good bike real cheap, from a bloke he knew.

'He can do papers, driving licences, too, if you need one.'

She shook her head. She would use the one Ben gave her. Anthea Gray, why not? No one else knew about it, after all.

'What else does this friend of yours do?'

'Passports. Exams. Anything.'

'You're a mine of information. Who else do you know who does stuff like that?'

'I know a good fence if you're into jewellery,' he offered, then cast a sidelong glance. 'Or a man who launders. You should sort out that paper trail before it's useless.'

She hadn't thought of that. She would happily burn it all, except it was useful, and meant she didn't have to steal, or fence goods as Jude suggested. Up to now she'd just been using the cash in hand, there was a lot of it, after all, but Jude's words triggered a new thought.

The bank issued different notes every few years, and these ones had been around for over five. He was right, she should do something with it while she could. She asked him who she needed to speak to. He said he'd speak to the man first.

Then she asked, 'Do you know men who deal in

214

drugs, big stuff, importers?'

He looked cagey. 'You into drugs, Jessie?'

'No.'

'Good. That's heavy shit. That's the guys you want to kill?'

'Maybe,' she said warily, not liking his intuitive understanding.

'I'll just listen out. I don't aim to ask, not about that kind of stuff. But I don't know what your lay is, Jessie.'

'Nor do I,' she finally admitted. 'I don't know what I'd be good at. I've never stolen cars or bikes. I don't know how to. In fact, I've never stolen anything except that money.'

'Do you want to learn?'

She shrugged. 'Why not.'

Jude immediately slipped into the role of mentor, taking Ben's place. He had jimmied locks at seven years of age, and gone on to more subtle methods of illegal entry at nine or ten. Not only that, he knew how to assess a place for possible value; he knew how to tell which alarms were just dummies, and, most importantly, he knew what to steal that would make the most cash with the shady dealers in stolen property. There was no point lifting something valuable if you couldn't move it on.

Jessie was impressed.

She was also a good pupil.

Time didn't dull the remoteness she felt for life, but the hurt part of her found a corner in her mind, lurking, claws sheathed, as other parts blossomed, and to an extent she began to enjoy the role she was playing. Ben had told her life was a pantomime, and a shallow one at times, but to survive it you had to be in control, not allow fate to rule you, but make use of the things fate sent you.

If Ben had been right, Jude was something fate meant her to have. She wanted to write her own script, direct the pantomime, and to call the curtains in her own time. He opened the door to a new stage, letting

215

her into a different world: that of thieves, fences, and dealers.

That scene was infested with drugs, too, so it suited her purpose. She was interested in getting to know who and where, but was never tempted to use. Once Ben had dried her out, she had no intention of letting anyone do that to her ever again. Drugs were a mugs' game, and she was out of it. She'd worked out that where drugs were concerned, the rich chose to be stupid, but others were forced into it to keep them under control, as she'd been. If she gave it much thought, she hated pushers and money-hungry power-seekers with equal intensity, regardless of their apparent status in society. They were all cut from the same cloth, using everyone else as their own personal rafts on the river of dirty money that kept them afloat.

And it seemed that the people who were involved in importing were not at the bottom of society's social pyramid. People like her father, with their houses, seemingly bonafide sources of income, and unimpeachable pedigrees were the worst of the lot, because their veneer of glamour hid hypocrisy.

She wasn't bothered about working within the law. It wasn't law that was an ass, it was the people who followed it like lambs, knowing the people who promoted it most fiercely were those who made full use of any available loopholes.

That was what Ben had been teaching her, in those long, silent lessons: you had to know and understand *self,* but you also had to understand how society worked, so that *self* could slip through the net, bypassing society's ineffectual pretence at following its own rules.

It was what her father did, after all.

Jessie, for the last few years had lived, by and large, in a time-slip, but now her worlds had collided – the past and present.

But she was now equipped to cope.

She was afraid of neither people nor authority,

216

because there was always a way out.

Her life was her own to dispose of, and the ability to destroy something gave you ultimate power over it.

Chapter 41

As Jessie developed her outward persona, men began to take interest, but she kept them all at arm's length, just sounding them out for contacts in the drug world, for the names on Vince's list. So far she'd found not a single one of the people she really wanted to kill. But if Ben had taught her nothing else, he'd taught her patience and dedication to the task in hand.

Jessie never stayed long in the house, she slept there, trained there as well as she could in the cramped space, and ate her food there.

Jude disappeared often, sometimes for days on end, always returning, but never offering any explanation, nor was one asked for. She was vaguely pleased to have her space back at those times. That he was back into prostitution, she didn't doubt, but he'd learned something from his mistake.

He now assessed his clients more carefully, and after the experience that in all probability would have ended in his death, armed himself with a knife. Jessie tried to teach him how to wield it to effect, but whether he would when time came, she wasn't sure. Jude's biggest asset and his biggest shortcoming was his absolutely passive nature.

He hated violence of any kind.

Jessie did try to teach him a few tricks for self-protection, but he would squeak and jump back if she was anything less than gentle. As he didn't have the inclination or the patience to learn any other of Ben's lessons, Jessie carried on fighting her invisible opponent in solitude.

Taking Jude's advice, she set about disposing of the contents of her kitbag. Dressing with care, and using her accent to open bank doors, she set up various accounts in the name of Anthea Gray, and started to deposit a few thousand here or there at weekly intervals, no more than she could earn in reasonable employment. Over time she could gradually move the money around and pull it together, but for now, little and often seemed a safe bet; but after a few weeks she realised it wasn't disappearing fast enough.

Jude set up a meeting between herself and an unsavoury man with a receding hairline, called Mr Smith, whose well-manicured hands were probably deep in shit, and who probably wasn't called Mr Smith at all. He knew where he could sell the bonds, he said, rubbing his hands, and advised her to invest the bulk of the money in a property, which he could facilitate without the money hitting a bank account in her name.

She'd been half inclined to burn the bonds, wondering if they'd lead the dealers back to her, when it occurred to her that triggering an alarm somewhere was exactly what she needed to end the present stalemate.

She didn't know who they were, but if they came looking for her, she would. And if they didn't, well, job done, bonds laundered. She gave him all the bonds, which he quickly transferred into significantly less cash than the value written on the paper, and banked it in a client holding account against the day she found a property to invest it in. She didn't trust him, but guessed he dealt with enough bad guys and illicit money to be afraid to rook her beyond what had been agreed.

Again with Jude's help, Jessie bought a motorbike, a Yamaha 750 that was several years old. It wasn't too big for her physique, and it wasn't so heavy that she couldn't recover on a corner taken at speed. For inner city use, it was better than some growling monster that wanted a freeway.

The bike lent new-found freedom. It enabled her to reach further out into the Birmingham suburbs, both to steal for the hell of it, and to carry on her search for the drug syndicate, which still remained elusive.

Chapter 42

Jude had been absent for a couple of weeks when Jessie found herself pulling into his favourite pub, realising with irritation she was actually worried about him.

She didn't need that kind of complication.

The Old Fox was frequented mostly by the local gay-male community. Whether Jude picked his clients up from there, or felt safe amongst them she didn't know, but the regulars seemed to have a soft spot for the under-age prossy with the eyes of a deer.

She'd hardly been welcomed with open arms until Jude let them know she'd saved his life from a bad trick, and then they'd done a strange about-turn, accepting her into their fraternity with an openness she found confusing. It was weird being in a crowd of men who didn't make sexual advances, but comfortable. She was further tolerated as although Jude boasted of his friendship with her, she presented no threat to his business relationships.

The pub, strangely, also attracted an element of motorcyclists, a group of men who were not gay, but somehow didn't challenge the gay community. They didn't frequent the place often, seemingly descending at random on one of the few pubs that catered for their grease-and-leather attire, which wasn't so very different from that which the gay community preferred.

On their part, the gays were happy to gaze with un-reciprocated admiration upon the broad shoulders of the bikers, knowing they were out of bounds. It was a friendly and tolerant attitude that Jessie hadn't expected from either group, one she found hard to

221

understand.

This evening, she was greeted in a familiar and friendly manner by some of the regulars, and one of them bought her a drink.

'Have you seen Jude around?' she asked.

'He's OK,' the man replied, and she didn't ask further.

A beautiful young man with wide-eyes and a pout came up to Jessie's companion, put his arms around him, and stared possessively up at the taller man.

Jessie shook her head and grinned.

The tall man winked as he turned away, and Jessie found herself standing, for a moment, alone. Music pulsed out into the night, and she leaned against the wall, eyes half-closed, appeased by the knowledge that Jude was, this time, all right.

When the voice asked if she wanted another pint she didn't realise it was speaking to her at first, then her eyes focused on a leather-clad man who stood before her. He asked again, and Jessie saw interest and speculation in his gaze. He was of the biker-fraternity; definitely not gay.

'I'll buy myself one when I'm ready,' she said in a tone that would have frozen ice.

The man shrugged and turned away.

Once his attention was elsewhere Jessie really looked at him. He was big, but not with over-developed muscles, and not with rolls of fat or an overflowing beer-gut. He was just large: big boned, long-legged, built like a bear. He wore a leather jacket and the obligatory oil-stained jeans, but there wasn't a hint of aggression in his stance, his manner, or his speech.

She wasn't quite sure why she looked, but the way he'd turned so easily from her was almost an insult. Unreasonably, after spending so much time developing an unbreachable wall around herself, she was annoyed he'd given up so easily.

Jessie cuddled her empty glass, and wondered why she cared. He seemed relaxed with the other bikers, they were laughing now at some anecdote of his, and it seemed as if he'd forgotten her presence totally. He didn't need her any more than she needed him.

Then, as if sensing her gaze, he swung his head and caught her stare full on. Irritated to have been caught looking, she was even more annoyed when a faint flush rose to tinge her cheeks. It was doubtful whether anyone else would have seen it, but she pushed herself away from the wall, angrily going back out to her bike. He'd ruined her evening, and now she had to face the problem of what to do, where to go.

Now would be a good time to work out, get rid of that sense of frustration that was building up. She needed to get on with her life plan, such as it was, but she couldn't kill people she couldn't find.

She straddled her bike to put her helmet on, staring into the distance for a moment before standing absently on the kick-start, causing the engine to throb easily into life.

Perhaps she should steal something, for the hell of it. She realised she was getting quite proficient at recognising good hits. Little things gave them away, like the style of the curtains, the car, and the routines of the owners. She would watch a prospect several times before going in, and had learned, lately, to recognise those who were away at weekends. It was easy if you had the gall, to go in at your leisure to take what you wanted.

The returns on these jobs were not important to her, they were simply part of her present, on-going education. Often she would steal some small item that wouldn't be missed, the house-holders never knowing they had been burgled. It was a challenge, a game. She ran her list of prospects through her mind, then dismissed them. Without Jude to share the experience, it didn't seem worthwhile. Recalling her life with Ben a wave of loss hit her.

She was actually lonely.

As she pulled on her gloves another engine broke

223

into life, a beam of light spilling her shadow along the road before her. She glanced behind, startled. In spite of the light in her eyes, she couldn't mistake the bulk of the person who straddled the bike thirty yards behind her. A flash of adrenaline rushed through her body.

She wasn't bored anymore. He had no more been ignoring her than she had him. Jessie's fear had always been of the unknown, not the challenge or the threat itself. That she could deal with as it arrived, she knew, and it had now arrived, along with a fleeting white smile flashed from the darkness behind her.

She pulled away slowly, and he pulled out behind her. She drove steadily for a few miles, turning this way and that, not trying to lose him, but just seeing how persistent he was going to be. He didn't alter the gap between them by an iota. Then she accelerated through an amber light, and her shadow followed through a light that must surely have been red.

A smile lit her face.

She wondered what sort of bike he had. She didn't like not knowing, so without warning, she did a U-turn, carried on around in a circle, and came up to drive alongside him. He watched her progress. As if he'd known what she was doing, he neither changed gear, nor looked as if he was going to brake and turn to follow what might have been an evasive manoeuvre. She looked over at the bike in the dark. It was a Moto Guzzi, but she wasn't familiar with the model.

'What cc?' she called over the noise of the two bikes.

'Thousand,' he answered, his teeth gleaming once again in the darkness.

Jessie calculated the odds. He had a bigger, newer bike, an advantage for speed alone, but hers was lighter, more manoeuvrable in a city environment. He was stronger which, despite what anyone said, was useful when you were throwing a bike around corners, but she knew the back streets of Birmingham like the back of her hand, which she doubted he would, along with every footpath, tow-path and lane, until she could

224

have done them blindfolded. And all those places she'd run, she could drive. No, she wasn't scared, she was exhilarated.

The two bikes travelled side by side, as if their riders were bonded by companionship, and Jessie wondered if she was being a fool. If she went back to the pub there were a lot of people there who would stand before her in a crisis. The gay community would close ranks to protect the woman who had protected one of their own.

If she accepted the challenge and won, she would have lost him, so the unknown man would no longer be a threat. If she accepted the challenge and didn't lose him, what was the penalty? Would he force her off the road, off her bike? What did he want? Was she the prize?

She smiled fractionally to herself. If he thought so, he'd no idea what he would be letting himself in for. Of course, she could simply climb off the bike and floor him right now. Big as he was, he wouldn't be expecting it. The man didn't pressure in any way. He just drove, glancing sideways at her from time to time, waiting for her to decide. Jessie shrugged mentally. What the hell?

She raised a gauntleted fist.

She pulled away from him and drove faster now, not at any great speed, but just to test his knowledge of the roads. She took turns with no indication, no warning. He followed, not close enough to overshoot, yet not far enough away to be outmanoeuvred. He drove easily, carelessly almost, as if the bike were a part of himself. Frequently she turned her head to assess his knowledge. She could tell by the way he tested the angle of the bends, by the almost imperceptible flick of the head as he glanced aside at unknown streets that flared out of the darkness, that he didn't know Birmingham as well as she did.

The adrenaline that had overtaken Jessie now faded. She slowed her breathing, and repeated the litany of concentration and focus, as if she were about to start a free fight with Ben. Her muscles unwound, her mind

225

expanded with the freedom of flight, her body-awareness ready for battle.

She turned into a pedestrian precinct. He followed without hesitation. A few startled night-walkers stopped and jumped out of the way as the two bikes throbbed illegally over the broken paving stones. Someone screamed abuse, but she ignored it. Then out of some sort of childish devilment she wound her bike in an out of a set of bollards, wondering if he would follow. He did, and riding full circle, she could see amusement in every line of his body as he manoeuvred the big bike proficiently around the obstacles without putting a foot to the floor.

Then she opened the throttle. She pulled away fast, the bike growling with the pleasure of being raced. Down into the High Street, past the cinema, up through Broadwhite road, in and out of the horn-blaring traffic, towards the tall brick warehouses that used to be the mainstay of industrial commerce, and out towards the canal. There, she slipped over a bank onto a bridleway, flying over the brow of a mound, slithering, foot to the floor, into a right-hand bend where a footpath disappeared through a hedge. There were no pedestrians here, at this time of night.

He kept to the road.

She sensed the distance building up between them. So, he knew this footpath, knew there was no gate, no opening until she reached the other end. He was taking a chance she wouldn't simply do an about turn and run in the opposite direction, but it was too soon to concede, and if she did he would assume it to be through fear, and that she couldn't allow. As the bike flew over the kerb and back out onto the road the wheels lifted and the engine screamed.

Knowing that on the straight he would catch up, she made the most of the bike's speed for just a few hundred yards, then slammed the brakes on, and rammed it into a left, then a right immediately. A small car coming down the hill screeched to a halt and

226

stalled. She caught the oval shock of the startled driver's mouth out of the corner of her eye. The biker was barely in sight as she crossed the road, belting down into the maze of streets below. She saw the flicker of lights follow her, and knew that he was now desperately trying to close the gap.

She wouldn't be at all surprised if by now someone had called the cops. Two bikes screaming through a residential area would cause annoyance, if nothing else. She threw the bike up a double kerb and onto a steep and winding sidewalk that paralleled the road around the hill, separated from it by a good four foot drop and a row of iron railings. That was when the biker caught her up, she on the path above, he on the road below. She could sense his indecision. Should he backtrack and jump the kerb, or should he keep going, hoping she would have to drop back on the road around the bend? This was the old part of town, a maze of streets barely wide enough for cars, and he didn't know the area. Logic should have told him to go back, but to do so meant having her out of sight, so he didn't.

Jessie slowed and turned into a tiny pedestrian walkway, the wide handlebars just fitting between the stone walls, and she bumped the bike down the ranks of steps that lay between two sloping widths of old paving.

She heard the other bike roar away behind her. He was putting speed on, following the road around, hoping to find a turning to take him down into the street below. His instinct was right, but Jessie knew she would be there before him. She shot out into the main road, once again crossing it with a complaining squeal of tyres, and belted into the winding streets beyond a row of local shops.

She could hear him still there, following, but he must have been working on instinct alone, for she could no longer see his lights. Crashing down onto the main dual carriageway once more, hoping to cross it while he was still out of sight, either she was unlucky, or his instinct was on overdrive. The Guzzi shot out of a side turning behind her.

Seeing her at the last instant, the man threw the bike into the bend with such force that she heard the screech of metal on the road as his exhaust bottomed out.

Before he pulled out of the bend, Jessie had turned up the steep hill to the right, bumped over the pavement at the top, and crossed into a pedestrian walk between two cul-de-sacs. In front there was a row of back gardens. She slowed down, killed the engine, coasted through an open gate, and dropped the bike and herself flat on the ground.

As she hit the deck, the Guzzi shot through the pedestrian way with a flash of lights. He'd been very close; too close for that last minute decision. Her breathing slowed. She heard the angry growl of the engine as the man knocked his bike into neutral.

Then he killed the engine.

He was listening. She hoped the people whose garden she'd invaded were too engrossed in the blaring TV to worry about the outside world. Finally the engine throbbed into life again, and he pulled away. She heard him stalking the streets up and down, moving further and further away, seeking his lost prey.

She waited for quite a while, listening to the interminable babble of a game show from within, and the distant sounds of traffic around. Then finally she pushed the bike back out onto the road, free-wheeled down to the main road and glancing suspiciously as she went, bump-started the engine, at the foot of the hill, to drive home.

She spent a disturbed night thinking about the chase through the dark streets, and nearly as much time visualising the rugged face of the large stranger. The chase had been exciting because it was distanced from personal contact, but now she felt all the more lonely, and was angry with herself for being emotionally confused by the encounter. Almost, she was annoyed with the big stranger for not winning, for in the solitude

228

of her home, later that night, unknown aches burned inside while her consciousness fought the treacherous instincts.

Some part of her wanted to know what it felt like to be held by a man you wanted to hold you, but despite what Ben had told her, she knew that if he'd made any attempt to do so, she would probably have killed him.

Chapter 43

David Stone met with a blank wall when he tried to find the girl. He'd thought of nothing else for the last three days, and was becoming consumed by her, which distraction, at present, wasn't good for his health. He'd never met anyone like her before, and didn't know how to classify her. Her attitude towards the law was flagrantly dismissive, and through little more than intuition he was pretty sure she operated on the shady side of the law, but in what way he had no idea.

Her level of camaraderie with the bum bandits in the pub was unusual, and that chase, which had been amusing and probably stupid, had been entertaining.

He smiled in recollection.

She'd been testing him, seeing how far he would go, and at that moment he would have blown everything to prove how fascinated he was. She was vibrant, beautiful and probably dangerous as a tiger, and he was smitten in way he'd never before experienced. He didn't just want to have her, he wanted to know her. Though she was also antagonistic, she'd challenged him with a capacity for enjoyment he hadn't expected. He was, when all was said and done, confused.

What she did for a living he didn't like to guess, and where she lived he would love to know, but whatever it was about her, she wasn't a woman he could forget in a hurry. And the knowledge that she'd actually lost him, on a bike, was irritating.

He wanted her as he'd never wanted a woman before.

His reaction hadn't been sensible, when he was in a

pub specifically to move stock, but the desire to knock the superior and cold expression from her face had been overwhelming. Had he simply meant to scare her, knock the supercilious expression from her face? He wasn't sure. Encroaching sobriety told him she wasn't scared, never had been.

Initially, he had been going to follow her home, a thought born of one drink too many, added to the insult of being spurned. After following her for a bit to put the wind up her, he would probably have driven on, but she'd called his bluff.

He realised now that she didn't scare that easily, and was all the more intrigued. Once the challenge had been accepted, and the rush of adrenaline had warmed him to the core, he'd realised she could lose him any time unless he cheated, knocked her off, or something. That was a development he hadn't expected. He also hadn't expected to be haunted by her to the point he could think of little else.

Chapter 44

The following day Jessie's thoughts shunted to the reasons for being here at all: the names in Vince's book. She'd met plenty of street sellers, and bought plenty of hits, flushing them down the loo when she returned, but still she'd heard nothing, not a rumour, not a hint, of any of the names on Vince's list. How long should she stay in Birmingham watching and waiting? Five years, ten? Perhaps her best bet would be to go back to London, start again from that end.

She took the Katana from its hiding place, and stilled her mind. Straight backed, feet spread, knees bent, she drew it in a single fluid movement across her body. She knew the movements like ballet, she knew the reasons from Ben's litany of explanation, day in day out.

And she knew the Way of the Warrior. Practice, practice, practice, until you don't hold a blade, you are one with the blade. The ultimate goal was not to win, but to kill the enemy. Otherwise the sword should not be drawn.

Whereas during real fighting the blade would be a blur of silver, it now moved with slow precision, training the inner self to know the movement down to microscopic level. She lifted the blade slowly, out and across her opponent, not to kill, but to slice the forehead open in a shallow cut to allow his own blood to blind him.

It was a game you played, an insult to your opponent. An opening move. Then slice down to sever a cut in his cheek. Step back, allow him a movement, and counter it, sending the tip of the Katana to slit a vein in his arm on the way back. You pricked him like a pincushion, you made your opponent your toy. You made him know he was going to die, because you were the Master of the Art and he'd challenged you.

And you had the ultimate power, because you were not afraid to die. Death was already assumed.

Her movements slowly increased in speed until eventually the murderous blade was spinning around in blurred speed, the hand nearest the hilt firm, the one at the rear pushing and pivoting the blade with a force that would decapitate a person in the wrong place at the wrong time. Sweat rose, her breathing increased with the effort, but her body was in total control.

Eventually the sword came to an abrupt, planned halt before her, parallel to the floor. She bowed to her invisible opponents, and put the Katana gently down. She cleaned the handle of sweat and the blade from any speck of dust before returning it to the old scabbard with a measure of reverence.

Ben still lived, in her.

Still there was no word from Jude, and she admitted to herself she found it hurtful when he made no effort to let her know that he was still alive. Perhaps Ben had felt like that about her, she reflected, caring about her, never knowing whether she cared back. She stared at the bare floorboards of her barren living room as if she'd never seen them before.

Chapter 45

The next day Stone's boss hauled him over the coals for fetching the wrong car, and he reflected grimly that he would have to snap out of his daydreams or it was going to cost him more than a reprimand. He was both chauffeur and bodyguard, when not being used as a courier, and had his talents been required, any lack of concentration was as likely to end in his own death as that of his employer.

'What the fuck's the matter with you today, Stone?' Chalmers asked.

'It's a girl,' he admitted honestly.

His boss glared at him a moment, then his features relaxed a little. 'Then go out and roger her, you silly cunt, before you end up without a job.'

'You don't mind?'

'What do you think I am, inhuman? Just don't let me catch you blabbing to any bird about my affairs, that's all.'

'It would be more than my life's worth,' Stone agreed, knowing he wasn't lying.

He'd worked for Chalmers for three years, now, taking over the job from that nasty little shit, Cary, whom, the boss said, might have the inclination to protect him, but was simply not big enough to scare people.

His boss was no nice guy.

He needed people to be scared of him, and scared of the people who worked for and protected him. Stone grimaced, for Cary was a much scarier person than himself all round, even though he didn't look it. He was an evil little sadist, in fact.

But, regarding the girl, Chalmers was right, the logic was simple. He wanted her, and the only way he was going to straighten himself out was find out whether she interested back.

A seduction was always good fun, even if it didn't bear fruit. The fact that it was likely to turn into a challenge itself just added spice to the adventure.

In his mind, she was his already, she just didn't know it.

He needed a girl with attitude, not some simpering Barbie, and she was that all right, all muscle and agro. He'd bet his bottom dollar she worked out some. No little Marks-&-Sparks floozy with high heels, but a real go-getter with a temper and a bike, even though it was a bit of a pussy bike. And once he saw what she could do with it, he'd to concede her choice. She couldn't have thrown his Guzzi around as she could the light-weight easy-rider.

He wanted to find her, big time, but the only place he'd seen her was the Old Fox, and for some reason the bum bandits were all ganging together, not telling him a single thing about her. Strange in itself, that. They were not usually so accepting of a woman, and he wondered what she'd done to earn that level of close-mouthed protection. He'd only learned her name by overhearing it by accident.

Jessie.

He rolled the name possessively on his tongue, and liked the feel of it.

Stone knew that the sort of confusion that was presently playing havoc with his awareness could end up killing him, but he was unable to put a lid on it. In some hidden corner of his mind he'd hoped she would try to find him, but after several evenings of sitting in the Old Fox, drinking more than was good for him, he decided that she wasn't going to. If the truth were known, he was slightly peeved that she hadn't, sensing a kindred spirit in her love of adventure and lack of fear.

He could try to trace her through the bike, of course, he knew the number off by heart, but he had a suspicion it wouldn't be registered to her current address, or even to her.

And what would he do if it was stolen?

He didn't want to open that can of worms, he would have to have a good explanation handy as to how he'd found her address, so the starting point was obviously the Old Fox, which was where he'd first discovered her.

Eventually, because he wasn't shielded by the other bikers he hung out with, he found himself the target of a persistent young man's attentions. The fool wouldn't take no for an answer until a broad-shouldered, bearded man with narrow eyes, interfered.

He shoved the indignant young man aside, and sat down next to Stone. Greeted with no more than a hard glance, he stared into his glass for a second.

'Just wondered what you were coming here for buddy, if you know what I mean.'

'Perhaps I just want a drink?'

The man shook his head. 'Not here.'

Stone looked fully at his companion, now. The man had sussed him out for a straight, and was probably trying to point out they'd all be happier if he buggered off, so to speak. He was definitely a fly in the K Y.

'I'm looking for a girl.'

'Here?'

Stone ignored the sarcasm.

'A tall fair-haired girl. Drives a bike.'

There was a small but significant silence. 'And what makes you think anyone here knows such a girl?'

'She's known here, I could tell. I met her a week ago Friday. I want to know how to find her.'

'Why?'

Stone opened his mouth to tell the other to mind his own business, but before he spoke he'd the sense to change his tune. He looked over with a lop-sided grin. 'I want to fuck her,' he said.

'Ah.'

'I can't help being straight, you know.'

'No, no, it's not that. It's just that she doesn't, at least, I don't think so.'

'Doesn't what?' Stone was confused.

'Fuck men.'

'She's a dyke?'

He was startled out of his complacency. That would account for her lack of interest in him, and perhaps gave him an insight into her strange tolerance for the gay community, but if that was the case, what a bummer.

The man gave another of those eloquent shrugs.

'Who knows what she is. Jude says that she comes to us because she feels safe, which tends to suggest she's been given a hard time by some man at some time. All we know for sure is that she saved him from a beating or worse, so we look after her if she's here. Not that she needs us to.'

'Who's Jude?'

He was cagey. 'A boy we know.'

Stone read between the lines. 'A prossy?'

'I never said so.'

'I've got no beef about it. What do you mean, she saved him?'

'He said she took on two men who were taking advantage of him, but he was probably exaggerating. Let me give you a bit of advice, big fella. Go find yourself a tart, because Jessie's not for sale. Rumour is she's looking for some guys, and not for what you were suggesting.'

'Who's she looking for?'

He thought.

'A guy called Porter, I think Jude said. Apparently she looked up all the Porters in the phone book and checked them out, but none of them turned out to be the one she wants.'

Stone felt coldness slide through his gut.

'Do you know why she's after this guy?'

237

'What are you, a cop?'

He shrugged. 'Curious, is all. I'll ask her myself, if I can find her. Do you know where she lives.'

'Nope. I guess Jude does, but he won't say. I think he's more than a little bit scared of her himself.'

'Maybe with good reason.'

'Maybe. Oh, and another thing.' His glance was candid. 'She doesn't like dealers. I mean *really* doesn't like dealers.'

'Point taken. I'll be careful. So where will I find this Jude?'

The man's face closed slightly. 'He's had troubles enough. You hurt him, you won't know what hit you.'

'I just want to find Jessie. That's the honest truth. I won't hurt your kid.'

He pondered for a moment, then shrugged. 'I guess she'll tell you to go to hell in her own way if you find her. Jude's hanging out in the Regency, these days. He's found some dude who pays well.'

'How will I know him?'

'Everyone knows him. Tall, thin afro kid with eyes to die for.'

Stone stood up. 'Buy you a drink?'

'No, just get out, eh?'

'Thanks.'

Chapter 46

The Regency might once have been a nice place, but just now it was a dive. A large, single room with a television dominated the ground floor with its torn, red Rexine seats and pitted tables.

The faded remains of an expensive flocked wallpaper still clung to the walls, yellow with cigarette smoke leftover from days gone by. Sawdust on the floor would have been appropriate, Stone thought in disgust, as he wandered up to the bar. They did have good draught beer, though, so it had some redeeming features. He sighed with true pleasure as he downed half the pint in one.

The man behind the bar smiled with effortless efficiency. 'Nice pint?'

'The best,' Stone agreed. He perched his backside on the barstool.

The bar-tender smeared the spillage around Stone's part of the bar with a greasy cloth.

'Passing through, are you?'

'Actually, I'm looking for someone. Chap called Jude. Do you know him?'

There was a brief pause, then the man said, 'Don't know a Jude.'

He turned his back on the man, and surveyed the bar. The men there were all old, seedy, and watching the television as if it was an obligatory end to a boring life.

The bar-keep's eyes had flicked around the room when he'd mentioned the boy's name. He hadn't asked what the kid looked like, and it was obvious that he knew exactly who Stone meant, and what he wanted him for. It was also obvious that the boy wasn't here.

Stone wandered into a corner, and from that vantage point he watched the evening drift away. Customers came and went, a strange mixture of clientele, as if some of them, like the bar, were left over from better times. The music box spouted tunes from time to time, obliterating the noise from the television, and the crowd talked louder to compensate for both.

It was running towards midnight, and beer was still flowing over the bar, when Stone felt eyes upon him.

He looked to the left, and saw Jude through the thinning crowd. It could have been no one else. The bar-keeper had his back to Stone, and was gesticulating towards the door behind the bar, but the boy shook his head adamantly. The bar-keep almost stamped his foot he was so angry, but the boy, his eyes meeting Stone's across the sea of people, silenced him with a gesture.

Looking around, the man saw Stone watching.

He stalked back to his bar, and ignored the boy pointedly. His body language was saying he'd tried, and if the little fool walked into trouble, it wasn't his fault.

The boy was tall and thin, had the face of a model, a mop of curly hair, and large doe-eyes. If he was as talented as he was good-looking, Stone thought, he would probably make enough to retire on early; that was if he didn't die in the meantime from aids, a violent customer, or drugs. Stone didn't move. He'd the feeling that the boy would bolt if he stood up, so he waited.

Jude came a few steps closer, hesitantly, and stopped, out of arm's reach. 'What do you want?' he said.

'What do you think?' Stone asked.

He shook his head. 'I know you from the Old Fox.'

Stone stretched back, and the boy jumped, startled. His whole body quivered with indecision, his inner radar, maybe, telling him to run.

'I'm looking for Jessie.'

'I don't know anyone of that name,' the boy denied,

and turned away.

Stone was out of the seat, and had grabbed Jude's arm before the boy could so much as lift a foot to run. For a large man he moved with deceptive speed. He spun Jude around, and shoved him into the seat behind the table. The boy gasped, but didn't cry out, used, perhaps, to being treated like an object. Stone put his bulk between the boy and escape, and his arm around the boy's shoulders. His left hand squeezed the thin wrist that strove ineffectively to free itself from his grasp.

The bar-tender walked purposefully towards them.

'Tell him to butt out,' Stone whispered into the boy's ear. No one else had thoughts other than disgust that they were being so blatant, but the boy did as he was told, with the flick of a finger. Stone's grip eased as the bar-keep sidled suspiciously away, muttering.

'You know her,' Stone said.

'Why do you want her? Is she in some kind of trouble?' The boy looked sideways at Stone. 'You've got the smell of a cop about you.'

Stone looked interested. 'Would the police like to find her?' he asked softly.

The boy winced at his mistake, and muttered, 'I don't know.'

Stone twisted the boy's arm behind his back, and held it there easily. The gasp of pain was smothered as soon as it was made. Jude didn't try to pull against Stone's strength, he tolerated the violence with acceptance and a touch of irritation. 'You don't have to break my arm.'

'Then talk.'

'Not until I know why.'

Stone let go of the arm, if he leaned on it any more he would have broken it, but he sensed the boy would let him do that rather than split on Jessie. It seemed that the whole lot of them wanted to protect her. Either that, or he was scared of her, just like the queer said.

'I met her the other night, that's all. I'd like to meet

241

her again.'

The boy rubbed his wrist, and stared at Stone. 'Does she want to meet you again?'

'I'd like the chance to ask her. That's all. I'm not out to hurt her.'

'She'll kill me if I say anything.'

'I'll kill you if you don't. And I'm here and she isn't. Why are you all so loyal, anyway? I heard a story, that she saved your arse, but it sounds a bit far-fetched.'

Jude was silent for a moment, then shook his head. 'It's true. I accepted a car job, two blokes. I'd know better now. She just happened to come by, and,' He hesitated, then shot a sour glance. 'She's not going to like this.'

'And?'

'She mashed one of the men into a wall, broke his neck, and put the other one in hospital. She said they were going to kill me. I think she was right.'

That didn't do anything but stir Stone's interest.

'Did she now? You know, I think I believe you. But, I'm being honest with you. I just fancy her. I want to see her, chat to her, fuck her, whatever. Isn't that OK with you? She can always say no.'

The large eyes widened with incredulity.

'She'll bite your head off and watch you bleed to death rather than let you touch her. She doesn't have normal feelings, man.' Then he gave a half-smile. 'She's off with the angels, somewhere. Perhaps she could do with a good lay, though. It might bring her back down to earth. But if you hurt her, you'll have the whole community down on your back.'

Chapter 47

Godfrey was slightly stunned when the name Jessie popped up on a routine, automated trawl which had been set up over a year ago, with little expectation of a catch. After a year of absolute blank silence, during which time he'd almost reluctantly decided the girl was probably long dead, someone had run a search on the name 'Jessie' through the police database, and the accompanying description could have fitted no one else.

'The query originated in Birmingham,' Oscar told him.

'Do we know who?'

'I traced it to Customs, but when I rang them I got an absolute brick wall.'

'We'll see about that.' Godfrey reached for the phone.

After an irritating half an hour spent crawling up the internal hierarchy, he ended up speaking to a woman called Deborah Madden. Although she didn't tell him exactly what her function was, he was pretty sure he'd reached the person who had run the search. He explained, briefly, about his interest in Jessie, adding that they wanted to speak to Jessie with regard to Ben's death.

'I can't tell you anything about her, I'm afraid,' she said.

'Can't or won't?'

'Can't, as it happens. We actually know nothing about her, hence the search, but what I will say, and this is absolutely confidential, is that we have an on-going operation here, and this girl seems to be implicated in some way.'

'You think she's a dealer or courier?'

'I don't know what she is, and that's the truth. But what I'm asking you to do, very politely, is back off. I'm not very clear about your capacity in the system...' she paused giving him time to answer.

'I appear to be in the same boat,' he answered dryly.

He could hear amusement in her voice as she realised they were at an impasse.

'Well, I will warn you that if you do anything to compromise something in the order of three years' work, not to mention the lives of certain of my agents, we will come down on you like the proverbial ton of bricks. You know that Customs have absolute power when it comes to a conflict of interests.'

Godfrey reflected that she hadn't come up against him before, but didn't put her wise on that point.

'Point taken. But if we were to find Jessie and lift her out of the equation, would it compromise anything?'

She was silent for a moment.

'Possibly not. She might even just be a free radical. Her name just popped up fairly recently on our radar in connection with a courier we're monitoring. If you can find her and make her disappear I don't think the people I'm tracking would lose any sleep over it.'

'I think we're in accord, then,' he said.

'And you'll keep me informed of any action? I'd also like to know the names of the individuals involved so that my team don't find themselves wrong-footed.'

'I can go along with that,' he agreed.

They exchanged mobile numbers and parted amicably enough, but as he put the phone down, Oscar, who had been listening to his side of the conversation, added his own thought.

'So, she's putting a spanner in the works of a customs operation? By accident, do you think?'

'Coincidences set my nose twitching. She's in Birmingham, for a reason, and I'd hazard a guess if she's getting in with some courier it's because she's found who she's looking for – or has a lead, anyway. And that means we have to move quickly.

'We need to tread carefully, we don't want to lead anyone else to her by accident. She's a highly volatile loose cannon with more guts than experience, but she's no fool.'

'So what are we going to do?' Oscar asked.

'Find her; quietly. I don't want to tread on any more toes than I have to. I'll call Chief Inspector Northolt of Birmingham Central and ask him to work with us on this. Once we know where she is, we'll decide how to handle it. My gut instinct is simply to pluck her quietly out of the system. Once we have her here we can decide how to handle things.'

'Do you think I ought to involve that Redwall chap?'

'Why?'

'He knows much more about her background than we do; met her father and all. He has a lot of empathy for her, and might just have some kind of insight when it comes to a confrontation. If he can handle it, of course.'

It was a sensible suggestion followed by a very valid question, Godfrey realised. After he'd tempered his initial dislike for Redwall's sloppy manner, he'd discovered the man had lost both his own kids within the space of two years, a motorbike accident taking his son in a fleeting second, Leukaemia paring his daughter away over two years, day by terrible day. The logic of that coincidence defied belief.

Some people were just unlucky.

No wonder he hadn't cared about what he looked like. Yet with his daughter not cold in her grave, he'd still cared enough about a child prostitute he didn't know to drive all the way to Southampton last year to try to help her.

'Good call,' he decided. 'He said he wanted to know if she turned up. I guess we owe him that. It might actually do him good. See if he wants in.'

245

Chapter 48

Northolt allocated a detective called Branlawe to be the liaison in Birmingham. He was at the station, waiting for them. He turned out to be a pleasant, middle-aged man with a loud laugh a ready smile, and a good track record. They met him in a tiny meeting room in Birmingham's central, along with Redwall, who had accepted the challenge without hesitation.

Godfrey ran through what he knew, which was little enough, though it had Branlawe leaning his chair back on two legs, listening avidly. When Godfrey stopped, he plunked the chair down decisively, and clasped his hands on the table. 'A karate-chopping blonde stunner of a girl? Shouldn't be difficult to locate, wouldn't you say?'

Redwall smiled. 'Put like that... She is, however, bright and, I would suspect, pretty determined. I doubt very much if we're going to find her walking up the high street punching people.'

Godfrey added, 'Of course, we're not entirely sure why she came to Birmingham in the first place, but she must have had a good reason.'

'It's obvious,' Redwall offered gently. He'd come post-haste at the invitation, his interest obviously not diminished by time or by his own tragedies. 'In fact, I should have thought of it before.'

They all looked at him with raised brows, but it was Godfrey who asked, 'It is?'

'Assuming the whisper was correct, the money she appropriated in London was destined for a drug consignment that came from Birmingham, though we never discovered anything to support that. But assume for a moment that it's true. In which case the drug syndicate won't have forgotten or forgiven. While she was with Ben she was effectively hidden, but now she's back out in the world, she's made herself visible again. She knows she'd be on the run from them for the rest of her life unless she takes them out.'

There was a stunned silence.

'Christ almighty,' Oscar said eventually, speaking for all of them.

'It's what Ben would have taught her,' Godfrey confirmed grimly. 'Take the initiative, don't let anyone else pull your strings; but I don't think he intended it to apply to drugs cartels. If you're right, Inspector, this could be amusing if it wasn't so serious. While they're down in Southampton and London looking for her, she's up here looking for them.'

'It's a possibility. Let's hope to Christ she doesn't find them.'

Oscar's phone went off, and ignoring Godfrey's glare, he exited the room, the phone glued to his ear. He was only gone for a brief moment, then waited just inside the door, obviously itching to speak.

'We're making assumptions, putting ideas on the table, I might be totally on the wrong track,' Redwall was reminding them, but it was clear no one believed that. 'Did the initial search on Jessie bring up anything at all? An address would be useful.'

'That would be too much to hope for. No, the search drew blank. If she's here at all, we don't have a clue where.'

'But I think we know who,' Oscar interrupted.

The sparkle in his eye made Godfrey suspicious. 'What do you mean? Have you been holding out on me?'

'No, Sir.'

He couldn't contain the grin that broke over his face. 'But when Jessie's name search was instigated, I discovered another search for a Virago motorbike at the

247

same time from the same log-on, and put a trace on it. It came up as registered to one Anthea Gray, which didn't really mean anything, but I thought it was worth checking out.'

Godfrey was annoyed. 'Deborah didn't mention that. Is it significant?'

'I had a hunch. I checked on our own database on any activity from Ben over the last few years, and got a hit. Ben obtained a driving licence for a female with blonde hair under the name Anthea Gray. We might have found it before, but weren't looking. We had the information there all along, in our own database. It's fully legal and accounted for, so wouldn't ring any bells if anyone stopped her.'

'Bloody hell.' Godfrey's hand slapped the table. 'Damn. Hell. Excellent. Well done, Oscar. Right: rent, purchases, convictions, bank accounts, anything under that name. Let's find her.'

'We can put out an AP on the bike, with a proviso to not make contact.' Branlawe suggested.

'Let's run the searches first,' Godfrey decided. 'I don't want her spooked by some zealous traffic cop. If she goes underground we might not find her again.'

'These drug importers you think she's looking for, do we know anything at all about them?'

'Not a thing. Birmingham was just a reference that cropped up in passing. I wasn't even sure it had any relevance until now. And now Jessie is here and we know there is some kind of drug bust going down, that's too much of a coincidence for me.'

Branlawe was silent for a moment, then said, 'OK. Here's another thing. This may be a long shot, but about the time you say this girl might have arrived in Birmingham a man was killed, and another badly injured. The man who died was a known thug, and Derke, the one who survived was also suspected of being involved in some rather underhand dealings. He got off lightly broken nose, smashed cheek and jaw.'

'Where's this leading?' Godfrey asked.

'Bear with me. We were never too sure about the details because the men were victims in the case and had to be treated as such, whatever we suspected. They were discovered the next morning by a jogger, and the car, a limo, was found a couple of miles away. Well, the official story on record is that they were hit by a gang of thugs, but we assumed it was a hit, or a falling-out amongst thieves. No one was ever convicted of the killing, we couldn't find any trace of a gang the like of which our man described, and Hughes' story varied quite dramatically from his first statement to the rest. In his first, unofficial statement, when he was still only half coherent, he said it was a girl who did it.'

Now he'd their full attention.

'As he was pretty badly concussed, we thought he was confused... but perhaps he wasn't. There was plenty of speculation as to why these two men were out together in that area at that time of night. The story about them just having a drink and a quiet business meeting in the back of a limo in a somewhat seedy location is thin. It didn't make sense at the time, but what if that was your girl? What if she actually found one of the dealers she was looking for?'

'You said the men were beaten?' Godfrey asked.

'They were, but not with weapons. As far as we could make out, the attacker or attackers just used fists and a handy brick wall. Could one female attack two grown men, one of them who we suspected to be pretty nasty himself, killing one, and seriously hurt the other? Is it possible?'

Godfrey grimaced. 'Just about anything is possible if you've been taught well.'

'Well, it's a long shot. I knew Derke's story was a load of hooey, but we never had anything except his word, and by the time he was out of hospital, other things got in the way, like his bloody solicitor. Shall we have another go at him?'

'It's worth an interview, I guess. Get him in. I'll do it, if you don't mind,' Godfrey offered.

Chapter 48

It was after one in the morning when Stone stopped his bike near a small end-of-terrace property. He pushed it down the last bit, the engine off, and prowled around the outside. His teeth bared in triumph as he found her bike in the back yard.

Jude hadn't been lying.

There was a light on in one of the rooms, and he sneaked around the back to see if he could peer in through a window. Because the house was on a slope, the darkened and grilled windows of a lower storey came up to his knees, and the sill of the street level window was out of reach. He whistled softly to himself and tried the back door. It was firmly locked. He could pick the lock, of course, it wasn't even a dead bolt, but that wouldn't win him any favours.

He went around and knocked at the front door. Eventually he pushed the letter box in with his hand, and looked into the dark hallway.

'Jessie, are you there? Come on, open the door.'

There was silence, but he sensed she was there, listening.

'Little pig, little pig, let me come in,' he called softly. If she wanted to play games, he was only too willing. The stillness was unnerving, but he sensed that she was within eye-shot, only he couldn't see her.

The kid had sworn she lived here alone. He'd described the place quite accurately.

'I know you're there, Jessie,' he said softly, his eyes straining into the darkness. 'I just want to talk.'

There was the flicker of movement, something

white.

'About what?'

So she had seen him, she knew who it was. 'Not through the damned letter box,' he complained. 'Open the door, come on.'

'Go away.'

Her voice had the hard edge of fury. She really was pissed at having been found, he thought, but it was obvious she did need him. Or someone, anyway, just like Jude said.

He put his shoulder to the door and leaned his weight inwards until there was an unhealthy creak in the wood surround.

'Come on,' he begged. 'I just want to talk. Don't make me break the door down. I don't mean any harm.'

There was silence from within.

Stone pulled back to shove his against the door once more, not really intending to break it, when he felt a breath of cold wind touch him from behind.

He whirled, but not soon enough.

Something belted him on the side of the head with enough force to melt his knees and turn his eyes to the heavens. He slumped down onto his knees on the doorstep. Pulling his senses back with an effort, he turned and sprawled onto his backside, his back against the porch wall. Putting a hand to his head, he felt the warmth of blood trickling down on his ear.

'Fucking hell,' he swore. 'What the hell did you do that for?'

His heart was hammering in his chest in a way that was definitely unusual. It wasn't lust, either. He recognised fear when it was on him. He sat there in the darkness waiting for the dizziness to go away or for her to finish the job. They were right, everyone who had warned him. She wasn't just barking mad, she was dangerous. The street light just outside the house wasn't working and his eyes adjusted to the empty road.

He sat in the darkness of the porch waiting for his

head to clear. Jesus, wept, he hadn't expected *that*. But he was no longer just thinking about wanting her as a woman. He had to find out what she wanted with Porter. He had a good idea who she meant, and if he was right it wasn't good news for any of them.

A light went on in the hallway behind him, and the door opened silently from within. She stood looking down at him, an avenging angel in a white judo outfit tied around the middle with a belt of the same colour. Jesus.

He looked down at his clothes. He seemed to be leaking an awful lot of blood. As he swore under his breath, she handed him a towel. He pressed it to his head and struggled to his feet.

'What do you want? How did you find me?'

Stone glared at her. She was stunningly, devastatingly beautiful, but nutty as a fruitcake.

'I came because I thought you were the most interesting woman I've met in a long time. I came because I wanted to make sure you were real. I guess I found out. I'll come with a strait-jacket next time.'

Irritated at himself for being taken off-guard, he dropped the bloodied towel, and turned. Still slightly woozy from his head injury, he took a single step, then wobbled back against the stressed door-frame.

Fuck, he wasn't even going to be able to drive. To his surprise, she opened the door wider and put her shoulder under his.

'Walk, damn you, I can't carry you.'

She kicked the door shut behind them.

He was thrust onto a hard wooden seat in a tiny kitchen, and those same cruel hands that had wielded whatever lump of metal that had knocked seven bells of shit out of him now proceeded to clean the wound.

Her hands were surprisingly gentle.

'What did you hit me on the head for? You might have killed me.'

'If I'd wanted to kill you, you'd be dead.'

He winced as she touched the swelling lump.

'You're aptly named, it seems. I was too stupid to be warned, though.'

The hands stilled. 'What d'you mean?'

'Down at the Old Fox, they call you the Black Widow.'

Her expression told him she hadn't heard that before. 'Did they tell you how to find me?'

'They told me how to find Jude.'

'I'll kill him.'

'I made him tell me.'

She froze again, eyes narrowed. 'Did you hurt him?'

'Does it matter? A minute ago you were going to kill him.'

She glared, then turned her back on him to rinse the cloth out at the sink. 'What do you want with me?'

'You. Is that so very wrong?'

He saw the stiffness of her back, and realised that her cuckoo brain must be going into overdrive. He would have given a monkey to see what was going on in there at this time. But something must have sunk in, because, although there wasn't anything he could pinpoint, it was as if her whole body relaxed.

'Not wrong,' she said finally. 'Just not something I can handle.'

'I can see that,' he said dryly. 'I had no idea. When you accepted my challenge the other night, I thought we were more in tune with each other than this. Why did you?'

'I don't know. Because it was exciting. Because I was bored. But I wouldn't have let you catch me.'

She added the last phrase on with a degree of uncertainty, which Stone noticed with malicious pleasure. She'd been speculating on the consequences of that end game, just as he had. Not so cold, then. She turned to face him, arms hugged protectively around her chest.

'Why have you got an aversion to blokes liking you? I don't think you're a dyke.'

A sneer crossed her face.

'I was a whore when I was fourteen, hooked on crack by fifteen, and didn't expect to see sixteen. Shocked?'

Now he understood what the bloke in the pub meant by she didn't like dealers. If she'd been hooked, and kicked the habit, she was one of a very small percentage.

'I'm surprised, saddened, and sorry.' He said honestly. 'And yet you're educated. What happened?'

She clammed up. He read the language clearly: one question too close to home, time to back off.

His voice became gentle. 'I don't know who hurt you, but it wasn't me. I wouldn't have tried to rape you, if that's what you thought earlier.'

'Just as well. You'd never have tried raping another woman.'

The words weren't for effect, she meant them.

He was aware that in spite of his size he might have come off worse in the encounter. Jessie stared intently into his face as if she would read what was in his mind. He realised her eyes were absolutely stunning, and in spite of his aching head, he still wanted to make love to her. Perhaps he was the one who was mad, here.

A faint smile slipped into being at her scrutiny.

'I'd better go. I don't want you to be afraid of me.'

'You can't drive yet.'

'I'll manage, thanks. But for future reference,' he held his hand out. 'I'm David Stone. And you are?'

She ignored the hand.

'What are you? A cop, or something?'

'Do I look like a bloody cop,' he asked, annoyed. 'That's what Jude said.'

'He's got a good nose for these things.'

'OK. I was a cop once, very briefly. It didn't work out too well; too many rules. Presently I'm a chauffeur and bodyguard to a geezer called Chalmers.'

To his surprise she gave something as near a smile as he'd yet seen.

'Don't tell Jude that. He'll become your personal limpet.'

'He wants to be a chauffeur? If I gave him a few lessons in driving a limo would you go out with me?'

She bit her lip in a surprisingly hesitant manner. He nearly smiled, but guessed she would hate to be laughed at. This impasse was stupid. He leaned on the table, pushed himself to his feet and waited a moment until the dizziness passed before walking around the table, removing the physical barrier she'd placed deliberately between them.

He dwarfed her, despite her being fairly tall. She backed as he advanced, one step at a time, not because she was afraid he'd hurt her, he guessed, but fear of the unknown. The gay in the bar had been right when he said some man had hurt her in the past. He just hadn't realised how many men. That's why she was so aggressive. She was afraid to let herself feel because she'd seen the side of men that made him ashamed to be one.

Because she wasn't belting him around the head again with whatever she'd used to crack his skull the last time, he advanced until she was pressed up against the wall.

He moved slowly, as one would to gain the confidence of a wild animal. Her chest heaved, her breath shortened. She was wide-eyed, ready to bolt, yet she'd let him come close. Very gently he reached out and stroked the errant blonde hair from her forehead, and touched her lips, her eyelids, her high cheek-bones, feeling her softness with blunt fingers.

His body pressed close enough to feel the contours of hers, and he could feel her shaking. He put his hands under her armpits and slid her up the wall until their faces were level, and pressed his body to hers, holding her there. Her hands rested uncertainly on his shoulders and he could see she was fighting her own instinct to react with violence.

That was something, anyway.

'Whatever happened in the past, perhaps it's time to mend it?' he said softly. 'Is it possible to try? I really

255

need to know. And I think you need to know, too. I'm not making any kind of promises, but here and now we can make things a bit better. You don't have to fight this thing all alone.'

Her eyes were greener and deeper than the Mediterranean. Her body smelled of soap and sweat and fear. He had never been so aroused.

He waited a moment, then leaned his face into hers and kissed her gently, a superficial butterfly of a kiss. He knew she must be in no doubt as to the level of his desire. His erection was thrusting imperatively at the heavy-duty zip of his leather trousers, but she remained rigid and unresponsive. He gave a wry smile as he lowered her down again, and backed away, hands up.

'Don't worry. I'll suffer in silence.'

'You don't understand. I just can't.'

'I do understand. I can be patient.'

He hitched his trousers at the front, thinking, she didn't say she didn't want to, though.

'I'll go now, but I promise I'll be back. By the way, what did you hit me with?'

She pointed at the curved sword that lay on the worktop.

'Fucking hell.'

She gave the hint of a smile. 'It was the blunt side.'

As he left, Stone realised he wasn't altogether unhappy about the way things had gone with Jessie. He wanted to interrogate her about Porter, find out what the hell she thought she was going to do if she found him.

Whatever it was, he was going to have to put a stop to it, somehow, because he really, really wasn't someone she wanted to find. Not that she was likely to, in all honesty.

Touching his head, he realised just how carefully he was going to have to tread. Thank God she'd only used the flat edge of the sword. He realised he could have come off rather worse in the encounter if she'd decided he was dangerous, and wondered what it was about her

256

that made him so determined to get through to her.

He had come here to find out what she was about, and was leaving with the knowledge that she was big, big trouble. The best thing would be to simply walk away, steer clear, but he had a pretty good idea she didn't have a clue what kind of trouble she was heading towards.

Jessie was uncomfortable for days after Stone's visit. Although she really did believe it was for no more sinister reason than he fancied her, she felt violated and exposed simply because he'd discovered her address.

In spite of his biker persona and the underlying violence she sensed in him, Stone had treated her with gentleness, deference almost, and in a strange way she was fascinated by that. She hadn't expected it. He was an enigma. The soft memory of his hands on her face also spooked her. No one had touched her that way, ever, and her body even now tingled in recollection. So why did she have this confused feeling in the back of her head that she'd also wanted him to do it again?

Chapter 49

Derke Hughes was a florid man with an overbearing attitude. On being asked to come in to answer a couple of questions, he'd said, *Make it quick, I don't have time to waste*, which is exactly why Godfrey had kept him waiting.

It was immediately obvious Derke had been in some kind of accident. His jaw was slightly distorted, and his nose had a distinct list despite the care and time the hospital staff had probably spent patching him up. You could forgive him for trying to make it out to be something more than getting beaten up by a girl, if that was what happened.

He held out his hand.

'Godfrey Kyam. Thank you for coming in, Mr Hughes. May I call you Derke?'

He was treated to a brief handshake, followed by a pantomime of huffing as Derke checked the time.

'Perhaps you'd like to tell me what this is all about. I have a business to run.'

'Please sit down Derke. This shouldn't take long.'

'Do you mind if we tape this session? For the record.'

Branlawe fussed with the recorder, told it the date and time and who was present, without waiting for an answer.

Derke glanced at him suspiciously, before sitting with reluctance, again glancing at his watch.

'This is about last year, when I was attacked by those thugs? I hope you've got some good news for me. It's about time the police did some bloody policing around here.'

'Thug, singular, I think you mean,' Godfrey corrected softly. 'An expert in martial arts who has killed quite a few people apart from your friend. We would dearly like to put her behind bars.'

Derke jolted fractionally. 'What're you talking about?'

'There was no gang, was there? But you shouldn't be hard on yourself. She's probably the most dangerous killer you could have had the misfortune to meet. You were lucky to come out of it alive.'

'But I told the police at the time...'

'Derke, we have a witness.'

'A witness?'

Godfrey had just been fishing, but he pushed home at the panic which lurked behind the denial.

'You know exactly who I mean, don't you? Now, perhaps you'd like to tell us what really happened? In your own words. Take your time. We'll see if it matches the story the witness told us.'

He'd hazard a guess that Derke was the kind who threw his weight around during interviews just to watch people squirm, as he was squirming now.

'Whatever he said, it was all lies,' he muttered.

'Do you want me to bring him in?'

Derke's eyes flicked to the door. 'Do I need a solicitor?'

'I don't know, do you?'

'We weren't hurting him, whatever he said. Jenkins was just having sex with him, which is what he was paid for.'

Godfrey would have put money on a prostitute, given the location and time, but he hadn't expected *that*. He hadn't taken Derke for a homosexual, but some liked their bread buttered both sides. He might have gone along with the idea for the novelty value of doing something risqué.

'Were you in the habit of picking up male prostitutes in the evening, the two of you?'

'No! I'd never done it before. I, ah, I prefer women. It was Jenkins, he'd done it before, he told me.'

'What was the boy called, Derke?'

'I don't know. I can't remember.'

Godfrey's voice hardened uncompromisingly.

'But you knew he was under-age.'

'No! He was older than that, I swear! I never had sex with a child. I didn't.'

Realising he'd further condemned himself, he went silent, the arrogance slumped out of his stance..

Godfrey got up and paced the room. He spun abruptly.

'Tell me, did you sell meth, too, or was it just Jenkins?'

He looked genuinely shocked.

'Jenkins was never into drugs. If he was, I didn't know about it.'

Godfrey believed him.

'So, let's get back to the boy. You've just admitted to having had sex with an under-age boy, who is, incidentally, willing to testify. Do you know what will happen if this goes to trial? The publicity, prison? Even criminals tend to dislike child-abusers.'

Derke's skin was grey, his breath laboured.

Don't have a heart attack, please, Godfrey thought.

'If you tell me exactly what happened, give me some way of finding this girl, it will go a long way towards helping your case.'

Hughes was broken, his voice monotone.

'Jenkins had been told about this kid, Jude. He made the arrangements. We picked him up by the Regency, and drove out to the warehouse.'

'Do you know his full name?'

'No, Jude was all we were told. Frank had had sex with him, but I couldn't. And then he was burning him with cigarettes. The kid will tell you, it wasn't me.'

He looked for confirmation. Godfrey said, 'Go on.'

'This girl just came out of no-where. She opened the door and just looked at us. Then she grabbed a brick and scratched up my car. Of course, I jumped out to stop her, and, Jesus, I don't even know what happened then. I woke up in hospital with a broken nose, jaw, and cheek bone. I'm told she broke Frank's neck.

He shuddered. 'It was so quick, and so crazy, I mean, a girl...'

'Describe her.'

'Well, it was dark. All I remember is, well, I think she was blonde. Her hair was in a ponytail.'

'Had you ever seen her before?'

'No. And I hope I never see the bitch again.'

Branlawe bit off a smile.

'So you don't have any idea where we'd find her?'

His eyes darkened. 'I wanted to find her myself. I asked around a bit, but no-one knew.'

After Derke had left, almost surprised to still be free, Branlawe commented, 'That tape's no use. There was a lot of leading going on. It would never stand up in Court.'

'You don't really want to charge him, do you?'

'If I thought I'd make it stick, yes.'

'Well, what I suggest is you bury that tape for now. We got one lead, which might or might not be of use.'

'Jude.'

'Yes, and if he was picked up outside the Regent, he's likely to be found there again. They tend to have their stamping grounds.'

But the interview had unsettled him.

Unless the tub of lard had been lying, Jessie had put him down in a second, without hesitation, then gone on to kill Jenkins, who had a reputation for being handy with his fists.

His earlier comment that she was a dangerous criminal who should not be on the street was beginning to sound like the truth.

Ben, what kind of monster have you created, he thought.

Chapter 50

Stone buzzed the gate open, and drove slowly, the big bike purring as quietly as it could. He glanced at the front of the big house, way up the drive, and was pleased to see it was free of cars. For all their fancy suits and cars, Chalmers' cronies were a bunch of bastards, one and all. Just the sort of people Jessie didn't need to know he was working with.

Knowing the cameras would be trained on him, he gave them the finger as he coasted into the parking bay behind the gatehouse. He leaned the bike onto its side stand, and ducked his head as he went in through the kitchen door, chucking his satchel on the Formica table. He guessed people came smaller back along, either that or the mill owners who had built the estate thought servants didn't have the right to walk through doors with the head anything less than bowed in deference.

Oh, cynicism, chastise thyself, he thought.

And what about Jessie?

He could hear the plum in her voice, all right. He had thought her an enigma in the pub, but now? He was totally baffled. With a background somewhat different from his mid-terrace existence, she'd made whore at fourteen? No scenario he could visualise remotely computed that piece of logic.

He'd always known where *his* dad fitted into society.

A brute of a man, a labourer and drinker with the clichéd set of behaviours: violent one moment, apologetic the next. He'd had tears in his eyes at his son's graduation at the police academy. A couple of years later he'd got pissed once too often and fallen under a taxi as he was staggering home.

It had been hard to grieve, and hard not to grieve. And that confused legacy was exactly what had got him where he was today.

The once-huge estate had been long dismantled.

The Big House, the stables and several acres of garden, surrounded by a six foot wall, were all that was left. The stables had been renovated long ago, turned into garages, with apartments above for the staff. Stone had the gatehouse, which was lucky, really. In his capacity as chauffeur, and more usually courier, he was called in to the big house on a daily basis, but just to exchange packages, never to be included in the meetings that went on behind closed doors.

He stuck the kettle on and fished in the fridge for milk.

What was it about Jessie?

He was being stupid, and he was never stupid.

Well, aside from taking this job on, that was.

In all his varied career he'd steered clear of girls not for any other reason than he wasn't too good on the commitment angle, and that's what most of them wanted before you'd even discovered what kind of toothpaste they used. Mortgages and kids weren't in his make-up. So to now be really hot on a chick who was out of the way barmy... Not a good move, and a bad time to be doing it. Things were hotting up on the Birmingham drug scene. It was likely there would be some action soon, and he'd have to jump ship and run.

Stuff like this could get him killed.

So why Jessie?

Sex was great, but not something he chased, as some men did, so it wasn't that. He'd never been with a hooker, either; it seemed pretty demeaning to use someone's body like a tool when you had a perfectly good hand. Once he'd even gone out with a policewoman, but that was back when he'd been in The Force – How did people like Jude and Jessie *know*? –

263

before his career had lurched off on a totally unexpected tangent.

Jessie was messing with his mind, and other things. He hadn't got such a raging hard-on for someone in a long time, not like this.

True lust, it had to be.

He did hope she wouldn't be too hard on the kid, Jude, then shook his head at the mental picture. She was a fruit cake all right. He knew he'd be better off steering clear, but the thought stuck in his head. He didn't just want *her*; he wanted to help her.

He went to sleep dreaming of being tangled up in a mesh of steel webbing, and Jessie was there, laughing at him, brandishing that weapon of hers, which looked as if it had materialised out of some fucking kung foo movie.

He woke up with a splitting headache. The chef up at the big house found him a couple of aspirin, and was looking at the lump on his head with admiration when Chalmers came bursting in looking for him.

'What the fuck are you doing in here? We're supposed to be at the Town Hall. The Session starts at nine.'

'Oh, shit, sorry. I forgot.'

Chalmers noticed the wound, and the thin red welt that crept along his brow from somewhere in his hairline.

'Have you been brawling?'

'Not exactly,' Stone said, unashamedly using Jessie as an excuse. 'You see, it was this woman I told you about.'

'A woman? What did you do, rape her?'

'That was just a love bite, you should see the other wounds.'

'Bloody hell. No wonder you're late. Shift your ass, Romeo.'

He led the way rapidly out to the Mercedes that waited at the front of the house, Stone almost trotting behind him.

264

The day was longer than he could have imagined, sitting around in the car waiting for his boss to do his act around town more frustrating than he recalled.

Councillors, politicians, they were all the same, wallowing in the importance of it all, and in style, too. But when it came to the crunch they were all running their own casinos, and the house always wins.

His boss's house was proof enough of that.

But you couldn't have your cake and eat it. If you wanted this kind of job, then you had to work for that kind of person. Thinking about it, the boy Jude could do worse than be a bodyguard. He knew about the seedier side of life and wouldn't be fazed by the underhand goings-on of the cream of society.

But he'd have to find his courage from somewhere.

Chapter 51

Stone was polishing the limo a couple of days later, and could feel Cary's eyes digging like needles in his back.

The runt didn't trust him. Like Jude and Jessie, his instincts, honed at the lower end of civilisation, were probably telling him something wasn't quite solid about stone, which was worrying. He whistled as he polished. Perhaps it was time the runt disappeared.

Chalmers was beginning to trust him, or would if Cary didn't keep slipping snide remarks about him into his boss's ear. As far as Chalmers was concerned, he had all the right credentials, and he intended to keep it that way.

He was going to ignore all the little arse-lickers and go straight to the top this time. No weasel with a wall eye was going to stop him. The thought of snapping the little git's neck was quite enticing, but he'd to do a little sleuthing first. He hadn't quite pinned down Cary's job in the outfit, but he would.

Cary knew Stone disliked him. Perhaps it was just mutual antipathy, but Stone often caught him staring in a way that would have curdled milk. Your time will come, pal, he thought, smiling back pleasantly.

Stone admired his boss in a strange kind of way.

As crooks went, he was pretty straight. Deal right by him, and you'd make a mint. He had a single-minded determination to succeed, which is why he was where he was today, in his big mansion with Staff waiting on him. Stone could identify with that. Wasn't it the dream buried deep in the heart of normal lives?

And the other reason Chalmers had made it, was

because he didn't get caught up in his own shit. He didn't do drugs, sleazy sex parties, or gamble.

And that went for his staff too.

He employed men who were strong enough to ignore the lure of the magic dust and stick to the rewards of hard cash. Stone was happy to toe the party line. He knew everything there was to know about supply chains and distribution, but he'd never indulged, except once, just to know what it felt like. And that had been in a controlled environment.

Chalmers came trotting out of the house, the ever-present phone to his ear. What mischief was he brewing up this time?

He stood up, hoiked the gun into a more comfortable position under his armpit, and opened the car door. Chalmers gave a nod of approval. He liked his men to be dressed well, and capable of using hardware. It didn't do Stone's credence any harm to remind him now and again of what a good bodyguard he was.

'Where to?'

'London.'

Stone paused for a fraction of a second.

'Got a problem with that?'

'Nope,' Stone said. 'I just didn't pack my nighties.'

Chalmers gave the snort that passed for laughter. 'We're not staying. Got a business meeting, dropping off some papers, then we're coming straight back.'

For papers, read dough. Stone shrugged himself into his jacket. He collected on a regular basis, but Chalmers always looked after the big wadge himself. It was the only thing his boss handled, he'd never be caught with any hard stuff in his possession. For that, there was a dented little Fiat owned by someone not connected to Chalmers, and driven by someone who didn't know who Chalmers was.

He was careful, all right.

Stone slapped the cap on his head, and drove with professional care. Normally he would have sat out all night in the car without blinking an eye, if that was

267

what the boss wanted, but for once he minded being away from home. He was pleased it was just a day trip.

But it didn't work out that way, in the end.

They were three days in London as it turned out, and Stone fretted quietly. Having got as far as he had with Jessie, he was afraid of losing ground by not being there.

Did she care that he hadn't called back, after that first mad-cap meeting? He imagined her standing there with the bloody sword in her hand, like some avenging goddess. She was a loony, and he was going to end up chopped into mincemeat if he wasn't careful. Yet there was something about her violence that appealed to him. Perhaps it was the very danger of a liaison with her that was attractive.

Was he that stupid? He didn't know.

Far from having his thoughts sorted out by a few days' enforced absence, he was more confused than he'd been before. He should have known when to steer clear. She was trouble with a capital T. Only he wanted more. The black widow could have her bite of him, and he'd smile while she did it.

He leaned against the rolling door of a warehouse where the deal was finally going down, and heard the low rumble of voices from within. Chalmers had some fairly nasty business associates in London, but these were the worst: smooth, expensive, with eyes like flat, black pebbles, and not an ounce of humanity between them.

He put his hand on the smooth handle of the gun, reassured by the weight of the silencer. He didn't trust the creeps an inch, and they didn't trust him.

He'd sussed out the guy covering him from the corner, and there were bound to be more. He didn't like the vulnerability, but it was the price of being bodyguard to someone like Chalmers. And the big, fat wage that came with it. He hoped to live long enough to spend it.

He'd been to several of these drops now, but still he

wasn't trusted to do more than stand watchdog over the car when the big stuff was going down. He was peeved, but swallowed his pride.

Next time, he'd do more than just stand outside. He wanted to be in with the dealers, he wanted to join the gang. He wanted to prove to Chalmers that he was a reliable, trustworthy sort of criminal.

Perhaps he'd succeeded in some respect, because on arrival back in Birmingham this time he wasn't sent straight to bed leaving Cary to do the work. He drove them to the warehouse and when the Fiat arrived, he watched the crap being bagged and tagged. He felt exhilaration fill him.

One step at a time.

The bags were large, a pound or so in each, and as he began the weary job of distributing, he knew it would be cut and cut again, stretching that pound so slim it would be almost transparent by the time it was on the street.

The bike had been his ticket for this job, actually.

His size helped, and his record, both as a police officer and the stuff that went down after, when he was kicked out of the force. Chalmers liked that, of course. There was nothing like someone who knew the ropes from both sides.

He'd been recommended by a colleague from Liverpool, who he'd done a few jobs for. There were plenty of heavies around, of course, and some who'd chauffeured, but none that drove a bike, too. It was his biggest asset, as far as Chalmers was concerned, but he'd known that when he approached the guy.

The first time he'd made the deliveries, he'd been led by the little creep, Cary, on his Honda, but the next time he'd done it on his own. It was easy from the bike. The dealers would be waiting for the sound of his engine, and would present him with their brown paper parcels, and he would present them with his.

Out of one pannier, into the other.

He had no heavies to back him up, because none of the buyers would dare to try to mess with the main man, even if they didn't know who he was.

They all knew where that would lead them.

Stone hadn't been involved in that kind of action for real, and didn't want to, but he'd seen the photographs of the men who had crossed Chalmers.

The gun wasn't far from his hand at each drop off, all the same.

That brought his thoughts, inevitably, back to Jessie.

Exactly why was she looking for Porter, and where had she even got that tag from? She said she didn't do drugs, but had once, and kicked it. There were not too many like her around. So how had that come about? You didn't kick drugs without help. You couldn't.

She dominated his thoughts as he drove around the back streets, making him dangerously uninterested in the job in hand, and he was pleased when he finally handed over the packages back at the house so that Cary could count the piles of dirty money.

Chapter 52

It was three in the morning when Stone arrived at Jessie's small house on the hill. He checked around the back, and her bike was gone. For a fraction of a second he felt a panic that threatened his equilibrium.

Had he spooked her so bad she'd done a runner?

Something jolted in his stomach. He had the feeling that if she chose to run, she'd disappear like a puff of smoke. Knowing that she wasn't in, it took him about two seconds to open the lock at the back door.

He strode into what must have once been a dining room, and there was that black-handled sword in the corner, and her white togs hanging behind the door. He let his breath go slowly, and decided to wait.

She didn't have much in the way of furniture, this strange woman of his, so clambered up the stairs and lay back on her futon, fully clothed, and rested his head on his hands while he waited.

He didn't realise that he'd dozed until he came to with a start to find something pricking him under the chin. He moved involuntarily at the discovery, and the point nearly drove into his windpipe.

'Hold up, there, Jessie, it's only me,' he whispered, hardly moving his mouth, his voice rubbed into harshness by the pressure on his throat. A small amount of light came through the un-curtained window, but he could see nothing but the gleam of the blade.

'I know who it is. What are you doing here?'

Her tone was cold, unpromising, and came like a ghost out of the blackness where she must have been

271

standing.

'If you don't know why I'm here, I might as well go.'

There was a fleeting hesitation before the blade slid away into the darkness, and he winced from the glare of the overhead bulb as she flicked the switch.

He knew better than to move, and twisted his head to look up at her. She was dressed in black from head to toe: ski-pants, polo-neck jumper, soft climbing shoes, and a balaclava. Fuck, what did she do in her spare time? But there wasn't anything at all funny about the way she stood the blade into the corner, and pulled off the balaclava to glare at him with her full anger.

'Where the hell have you been?'

Well, now. That was interesting.

'Had to go away. It's my job. My boss doesn't ask if I'm doing anything, he just snaps his fingers.'

She fairly pulsed with anger, or something, and suddenly lashed out with her foot. She was quick, and the only reason he caught her ankle was because he'd foreseen the movement. He yanked hard, and she came down on top of him like a cat, spitting and clawing, science to the wind. Stone rolled over and squashed her with his weight, catching the talons that would have gouged him, and stilling her legs with his own. Her body vibrated with violence, every muscle in her body tuned to hatred, destruction.

He smiled down at her.

'I would have called but I don't have a number.'

He leaned down and kissed her. Not on the mouth, for she would have bitten off his lip, he was sure, but at the side of her neck under the chin. His soft and gentle touch belied the strength with which he held her.

For a second she remained frozen, then her rigidity melted. He was wary, though. He didn't let go of her arms in case it was just a ploy. He drew his head back and looked at her, searching for clues. She stared up expressionlessly.

Stone made a wry face.

'What do you do when you catch a tiger by the tail?'

272

Her smile was like sunshine on a winter landscape. His breath caught.

'Let it go and see if it's hungry.'

Stone did more than that. He rolled over, and pulled her on top of him, giving her the advantage. She sat up over his thighs, folded her arms protectively over her breasts, and stared at him.

'You ever hurt me,' she said, 'and I *will* kill you.'

'I know.'

She dropped her hands to his front and undid the shirt buttons while he lay there, quivering with anticipation beneath her. She reached her hands around his shoulders to ease the fabric back, and Stone assisted by lifting his weight fractionally.

He reached up to touch her, but she slapped his hand back. She then removed his boots, his trousers, his underwear. He hadn't been undressed by anyone since childhood. It was amazingly arousing.

Then she stood and removed her own clothing. Not sensually, just with practical lack of nonsense. By the time she was naked, Stone was rampant. He'd known she would have a good body, but the reality stunned him. Her body was creamy white and carved with muscle. The temptation was to grab her and thrust himself into her my God, it felt as if he'd waited a lifetime for this moment but he held back. There was a kind of vulnerability in her display of confidence.

It was almost a challenge.

His eyes didn't leave her as she knelt at his side and reached out tentatively, as if she'd never done this before. Perhaps she hadn't. Not the sex, he mentally amended, just the wanting of it.

She used her long slim fingers to touch, learning his every muscle, almost as if trying to understand him in the way a blind person would.

He groaned, and closed his eyes. He had never been touched, explored in that way before, and the pain of lust was exquisite, but there was also the tension of indecision on her face.

273

In spite of their nakedness, he realised she was still wondering whether she could go through with it. Jesus, what had done this to her?

'You don't have to ' he began.

She put a finger on his mouth, silencing him.

His body had no doubts. He held his breath as she climbed over, and slowly lowered herself onto him. There was a moment of warm stillness, then she began to move gently, teasing him inside herself.

He reached up and touched. As she'd set the scene, he followed. He used the tips of his fingers to brush the hair follicles of her arms, her stomach, her breasts, until he felt the tension in her change to something else. He opened his eyes. Hers were now half closed; he knew that look.

Then neither of them was gentle anymore, but lost in the animal world of lust, biting and thrusting, crying out with basic animal necessity.

Finally, when he stilled, when his heart had slowed to a more normal rate, he reached up and touched Jessie's knees where they straddled his abdomen, and stroked gently. Neither of them wanted to move, to break the spell of contentment that still joined them.

'Can I stay?' he finally asked, in a small whisper.

In quiet assent, she rolled from him, and he pulled the covers over them both. She nestled into the curve of his body, but neither of them slept for a long time.

As always, when he awoke, Stone was fully alert, with instant knowledge of where he was. But this time there was a new feeling, a sense of wonder. He hadn't truly ever expected to be here, and it was good.

He turned his head. Jessie had awoken with the same instant clarity. She was the same type of person, living on the edge of society, her instincts keeping her alive. He smiled, but there was no smile back.

What had happened last night had happened, and was gone.

'I should go,' he said.

'And I should be working out.'

She climbed into the white cotton suit.

'Shouldn't you have a black belt?'

'I don't need to prove anything to anybody.'

She was right, there.

'Is that get-up necessary?'

'My teacher...' She stopped short. 'It puts me in the right state of mind.'

'Your teacher? Who was that?'

He guessed that whoever it was had given her this gift to replace the whoring and the drugs.

She padded downstairs without another word.

He sighed, forcing himself to leave the warmth of the futon, and followed suit. Whatever kind of communication he thought they'd shared yesterday had evaporated.

Maybe she even regretted last night.

He didn't.

She was standing in the kitchen when he went down, as if wondering whether to ask him if he wanted breakfast. How deliciously normal, like an old married couple. She managed to restrain herself, though.

After a slight pause, he said, 'Well, I'd better be off. Don't want to be late.'

Was she going to ask him if he was coming back? No chance. He shrugged himself into the leather jacket, and picked up the helmet, and opened the door. He wanted to ask, what do you do all day? What were you doing last night? But he knew the question would be greeted by a brick wall. She did that so well. Actually, it was obvious that whatever she'd been doing last night was illegal.

'I have a day off on Saturday. Will you come out with me? For the day?'

She froze. 'Where?'

'Anywhere. It doesn't matter does it? I would just like to be with you. We could walk around the shops. Walk along the canal. Go to the cinema.'

'A date?' she said blankly, as if she'd never

considered such a thing.

'You could look at it that way if you wanted.'

Her lips tightened.

Irritated, he snapped, 'I'm not buying you. Going out doesn't have to mean sex. I don't buy sex, Jessie. Not now, not ever.'

She turned away a moment, and when she turned back she looked different, somehow, smaller, as if she wanted to apologise, but couldn't get the words out.

He relented, and pulled a coin out of his pocket. 'Tomorrow. A date, nothing more. Heads you come, tails you don't.'

He almost got a smile as he threw the coin.

It flipped over and over before landing squarely in the centre of his palm. He slapped it onto the back of his hand, and peeped.

'Heads.'

Jessie frowned. 'Let me see.'

'Don't you trust me?'

But that was asking too much. She reached out, took the coin and turned it over and over. It had heads both sides. Stone shrugged at her quizzical expression.

'I never said I was honest.'

She turned away, shutting him out as surely as if she'd slammed a door in his face. Did that mean yes, or something else? He wasn't sure. She tied the worn belt twice around her middle and pushed it down onto her hips before padding through to the other room. After a moment he heard bare boards creaking. He went to look, unable to help himself.

She stood, her back to him, one strong hand wrapped firmly around the leather-whipped handle of the curved blade. Her knees were bent, and she faced sideways, one arm stretched out before her. The blade hovered over a body poised with grace and power, as still as a stalking panther.

When she moved forward, the sword arced through the air with a flash of silver, halting without a quiver, as she found another strange and beautiful pose.

It wasn't just that she could do that which was disturbing, it was the whole ethos of the thing. She must have done nothing else all her life except. She didn't seem old enough, somehow.

'I'll be here at eight,' he said finally. But she didn't acknowledge the words, and he left, aware that for this moment in time, if not always, he lived outside her sphere of existence.

Chapter 53

'The boy's called Jude,' Godfrey told Redwall and Oscar. 'Not a common name, I think, in spite of the song. Derke gave us a fairly good description. He'll maybe have filled out a bit by now, if he was somewhere in the region of fourteen years of age; if he's still alive. The way he was carrying on though, he might not be. Get out there and find him. Quietly. I don't want him spooked.'

Oscar was picked to be the contact.

'Not only are you able to take care of yourself,' Godfrey said, 'But the men out there might very well believe you're looking for a nice young black boy.'

'Thanks.' Oscar was not amused, but as with everything he did, he took the part on with detailed thoroughness.

For several nights he visited the known gay pubs, including the Regency, which was where Hughes said they picked up the boy, just to show his face around. To the odd question that came his way, he was simply new in the area and looking for action. He didn't quite mean the action they had in mind, but they didn't know that. With true comradeship, he was given lots of advice, and skilfully had to side-slip the advances of a couple of interested men in the meantime. He liked younger boys, with, ah, a bit of colour, if you know what I mean.

Oscar must have been very convincing, because the barman at the Regency offered him a couple of other contacts, but Oscar said he'd heard Jude was a sweet kid who knew how to make a black man feel good. Did he know him?

No, the man didn't know who he meant, but if he saw someone who fitted the description, he'd pass the message on. A couple of days later he was less cagey.

'He might get back to you if he's interested in some work, but he won't do car jobs. Just thought you ought to know and he 'aint cheap.'

'And I'm not short of readies.' Oscar was all puppy-dog eagerness. 'Tell him I'm here on business for a while, renting a house. He can come for the evening, watch tele and stuff, all nice and civilised.'

He pulled a banknote out of his pocket, and handed it over, along with a telephone number.

'If you should just happen to see him.'

The note disappeared, and so did Oscar.

He didn't want to seem too eager, and he didn't want to get picked up by any of the other men listening with interest to the conversation while pretending not to.

The call came two days later while they were in conference, and he swallowed hard before speaking. It was one thing taking liberties with his sexual inclinations out on his own, but this time three other people were listening in.

He held up his hand for silence.

'Yeah, it's Oscar. Is this Jude?'

'Why's it sound funny?'

'It's on speakerphone. I don't hear so good D'you mind?'

'Nah, I guess. I was told you want some action?'

The boy had a soft, vaguely feminine voice that effused sex even down the line, making his skin crawl. He made the arrangement as if they were just going to buy a pizza. Oscar was glad he hadn't had to do this face to face, because he would never have disguised his shudder of distaste.

However, he arranged the meeting with as much enthusiasm as he could muster. The boy seemed happy enough to come to Oscar's house, and to further lull his suspicions, if there were any, Oscar accidentally dropped the name of another gay he'd been offered as a substitute for Jude at the Old Fox, vaguely suggesting that he'd been with the man.

Branlawe was taken aback by the level of promise in the boy's voice.

'Christ, I could almost have gone for that myself,' he said. 'No wonder he's put his prices up, the little shite.'

'Tell you what ' Oscar began.

'No,' Godfrey said firmly. 'We'll stick with the plan. Branlawe can have a go later if he's still so inclined.'

Branlawe flushed faintly, but grinned. He'd let himself in for that one.

Chapter 54

Jessie emerged from the shadow of a wall, as Stone arrived. He'd guessed she wouldn't wait indoors, she'd place herself somewhere not confined, in case he hadn't come alone, in case flight was necessary. It's what he would have done.

He'd known she was there, but only because he was expecting something like that. Even so, her very stillness was unnerving to watch. He swung the bike in a tight circle, and held out his hand. She glanced over at her bike, and made that little frown, a wrinkle between the eyes he was beginning to recognise as indecision.

'Come with me?' he asked.

She fitted her helmet, and climbed gingerly up behind him, clutching tightly at his jacket for the first couple of miles, gradually relaxing into his back as she got used to being a pillion. He guessed she'd rather have her hands on the controls, independent cuss. Because he was enjoying the warmth at his back, he made it last, driving up onto the motorway and revelling in a burst of speed before sense overtook him. Now wasn't a good time for getting stopped for speeding.

He drove to the place on the canal where it had been tarted up, where warehouses had been turned into shops, and the path was lined with flowers. He liked the dark ribbon of water, for all it wasn't salt. It reminded him of the village where he spent his first few years. When his dad fished out on the trawlers, before his mum died, and the fishing trade died.

The small quay here, where working barges used to linger, was a tourist trap. There was no work here for a man any more.

Stone wanted to know more about Jessie, but though his curiosity burned like a canker, any attempt to delve into her past was greeted by silence.

In fact it was very difficult to find anything to talk about at all. She never watched television, and had never owned one. She was an enigma. She had no past, no aspirations, no job, no nothing, and he was being equally as cagey.

Work subjects were taboo on both sides.

What the hell was he doing?

He had the strangest sensation of being in a time warp, a bubble that was about to burst. The only thing about Jessie that was real was the solid fact of her presence.

But still, somehow, the day was wonderful, something he had never experienced before. Just being with a woman, strolling side by side, not touching, often not talking, but somehow more together than he'd ever been with anyone.

He bought sandwiches from the dockside café, more than half of which they fed to the pigeons that clustered noisily around them, and he took her into the shopping centre where suspicious glances were often cast their way, where women steered pushchairs in a wide berth around them.

'They're scared of us,' Jessie said after a while.

'Perhaps they have reason.'

'I wouldn't '

She stopped short.

Wouldn't what? Hurt anyone? But she had and would, he knew that, and probably the people who avoided them felt it.

'No one should be scared like that,' she said finally.

'Maybe, but life teaches us all to be scared. It's how we survive. Hey, look at that. A black widow!'

He dragged her to the window of a jewellery shop,

282

and showed her what he'd spotted; a watch, made in the likeness of a spider's web, and the spider was clicking around the outside, counting away the seconds.

She smiled. 'Cute. But pointless.'

'Does everything have to have a point?'

The door chime tinkled as he went in. The shopkeeper's face was the picture of panic for a second. Stone's brow lifted.

'I'd like the watch in the window; the cheap one with the spider. I'm not going to mug you for it.'

'Sorry,' the man muttered.

'It's just a gift,' he said, handing her the package. 'No strings attached.'

She didn't put it on her wrist, but wrapped the watch reverently back into its paper, and put it in her pocket. There was something so poignant, so sad about the moment, something did an about-turn inside, chilling him.

In spite of Jessie's lethal abilities and hard protective shell, she was vulnerable. Her attitude today was that of a child being shown Christmas for the first time, and he realised that he was leading her down a road he would rather she hadn't entered, towards a destiny she hadn't envisaged, and that he was in some way responsible.

This was all a big mistake.

She was damaged goods, and he would damage her further. He shouldn't get involved. For her sake, and for his. She was streetwise, a thief, maybe, living outside the law. But she wasn't a dealer, she wasn't living outside of morality. He'd justified to himself that all the shit he was involved in couldn't harm her, because she was already there.

When they headed back to the bike it was getting dark, and the lights were strung like orange globes above them. They walked in silence. Perhaps Jessie, too, knew this was the eye of the storm, and that things would change all too soon.

She reached into one of the cavernous panniers to

pull out the helmets, and when she drew out her fingers, he saw her lift them to her mouth. He watched helplessly, knowing what she'd discovered. Warily, he watched for her reaction, wondering if she would be angry enough to kiss his ass goodbye, or ask for a cut. He didn't know which would be worse.

'One of the bags leaked,' she said.

'I'll be more careful next time.'

He thought he was prepared for a reaction, but hadn't expected to see the glint of tears as she turned away from him. He cursed under his breath.

'Come on, let's go back,' he said gruffly.

But she began to walk. He followed, not used to feeling so inadequate, so unable to respond with the things he wanted to tell her. She knew he was following, but kept walking until, presumably, she'd conquered her weakness.

When she turned, the cold mask was in place.

'Don't ever come near me again.'

He stared at her in silence, knowing nothing he said could take this away.

'Jessie. At the Old Fox they told me you were looking for a man called Porter.'

'Jude.' She said flatly.

'I suppose it must have come from him initially. But Jessie, stop looking. Go back where you came from. Leave it alone. Trust me, you don't want to find him.'

'You *know* who he is?' The stunned comprehension on her face gradually faded. 'Of course you do. Why didn't I guess? Who is he? Where will I find him?'

'You won't find him. That's not his real name. It's just the name he uses when he's dealing.'

'Tell me.'

'No. Whatever your beef is with that man, leave it alone. You'll end up dead. You have no idea what kind of person he is.'

'Tell me who he is. Now.'

She took a step forward, her whole body vibrating with emotion. He almost backed at the murderous fury in her eyes, but stood his ground as she nearly bumped into him.

'Or what?' he asked gently.

They were face to face quivering like rabid dogs for a long moment. 'I'll find him,' she promised in a low voice. 'And when I do, I'll kill him. And when I find him, you'd better not be there or I'll kill you, too.'

Then Jessie backed, and began to walk away. He knew better than to offer her a lift, but there was one thing he needed to know.

He called after her, 'Are you going to grass on me?'

She stopped dead, several paces away from him, turning slowly, her disgust hitting him like a punch in the stomach.

'No,' she said, 'You can go to hell in your own time.'

He watched her walk away into the darkness, and felt as if she'd taken his soul with her.

Chapter 55

Godfrey suggested there were a lot of reasons for not bringing the boy in through official channels.

'Unless you're going to charge Derke?' he added.

'We need to hear Jude's side of the story before I know what to do about him,' Branlawe said. 'He's not likely to confirm he's a rent boy, and even if he does, Derke's got a bundle of solicitors who will discredit him as a witness.'

'So let's hear what he has to say. We can put the frighteners on him, and make a decision once we know a little more. It's not as if he's going to complain to the police, is it?'

Branlawe agreed reluctantly. It was his job that would be jeopardised, but Godfrey assured him he had the clout to sort any problems that might arise.

Oscar waited with Branlawe, watching the street from an upstairs window in the rented house.

When Jude arrived, he was in no doubt.

'That's him.'

'I guess it must be,' Branlawe agreed.

Jude just had that air about him, Oscar thought as they made their way downstairs. You'd just know. He had an androgynous appearance, neither muscled nor feminine, and his face, even from this distance, appeared truly angelic, with large eyes and a sensuous mouth.

He was humming happily to himself as he made his way up the front path of the end-of-terrace, filled with the confidence of youth, obviously having put the memory of his previous bad experience far behind him. He looked easily sixteen, but was probably less, it was hard to tell with youngsters who had seen the underbelly of life.

Oscar could see why the boy was popular, and he'd silently agreed with Branlawe's comment about the voice on the telephone, though he hadn't been dumb enough to say it out loud.

After the boy knocked, he took a deep breath, and managed a diffident, almost shy smile as he opened it, making it clear to the boy he'd only just discovered the gay man inside himself, and was still slightly nervous about it all.

'Jude?'

'Hey, man.'

The boy stood there, smiling distantly, and it took a moment for Oscar to twig. He reached into his pocket and pulled out a bundle of notes. As the notes disappeared, so did Jude's attitude. He lit into action like a shop store toy that had just been fed coins.

Startled by the suddenness of the change, Oscar backed hastily into the house as Jude almost popped him a kiss right on the mouth, and Jude followed, laughter in his voice.

'You don't need to worry, no one's going to look.'

He patted Oscar on the backside as he went past, and surveyed the three shut doors and the stairs.

'So, where do you want to go?'

Oscar pointed to the door on the left. Jude opened it, saying, 'I get the feeling you're new to this game. Don't worry, just lie back and enjoy. I'll even get it up for you if you've got a problem. You'll like me, I promise. All my clients do. Just relax, and let me do what I'm good at.'

As he stepped through the door, Oscar took hold of his arm, swallowing the bile that had begun to rise in his throat at the thought of all Jude's other clients, and twisted harder than he intended.

As Jude folded into the room with a shocked mewl

of pain, Branlawe took his other wrist. Before Jude knew what was happening, his wrists were cuffed neatly behind his back.

He froze, and they hauled him upright.

He looked quickly from one man to the other, wondering what their game was, knowing that whatever it was, it was far too late to mind.

'I don't do bondage stuff, and I only do one client at a time.'

His voice shook slightly, but Branlawe held him by both biceps from behind whilst Oscar frisked him. They removed his knife, his freedom, and his confidence in less than a minute.

'Please, don't.'

'Shut up. If you make any noise at all, you'll be sorry,' Oscar said in a low growl. His words had the desired effect. Jude became a pliant puppet in their hands, but his look of resignation, coupled with the expectation of something nasty about to happen to him didn't make him feel good.

Branlawe made a call.

'Bring the car round. We've got him.'

They remained grim-faced as they man-handled the wide-eyed, silent youth out through the back door, to where Godfrey's limo waited, silently purring. Redwall climbed out and opened the back door.

Jude swallowed hard as he was sandwiched between Branlawe and Redwall. They buckled the seat belt around Jude, while Oscar took the driving seat. He wasn't trusting anyone with this limo for more than a block.

Glancing into the mirror as he pulled out, Oscar thought Jude seemed years younger with his air of confidence stripped from him. He was scared, there was no doubt about that, but not in the way a child of his age should be. He'd obviously been in similar situations before, and it showed in the resignation with which he accepted the situation. He was simply hoping he would get out of this mess alive, and they all knew it.

'Where are you taking me?' he asked in a small voice.

'Shut-up,' Branlawe snapped. 'I'll let you know when you can bleat.'

The street lights went on as he pulled out into the traffic.

Oscar wondered what made boys like him go out on the street, on the game, knowing the kind of pervs who would be seeking their services. They were the vulnerable ones, the easy targets for people with twisted needs, and he'd obviously been there a while. What the hell sort of life had he run from?

He kept his face an emotionless mask.

Following Branlawe's instructions, he eventually found himself driving along a small, muddy track littered with old furniture and shopping trolleys.

The car headlamps highlighted the tunnel between derelict warehouses, which leaned in to dominate the skyline either side. The car lurched from side to side as he tried to save the tyres.

In the encroaching darkness, Jude gave an audible intake of breath. That small sound alone was enough to convince Oscar that Derke's story was true. Hearing the increasing pant of Jude's breathing, he didn't feel very proud of himself. He guessed the other men wanted to stop this right now, but Jessie's life was at risk.

He stopped the car, turned out the head-lights, and found an internal light that wasn't much more than a glow. He climbed out, slammed the door, plastered a hard expression on his face, and got in the back, facing the other three men.

Jude licked his lips, glancing from one to the other in the thunderous silence.

Oscar reached over and took the boy's chin in his hand.

Frightened, wild eyes stared straight at him.

'You remember this place?' he asked.

'What do you want of me?' Jude whispered.

'A while back a friend of ours came down here, and

289

was severely hurt. A little bird told us that you were responsible.'

The soft menace in his voice reached out and hit the boy hard with knowledge.

'I don't know what you mean.'

'You do, pretty boy,' Oscar's fingers dug into his cheeks. 'His jaw was broken in three places and had to be wired together. His nose was plastered across his face, and his cheek-bone was snapped.'

He turned Jude's head one side to the other as if assessing what the damage would look like, there.

'It made a bit of a mess, actually. Do you read your bible, son? Eye for an eye, tooth for a tooth? Wouldn't you do the same for one of your friends?'

'Oh, Christ. Oh, no, please...'

His voice tailed to nothing. His dark eyes were haloed with terror.

'What did you use, you little whore, was it a brick?'

Branlawe opened the car door, leaned out and picked up the broken half of a brick, and closed the door again behind him. He tangled his fingers in the boy's hair, held his head still as he waved the brick closer and closer.

Jude's eyes followed, mesmerised. He was sucking air, hard.

'Shall I do it, or do you want to?' he asked Oscar.

'I didn't do it!' Jude screamed suddenly. 'They had me tied like a fucking pig in the back of their sodding car, how could I do it? Your friends were burning me with cigarettes, and they were going to kill me. Jessie killed the bastard, not me!'

Oscar's eyes leapt to Branlawe's. The boy *knew* her?

Branlawe tightened his fist in the boy's hair so much that the skin around his eyes drew tight.

'Where can I find this Jessie? Tell me where I find him, or you'll end up looking like Frankenstein, and you'll never turn another trick. I'll break your jaw, cut your lying little mouth, and slice off your frigging ears if you don't tell me where to find him.'

290

Oscar was startled.

He almost believed Branlawe himself.

Jude's eyes grew moist. 'You don't understand. She saved my life.'

Redwall looked over at Oscar, brows raised: enough?

Oscar gave a faint shake of the head.

'I'm waiting,' he said softly.

Jude's mouth opened and closed a few times, then said, in a rushed whisper, 'Stebbings Avenue.'

Hot tears silently followed the words.

Oscar climbed back into the driver's seat, and put the car into gear.

'Calm down,' Redwall told Jude. 'It's over. We're not going to hurt you or Jessie. We want to help her.'

He felt Jude stiffen.

'You're cops?'

'We're cops, and if you tell anyone about this incident, you'll be in a special home for boys before you can look around. Do you understand me?'

'Those men were going to kill me.' Jude said after a moment. 'She saved my life.'

'And we're trying to save hers,' Redwall told him. 'There are people who want to kill her, and we just needed to get to her first, whichever way we could.'

He didn't know if Jude believed it, but he felt almost obliged to give the boy some sort of explanation for having scared him half to death.

'O.K.,' Branlawe said. 'We're here. Which house is it?'

Seeing the mutinous look on the boy's face, he added, 'No one's playing games here. If you aren't co-operative, we *will* take you in.'

'Down the end, on the right,' Jude said sullenly. 'There, that one with the green paint.'

He pointed with his chin, his voice dull with disgust at his own weakness.

Branlawe pulled out a wide length of plaster and pressed it over Jude's mouth as they drove slowly past the house and turned around and parked. The boy leaned his head back against the seat-back, staring at nothing.

Oscar climbed out of the car with Branlawe, leaving Redwall to look after the boy. He popped the front door in seconds while Branlawe went round the back, but the house was empty, with little sign of occupation.

'We'll wait.' Oscar said. 'Bring the boy in. I'll park the car round the corner. I don't want to lose him until we have her, and he'll go under cover like a rabbit down a bolt-hole if he gets away.'

They brought Jude in, and sat him on the floor, in a corner. His eyes widened, and he began to make insistent grunting noises, until Oscar crouched down before him.

'OK. You've got something to say, I get it. But you say anything louder than a whisper, and you'll regret it.'

He ripped the plaster from Jude's mouth.

After wincing, Jude said, 'She's gone.'

'What do you mean, gone?'

Jude indicated with his chin. 'The sword. A Japanese one, she leaves it in the corner. And that white suit of hers. That's gone, too. You've spooked her. She's gone.'

Redwall slapped his hand into a wall.

'Dammit. Do you think she saw us? Christ, we should have got back-up, had the place surrounded.'

'Kid,' Oscar said. 'There are some seriously nasty people after her. People who are into drugs. They won't just kill her, they'll make sure she stays alive long enough to wish she was dead. Do you hear what I'm saying? You think by helping us you're betraying her, but you're not. Believe me; we're trying to save her life.'

Jude's mouth pinched together, he said nothing.

Oscar stood up, his body tense with frustration.

'What now?'

'Christ knows. She could be anywhere.'

'Someone else was looking for her a week or so back,' Jude said in a small voice behind them. 'A biker. A big guy called Stone. I knew he was a dealer, but he said he just fancied her. I gave him this address.'

'Goddammit!' Redwall swore.

'No,' Oscar said, looking around. 'It's not that. They wouldn't have given her time to pack. For some reason she's scarpered. We've just got to find her again.'

'Just? It took us a year this time, and five years before that.'

'Why would these drug creeps want Jessie, anyway?' Jude asked. 'She never interfered with anyone, apart from those pervs who were hurting me. She was good to me.'

'She stole some of their money,' Redwall said.

'Oh, Jesus. It was *drug* money?'

They all looked at him.

He swallowed.

'Upstairs. Middle bedroom, under the floorboards. It came out of an army kit-bag she keeps in the cupboard.'

They found where the boards had ben prized up, but the cavity was empty.

'Great, so now what are we going to do?' Branlawe said.

'Find that biker chap Jude was talking about.'

Oscar turned to Jude. 'Well? Any ideas?'

Jude swallowed.

'I need to go to the bathroom.'

Chapter 56

Godfrey was sitting at the head of a large functional table, with Redwall, Branlawe and Oscar. The indecipherable ink stains of past operations imprinted on its surface reflected his present sense of being on a ride to nowhere.

They had found her, then lost her again all in the space of a few minutes. He wondered what had spooked her this time.

'Well, the reason we're all here is Stone. I've managed to get a handle on him, and it doesn't make good reading.'

He opened a file, and drew out a closely typed sheet, and slipped on a pair of half-glasses to read the bullet points out loud with staccato lack of emotion.

'David Stone. Brought up in a large family in Leeds, with a history of violence. Had up for stealing at ten, nearly killed his own father when he was twelve., left home at fifteen, did a six month juvey stretch for breaking and entering, ended up in Borstal for attempted armed robbery, but has never done real time. He's so far managed not to be convicted of any serious felonies, but the file suggests he's been involved various gang- or drug-related activities. After that he spent several years dabbling in various scams in Leeds before leaving to seek new pastures, ending up in Birmingham.

'He's ambitious, ruthless, and is reputed to be a fast and accurate shot, but that hasn't been confirmed. He's also thought to have been responsible for the disappearance of at least two men in the last few years, but there's no proof, no convictions. He's been known to handle situations with extreme violence, on one occasion using a knife. The man survived and Stone was charged with attempted murder. He was acquitted because his actions were deemed to be self-defence and he was in fear of his life.'

There was a small disbelieving snort from someone at the table.

'Quite. According to the report he doesn't hold anything about life very sacred, and has been known to deal in both drugs and prostitution in the past. It says here, and I quote, *his bear-like appearance often gives the impression of stupidity, but he's extremely intelligent, and that makes him doubly dangerous.* His present occupation is as bodyguard for a man called Chalmers '

'Benjamin Chalmers?' Branlawe asked in surprise.

'Know him?'

'Know of him, more like. He's out of my league, multimillionaire, entrepreneur businessman. On the City Council, too. I met him the once. He's a bit blunt, and has a reputation for ruthlessness in his business dealings, but I've never heard of him attached to anything illegal.'

'Makes you wonder why he'd employ someone with Stone's record, though, doesn't it? I don't believe a man in that position would take on an employee without checking his credentials.'

'Perhaps that's *why* he took Stone on. No point having a bodyguard who's afraid to act.'

'There are reputable men out there,' Redwall commented. 'But the other question which begs an answer is, if this Stone chappie is looking for Jessie, is it on his own behalf, or that of someone else?'

'That remains yet to be discovered,' Godfrey acknowledged. 'But there's something else you should know. When Oscar was delving into certain files recently, he came across the name of a man he recognised. One Luther McCormack, private eye. It turns out that Edward Stowleigh hired him to look for Jessie when she ran away over six years ago. He reinstated the guy when she surfaced in Southampton a year ago, because the man already had knowledge of the situation, and it now seems that commission has never actually been rescinded, because Luther has turned up in Birmingham, and we have to assume it's because Jessie is here. Whether he followed Redwall, here, or whether he has information from another source, I don't know. But it worries me, because if he's already discovered she's here, then so will others. I propose we put a tail on Luther. If, for some reason he finds Jessie before we do, it will save us a lot of bother, but he might inadvertently put her in jeopardy.'

'If he finds Jessie before we do, it's likely he'll be in jeopardy *from* her,' Oscar commented.

Godfrey smiled fractionally.

'It pays not to take some things for granted.

Chapter 57

Decisively Jessie embarked on a course of action predetermined months ago. The house she chose was a Victorian affair, solid stone, with a couple of outbuildings and several bedrooms. She wasn't enamoured of the house itself – wrangled over by avaricious beneficiaries for so long, it was barely habitable – but for the large garden; a field of waist-high grass that had once been a lawn, surrounded by a wall lined by trees.

The outside of the boundary wall towered many feet from the pavement outside, but the garden inside was raised to within a few feet of the capping stones. The whole of the wall, as far as Jessie was concerned, was an escape route, providing easy access to any number of streets that could be used to bolt into in the event of a catastrophe. At no single point on the property could she be cornered.

Like Ben's property in the New Forest, it was both a haven and wide open door.

She contacted the solicitor who had handled her stolen money, and instructed him.

He assured her that by greasing the right palms it could all be sorted out in record time, as long as she didn't want surveys and the like. House purchasing transactions, the bane of the working man, were only extended so that the solicitors involved could make more money, he said, adding magnanimously that he'd already made enough off her to buy a luxury yacht.

A week later she stood in the long grass half way down the garden, a tiny seed of regret filtering through her mind as she viewed her house. As a little girl she'd dreamed of owning her own house, her own private space in a world that was too busy to see her, and this was as near to her dream as she'd ever seen. Even to the field of a garden, and the old stables. The only thing she missed from her past life was Rocket, but her little pony was probably long sold.

Something hardened inside her, thrust the past aside. Though she'd bought the place, she would never be able to live in idyllic peace here, isolating herself from the outside world as Ben had done.

She was about to stir up a hornet's nest of trouble, and the only consolation was that the syndicate would never get their money back, either. It gave her more malicious pleasure to tie the money up in some way that would get right up the drug lords' noses; she hadn't quite worked out what, or how, but this place was it. If she died, it would be tied up in a legal wrangle that would grease many pockets before they ever saw a penny. But then, they didn't want or need the money. They had done without it for six years, now.

What they wanted was her.

She didn't tell Jude where she was, the little sod had been the one to lead Stone to her the last time, and she couldn't trust him anymore. Not that she blamed him, he was a tool, there to be used. You just had to prod him in the right places, threaten him, and he did what he was told. She'd seen his eyes fill with tears, his soft lips quiver just at a harsh word. No, he'd sell her down the line to save his own skin, and the fact that he hated himself for his cowardice was no consolation.

No, let him stew.

That Jude would come back to the rented house and find her gone, she didn't care, it served him right. The rent was paid up for a few months, and he was earning enough, now, to look after himself. Yet, once she went back to the terraced house, and checked, but the house remained silent. Maybe having given her away to Stone he was scared to go back.

She shrugged. It was his choice.

There was, of course, another big reason for sorting out a bolt-hole Stone didn't know about. Never one to take things at face value, she'd made her own enquiries.

It hadn't been difficult to trace him. She discovered he was exactly what he said he was, a chauffeur for a local big-wig called Chalmers.

What he hadn't told her about was his violent past, which hadn't been too easy to dig out. Once she slotted that piece of information into the equation, it didn't take long for her to connect all the dots: Stone's boss, that pillar of the establishment, was importing or buying the drugs Stone distributed.

When the penny first dropped she'd stared at Vince's little notebook for a long time, so still she was hardly moving. Vince, the ignorant little shit, had been barely literate, he certainly couldn't spell. But the truth leapt off the yellowing page: Jalmers equals Chalmers equals Porter. Because Stone worked for Chalmers and knew not only what Porter was, but who he was.

Adrenaline buzzed in her loins. Life dealt you some strange hands. The connection might never have been made had she not discovered that Stone had been moving drugs, and if he hadn't warned her off Porter.

He knew Chalmers was Porter because he worked for him.

She went to an internet café for the first time in her life, and began to press buttons. Chalmers was everything a rich business man could be, a mainstay of the Chamber of Commerce, an active member of the Round Table, and probably the Freemasons, too, she thought derisively. All these things added fuel to her belief that this was her main target. After all, had she not known another pillar of society in another life who had been all those things?

Loathing for her father rose for a moment.

She wondered if he was tense with the knowledge that she was out here somewhere, watching and waiting.

299

Let him worry. His time would come.

Hell, they were all crooks, she thought: the politicians, the businessmen, the rich bastards. You only had to read the history books to see how these people had got where they were.

Almost everyone who inherited riches these days had an impressive family tree of crooks behind them, who had murdered for it in the name of the crown, or religion, or whatever other motive worked in their favour at the time.

Never mind that her father's potential title and real wealth were long gone, he still belonged to the blue-blood club, unlike Chalmers who had crawled out of the gutter more recently.

She was tempted to go in and pop the bastard's clogs for him right now, but first she needed to expose the other men were who were helping to manage his personal pension plan.

Once she had that information, she would kill the lot of them, one by one, and that would include Stone, if he got in her way. Just thinking about him made her eyes tear-up with anger for the second time. She would never be taken in again.

Chapter 58

It had been a while since Jessie had found out about the drugs, and Stone had never forgiven himself for the slip. He was angry with himself that this had to happen now, of all fucking times, and with her, of all fucking women.

He'd known from the get-go she was trouble personified, but she intrigued and confused him. There was also something ingenuous and childlike about her despite the fact that she could take on a biker nearly twice her weight and show no fear whatsoever.

But he was glad he'd had that one day with her, short though it was. He sensed that she'd enjoyed the novelty of being *normal* for a brief moment in time, as he had.

Swallowing his pride, he'd finally gone to her house, just once, prepared to go down on his knees or let her beat the shit out of him if that was what it took. He'd been prepared for anger, recriminations, anything she'd to throw at him.

He hadn't expected to find her just gone.

She had fled because of him, and he had a nasty suspicion that if she wanted to remain hidden, she would probably make quite a good job of it.

He did try to get her via the grapevine, but down at the Old Fox, no amount of wheedling brought her to light. In fact, his attempts to trace her had been greeted with outright antagonism, because Jude, too, had disappeared from the face of the earth, and they seemed to think, in some indefinable way, that it was his fault.

Perhaps it was.

So he lay on the single bed in his sterile apartment, arms behind his head, thinking about life, his job, and Jessie, and wondered how it had all got so complicated so quickly. When he took this job on, he'd only meant to stay for a year or so, then move on, but it hadn't worked out that way.

Suddenly his situation felt overpoweringly depressing.

Jessie's over-reaction to the discovery of the drugs, though, was a plus in a long line of minuses. The chap at The Old Fox had warned him she didn't like dealers, a point which could have been debated on another day. It was just unfortunate she'd found out when she did, the way she did.

He'd give up everything, right now, to know that she was alive and well if only he wasn't so deeply entrenched in the whole thing. Chalmers was giving him a hard time of it too, lately, as if sensing that his bodyguard had things other than his boss's well-being on his mind.

Stone's real reason for not looking too hard for Jessie was that he didn't want to jeopardise her safety any more than he wanted to jeopardise his own, because any action on his part would make the people he worked for look at her, look into her, and that would be bad.

He wanted to do that for himself before deciding what the hell to do about her.

But one thing he knew: he wouldn't rest until he'd seen her again. If she told him to go to hell at this moment, it would be music to his ears.

A small sound on the window made his eyes flick over. When the sound repeated itself, he rose to his feet with more grace than anyone would have given him credit for, and reached for the familiar handle of his ever-present firearm.

He peered cautiously into the darkness, squinting sideways through a small window to present as small a target as possible. But logic reasserted itself. If he was being targeted by a marksman, he would have been dead meat before hearing the window smash.

He could see nothing, but the buzz of adrenaline didn't diminish. From this window all he could see was the endless sweep of the property wall, and the garden climbing into darkness.

The security lights were on, making a mockery of anyone trying to skulk around the property, and Stone shrugged. Maybe it had simply been a bug hitting the window; but he didn't think so. Someone had thrown a small stone at his window, which had been his first thought, and he'd been meant to hear it.

So, someone was waiting out in the darkness.

He donned his dark leather jacket, presenting a darker target, turned off the light, and took a deep breath before opening the door.

He didn't like the exposure of the entrance to his apartment. It consisted of a couple of steps through a porch edged by a row of open railings. Not good at all, but he'd been given no choice in the accommodation. It came with the job. He felt a jolt in his stomach as he ran down the steps two at a time, fast, in the hope of outrunning a bullet. Stupid, he knew, but to walk down slowly was more than his nerves could take.

A shadow bolted towards the wall.

Whoever it was surely didn't know that the wall was topped with pressure pads. He ran, but the dark figure glided before him, and was up and over the wall before he could catch up. The multi-thousand pound security system remained silent.

'Shit,' he muttered to himself.

He put the gun in his pocket, and ambled to the gate. If he was still alive now, he probably wasn't meant to die today. He pressed the buzzer and lifted his face to the camera

'What?'

Cary was on night duty. The man was a sadistic little shit, and made no secret of the fact that he didn't like

Stone's increasing familiarity within the business.

'Open sesame.'

'Where the hell are you going?'

Stone shrugged, he'd squash the man underfoot right now given a chance.

'Bored. Just thought I'd go get a pint,' he said.

'All right for some.'

The buzzer went.

He walked on down the road, turning to follow the sweeping brick wall, his eyes scanning for movement. His finger was wrapped around the trigger of the gun in his pocket as he stalked the elusive figure.

Blinded for a second by a passing car, he backed into the shadow of the wall until his eyesight cleared. It was as if the shadowy figure had existed only in his imagination, but he knew it hadn't. Someone was playing games.

Could it be?

When he heard the sound of a Jap bike start up somewhere ahead, he dropped his pride, and ran.

But she didn't just zoom off into the night and leave him cold as he feared, she waited. He slowed down as he approached, and stopped just short of the black figure on the Virago, relief scalding him for just a second. He controlled his erratic breathing which had nothing to do with running. He was fitter than he looked.

'Jessie.'

She handed him a helmet in silence. He thrust the helmet, which was too small, onto his head, and climbed awkwardly on behind. With his greater weight over the back wheel, the bike wobbled slightly as she pulled away. He didn't ask where they were going, he didn't care. His body was fired by the electric contact with hers, even through the double layer of leather.

Jessie drove down to the park and stopped in a dark corner where the lights had been smashed. He wondered whether she'd smashed them herself before picking him up. It was the tiny attention to details he would have expected from a professional.

They climbed off, removed their helmets, and stood awkwardly for a moment in semi darkness, and Stone sensed she was unnerved by the meeting.

It wasn't to be a happy reunion, then. No kiss and make up tonight. She baffled him, this strange woman, with her desires, her fears, and her strangely immature inability to handle either of them.

'You didn't have to run, because of me.'

'You know I did. You found out where I lived. And you wouldn't know I'd gone unless you'd broken in.'

'I wouldn't hurt you.'

'Maybe not knowingly.'

That was almost a compliment. He buried his irritation as she walked a few steps away from him, towards a slight ridge. From there, the city lay twinkling in a solid wall of lights below them.

'I was worried about you.'

'You should be worried about yourself. People like you don't tend to live long.'

What did she think he was for Christ sake?

Oh; of course. She knew exactly what he was, which was more than he knew about her. She was more paranoid than him, and that took some beating.

He ran a couple of steps, caught up with her.

'Look, you're in some kind of trouble. Let me help. Don't tell me anything if you don't want to, but please don't just walk out on me again.'

Her eyes flashed, her voice chilled even more, if that was possible.

'I don't need your help, or anyone's. Shut up and listen. I came here to warn you, that's all. The police are looking for me about something that happened a long time ago. Some inspector from London. They got to Jude, and he told them where I was, so I guess you did me a favour. He gave them your name, too.'

Stone went cold, and stopped short.

'Christ. What did he tell them about me, exactly?'

'At the moment nothing other than he thinks you

might be able to tell them where I am. He doesn't know anything else.'

'I'll kill the little shit.'

'Get in line.'

She fumed for a moment.

'At least he got word to me.'

'How?'

'Don't be daft.'

Jude had contacted the dodgy solicitor, who had a post box number, but Stone wasn't going to be privy to that information.

'Well, it was worth a try. Why *did* you come to warn me tonight, Jessie? I got the distinct impression you'd like to see me behind bars.'

'Because I don't bloody know. Maybe I think you could change. Turn over a new leaf.'

'Get a job lugging bricks on a building site?'

'You're not stupid. I don't know what you could do. But not what you're doing now.'

'And what about you? What do you see yourself doing in the future, aside from stealing. Incidentally, why do you steal?'

'I like doing it. I'm good at it.'

'H'm. And while we're looking at reasons, there's only one reason I can think of that you warned me I'm being looked into and that is you care about me.'

She threw him a sour look, and he grinned. She was no more capable of admitting feelings than flying, but she did care. She cared about him, albeit in some crazy way, and he felt something blossom in his chest. Without knowing how he would do it, he knew he'd work something out.

In a spirit of unholy amusement, he wrapped her in a bear hug, lifted her up and gave her a smacking kiss before her startled gaze even registered his action. He dumped her straight back on her feet, and the next moment found himself writhing on the floor, his knee shooting with agony. 'Oh, shit, Jessie,' he gasped, and clutched at his leg until he could breathe again. 'What did you do that for?'

'I told you never to touch me again.'

He clambered carefully to his feet, favouring his left leg, hands out in supplication.

'OK, OK, I won't, for Chrissake.'

They stood close but not together, listening to the distant night noises, the ever-rumbling Motorway, the odd cry, bark of a dog, screech of brakes. From their vantage point they could see fingers of lights clutching the dark, jewelled buildings.

'I hate this city. The people, the noise, the filth.'

'Why can't you just leave it and move on?'

'I'm going to find Porter, kill him, and anyone who gets in my way.'

Was that a warning? Had she somehow worked it out? But he couldn't see how.

'And what then, Jessie?'

'Then I'm going to find who killed Ben, and I'm going to kill him, too.'

He closed his eyes momentarily as she paused.

'And what then?'

He pulled her to face him, taking her shoulders with hard fingers, holding her furious gaze in spite of her intake of breath.

'Don't lash out at me, please. Just answer. If you finally do manage to kill all these people without getting killed yourself, what then?'

Her lack of answer was all the answer he needed.

'Revenge won't bring the peace you're seeking. It won't make you happy.'

Her lip curled. 'Happy? Has anyone got a right to be happy? Ask all the people that take that shit you sell. Ask them about happy. I just won't be able to rest until I've done this thing. It's what I live for. There is nothing else.'

He felt more helpless than he'd ever felt in his life. 'There are always things worth living for. Wouldn't that teacher of yours have told you that? Was that Ben?'

He felt her wince and knew he'd hit home, but she

307

snapped back.

'You deal drugs. How can you even presume to lecture me?'

Jessie's answer hung on the cold air between them.

She was racing backward into the distance, and he was unable to keep up. Somehow he knew his words were going over the top of her head disappearing into the ether.

'OK. I'll stop. Let's both leave, put this all behind us. I'll get a proper job.'

She pushed his hands away.

'And a cottage in the country with roses over the door? What about a few pigs and chickens and babies?'

'I'm not joking.'

'You'd leave with me?'

'Right now. Before you get yourself killed.'

There was a long pause. Her voice was a sigh of white mist on the air.

'You're too late, Stone. I died a long time ago.'

'Jessie, trust me, it's not '

Her voice cut through his. 'Trust you? A hired gun, who deals in death as a sideline? I might be going to my own destiny, but I'm sure as hell not taking a whole load of kids with me.'

Stone grimaced. She had a point.

'Jessie, if you don't trust me, trust your instincts. When I first met you, I didn't know what you were, but I asked myself if you were all right, and I told myself you were. Do the same for me, Jessie. Trust your instincts.'

'Go sell some drugs, Stone.'

'But Jessie, listen

'Stop. Now. I came here to warn you, and what you do with that information is up to you. You can either have a lift or walk, I don't much care,' she said coldly.

Stone shrugged, defeated, and followed her to her bike. She dropped him short of Chalmers' entrance, and he stared at her for a moment, knowing there was so much he wanted to say, yet couldn't.

When the whine of her engine was no more than an echo on the air, Stone pulled out his mobile phone and tapped the buttons quickly.

'I've got a problem. There are some cops looking for Jessie, the girl I told you about. She said they've been given my name.'

There was a babble of consternation at the other end.

'No: David Stone. It could be serious. I don't care what it costs. You have to get them off my back. Get rid of them.'

He thrust the mobile back into his pocket, knowing that it was all going to go belly-up, and that didn't bode well at all.

Chapter 59

Godfrey said, 'Redwall has been recalled to London, and I couldn't understand the urgency, so had a, ah, discussion, with his boss, and told him he was vital to finding Jessie.'

There was a heavy pause as his words sank in.

'They told me that they wanted him out of Birmingham. Pronto, as someone up here has put a contract out on him.'

'What?' Branlawe's disbelieving comment said it all.

'Rubbish, of course,' Redwall said. 'I'm not going.'

'I think a rumour that a contract has been taken out on your life should be taken seriously,' Godfrey commented.

'Yes, but where did this rumour originate? Look at it logically. The going rate for a professional hit is at least thirty grand. Who's going to pay that much to take a cop out of the system? There's plenty more where I come from.'

'I doubt your wife would agree,' Godfrey said.

'Maybe she's the one who's taken out the contract.'

Oscar maintained an innocent expression as he spoke, but Branlawe's lip twitched.

Godfrey glared at both of them in turn.

'Someone knows I'm looking for Jessie, and is putting a spanner in the works, but there isn't a bloody contract, I'd stake my life on it.'

'Exactly. It's too big a risk. Even if you're right.'

'Look, everyone's responding to the rumour in the way they're supposed to for goodness sake! Can't you see that? They want me gone, and next they'll find a reason to take Branlawe off the case, and so on.'

'If means we're treading on toes,' Godfrey mused. 'Is that good or bad? And whose toes?'

Redwall took a deep breath as if mustering patience.

'All I'm asking is that you use some of your clout to find out what's behind it, if you do that it will go a long way toward finding out who the hell Jessie is after, because you can bet your life that's who's spreading this rumour.'

'I really don't have the clout to '

'With respect, I don't know who the hell you are, Godfrey, and I don't expect you to answer that, but you do have the facilities and you do have the clout. I'm not stupid. I'm just asking, very, very politely if you'll do me a favour.'

'That was polite?'

The note of surprise in Oscar's tone increased the colour of Redwall's ire by at least a tone. 'If you'd like to hear me when I'm not being polite, you just keep that up, son.'

Godfrey held his hand up, palm out, silencing him, then addressed himself to Oscar.

'There are times when levity relieves a tense situation. I believe this is not one of them. You have my permission to leave the room.'

In stunned silence Oscar stared for a second, then rose slowly to his feet.

Redwall looked at his hands, embarrassed by Godfrey's overreaction to his own bluntness.

'And while you're out there get on the phone and see if you can find out who was behind the order for Redwall to be pulled, and where the information about the contract came from. Don't come back until you've got something.'

'Yes, Sir,' Oscar muttered.

'Is there anything else?' Godfrey asked, glancing around the table.

'What about the boy, Jude?' Branlawe asked.

'Ah yes, the one you *and* Oscar *and* Redwall jointly

allowed to escape.'

Oscar slid out of the room, and Branlawe squirmed uncomfortably.

'That window looked far too small. He must be a bloody octopus to have wriggled through that gap. What I meant was, do we need to get him back for any reason?'

'Well, he served his purpose, I suppose. As we weren't going to book him with anything, I suppose we'd have had to let him go, anyway. We can pick him up again if we need him. But out of interest, do we know his surname? I'd just like to run his name through the mill, see what comes up, if anything.'

'He's probably not registered on anything anywhere. Kids like him are like ghosts in the system, but I'll see if I can find anything,' Branlawe said.

Chapter 60

Stone was right about one thing. Jessie had warned him because no matter how hard she tried to hate him, she couldn't. He'd wormed his way past her defences, and when she found he was protecting the very man who she'd sworn to kill the bottom had dropped out of her world.

Yet still she couldn't hate him. She warned him, though, and that was the end of it. If he didn't leave, what more could she do?

She slid over the wall, black and silent as a shadow.

Her feet made no sound as she landed, crouched and ready to run. The building ahead was bathed in the white glare of security lighting. The guards traipsed around the perimeter once in a while, at approximately hourly intervals, though it wasn't that regular. She'd watched now for several nights.

They were so confident in the protective powers of their security systems, that they thumped around the estate, chatting about TV programs and football, with little regard for stealth, and were looking more towards the drink at the end of the beat than for intruders.

Like a wraith she ran past the gatehouse, wondering if Stone was dozing within. She had a fleeting moment of guilt, but hardened her heart. Stone dealt in drugs, and was as bad as Chalmers. To do him credit he'd neither denied nor justified what he did, but it didn't change anything. Perhaps she would have to kill him, too, after she'd got the others.

Because killing him would be the hardest thing she'd ever done in her life, she put that thought aside.

Concentrate on the moment.

Don't be side-tracked by wayward thoughts, they will get you killed.

Yes Ben, I'm listening.

In the darkest part of the night, when the guard had finished his rounds for a while, and when a cold wind bit through the grounds, she ran silently from cover to cover, and made her way to the main house. Chalmers should be in bed now, like a good little drug dealer, happy with his haul.

There was a small side door that led from a conservatory and store room block into the main house, and Jessie ran for this now; it was the weak point of the whole system. She picked the lock with fluid ease, and with her heart in her mouth ran for the small box on the wall, which shone with a baleful red light. It was equipped with a set of numbers, like that of a telephone key-pad, but she ignored them and jimmied the lock on the small and inadequate box, being careful not to damage the outer casing. The seconds were ticking by, but she remained calm.

What Ben hadn't taught her, she'd learned from Jude.

There would be a delay of two minutes at the minimum to allow someone to enter the house and disable the system before the alarm sounded. She'd been about twenty seconds so far. Inside the box was no complicated tracking of wires, just a wide open space filled with no more than a circuit card. She took the screwdriver and levered it gently under the deceptively simple piece of electronics, and broke the connection. She waited, tense, ready to run, should she have bungled it.

There was an endless silence. To Jessie's alarm a baleful red light above the door began to flash in frustrated silence, but no siren split the air with its warning sounds. She levered the cover off and smashed the bulb. She waited, but the small noises had been lost in the night.

A rush of adrenaline pounded in her ears as she made for the internal back door. She listened for sounds of people, then, hearing nothing, opened the lock with the fine-pointed steel pins.

Inside the house was a rich and plush silence. Her small pencil beam picked up doors that were of solid dark red wood with inlaid patterns around the edges, and handles of polished brass. Small ornaments, tables and oil paintings decorated the hallway with sparing taste. Everything was quietly expensive. Jessie was surprised to find that someone who dealt in death at this level should have good taste. And Vince, the daft git, had thought he could blackmail these people?

She trod silently to each room, listening at the door of each before opening it on the noiseless hinges. She found a cloakroom, an enormous reception area, a dining room with an impressive chandelier, and a real show-piece of a kitchen. He either liked his food, or entertained a lot, she thought. She listened carefully to the noises coming from the kitchen, poised on the toes of the soft leather shoes. Their voices were loud, and there was the sound of laughter.

Whoever was in there seemed well involved in whatever they were doing, sorting something. Money, perhaps. Besides which, she'd burned her bridges for another try. They would know someone had broken in, even if she got out unscathed. She ran silently and swiftly up the wide, curved stairs, and listened at the upstairs doors, too, before trying each. There it was; Chalmers' study, on the first floor, where she'd expected to find it. She pulled down the blinds, and drew the curtains. The room was on the far side from the guard's domain, and for fifteen minutes she should be safe with the light on. She allowed herself five, and began to search carefully and quickly.

There wasn't anything of importance in the drawers, which were not even locked. There was a safe behind the picture, where she'd expected it to be. She noted the type for future reference, one never knew. She doubted that there would be anything in it, not if he'd any sense. But there was something about the immaculate room that didn't ring true. She stood back and assessed her doubts for a moment until the aura of the room told her. It wasn't used. Not now, hardly ever. It was a decoy, a blind. She swore as she noticed the clean work tops, the unsoiled mat around the swivel chair, and the rows of books that had been bought by the yard, and not for their literary value.

The books. She looked again. The bookshelves themselves had been custom built into an alcove. She glanced at her watch. Time was nearly gone.

One minute, just one minute.

She ran her fingers along the book tops, and under the wood of the shelves, seeking for what should be there. Logic told her that the door would be at the near end of the shelves, or the other shelves would surely show some signs of wear.

She was wrong.

The catch lay at one side of the middle set of shelves, and when the latch fell, the shelves simply rolled backwards with a silent electronic swish into the hidden section of the room. Jessie felt her heartbeat increase. She stepped through, and the light from the study followed her. This was the working room. The shelves were no more than rough wood on bolted angle iron, and they were all stuffed full with papers, boxes, old ledgers, and even an ancient handgun.

He was so confident no one would ever get into this room, it made Jessie wary. She searched with hasty expertise, but there was no great pile of money waiting to be lifted, no ledgers with his shady deals. She was annoyed, for she wouldn't get a second chance.

Then she noticed two small polythene packages in a cardboard box on the table. She swore under her breath, and stared for just a second. Not money, but drugs.

Jesus Christ, they actually were here, on his premises; but not much, not enough. No, this was a

316

small, private cache that Chalmers probably used for bribes, or whatever, but even that wouldn't remain here long, she reasoned. The goods didn't stay with the importer, but were pushed on immediately so that others could take the fall. The higher the dealer was in the hierarchy, the less time the stuff stayed in his hands. Here today, gone tomorrow, except that he was richer, and some sod down the bottom of the pile was going to abuse others to get their hands on it. Well his hands were not going to remain unsoiled this time.

She thought for a moment about killing the man. Should she do it now? Hell, no it was too quick, and besides that, she still had no clue as to who he was working with. No, tempting though it was, she needed to force them all into the open, expose them. She slit the packets, sniffed, then damped finger and tasted. Not heroin then, as she'd discovered in Stone's pannier, but crystal meth. Silence fell in her ears like lead as she made her way back to the entrance through which she'd come, spraying the powdered crystal liberally as she ran. That would make the bastard shit bricks.

There wasn't anything she could do now but get out fast, and not come back. She opened the external door carefully, looked out into the silence, listened, then touched the wires of the alarm together before stepping out into the screaming noise of the night. She pulled the back door closed behind her. She heard the lock fall into place, and stood in the darkness of the entrance, adjusting her eyes to the white, pulsating light beyond.

She paused for no more than a fleeting moment, then stepped out, toes poised for running. Sensing rather than seeing movement to her right, she dived without thought as the small popping sound of a silenced pistol preceded the twang of a spent bullet as it ploughed into the wall where she'd been standing a moment before.

Jessie had never been shot at, for all her training with Ben, and the shock of it stunned her for a second. Survival instinct rushed into the gap, however, and her

317

body reacted where her mind failed. Out of the darkness a shape plummeted, and Jessie ducked fast as a fist contacted the thin air above her head. She fell heavily, out of balance, but immediately rolled over as the foot lashed out towards her.

She grabbed it and twisted hard. There was a scream of pain as bone and cartilage scrunched under her hands, and something metal rattled off into the night. Jessie turned her attention outward, immediately ignoring the disabled man.

She rolled back to her feet in one fluid movement, but didn't stand, presenting as small a target as she could to whoever else was out there. She could sense him, but the strobing light was her enemy. A second later she saw him, and remained frozen in a crouch.

He stood just fifteen feet in front of her, feet apart, the gun rock steady as it pointed directly at her. There was a feeling of menace in the air so palpable that she could almost reach out and touch it.

They stared at each other.

The man before her wasn't large, rather he was wide with excessive eating, but his clothes and his attitude gave him away: Chalmers. She'd never seen him, but she knew.

He didn't move his eyes a fraction as he shouted behind him.

'Cary? Stone? Get your asses out here, now!'

Then he turned his attention to his wounded henchman. There was no pity, just irritation.

'Sandy, get the fucking alarm, and sort the lights out.'

Jessie didn't move a muscle as she heard the injured man drag himself to the door-way, fumble up the wall. Silence hit the air, and she was bathed in a blinding spotlight as she still crouched, both hands on the floor like a runner waiting for the starter gun to fire.

The injured man's gun lay before Jessie on the gravel.

Her eyes flicked towards it.

318

Chalmers saw it at the same time, and walking sideways, he went over and kicked it further from her reach. Using the gun as a finger he indicated that Jessie should rise.

'Stand up,' he snapped. 'Keep your hands out or I'll blow your fucking head off.'

Jessie obediently unwound from her near foetal position. That was when he realised. In the tight fitting outfit the womanly shape would have been hard to disguise. He sucked in breath.

'By Christ, he was right. You *were* trying to find me. Well done, Jessie my girl.'

She froze at mention of her name, shocked.

'Who told you I was trying to find you?' she hissed.

'Why, Yellow Streak, of course.'

'I don't know anyone by that name.'

For some reason he found that hilarious, and gave a shout of laughter.

His attention was distracted for a nanosecond.

As he unconsciously registered his superiority in strength and dominance she threw the two handfuls of gravel straight into his face, springing forward at the same time. She slapped her right hand hard up against his wrist knocking the exploding gun into the air.

The report echoed through the depths of the garden and out into the city. No silencer on that one, she thought. Her momentum carried her right hand into the side of his face, and she felt her knuckles grind into bone, but she'd no thoughts of going in to tangle with him.

The gunshot would have achieved what his shout hadn't, and would bring his whole army into the battle.

As Chalmers fell back with a grunt of pain and anger, Jessie ran.

She sprinted across the wide expanse of garden, and ran at the wall like a cat, using the momentum to carry her up and over. Chalmers lost precious moments retrieving his gun, but now the bullets flew, hissing past like angry gnats. Jessie scaled the wall and set off a whole barrage of alarms as she landed fully on the pressure pad. Something yanked her arm and dropped her with violence on the other side of the wall, but she rolled, and was up and running before the shot registered.

Two youths were strolling past as Jessie appeared, falling over the wall in a snarl of limbs, and she knocked them flying before their expressions of amazement finished forming. Jessie heard their footsteps patter rapidly behind hers, then disappear.

The youths, recognising trouble, had run.

No witnesses there to worry about. A short way down the road, Jessie leapt onto her bike, kicked it into being, and was gone into the night before any of Chalmers' men made it to the gate.

Chapter 61

Stripped to the waist, standing by the crude white kitchen sink of her old property Jessie assessed the damage.

The wound was a gash across the muscle in her upper arm, and was bleeding profusely. Having no alcohol to hand, she gritted her teeth and tipped neat disinfectant onto it. She swallowed a strangled scream and stood rigid until the fire diminished to bearable pain, then tied a rag tightly around her arm to hold the edges of the wound together and stem the bleeding.

It would probably go septic, Ben said bullet wounds usually did, but there wasn't anything else she could do. But even the pain and the resultant lack of mobility couldn't diminish her shock. She'd just intended to rattle his cage, make him insecure, but he already knew who she was.

They all did.

How?

Jessie sat there thinking for a long while.

Yellow Streak, obviously a code name for someone who knew her.

She hoped it wasn't Stone.

No, she knew it wasn't Stone.

She wished, just for a moment, that she could tell him she had that much faith in him. She hoped it hadn't been him who shot her. She rather thought he might be a bit upset, but she thought she knew where his loyalties lay at the crunch.

Self-preservation would come to the fore; he'd probably already joined the army of thugs looking for her. On the other side of the fence good and proper now, Stone, she whispered.

Chapter 62

Godfrey was awoken in the small hours by Oscar's harsh whisper. 'There's been action at Chalmers' house, Sir. Gunshots.'

He didn't hesitate, but dressed silently and quickly. If Oscar said 'Sir', something serious was up.

In the car, Oscar updated him.

'Branlawe's out there already. Our men heard the alarms go off, and the sound of gunshots. Someone came flying over the wall, and off the property. All hell broke loose. One of our men stayed at the stakeout, the other followed the figure, and called it in.'

Godfrey heard triumph rise in his voice.

'It was a female. She got on a bike, and he followed her out to a big property up on the South side. He's there now, and she hasn't exited. He said the place is wide open, though. We need an army to surround it, or we'll lose her.'

'Are they sure?'

'Not identified, but pretty likely.'

'What about Stone?'

'We don't know, but one of the men thought he took a bullet. The police are there now, in response to the alarms. Branlawe's with them.'

He considered the implications.

'OK. Get the team in, everyone we can muster. Let's pick her up now.'

'You don't want to just put a surveillance on her, see what else she's discovered?'

'Christ, no. Let's get our hands on her before she does her disappearing act again.'

323

Chapter 63

Early morning sun was driving the city glow from the sky. Godfrey glanced at his watch. He was afraid to wait any longer. There were too many men around the property to remain inconspicuous for long in daylight. He gave the nod.

From a discrete vantage point he saw one of his operatives walk up the drive to the house and knock on the door. His operative had been versed: He was looking for a Mrs Armitage, was that yourself? Oh, she died, did she? He hadn't been informed. Sorry to have troubled you, miss.

But there was no answer.

Somehow that was what he'd expected. As the operative waited by the front door another watcher alerted them.

'She's bolting! West wall!' he yelled, and the time for discreteness was over.

What had alerted her, Godfrey didn't know. She must have the instincts of a cornered fox. She didn't attempt to get the bike out through the gate, which was partially what he would have expected.

Instead she was just leaving, virtually empty handed, over the wall. And now, when she saw the darkly clad men moving out of the trees, she turned in a single motion and legged it like a startled deer down the slope of the garden. He knew she intended to fly over the end wall and lose herself amongst the maze of streets.

He whispered under his breath, 'Catch her, come on, don't let her do it.'

She was fast, but the man behind was faster. Godfrey saw him gradually gain on her, then she stopped in her tracks, turned, and lashed out with a weapon of some kind. He couldn't identify it from that distance, but guessed what it was. The man dropped silently in his tracks.

Christ, she's killed him, he thought in disbelief, and raised the walkie-talkie to his mouth.

'She's armed!' he yelled. 'Bring her down.'

Jessie didn't even look at the downed man, but ran on.

From the bottom of the garden more figures materialised, three from one corner, one from another.

There was the briefest hesitation, then she aimed for the single figure. The man reached out to stop her, but the weapon swung again, the man's arms flew up, and she leapt over him as he fell.

Godfrey had given the order not to use firearms, but sensed the men around him stop and pull their weapons. He was running hard towards them. Damn it, he wasn't young enough for this! Gun in hand, he stopped and took aim. She wouldn't kill another one of his men. But even as his finger tensed on the trigger, the man on the ground rolled and grabbed her foot as she jumped.

She took a nose dive, and he cursed and ran towards them again, ignoring the gun in his hand, for his men were all over her.

Jessie was a dark shadow on the ground, biting and punching and kicking at anything that moved, but she was overwhelmed by sheer numbers.

They forced her onto her front and held her.

She fought like a wild-cat for a moment then stopped struggling and lay still, the sound of her harsh breathing loud on the air. Godfrey looked behind and saw the man he thought was dead lift himself groggily to his feet. He picked his way to the tense scene and saw the Katana lying a short way from them, still sheathed in its case.

Thank God she hadn't had time to take it out.

But that was wrong, and he knew it.

If she had wanted to use steel she could have, and probably would be away, free, leaving in her wake a pile of bloodied bodies.

One of the men lifted a syringe, sprayed small droplets into the air, then plunged it into her thigh. Her scream was the chill embodiment of wordless rage, that of an animal, and her sudden burst of fury almost dislodged the six men who were holding her.

Gates put the syringe back into the little case and snapped it shut.

'We didn't establish whether it was the right blonde chick,' he said.

Godfrey bent down, turned her over in a soft flop of limbs. For a moment time stood still. She was just as she'd been five years ago, in the garden of Ben's house. It was hard to imagine that this deceptively slender girl who could be barely twenty, had been the cause of so much expended man-power over the last year.

Then Madden bent down, heaved the slack body over his shoulder, and carried it to the black van.

Chapter 64

Hearing came back first.

Jessie heard people talking over her, a clinical burble of blood pressure and eye reflex. Confusion took her back to hospital, to being relieved of the flame of life that had been lit within her body. She had wanted to keep that life so much. They couldn't understand that it hadn't been an accident, that she'd chosen to conceive it, something of her own to love, something that would love her back as it grew. Her father had insisted, and they had taken it from her, leaving her so empty inside, more than anyone could ever realise.

Her head ached; and her mouth was unnaturally dry.

Time flashed past with blinding clarity.

Oh, yes, that was a long time ago.

Now she remembered: the garden, running, being injected. It hadn't been heroin, after all, just something to knock her out. She felt incredibly sick, and there was a pain lashing behind her eyes. When would they start on her? Punish her. She didn't care. It was easier to go back to sleep.

When she awoke again the sickness had dissipated, and the headache was a dull throb in the back of her skull. This time her faculties returned in full, and with them a new understanding. If she'd been picked up by the dealers she surely would have been in a warehouse or something, trussed like a pig ready for roasting, whereas a single cognisant glance told her this was institutional.

The painted walls, iron bed, steel toilet, steel sink,

and above her, a light set into the ceiling with no loose flexes she could hang herself on.

Institutional, without a doubt, but what? Prison?

No, the police would have come knocking at the door with cars and uniforms. She would have been over the wall and lost in the concrete jungle before they realised she was gone. The men who had taken her were something else, but what?

She looked down at herself. She was dressed in blue cotton pyjamas, and the wound on her arm had been dressed professionally. She pushed herself up in spite of the sinking feeling in her gut, and stood up on shaking legs, annoyed to find that she had to use the wall to get herself to the sink. She sat on the loo for a moment and put her head between her legs before she was able to run the tap and swill some life back into her swollen tongue.

She forced herself to move, to exercise, to get the blood into her brain, to remove the toxins that poisoned her. At first it was hard making herself do anything. She'd never experienced lethargy like this in her life.

Partially it was the drug, partially a sense of failure at ending up in the hands of the powers that be, whoever they were. She exercised hard, ignoring the wish to simply lie down and die, and the pain of the flexing wound. Blood began to seep through the bandage and pyjamas alike, letting her know she was still alive.

Then the hatch in the door fell away. A pair of brown eyes stared through a grill for a second.

'Step back from the door, please.'

The hatch closed with a bang. The door opened.

She was wary, ready, but relaxed instantly with a faint shrug, because aside from Mr Innocent, in his suit, with those cow eyes, they'd sent three action men complete with uniforms, square chins and iron muscles.

Mr Innocent came forward with a waist belt sporting

handcuffs.

'Hello, Jessie. My name's Oscar and I'm your friendly jailer. Please behave yourself, because we don't want to have to hurt you or use force again.'

'Where am I? Who are you?'

'You'll find out. Hands, please.'

Jessie complied, and as he cuffed her wrists to her waist giving due consideration for her injured arm, she realised he was too soft. It was a weakness she would use against him.

He took her good arm to lead, and maybe to hold her up if she was still weak from the drug.

She padded barefoot beside him, the guards following a couple of feet behind. The corridors were a featureless, light green with starkly functional lighting, and the doors were fitted with security wheel-and-bar locking systems on the outside. Horribly secure. She sniffed. Underground, too. A slight pressure and they turned right into another corridor. Here the doors were wooden, and had glass in them.

Out of the cell-block.

A slight pressure on her arm, and they halted. Her escort knocked and opened the door. The room was barely functional, sporting a desk, two chairs and one old man standing by a window.

Her eyes assessed him as fully as he was assessing her.

He looked like a retired soldier. There was a hard look about the eyes, and the face was the sort that had been trained to show no emotion.

She'd seen him before.

Jessie was steered to a chair opposite the desk

Mr Innocent moved to stand between her and the door, just out of her line of sight. Did he think she was going to try to scarper chained like a bloody dog? The old man came and sat on the desk, in front of her, and Jessie sensed a challenge in the movement. She could have taken him out with a single movement. But he must have known that, so he was either confident of his ability to protect himself, or he was testing her.

'Do you know who I am?' he asked.

'Ben called you Godfrey.'

'My name is Godfrey Kyam. Do you know where you are?'

Was he playing games? She answered him in a flat monotone. 'Institution: narcotics, police, maybe, but I don't think so. This place stinks of government or army, I'm not sure which. Why am I here?'

'What's your name, Jessie? Your proper name?'

'Anthea Gray.'

The silence lengthened for just a moment. The man didn't take his eyes from her.

'Elizabeth Jessica Stowleigh.'

Her breath caught. She hadn't expected that.

'Why did you kill Ben?'

She leapt forward to thrust her face into his.

'You killed him, you bastard! You or one of yours, not me. Never me. I would have died first.'

Mr Innocent had leapt, and grabbing her arms. She winced at the pressure on her wound. Her head swam. She shook him off and sat back down.

Godfrey hadn't moved.

Maybe he believed her, she didn't know, but he changed tack. 'But you don't deny you have killed?'

Her lip curled. 'So have you.'

'In defence of my country. What's your excuse?'

'Because I wanted to. Because it felt good. Because I could.'

Her voice hissed with venom, and as she glared at the old man, he glared right back, their eyes meeting in a clash of wills.

'When my men were trying to take you, why didn't you unsheathe your sword?'

'Against your guns? Don't be silly.'

'Did you see guns?'

'No, but they would have been there.'

He changed tack again. 'What made you think one of my men killed Ben, Jessie?'

'Because Ben welcomed him with open arms, like a son or a close friend. And he didn't have anyone except you lot.'

'Are you telling me you actually saw the murderer?' He sounded surprised.

'Not clearly, but I'd know him again, there was something about the way he moved,' she pondered, but couldn't capture the elusive thought.

'Whatever. I'd know him. And when I find him I'll kill him.'

'Let us deal with him.'

Her lip curled. 'Tell him he's been a naughty boy and not do it again?'

'You don't have a very high regard for the judicial system, do you, Jessie?'

'Nor do you,' she snapped. 'Or I wouldn't be here.'

She heard the faintest indrawn breath behind her and realised that Mr Innocent was smothering a laugh.

Godfrey seemed to look into the distance for a moment, and when he spoke, he sounded almost tired.

'Tell me, Jessie. What happened to make you the way you are now?'

'Nothing.'

'Something. No matter how silly it sounds now, tell me.'

She stiffened, gave an almost imperceptible shake of the head.

'I'm not a psychiatrist, but I'm trying very hard to understand you, to help you. I want to know what turned you into the person you are.'

'Ben made me what I am.'

'No, you were already that person. Ben simply picked up the pieces, and taught you some things we wish he hadn't. I'm trying to find out whether he created a human being or a monster.'

'What's the difference?'

'How do you live, Jessie? Do you just take what you want?'

'It's what everyone else does.'

'No, they don't. Only a small percentage of the population do that. We call them criminals.'

She felt a faint flush penetrate her skin.

Ben would have said the same thing, but she knew better. She'd seen them do it. And the biggest criminals, the biggest liars of all were the ones with the most status in society, the most clout.

'You've got a choice here, Jessie. You can decide to live within the law, or you can live outside of it. There's no other alternative. You can't go around killing the people you don't like.'

'I haven't yet. But I will. The men I intend to kill are not human, they're insects, and given the opportunity I'll crush them underfoot like the vermin they are.'

'That makes you as bad as them.'

'No, it doesn't. I don't kill for pleasure or financial gain. I'll kill them because the world will be a better place without them. Isn't that what you do?'

'But it's still not your job to be judge and jury and executioner. What if it turned out they were innocent? How would you feel, then?'

'I'd find out, wouldn't I?'

She leaned back in the chair, stretched her legs out, and yawned. Godfrey's eyes darkened dramatically.

'Jude told us what you did when you met him.'

'When I saved his arse, you mean. That makes sense. It was you that got to him, then, not the police. Tell me, should I have just walked away quickly like a good citizen? Most would have, you know. The little whore was getting his just deserts, anyway. What you don't see can't harm you. That's how most of your genuine citizens behave, Mr Godfrey. They turn their backs, don't get involved. Well I'm not like that.'

'What are you, Jessie? A vigilante, perhaps? Here to right the wrongs of the world?'

'Oh, no. The world can go to hell. I just intend to set my own record straight.'

'I would call that revenge, plain, simple, and selfish.'

'Fuck you.'

He sighed. 'Why did you break into Chalmers' house?'

She was tempted to say it was simply to steal the family silver, but for some reason she wanted him to know the truth. It galled her that these men Ben respected thought she was simply some low-life. Didn't they know better than that?

'Your pillar of society, that charming Mr Chalmers, is a drug importer. I wanted to make sure he really was who I thought he was. I wanted proof.'

'And did you find it?'

Her lip curled. 'Oh, yes. I found it. There would have been no doubt about that when the police went in.'

'Why should the police have gone in?'

'The gunshots? Someone must have reported them. And I set the bloody alarm off so they'd go in. It wasn't an accident. There were meth smeared over his fancy carpets like confetti. Even the police couldn't have missed that.'

'Well it backfired. Chalmers said nothing was missing, so even though it all sounded a bit suspicious, they didn't have the right to go in if they weren't invited.'

Her eyes rolled.

'Hell. No wonder people like Chalmers walk all over them. I should have just killed the bastard like you said.'

'So it was for nothing.'

'No, it wasn't. All that shit could never quite be cleaned up, only superficially. The evidence will still be waiting there when Chalmers slips up, one day. In the carpet, in the skirting, in the cracks of the floor-boards. He must have had his men working overtime with vacuum cleaners. Stone, Cary, Thomas. It was almost amusing.

'Why didn't you kill him when you had the chance? Instead of setting off all that commotion.'

'I wanted to know who the others were. If I killed him, someone else would have carried on. I thought

333

even if the police got him, he would have shopped them all in the end to try to save his own skin. I should have realised no one would do anything.'

'Tell me about David Stone. What does he mean to you?'

'He's nothing to me. He's a low-life scum-bag.'

'Then why did he save your life when you were running from Chalmers' house last night?'

She frowned in true puzzlement. 'What are you talking about?'

'It seems he took a bullet that was meant for you. Our man said it didn't look like an accident.'

She was silent, the implications running around in her brain, not making any sense. Stone had *helped* her get away? He'd taken Chalmers' bullet for her? He'd chosen sides after all, the bloody moron.

She thought he had more sense. 'Is he dead?'

'We don't know. Possibly not, he's in the house somewhere, as far as we can tell. No one called an ambulance.'

'You didn't go in?'

'It would have broken our cover. It turns out Chalmers is part of an on-going investigation. Not ours, the Narc's. He doesn't know about it, and you nearly blew it for them. We've been told to stand clear.'

She was silent again for a moment, then lifted bleak eyes to Godfrey.

'Chalmers wants me real bad. It was his money I stole, in London.'

'Then it's just as well we've got you here, all safe and sound, isn't it?'

She leaned forward. 'Don't you get what I just said? Stone could be in trouble in there. Chalmers could be torturing him to find me. You've got to go in and stop it.'

'Even if I wanted to, I've been told not to interfere. There's something big going down, and you were getting in the way. Anyway, Stone knew the score. He made his choice a long time ago.'

'After all your fine words about the value of a life, about it not being my place to judge people? What if Stone is innocent? My, what a hypocrite you are.'

Godfrey flushed faintly.

'Decisions like that aren't made lightly. If you know about Chalmers, you know how big his operation is. This is about countless lives, not just one, and I'm not going to jeopardise a whole operation to try to save a crook who may or may not already be dead.'

The telephone belled, and the old man turned his attention from her for a minute.

'He's here? I'll come now. No, reception will be fine.'

He glanced up at the man who stood by the door. 'Something's come up. I have to leave this for a moment. Take her back to the holding block and get her something to eat. I'll give you a call later.'

He indicated to the guards, preoccupied with whatever problem had materialised.

'You, come with me. Oscar can manage the girl.'

Chapter 65

As they walked back to the cell, Jessie stumbled just once. The blank look on her face wasn't a sham.

Stone, in Chalmers hands?

Being tortured for information?

Shot? Dying?

She hadn't thought she could possibly feel so numb or so helpless. And the people who could stop it weren't going to do anything. Worse than that, they were going to let it happen, knowingly. The man's hand on her arm tightened helpfully as she stumbled, and her disbelief at their inaction turned in the fraction of a second to black rage.

As she was released from the chains, she was compliant. She sat on the bench-bed, and put her head between her knees.

This time the confusion directed at her captor was calculated.

'Do you want something to eat?' he asked, his concern immediate.

'I don't know. I don't feel too good.'

She slumped a little further.

'Look, we're not all bad, you know. It'll turn out OK, you'll see. I'll get you something to eat, anyway. It doesn't matter if you don't want it. I won't be long.'

He touched her shoulder as he left, so very young and inexperienced. When he came back to her cell with a tray of food, he turned to put it down on the bed and she took him with an ease that was unexpected.

Rising and turning in a single fluid movement, she immobilised him with a jab to a nerve in his inner elbow, while twisting his wrist. In the next second he was on his front on the floor, an arm bent up behind him. Before he could do more than utter a startled yelp, her fingers had the pressure point in his throat. He passed out when she reached four, but she held it a couple of seconds more. Not long enough to kill, but long enough to make sure he wasn't faking.

Quickly and efficiently she relieved him of his outer clothing. He wore jeans and a fleece sweater under a padded leather jacket. He also wore a shoulder holster with a gun that the jacket was probably designed to disguise.

Who were these people?

She stepped quickly into the jeans and polo neck, a hint of her old assurance shining through with the adrenaline of action, and put the jacket over her arm. It was a shame about her bare feet, but his shoes were too large and would have been more of a hindrance than a help.

She looked at the gun, and shook her head.

Taking a deep breath, she plunged into the corridor, diving to the right and rolling, but the goons were not there. She secured the door behind her, and headed swiftly down the corridor towards the circular stairs she'd noted previously. If this place was underground, where she wanted to get was up. She raised her head, and listened. There were sounds of people talking, laughing, but after a moment she decided they were not coming her way. The stairs circled upwards into another row of corridors just like the first, except that up ahead she could see an entrance.

Corridors snaked off either side, and cold winter sunlight came blindingly through the plate glass. Again, there were no people. Doubt sneaked into her exuberance. The sunlight was just within reach, and although it beckoned enticingly, some sixth sense told her this was too easy, there was something very wrong. But she either had to go forward or go back, and that was no choice.

337

She stepped outside.

Without warning a group of young men came trotting around the corner in a bunch, lathered in sweat. It was too late to run, so Jessie put her head back defiantly, and waited, but they ran on past. From the cut of their muscles they had to be soldiers, so this must be some kind of training establishment, amongst other things.

Heartbeat increased by the encounter, she trotted on. Further along there was a car-park, but although she was quite capable of stealing a car, there was also a guard at the entrance checking credentials. A trap she would be better off avoiding. Jessie forced herself to walk slowly along the side of the building, nonchalantly, as if she had a right to be there.

Why had the alarm not sounded?

At an angle to the main building, and some thirty yards away, a tall wall stretched away to the right, and beyond it, past a wire fence, she could see open countryside. There was absolutely nothing she could do but cross the width of concrete, and the longer she stood there, the more chance she had of being found. She heard no cries as she left the cover, and was soon in the shadow of the wall.

Suddenly the sound of shots filled the air.

She shrank downward instantly; a small target, ready to roll. But the firing continued. Behind the wall was a range of some sort. Of course there would be if this was an army base, for Chrissake. She chose the place to cross the wire fence with care. The fence itself posed no problems, though it might have daunted another, as the top curved outwards designed to stop people from getting in, not out. It was eight feet, not so high, and there were notices pinned on the outside at intervals. She wondered what they said, what this place purported to be. It was likely the fence was wired to an alarm, but she doubted it was electrified.

Jessie looked back at the building, and when her line of sight hit the corner of the building, she knew that anyone looking out of their windows wouldn't be looking directly in her direction. She slipped the jacket on, not that it would add much protection, and ran at the fence, bounced two steps up, then dived in a backward somersault over the edge as her momentum reached its peak. She rolled over the top with little pressure on the fence, but didn't make it unscathed. Razor edges sliced deep into her back muscles as she tumbled over, landed on the balls of her feet, and rolled over her shoulder. Then she was up and running, ignoring the pain of stones in her feet and a hundred tiny wounds down her back.

Enjoy pain because it means you are alive.

Everything Ben had ever taught her came to the fore.

Her breathing came up to a controlled pant, her heart pumped at a steady rate, and her muscles drove her body forward with the ease of a machine, which is what the body was, he said. This was what the body was made for, running.

She revelled in the freedom, the action, and her teeth bared in a grin of determination. She realised she must have been brought up to the Yorkshire moors, or Derbyshire even while she was unconscious.

Somewhere big and wild and rugged.

It was early morning, and winter was approaching. The air was chill, yet the sound of birdsong followed her on the cold air, and she revelled in the smell of the frost-deadened leaves underfoot.

If they were following now, they didn't have the faintest idea which direction she would have taken, unless they had dogs, of course. And yet in spite of the gradually increasing distance, there was a little niggle in the back of her mind that shouted as she ran: too easy, too easy.

But perhaps it was easy because Ben's training was good, because she was just one girl, and they hadn't expected her to even try to run.

Jessie had never seen this rippling expanse of open countryside before, and was fascinated by it. She

339

breathed the scented air in deeply, freeing her lungs of the stale taste of institution. Ben had talked about freedom, and she'd always listened eagerly, thinking she'd been fighting for that elusive state—not realising she already had it.

Until today she hadn't known the meaning of lack of freedom: bars, walls, fences, manacles. Now she was outside she could allow herself to recall the fear of that confinement.

Fear was too simple a word: terror was better.

She would kill herself rather than be institutionalised, whatever Godfrey said.

Behind her she heard the slow thrum of a helicopter pulse into life. In the space of a second she'd crossed to the boundary hedge of a field and curled deep in the shadow of a hedge as it passed over and circled around. She buried her face in her arm, though the temptation was to look. A human face could be seen instinctively, for several miles.

The helicopter trawled, back and forth, gradually moving away.

They were looking for her, now.

Then came a sound that chilled: the distant yapping of dogs. She plunged through the hedge and ran on the other side across one field, a small road, running like the wind. The dogs began an excited frenzy of yapping. A faint sob escaped her throat when a small car zoomed past. She stuck her thumb up too late.

To her surprise the car stopped, reversed. She was poised by the driver's window ready to kill him if he was one of them. A youth beamed at her.

'In a hurry or just jogging? I wasn't sure.'

Without hesitation she ran around the front to stop him driving on, and jumped in.

'In a hurry,' she said honestly.

Just around the corner she could see the Motorway. 'Going south?' he asked.

'Yeah.'

The throb of the helicopter passed overhead.. She

340

held her breath, but it circled once more, then they were no longer on the slipway, but anonymously amalgamated into the steady stream of traffic heading south.

'From the army base,' he said knowledgeably, following her upward gaze. 'Those things are always buzzing around out here.'

Now she leaned back, and smiled at the driver. 'How far are you going?'

He only went thirty miles, or so. She considered stealing his car, but thanked him nicely, and almost immediately got another lift from an obese lorry driver whose thoughts were not so much on the road as on her.

She smiled at him, too, when the time came. Better to leave people happily unaware of what they were carrying. The further she got, the more diffuse her tracks, the better her chances. If they had been going to find her, stop her, it would have been before this.

Their next chance would come in Birmingham, because without a doubt, Godfrey knew where she was going.

Chapter 66

Knowing Chalmers was under investigation, and his lines were probably being monitored, Jessie called Stone's mobile from a phone box. It was answered by an unidentified male voice.

'Yes?'

'This is Jessie.'

'Who?'

'The one Chalmers is looking for. The one who sprayed his house with crystal meth.'

There was silence. She wondered who she was talking to, it certainly wasn't Chalmers.

'Where are you?' he asked eventually.

'Don't be stupid. You get Chalmers there and say I want to speak to him. How long will that take?'

'Half an hour.'

'Be there. I'll call.'

Jessie went out, stole a motorbike, and called again, from a payphone. It rang once before it was answered.

'It's me.'

She recalled his hard voice all too well.

'Hi, there, Chalmers. Get the house cleaned up, yet?'

'Wherever you are, you're dead. You know that, don't you?'

The time for playing was over.

'Where's Stone. Have you got him?'

She heard an intake of breath at the other end. 'Yes.'

'Is he alive?'

'Yes.'

'He doesn't know anything about me.'

'I was beginning to wonder that. But your little

sidekick knows a bit more about you.'

'Who?'

'You know Jude. A pretty little thing or at least he was.'

She went cold.

'Have you hurt him?'

'He's just a bit knocked around at the moment. The little prick didn't put up anything of a fight at all, just collapsed in a soggy heap the moment my men found him.'

'Neither Jude nor Stone know where your money is. I do.'

'Trading, are we?'

'You let them go and I'll come on in.'

'Do you think I'm stupid?'

Her voice echoed the open venom in his.

'Are we bargaining, or haven't you got anything left to bargain with?'

'Oh, they're here. Both of them, and they're still alive. But we're at a bit of an impasse, because I have no intention of letting either of them go until I get you, Jessie.'

'Let them go, and I'll come in. You have my word.'

'How far away are you?'

'In Birmingham. A couple of miles.'

'Then you get here, darling. I'll let them go when you come in, and to give you a bit of incentive, I'm going to have Cary cut a piece off Jude every five minutes until you get here.'

The phone went dead. Jessie closed her eyes once, swore, then kicked the bike into life.

She knew Chalmers' house was under surveillance by Narcs, but just how good, and how many there were, she had no idea. All her plans up the chute, she was spurred into directness by the knowledge that Chalmers really would do as he said. She drove straight for the front gate. Please let it be open, she thought.

The gate wasn't only open, but manned by two of Chalmers' men, and if Godfrey or the Narcs had anyone there, they kept out of sight as she screamed the bike straight off the road and up the drive, not giving anyone time to knock her off, or whatever else their plan might have been. She heard the gate closing behind her, and the sound of thumping feet. The drive stretched up towards the spot-lit serenity of Chalmers' mansion.

Chalmers: councillor, pillar of society, cheap peddler of drugs.

As she stopped, dark figures ran around the outside of the house from all directions, and she could see the glint of metal in their hands as she killed the engine, climbed off the bike and thrust it away from her. It flopped heavily onto the stone chippings in a cloud of dust.

She pulled off the helmet, threw it after the bike, and flicked her corn-coloured hair defiantly from her face.

Men surrounded her, patted her down for weapons, and almost carried her to the front door as the drive's stone chippings cut her bare feet causing her to stumble. Chalmers himself stood in the doorway.

With a flick of his fingers, she was released.

'Come on in, Jessie. I've been looking forward to meeting you. I've heard so much about you from various people. Stone, Jude, your father.'

She stopped short. 'My father?'

'Oh, he works for me, didn't you know?'

'Yellow Streak,' she said flatly, understanding his previous amusement.

He indicated, and followed her into a large drawing room, for all the world as if it was a social function, she thought. So proper, so very English. She turned to face him, and waited while Chalmers perused her face. 'You really are quite lovely, but very stupid. Why did you take the money?'

'I needed it to get out of the rat hole I was in. To get out of the game. I wanted to be free. It just seemed expedient at the time. I was very young.'

'H'm. We're one of a kind I suppose. But you never

344

had a chance of keeping it. I would have found you sooner or later.'

'As you said, I'm here. Where's Jude?'

'Ah, yes. The prostitute. You took ten minutes, by the way.'

He snapped his fingers to some unseen minion behind him. Jessie felt a chilled sense of expectation seep through her. Then Jude stumbled through the door, propelled by a hand in the back from a small weasel-faced man who grinned at her and deliberately wiped blood from a slender knife onto Jude's sweatshirt. The boy's eyes were glazed with shock, and blood dripped from his cradled hand.

He stood where he was thrust, a cowed and whipped animal.

'They're going to kill me, Jessie.'

'I'm sorry. It wasn't meant to be like this.'

She felt as if the world was receding around her. She felt so tiny, so insignificant. Jude was right, it didn't matter what any of them did, Chalmers would kill the lot of them. Stone had brought it on himself, but Jude's death would be right at her door. Chalmers fingered the long, angry scratch down his face, and she could see it in his eyes that she would pay for every millimetre.

He had every sign of a man enjoying himself, in total control of his domain, as he strolled to a cabinet, poured himself a finger of whiskey and savoured it.

His eyes never left hers as he lowered the glass.

'I'd really like to know why you came, I'd half expected you not to. I thought you were more of a survivor than that. As the whore said, I have to kill him anyway, you know that don't you?'

Jessie shrugged. 'I ran out of options,' she admitted. 'Let Jude go. You'll get your money back. And you've got me. That's all you wanted.'

'You know I can't do that. He knows far too much, judging by our little discussion just now.'

'Don't you know when to keep your mouth shut?' she snapped at Jude.

'It wouldn't have made any difference,' he replied.

Her anger fizzled out. She was forever directing it at the wrong people. 'No, you're probably right.'

'What's your connection with Stone?' Chalmers asked. 'Are you two in some scam together?'

'Didn't you get that out of him?'

His response was irritated.

'Cary didn't get a fucking dicky bird out of him. Must've lost his touch. Were you just using him to get in here?'

She shrugged. 'Not even that. The stupid git really didn't know anything about me. He just fancied me which was obviously not a clever thing to do,' she added dryly.

'Even if I believed that load of shit, it doesn't change anything.'

'Stone and I are your kind of people. You don't have to kill us, you know. We're on your side of the fence at the end of the day.'

His eyes gleamed with amusement.

'Are you asking for employment?'

She shrugged. 'Dead I would simply be out of your hair. Alive well, I have certain talents, and you wouldn't have to lose Stone, either.'

'And what about Jude?'

She gave a small curl of the lips. 'You could do to Jude what you've probably been doing to little boys for years. He really wouldn't mind.'

Chalmers gave a shout of laughter. 'I like you, Jessie. I really like you. I like you a lot more than your slimy git of a father, that's for sure.'

'Well, that's a relief.'

'But you see, I could never trust you, and I somehow don't think Stone wants to work for me anymore. Nice try, anyway. You've got such a lot of guts. I admire that. Thomas!'

The door opened, and a tall, thickset, scarred man came through it. He had a gun in his hand, and had obviously been waiting outside the door. 'Take the whore outside and kill her. Actually, you'd better let Cary do it; quieter than the gun.'

Thomas said, 'Yes, sir,' and Jessie saw his eyes light up as he lumbered towards her. She backed away, a hand up as if in supplication, but he reached in, confident that he was in charge, grabbed her proffered wrist and twisted her right arm up behind her.

Chalmers looked disappointed. 'I thought you had more fight in you than that, after all I heard.'

Jessie bent her knees, dropped her left shoulder and twisted her body in line with her captive arm, straightening it in a single lithe movement facing Thomas. His mouth was still opening in surprise as she rose, her left fist hammering like a piston into his groin. Slowly he released her wrist, dropped the gun and collapsed to his knees. Jessie didn't snatch for the gun as it toppled. When she turned Chalmers was pointing his unerringly at her, both hands rock steady.

'Like that?' she asked evenly.

'Something like that,' he admitted, admiration in his eyes, but at that moment she knew he was going to kill her.

Not later, after further discussion, but right there and then.

Giving a wry grimace, she sprang forward knowing she couldn't outrun the bullet, but even as she moved, Chalmers unexpectedly seemed to fly towards her. The sound of his shot filled the small room, and the bullet ricocheted somewhere out of vision.

Jude stood there, surprised at the efficacy of the brief shove he'd given the man.

Behind him, Cary's face twisted with loathing.

Her actions now were pure reaction, training taking her somewhere past thought. Even as a cry of denial began to wail somewhere deep in the darkness of her mind, her thigh bunched, and her foot came up under Chalmers' chin. From the snap of his neck she knew he was dead before he hit the ground.

There was a soft whoomph as the gun spat once

more as he fell on it, and she was still moving forward, trying to stop time.

It all happened in a split second, but each moment was an adrenaline rush of clarity. She was still running towards Jude, her mouth open in a yell of urgency, but he stood there, bemused by his own actions and the sudden cacophony of noise.

She watched Cary bring his knife up in a vicious movement, and she screamed in rage as the youth's face flowered with the endorphin rush of impending death.

Jude stood for a moment in surprise, before Cary pulled the knife out and thrust him aside, arterial blood spurting from his back as he collapsed.

She was vaguely aware of the harsh popping of more bullets, the crashing of doors, the wail of an alarm, but her conscious thought was filled with Cary's snarl of fear as he backed like a cornered animal before her, he armed with eight inches of steel, she with her bare hands.

'Jessie, stop!'

She froze.

She knew that voice. 'Jessie, step back. We've got him. You can stop now, it's all over.'

Oscar's voice was urgent, compelling, with none of the softness she recalled.

Her eyes focused, and almost imperceptibly she relaxed.

As she did so Cary sprang. She leapt back, twisting as he slashed. The wicked steel glanced like fire across her line of sight, just missing her throat. A gun thundered, and Cary collapsed in a screaming heap, the hands clutching his knee turning bright red.

She swivelled to find a sea of darkly clad men filling the room silently behind her, and began to sink into a half crouch, as if she would take them all on.

'Jessie, where's Stone?'

Oscar's voice washed over her like a cold dowse of water, and there they were, on the same side.

She bent down, took Cary's face in her hands and lifted the top half of his body from the floor with it. 'Where is he?'

'Cellar,' he squealed. 'Kitchen.'

Oscar found they were too late. Stone lay chained in a bed of dried vomit, and his skin had the cold blue tinge he'd seen all too often. There wasn't anything subtle about the way they'd tortured him, judging by the livid red swellings around his joints, and the black and yellow potato-shaped lumps that were his feet and hands. A crust of dried gunge surrounded a bullet hole in his abdomen, and his eyes were lost in folds of swollen tissue where dried blood and matter had seeped out of the wounds on his head, and dried like tears upon his face.

A figure pushed past him urgently, and searched for a pulse. He turned and trod slowly back up the stairs to the living room where Jessie sat on the floor, cradling the boy.

There was a look of vague astonishment on Jude's face, as if in death he was still wondering how he'd found the courage to act.

Jessie sat with Jude's head in her lap, her mind a dark chasm filled with guilt. If she could have traded places with Jude, she would have done it at any time in those last few seconds, but the action replayed itself over and over in her mind, never changing, irrevocably moving towards the same conclusion.

Ben had told her she couldn't stand on the fence of life forever, because sooner or later she would tumble, and the choice would no longer be hers.

He'd been right. Chalmers was dead, but it had brought her no joy.

The harbinger of death had won, after all. There was no sweet taste of success, just the bitter reflection that Jude was dead because of her.

Chapter 67

Finding a faint pulse, Godfrey's men treated Stone urgently, not stopping to remove the shackles; simply slicing the chains through with bolt-croppers.

He was swung onto a stretcher in the space of seconds, his mouth covered by a clear plastic mask, his body by a blanket. Godfrey let it be known he'd been discovered dead, it was the only way the man could be shielded from retribution, for the drug syndicates had an information network he would be proud to own.

He wasn't quite sure why he felt the need to protect the man at all, except that for some reason Jessie was in love with him, even if she didn't know it herself. And Stone himself probably wouldn't thank him when it became clear they could think of nothing better to do with him than lock him up forever.

If he survived, which was hanging in the balance.

Godfrey had trodden on toes that night, and there would be repercussions, he knew.

The feisty Custom's Officer, Deborah, would be after his head, and the police were banging on the door, while his men were cleaning up one mess, and her men dealing with another. They were, even now, hastily picking up everyone on their shopping list, including the two men suspected of being Chalmers' partners in crime. But with Chalmers' untimely death, many more would melt into the night, and the trade, temporarily interrupted, would find new channels.

Many of the ones they picked up tonight would no doubt slip through the judicial net, because the groundwork hadn't been finished, and would probably end up back in the circuit.

But Stone would never get to trial. She had no idea he was still alive, and it was going to stay that way. Godfrey liked having an ace in hand. You never knew when it might be useful.

If it lived, of course.

He trod back up the stairs to the room where Cary was being manhandled out on another stretcher.

Oscar had been told Jessie was his charge, to hang on to her at all costs, but he wasn't having trouble. She was sprawled on the floor, cradling Jude's body as though by will power alone she could bring him back.

Godfrey bent down, touched her gently.

'Stone's badly hurt, but still alive, Jessie. I just thought you'd like to know. Come on, it's time to go.'

To his surprise she obeyed, putting Jude aside carefully, and standing up.

He was shocked at the blank incomprehension that stared out of her eyes. The fire that had made her unique seemed to have been extinguished. She simply waited for whatever was going to happen, uncaring, unseeing.

He took her arm, and led her to the van. She'd been through so much and survived, though; he guessed she would pull through this. She was one of those creatures who had endless capacity for life, he'd seen it in her.

Yet this blank compliance was unsettling, and she didn't snap out of it even as she was ushered gently into the cell she'd vacated only that morning.

He was shocked to his core when he was given the startling news the next day that Jessie had tried to kill herself.

'How the devil did she do that?'

'When she stole my clothes she also stole a key from my pocket and hid it in the room, just in case she was brought back in.'

'A key? To what?'

'Nothing in particular. She was just taking hold of the opportunity to get something useful. It didn't matter what it was for, it could have been used as a weapon, or a tool.'

'Did she do much damage?'

'She managed to gouge a fairly nasty wound in her wrist before someone happened to check though the grill and just had a hunch things didn't look right. If she'd been left there with it for the night...'

His shrug said it all.

'Christ.' Godfrey wandered over to the window. 'What have you done with her now?'

'Put her in the infirmary for the moment.'

He arrived to find Jessie lying on her back, eyes wide open staring at the ceiling. His eyes gravitated to the restraints, and her bandaged wrist as he pulled up a chair and sat beside her.

He put his finger and thumb to the bridge of his nose, and pressed, trying to ease the tension.

'What the hell's driving you, Jessie? If you don't want to kill someone else, you want to kill yourself. I'm trying to understand why, here. Help me.'

She said nothing, but he could see the glint of tears.

He pushed a bit more.

'You killed Chalmers. Isn't that what you wanted all along?'

He was expecting one of her clenched silences, but maybe she needed to explain.

'I thought so, but it doesn't really matter, now, does it? Jude's dead because of me. Ben was right. You don't get revenge. It gets you.'

'David Stone isn't dead. He would be if you hadn't gone in when you did. He nearly died for you, and you saved him.'

Her lips compressed.

'You let me escape. You used me.'

'You wanted to get Stone out, and I had been ordered to let it alone. I merely helped by looking the other way.'

She yanked at the canvas restraints. 'I don't want your help. I made this whole bloody mess. Why didn't

352

you just let me get myself the hell out of it in my own way?'

'By killing yourself?'

'It's my life.'

'It's a waste of all that effort people have been putting in trying to help you, don't you think?'

'I didn't ask for their help.'

'Don't you think you owe a few more people a bit more respect than that?'

'Who?' she sneered. 'You?'

'How about Ben.'

'He's dead. So is Jude. Ask them about respect and see what they have to say.'

'I respect you. You could have killed Oscar when you escaped, but didn't. He believed you wouldn't kill him, so he put his life in your hands.'

'Then he's a stupid fuck.'

She glared, and looked as though she would have slaughtered him without hesitation had she been able to do so at that moment.

'That's more or less what I said, but not quite so succinctly. And then there's Inspector Redwall.'

Jessie turned her head to look at Godfrey, the confusion in her eyes palpable.

'Who?'

'A copper from London. Ever since Vince was killed, he's been trying to find you.'

'Why?

'To save you. He went to Southampton. He saw your father, your teacher, your sister, and tried to contact your mother for some clue about where you might be, what you might be doing.'

She gave a humourless laugh. 'I doubt he found *her*.'

'No, but I think you owe him at least a meeting.'

'I don't understand why he'd do that.'

'He heard your cry for help. Isn't that what it was all about, the wrist-cutting session when you were thirteen, the pregnancy when you were fourteen?'

She was silent for a moment, and he understood she

hadn't known what she wanted.

'The world isn't all bad people out there. There's good ones and bad ones and all the ones in between, and there's a lot who are just too busy to listen. But with all their faults, most people find something to care about. That's what makes them human. Redwall cares about you. And you, what do you care about?'

She turned her head away.

'I don't give a shit about anything.'

'You're not as bad as you try to make out, Jessie. It wasn't you who killed Jude, it was Cary. You can't take the blame for what other people have done. You've never killed indiscriminately, when you could quite easily have done so. And what about Stone? You felt enough about him to try to save his life.'

'He's a low-life. I shouldn't have bothered.'

'He stepped in front of a bullet for you, that's why you bothered. He told you he had faith in you. He was tortured for you. Doesn't he deserve even a little respect for that, if nothing else, Jessie?'

'I owed him. I've paid him back. When he's looking out of his prison cell in thirty years' time, perhaps he won't thank me.'

'Do you want to know how he's doing?'

'I don't care.'

'After the major one to remove the bullet, he's had five operations, and is looking at rather a lot more before he can walk again. They smashed his hands and his feet and his knees and his elbows. He's suffering, physically, Jessie. But more than that, he's suffering mentally. He can't pull himself through what those men did to him without help. You could help him if you cared enough.'

Her mouth went tight. 'He deserved what they did.'

'No one deserves that. And what of Ben's murderer? That's just one instance where justice isn't going to happen if you're dead. You're the only one who can identify him. What if I make a bargain with you. We'll help you find him, you let us deal with him, then you throw yourself down the pan.'

She glared at him. 'If I find him, I'll kill him.'

His tone hardened.

'Do that and I'll make sure you spend the rest of your life behind bars.'

He leaned over and undid the restraints.

'If you want to kill yourself, go ahead, there's a few nice sharp scalpels in the drawer, but it's time you woke up to the fact there's always something worth living for, if you've got the courage to go out and find it. Suicide isn't the kind of courage Ben would have advocated.'

She lay there, arms across her chest for a minute, then swivelled herself upright, and swung her feet off the edge of the bed. She didn't look up.

'What kind of life would I get? You said yourself I don't fit into society anywhere.'

'I don't know, but have you got the courage to find out?'

As he was exiting, he turned back.

'There's a gym up in the main block. Oscar will show you where. Ben's Katana is waiting for you there. Go and work something out with yourself.'

After a few false starts, Jessie began to rise at three or four in the morning, and work out until the first classes began to trickle in, then returned silently back to her room to stare at the wall, as if seeing her life printed there before her on the fading green paint.

Oscar became her shadow. Everywhere she went, he went, and his very presence reminded her that he'd once trusted her with his life. Strangely, after a while the black despair receded a little.

Chapter 68

A couple of weeks later, alone in the gym, Jessie knelt in seisi, ramrod straight back sinking into the vee of her bare feet, her mind focused inwards.

She liked the anonymity of the small hours, and the semi-darkness before dawn. The only lights that glowed were the soft access signs above the doors at either end, leaving the centre in shadow, as if she could hide her insecurity in darkness.

She placed her hands, palms uppermost, on her thighs, and breathed the higher awareness into being. The awareness circled her body, through her lungs, through one arm and around into the other; the endless circle.

Gradually calm descended, and she let it swallow her until there wasn't anything but a small spark of awareness of body. She floated. Then, from outside her awareness a small movement touched her.

She was no longer alone.

Another white figure knelt beside her. He too, sat in seisi, and a Katana flowed along the floor beside him from his hip. His awareness was that of a master.

It was Ben's ghost, or she was dreaming.

He unbuckled the scabbard and let the Katana lie.

Standing, he said in a soft command, 'Taikyoku Shodan!'

Together they moved in identical, fluid motion: block left, gedan barai, midriff punch, long turn and block, punch, punch, kai!

At the silence left in the wake of the last shout, the figure beside her spoke again, and his voice was that of a real man, no ghost.

'Heian Nidan!'

'Heian Nidan!' Jessie echoed.

Her tight muscles began to move with a design and purpose once more, and the remnants of uncertainty faded. They glided through the dust-motes and stirred the emptiness with movements that were beautiful in their precision and intensity.

Jessie had never known such unity of spirit with any except Ben. But even though she couldn't see the features of this man who moved with uncanny similarity next to her, she felt Ben in every movement he made, and from some place inside her, she knew that Ben had taught him.

The stranger bowed the formal cessation, feet together arms by his side as he bowed. Beside him, she echoed, and waited for his next move.

He knelt and made obeisance before lifting his katana with traditional reverence.

Something inside her wanted to cry out for loss.

It was as if Ben was there, trying to tell her something, but she couldn't work it out.

Who was this man? Something about the glance he cast towards her made her breath catch, but the fleeting memory fled.

She knelt by Ben's Katana and buckled it on.

Her shadow followed suit.

They stood as one, right hand on the hilt, left on the scabbard, rising forward onto the left knee, drawing the blade with a soft sigh of steel against leather. They rose, cut the air across horizontally, then diagonally before re-sheathing, honouring the invisible opponent.

Jessie turned to face the stranger for the first time.

He was familiar. Yet she didn't know him.

They worked together now, as a team, performing the kihon, attacking and blocking in well-rehearsed movements, steel never touching steel, blade passing within hairsbreadth of body, but never striking.

Who was he, that they shared such subconscious

357

harmony?

Jessie's hands touched fist to fist on the bound leather handle that was rich with her sweat, and gradually the dawn peered through the high windows.

The man opposite Jessie smiled again, and bowed.

Then he stood in the traditional fighting stance, and presented his intent to fight with swords, not the wooden practice bokkan.

What was he thinking?

Flushed with adrenaline, and tired of mind, and exhausted in body, comprehension finally dawned.

This was Ben's murderer.

He had come to find out if she would recognise him.

Her eyes widened with knowledge; he betrayed himself with a single flicker of uncertainty. Jessie's recognition of his self-betrayal gathered in a blinding flash of rage. She swung the katana behind her with more violence than skill and with every ounce of strength in her frame, brought it down on his head.

He simply stepped back, and parried the true killing force of her blade with his own. There was a ringing clash that echoed in the whole of the tall and empty room.

Jessie ceased to think as a human.

She had no fear of death, no conscious thought of her own mortality, and became the epitome of the Samurai Warrior. The Bushido, the way of the warrior, filled her soul. Her death was immaterial. Ben had been her Lord, her master, and she was going to avenge his death. The Ken-jutso Kata that she'd learned with minute attention to detail under Ben's tuition now blossomed into fruition with killing and murderous intent.

She was going to kill him if he didn't kill her.

That was the only truth.

Blind in her passion for revenge, Jessie was hardly aware as double doors opened and a laughing and joking group of young soldiers wandered in. They halted in the doorway at the clash of steel, and stood in shocked silence as their two white-clad figures thrust and parried with murderous curved metres of naked steel, their faces betraying nothing of the killing rage that prompted the action.

Jessie screamed with a life-time's pent up fury as her blade descended towards a naked shoulder in a sweeping arc that would have cut the man through to the chest, but he turned, parried, and her blade swept like lightening along the length of his own to split the floor. She dragged it free, and spun away again on agile feet, before he could turn his Katana against her. *split*

The hotness of her anger gradually cooled.

They circled, and she began to assess her opponent with more rational ability. She saw a man no longer as young as she had at first thought; maybe fifty years old.

A fit man, stronger than her.

An opening presented itself, and she lunged forward, narrowly missed, and spaced off again, taking in the new information. He'd parried her blade, but hadn't made the expected retaliation.

Brows beetled, eyes narrowed she realised that the man wasn't fighting her any more, he was just protecting himself. She attacked with renewed determination, intent on stimulating him to fight, but the more she lunged, the more the man blocked and twisted away without striking back.

Jessie felt a presence approach her left side, and she swung around to find one of the track-suited men approaching, hands stretched forward in supplication.

'Just hold on a minute,' he said in a reasoning tone. 'Whatever it is, I think we could just talk...'

He got no further. Jessie's blade flashed towards him and cut within centimetres of his chest. He flung himself backwards with a cry of alarm, and there was a rustle of movement from the doorway.

Godfrey's voice rang out stridently through the tense atmosphere.

'Jessie. Michael. Stop this nonsense now.'

'Leave us,' her opponent replied shortly, his

attention not wavering one iota from Jessie's advance. She was vaguely surprised when, glancing out of the corner of her eye, she saw Godfrey give way to the demand, and usher everyone from the room. The door closed, leaving them alone.

Her glance flickered back to the man who now had a name: Michael. She was annoyed by the knowledge. He was no longer an anonymous focus for her anger, he became a real person. Her feet slowed, and she pulled back the merest fraction.

'Why,' she breathed. 'Why did you do it?'

'Revenge.'

'But he trusted you!' Jessie hissed.

Michael dropped the point of his Katana to the floor, and left himself wide open to attack. 'I know.'

Jessie lunged in, and had to withdraw it in ungainly haste when the man, Michael, didn't attempt to defend himself.

'Fight, damn you!' she roared.

She attacked again, and had to break the motion with alacrity as Michael moved in towards the murderous thrust.

She pulsed with suppressed rage, knowing that this Michael would stand there, and let her chop him to mincemeat before retaliating.

Why?

Was he committing suicide in some strange fashion? He seemed to confirm this as he sank to his knees, put the blade on the floor before him, and placed his hands calmly on his thighs. He seemed to be at peace with himself.

Jessie screamed with an explosion of rage and swung Ben's Katana, around her and towards Ben's killer, but even as the steel whistled towards the man's neck, she pulled it back, and let go. It bounced half way across the gym with a dull ring before embedding itself in the floor. She couldn't stand there and cut someone down in cold blood. Not someone who had been taught by Ben, who had liked Ben, and who was filled by guilt at having killed him. She stood panting for a moment.

'Do you want to die?'

'No.'

'Then why?'

'I've been watching you suffer. This was the only way you could find out if killing Ben's murderer would bring you peace.'

She sank to her knees in front of him.

'Christ almighty, what kind of a fool are you?'

'Ben made a mistake, many years ago, which caused the death of someone I loved very much. I waited a long time to kill him, searching all the time. When I found him, he just stood there and let me shoot him, without trying to protect himself. I thought it would make me feel better, take away the pain, but it didn't. I just wanted to die, myself, because I'd killed a good man who had made a mistake. I'll have to live with my mistake for the rest of my life as he lived with his.'

His eyes met hers.

'I didn't choose to die here today, in spite of what you think. I came to see if you could rid yourself of your ghost so you didn't have to live with it as I do.'

'I could have killed you.'

'I was prepared for that. But do you want to kill me now?'

'Not really.'

'But do you feel better?'

The man gave a smile that betrayed no amusement. She could see the natural laughter lines around his mouth that had been flattened by the despair of the past year.

'I feel empty.' Her voice dropped to a whisper. 'Fate had me on a string, dancing like a puppet all my life, but Ben gave me a reason to live. Then when he died, killing you became the reason. Now I don't have a reason any more. What am I to do, Michael? What am I to do?'

The door opened and Godfrey looked in. He glared at the two of them for a second, as if wondering why there were no bodies lying around.

'When you two have quite finished,' he said flatly, 'I would like to see you in my room.'

As they both rose from cramped limbs, and limped to the doorway Michael held his hand out. 'I'm truly sorry,' he said.

After a moment, Jessie took it.

She considered running, but didn't.

Chapter 69

Of her own accord, she made her way to Godfrey's room. The General looked up from his notes as she knocked and entered.

'Jessie. Thank you for not killing Michael, when the silly fool went and handed himself to you on a plate.'

'I couldn't have killed him. He was better than me.'

'He would have let you.'

'I know. I thought I was angry enough to kill him in cold blood, but I couldn't. Then he told me what happened. At least I understand, now. It helps.'

'It might help you, but it leaves me with the problem of what to do about him, as well as you. Incidentally, why haven't you tried to run away? I thought that was what you did best.'

'I thought about it.'

'You wouldn't make it.'

'That wouldn't stop me from trying if I'd thought it was a good idea.'

A muscle twitched in the corner of his mouth in response to her grave humour.

She said lightly, 'So, is it the asylum, or prison? I'd like to know.'

'Are those the only alternatives you can think of?'

'You won't just let me go, we both know that.'

'Unfortunately that's true.'

She gave him a straight look.

'All this year I've been looking for revenge. Then, just as it's in my grasp, it seems so pointless.'

'Revenge usually is.'

She paused for a moment.

'I don't want to die, not really. I want to live. Really live, I mean. Not cooped up in some cell. I don't think I would be able to do that. Wherever you send me, I'll get out, one way or the other.'

'Are you threatening me?'

'No. Just telling you how it is.'

'There's another option. You could work for me.'

Jessie was rendered speechless as her mind somersaulted. She'd been running all her life, from people who lied and cheated, from those who wanted to use her or kill her. And now the people she thought wanted to lock her up and throw away the key were offering her a lifeline?

'Why would you do that?' she asked, finally.

'It would be a waste to have spent all those years with Ben, learning how to survive, then not put those skills to good use.'

Her look of distrust deepened, and he struggled to find the right words.

'Ben didn't just work for me, he was my friend. When he took you in, I thought he'd finally lost his senses. When I believed you had killed him, I blamed myself for not interfering. Not once did it occur to me to trust my friend's instincts, and it should have. He wouldn't have tolerated you in his home unless he thought you had integrity, honour and ethics.'

'I'm not sure I have.'

'I am. Everything you have done since Ben's death has been tempered by those characteristics, even if you don't realise it yourself. Well, what do you think? We could give it a try. We could always put you in prison, later, if it doesn't work out.'

Her grim look softened fractionally.

'Why would you trust me to do what you tell me to do?'

'I don't. None of my people do what they're told, but they get the job done. Some of them would be in prison if it wasn't for me, but not one of them is inherently bad. Some people just aren't made to conform, and

364

crime seems like the only solution. The freedom to choose a different kind of life usually makes better human beings out of them.'

She was silent for a moment, soaking up this new information.

'Ben wouldn't have worked for you if he didn't think your work was good,' she said finally. 'But who are you people, anyway?'

'The organisation is called Mayday. We're under the aegis of the army, but in matters not of military conflict, but social and ethical. When the law is hamstrung, we sometimes step in. If the general populace knew about us, they'd call us vigilantes. I suppose, in the true sense of the word they'd be right, but we're not. I prefer to think of us as society's safety valve, tipping the scales sometimes so that things don't slide too far out of hand. Only half a dozen people in government are aware of our existence, and to them as a committee we have to justify our actions. Everything we do is ultimately to protect our society, our freedom, our way of life. Would you be interested?'

Prison, or work for Godfrey? Was there a choice?

She didn't know how he did that: smile without moving his lips.

'Can I let you know?'

'Don't be hasty, it's a big decision.'

She stood up assuming the interview was over.

'Before you go, do you remember I told you about Inspector Redwall?'

'The cop from London?'

'He's driven up to see you.'

'Do I have to?'

'I think you should. He's been trying to help you for rather longer than you realise. It would be good for you just be nice to him, even if you're not ready to unload. Shall I call him in?'

She was startled.

'I suppose...'

He pressed a buzzer.

Chapter 70

When Redwall walked into the interview room, Jessie was waiting, with Godfrey. What he hadn't expected to see was a girl who quite clearly was her father's child and Catherine's sister. He would have known who she was if he'd seen her walking down the street. What he hadn't expected was a girl who just looked ordinary. Tall, shapely, and fit in the kind of way one would expect from someone who jogged and did yoga. What he hadn't expected was that unlike her manipulative father and superior sister, she had a pleasant face, which was presently openly curious.

Godfrey didn't make formal introductions, he simply waited.

'Jessie,' Redwall said. 'I was beginning to think you were a ghost. That I had imagined you.'

'And I had no idea you existed.'

She sounded like Catherine, too, except the accent less abrasive, and there was a hint of amusement behind the words. Now he was here, he wasn't quite sure what he wanted to say. Maybe she realised that, as she added, curiously. 'Godfrey said you've been looking for me. That you wanted to help me?'

'You have no idea.'

He was going to hold out his hand, but something made him take that extra step, and hug her briefly. He felt her body go instantly rigid. Her hands were spread slightly as if she didn't know what to do with them, and he knew no-one had hugged her in a long, long time.

There was a coffee machine in one corner, and Godfrey busied himself with it. 'Anyone want one?'

'I'd love one,' Redwall said. 'Milk and sugar, please.'

'I'm fine,' Jessie said.

Redwall couldn't take his eyes off her.

The years compressed from this manic few weeks back to the frustration following Vince's death, and his subsequent belief that she was long dead. It was only now, he realised he had actually grieved for the child, yet here she was.

As if seeing bewilderment on his face, Jessie said, 'Godfrey told me I should tell you what happened. When I was little, I mean.'

'You don't have to tell me anything.'

'I want to.'

'Do you want me to leave?' Godfrey asked.

'No. I'd like you to hear, too.'

She closed her eyes for a moment, then began.

'When granny died, she left Mum a substantial inheritance, I guess. Mum was an only child, and Granny had a huge house. I didn't know this at the time, I was about five, but I worked it out afterwards.'

'Of course,' Redwall said, with some satisfaction.

She was confused. 'Of course what?'

'The majority of crime is about someone wanting what someone else has got.'

'Oh. Well, I think granny's money was paid into their joint account. I think Daddy took it all out and put it into another account so she couldn't touch it. I think when she fell in love with George, she went to him with nothing.'

She made eye contact with him.

'I don't know the facts, of course.'

'It's OK. Carry on.'

He glanced over. Godfrey was obviously as enthralled as he was.

'She must have tried to take us with her, my sister and me, but daddy wouldn't let her. She came back a year later, to try to get us. I was about six, and I remembered her from before, but she didn't come upstairs to see us. I guess Daddy didn't let her. She was

367

with him in the lounge. They were arguing. Shouting. I was listening, watching through the banisters. I didn't understand it at the time, but as I grew up it fell into place. She threatened to go to the authorities with something he'd done, I don't know what, if he didn't give her some of her money back, and let her take us.'

Her eyes lifted to Redwall's.

'So he strangled her, there, in the living room, with his bare hands. He looked up and saw me, and just closed the door with his foot. Afterwards he came up and tucked me into bed and told me if I spoke to anyone about what I saw, he would put me in a home for bad girls and I'd be chained up and whipped every day. He told us both the next day that Mummy had come to get her things, and didn't want to see us ever again. He told Catherine and me such dreadful things about her. And all the time, he knew I'd seen.'

Redwall found he was holding his breath.

Edward Stowleigh had murdered his wife? And the child had seen him do it? Christ, no wonder she'd gone off the rails.

'And you didn't tell anyone?'

'I thought they'd take me away, put me in a home and chain me and beat me as he said. Of course, as I got older I realised just what he could and couldn't do, but it was too late by then. I couldn't tell anyone, because no one would believe me. And I didn't know what he'd done with her body. I still don't know.'

Godfrey leaned forward, his clasped hands tightening.

'Have you any idea what your father did that he didn't want your mum to spill the beans about?'

'No idea at all. Something that would impact on his career, his public face, I guess.'

'Did you tell your sister?'

'I tried to, but she didn't believe me, didn't want to hear. In her eyes Daddy can do no wrong. I don't think she wanted to believe me. Do you believe me?'

'Yes. It makes a lot of things clear.'

She stood up, suddenly, as though it was all too much.

'I need to go now. I need to see Stone. They told me he's finally decided not to die.'

Redwall stood and held his hand out. He didn't just shake hers, he clasped it hard for a moment.

'Thank you Jessie. Well, we can't change what you've been through, and my God, it's amazing you've come out the other side, but perhaps we can work towards finding out the things you don't know, and set the record straight.'

She hesitated.

'There's one more thing. Chalmers told me my father's working for him. I don't know how that could have come about. I really don't think he was into drugs, whatever scams he was running.'

'We'll find out.'

After she had gone, Redwall sighed.

'So, it's all done. I don't know if this is a long goodbye, but thanks for letting me meet her. It's closure of a kind.'

'I heard about your own loss.'

'Ah, well, don't start psychoanalysing. Jessie can't replace my daughter, and I'm not even thinking down those lines.'

'I didn't suppose you were. But if we're to take her story seriously, there's a body to be discovered. Any idea how we could go about it?'

Redwall's eyes lit up.

'It's in my patch. Maybe we could work together?'

'It would be my pleasure.'

Chapter 71

The infirmary was like a mini hospital, with its own operating theatre, and probably a couple of dedicated surgeons. There were some hefty doors around, but the prison-like security measures were hidden behind fresh paint and bright colours. Jessie found Stone alone in a small, functional room. The door was open. Van Gogh's *Sunflowers* smiled from one wall, and someone had gone to the trouble of putting a jam jar of flowers on the windowsill.

He was in an iron hospital bed, staring out of the window, but from his grim expression, he wasn't seeing the moor beyond so much as reliving experiences in an endless loop.

Jessie hesitated for a moment in the doorway, but he heard. He gave her an enigmatic look that said little. He'd been through a lot since they last met, when she'd rejected him, and hurt him.

And then he'd taken a bullet for her.

He wasn't going to make this easy.

Back at Chalmers' house, when Godfrey had told her he was still alive it hadn't meant anything. She'd been drowning in a sea of emotion, covered in guilt and Jude's blood. But seeing him now, alive if not fit, a surge of something inexplicable raced through her.

Perhaps it was happiness, she didn't know, but she was pleased he'd survived. She walked forward and stood looking out of the window beside him. They were on the second storey, looking out over what she now knew were the wild expanse of the Yorkshire moors.

After a moment she turned and assessed him

candidly.

She'd known his hands and feet and joints had been pulverised unscientifically with a hammer, and couldn't imagine the pain he must have experienced.

His arms were in plaster from wrist to biceps, his hands were heavily-bandaged lumps, and the fading remains of lacerations, burns, and bruises lingered on his face.

His torso was tightly strapped because of the bullet wound that had nearly killed him. A gut shot that hadn't been addressed soon enough, with all its associated infections, would have killed anyone less robust.

It would take a long time and a lot of remedial work before he would recover a fraction of his previous mobility.

'Cary gave you a good working over. I'm sorry about that.'

'Are you? After all, I'm a low-life drug courier, I'm scum. I deserved it.'

She winced at the sarcasm.

'You once said you stood back from my actions and decided I was OK in spite of appearances. You asked me to do the same for you. Well I think I did, only I didn't know it myself, not then.' She paused, and added, 'Godfrey told me you took a bullet for me.'

'He had no right. It wasn't his business.'

'He's a devious old bastard. That's the only reason you're alive. I couldn't leave you in there, knowing what Chalmers was doing, when it was my fault; and Godfrey knew it.'

'So out of the kindness of your heart you charged down like an avenging angel to rescue me, so that I could spend the rest of my life locked up. Thank you.'

His voice was acidic.

'Well, I'm sorry if it doesn't meet with your approval. I tried to save you. I didn't make you what you are. You did that.'

He dropped the antagonism.

'You decided to save me in spite of what I was. That was very noble. Only, you see, I never was that person. I was an undercover Customs' Officer, and even Godfrey didn't know that until it was too late.'

'Customs?' she echoed, stunned.

'Yeah, sorry to disappoint you. He told everyone, my lot, that I'd died, because he thought he could use me to gain the advantage of inside information no one knew he had. I think he was disappointed when he found out what I was, and annoyed. It's difficult to bring someone back to life when you've pretty much buried them.'

'Can he do that? What about your family'

'I don't have any family. That's why I was chosen. I'd been under cover for five years, working my way up the supply chain, and you rolled in and blew it; because you wanted to be a vigilante.'

'I didn't want to be a vigilante. I just wanted to kill the people who wanted me dead.'

He waited, expressionlessly.

'All that stuff I said to you... I'm sorry.'

'You didn't know. I couldn't let you know. But, hell, I'd been there so long, you were probably right. I was getting sucked into it.'

His voice was filled with self- loathing.

'At first it was so hard working with those people, knowing what they were capable of, but after a while I got distanced from the reality of drugs on the street. It gets to you in the end, people being afraid of you. It becomes a stimulant. You almost get to enjoy the fear in their eyes when you stand as bodyguard with a gun under your arm. I got lost in the vision of my own importance.'

He paused for a moment, remembering.

'Of course, you really know just how important you are when the people you work for make the decision to leave you being tortured so as not to compromise the operation. Deborah knew what Cary was doing, yet chose not to intervene. We'd all agreed to that at the outset, but when it came to me being tortured, it wasn't so academic. I believed that at any moment they'd burst in and rescue me. It was the only thing that kept me sane. Godfrey later told me they weren't going to. And when you came, I was out of it by then.'

His eyes closed briefly in recollection.

He shifted slightly, and grunted with pain.

'It's ironic, because Chalmers wanted information I didn't have, about you and some damned money. But I could have made him kill me straight off simply by telling the truth. Just shows how much you don't want to die, doesn't it?'

Jessie flushed guiltily, but he was staring, unseeing, out of the window. Then his eyes turned and met hers full on.

'Then, from what I've been told, you barged in to save my life, knowing the odds were that you would just die, too. I don't get you. And here we are; both unexpectedly alive. But for what? Where do we go from here, Jessie? I've lost everything.'

'Not everything. You have me.'

His eyes dropped to his bandaged hands. 'Would you have said that if I wasn't like this?'

'You think I'd say that out of pity? Think again, Stone. Or whatever your name is. I like you. I probably would have worked it out sooner or later. I'm a bit slow on the uptake when it comes to people and emotions and stuff. I didn't know I loved Ben till he was taken from me.'

'Who?'

'My teacher.'

'That still leaves us with the problem of being here. Maybe they can give me a new identity. I don't know. But what about you? I don't see how they can just let you go.'

'Godfrey has asked me to work for him.'

His brows lifted in disbelief.

'It was a choice: that or prison. I haven't made my mind up yet.'

He almost smiled.

'The man's a fool.'

'That's what I told him. I have a feeling he's going to give you an option.'

'I'm pretty much broken. I doubt I'll be much use to anyone anymore.'

She leaned over and gave him a peck on the cheek, startling him.

'You'll mend. We'll work on it together. You fix me, and I fix you. Bargain?'

'Bargain.'

Now, I have to work out. Don't go anywhere.'

'I won't.'

She left him staring out of the window, but the traumatised, blankness in his face had lifted. It only occurred to her as she was changing into her gi, that the traumatised blankness on her own face had probably gone, too.

Look out for Chris Lewando's next thriller....

Night Shadows

When Tom's adoptive mother dies, he learns something that shocks him into seeking information about his birth mother; a decision he previously vowed he would never make.

In seeking to understand his own history, Tom soon finds himself in a desperate race which threatens his very existence. For Helen, the reporter beguiled by Tom's gentle, artistic nature, it becomes a story of nightmare proportions.

Why would an adopted child seeking his roots spark a manhunt which spans continents? Why should a stained glass window made by Tom instil fear into those who seek him? And what could any of this possibly have to do with the latest routine manned mission into the earth's orbit?

Events draw relentlessly towards a climactic meeting which will have repercussions throughout the world.

If you enjoyed this first published imprint of Jessie Running, and discovered any typos, I'd be pleased to be informed.   westcorkwriter@gmail.com.

23325172R00213

Printed in Poland
by Amazon Fulfillment
Poland Sp. z o.o., Wrocław